International Bestselling Author
Emma Scott

Someday, Someday

Copyright © 2019 Emma Scott

All rights reserved

Cover art by Melissa Panio-Petersen

Interior formatting by That Formatting Lady

Proofing by ProofingStyle http://proofingstyle.com/

No part of this book may be reproduced or transmitted in any form or by any means, electronic or mechanical, including photocopying, recording or by any information storage and retrieval system, without written permission from the author.

This is a work of fiction. Any names or characters, businesses or places, events or incidents, are fictitious or have been used in a fictitious manner. Any resemblance to actual persons, living or dead, is purely coincidental.

ACKNOWLEDGMENTS

This book would not exist in your hands or on your Kindle if not for the help, expertise, and loving support of the following people who gave their time and energy to help make this book what it is.

Many thanks to my sensitivity reader, Robert Hodgdon. Thank you so much for your incredible support; your words allowed me to be confident in telling this story the way it needed to be told. Thank you, Nicky F. Grant, for your energy, enthusiasm, and insight, and for your uncanny ability to sense when I needed a boost. I'm forever indebted to both of you and love you so much.

Thank you to my intrepid beta readers who slogged through the earliest drafts and who saw through the messy bits to the story I was trying to tell. Your encouragement is everything so thank you, Shannon Mummey, Joy Kriebal-Sadowski, Desiree Ketchum, and Joanna Wright. I love and appreciate you all so much.

So many thanks to Jennifer Balogh for lending me your incredible insight and beautiful perspectives to the book process, and for your friendship and compassion outside of it. Much love.

Thank you, Angela Shockley, for forever putting up with my crazy schedule and making the insides of the book so beautiful.

A thousand thank yous and hugs to Melissa Panio-Petersen. As always, you keep my ship from veering off course and create beautiful art for the book, all the while being a real and true friend. I don't know what I'd do without you and don't want to find out. Love you so much.

And to Robin Hill. This book would not be what it is without you. The final form has so much of you in it—your time, insight, and love for these characters (and a lot fewer commas). I will never be able to read a page of it without thinking of how much time and love you gave to it, and me. Love you.

PLAYLIST

Weak, **AJR** *(opening credits)*
Missing Home, **flora cash**
Fell on Black Days, **Soundgarden**
Born This Way, **Lady Gaga**
Bohemian Rhapsody, **Queen**
Stay with Me, **Sam Smith**
Time, **NF**
When I'm Over You, **LP**
Someone You Loved, **Lewis Capaldi**
Courage, **P!nk** *(closing credits)*

Silas's piano music:
Rondo alla Turca, Wolfgang Amadeus Mozart
Pavane Pour Une Infante Défunte, Joseph Maurice Ravel
Piano Concerto No. 2, Sergei Vasilyevich Rachmaninoff
Moonlight Sonata, Ludwig van Beethoven

DEDICATION

This book is dedicated to everyone still fighting for the basic human right to love who you want to love without prejudice, censure, or torment. This is my small contribution to the enduring and indisputable truth that love is love.

PART I

"All great and precious things are lonely."
— John Steinbeck, *East of Eden*

PROLOGUE

San Francisco, seven years ago

Max

"Hey, man." Joey flashed a small baggie of white powder my way. Carefully, so none of the other guys milling around on the corner under the streetlamp could see it.

I hesitated. Not because I didn't want the high—I was desperate for it. Especially that night. But Joey's dope was usually cut with weird shit. Two nights before, Mel had overdosed after injecting something from Joey's dealer. We'd had to dump him in front of the ER and run. I'd lingered a second outside the hospital, Mel's puke on my hands and my heart pounding from the coke and fear. I'd wanted so badly to go inside that warm, yellow light. Outside, it was cold and black and dirty.

I wondered what it might be like, to be frantic and desperate to save someone's life, instead of being frantic and desperate just being alive.

"I'm trying to cut down," I told Joey, forcing a smile.

Joey didn't smile back. "Not tonight."

He was right. My nerves were jangling and my stomach was tied in knots so tight it ached. I could hardly stand straight—every muscle was tense, hunching me over, hands stuffed into my thrift-store leather jacket, making fists in the pockets.

Joey jerked his head into the shadows outside the streetlamp, toward the street. "You gotta be loose for your first time. Don't think about it too much. Just let it happen, collect your cash. Boom. Done."

I nodded and snorted the little pile of powder from Joey's palm. Like an animal eating out of its master's hand.

"What is it?" *I asked, only after the sting in my nostrils flared, making my eyes water.*

Then the mellow calm flooded my veins and I didn't care what I'd just inhaled. For a few, brief, shining seconds, nothing mattered. The night turned from black and menacing to soft and fuzzy. The fear of what I was going to do receded and I didn't give a shit about anything except this. This feeling right here. I wanted to live in it forever. And if I did this thing tonight, I'd have more cash to buy more of it.

Joey slapped me on the back. "Feel better? Ready to do this?"

I smiled lazily. "Are you my pimp now?"

"Just looking out for you," *he said, leading me back out to the corner, under the streetlamp.* "And we got rent coming up."

Rent. I chuckled blearily. We squatted in an abandoned building in the Tenderloin District. "Rent" was the payoffs we made to the other guys who'd gotten there first. Between them shaking us down and our increasing need to get high, funds were running low.

On the street corner, a couple of other guys eyed me up and down, not too friendly.

"They're jealous," *Joey said and cupped my chin in his hand and gave me a shake.* "Look at this face. Gorgeous *and* a hot piece of ass. You were born for this."

I was born for this.

The euphoric mellowness soured and my heart that had been thudding dully against my ribs sped up. My high was now cut with dread and disgust. What'd I'd actually been born for, I no longer knew. I was a million miles from who I was, so that I hardly recognized myself.

The cone of sallow light fell over me like a spotlight. I put my hand on the lamppost to steady myself. The concrete was pebbled and rough under my palm. It was real. It was the only thing that was real, as the drugs in my veins warred with the voice in my head that told me this was all wrong.

"Joey..."

But he was gone—folded into the night with the other guys on that corner. They'd become ghouls lurking on the other side of my cone of light. My fingers clutched at the lamppost until they ached. But the post was too wide. I couldn't fit it all into my hand. I couldn't hold on.

Sweat slipped between my shoulder blades and the night pulsed over the city beyond this corner, this light.

A car pulled up. The passenger window went down. I was dimly aware of the half-dozen guys around me instantly turn their attention to the driver. He was nothing but an indistinct shape behind the wheel. The orange coal of a cigarette glowed from his hand slung behind the passenger seat. The other guys made catcalls and bent over to shake their asses at him. In between their noise and over the rushing in my ears, the driver spoke.

"You."

Me.

The cigarette glow moved in the murky dark to the man's mouth. It flared as he inhaled, revealing a glimpse of his face. Middle-aged. Jowls. Heavy brows over black eyes that were locked on me.

"You pretend like you like it," Joey had told me in our shitty corner of the abandoned building. "Pretend like you like them. *It's all an act. You play pretend and get paid for it. Nothing easier."*

The light over me was a spotlight on a stage. The man in the car was my audience, waiting only for me. The other guys cursed and slunk off into the darkness. I gripped the lamppost tighter. The rough cement scraped my skin. If I let go and got in that car, I'd never be the same again.

Smoke wafted out of the open window. The city breathed like a monster in the dark. Whatever I'd snorted had been weak. The euphoria that was supposed to make this so easy was already gone.

Don't let go. Hold on and you'll be safe. Let go and you'll never be the same again.

Another voice countered, Same as who?

Max Kaufman, son of Lou and Barbara Kaufman, little brother to Rachel and Morris Kaufman. He no longer existed. That kid had already been kicked out of his life and into this one for the crime of sneaking someone into his bedroom. Not just any someone. Another boy. A man, all of nineteen years old. Didn't matter if the guy was a good person. Didn't matter that we only kissed. Didn't matter that I cared about him and he cared about me. Or that I felt more like myself with him than I had in all of my sixteen years.

There was nothing left of that me except for the need. The endless, desperate craving to remember what it had felt like to have been wanted once —and the even stronger need to forget what it had felt like to be rejected. I had to fill that empty shell with pills, X, coke. . .Anything and everything. It consumed every waking minute until there was no job I could hold, no schedule I could keep. Because that hunger had its own timetable, and it was always.

The man in the car, waiting for me, was the only way to keep feeding it. And what difference did it make if I sold myself? My parents thought this was who I was. Joey did. Maybe if I did it enough, I would too. Maybe I would get used to it. I'd already polluted my body. Why not let strangers take a turn?

I was born for this.

Nothing easier.

I let go.

CHAPTER ONE

Max

"I let go."

I blinked out of the memory and came back to the present, into a room in the community college, downtown Seattle, Washington. Not on that San Francisco street corner. Not in the car that smelled of smoke. Not in a body that smelled of that man when we were done. I was me again, and I was going to stay that way.

Twenty or so pairs of eyes were watching me. Some nodding.

"That was my rock bottom," I said, leaning into the mic on the podium. "Or the beginning of it. It took a lot of hard work and the benevolence of a total stranger to help me crawl out of it and see my own worth."

I glanced around at the faces in front of me that were waiting expectantly to hear the rest. My happily ever after. But I didn't have one, and I was done talking for the night. Telling my story—putting myself back on that street corner—turned me inside out. I didn't have it in me to keep going.

"But I don't want to eat up all of the time. I'll finish up next meeting."

The group offered a smattering of applause, and then Diane, the Narcotics Anonymous coordinator, resumed the stage.

"Thank you, Max, for that honest and deeply personal share. And welcome to our group. We are so glad you're here with us." She addressed the group at large. "Max was a sponsor in San Francisco, prior to moving here. . .what? A few weeks ago? We're so happy that he's willing to sponsor someone here as well. Please let me or Max know if you're interested."

More scattered applause and some tired nods. I recognized that weariness in the people assembled here. That bone-tiredness that came with the fight. Addiction thrashed you like a dog with a rabbit in its teeth, sometimes retreating but never slinking away for good.

Before I resumed my seat in the front row, I caught sight of a guy all the way in the back. He slouched in his chair with his long, jean-clad legs stretched out in front of him. He wore sunglasses indoors and a black sweatshirt with the hood pulled up over his head. A lock of golden blond hair had escaped the hood and hung over his brow. His full lips were pressed together, arms crossed tightly over his broad chest. His clothes looked plain enough, but his shoes and the sunglasses—not to mention the watch strapped to one tanned wrist—screamed *money.*

Hot Unabomber, I thought with a smile.

"Are there any new members who would like to introduce themselves?" Diane asked.

I imagined I felt the stranger's eyes boring into me. I suddenly itched to turn around and get a better look. No one responded, and I couldn't help myself; I snuck a glance over my shoulder. The tall guy shifted uncomfortably, arms crossed over his chest like a brick wall, his face a stony mask behind the glasses.

You're staring, I scolded myself. *Stop staring. Jesus, dude, this isn't a singles mixer.*

I faced forward as another person volunteered to share. The squeak of a chair brought me around again, and I watched the guy get up on long legs and stride out the door.

I was sorry to see him go. He might come back. He might not. Sometimes the desire for help drowned a swift death in the face of shame, guilt, and the vulnerability in asking for it in the first place.

The next group member took the podium to speak. I tried to give her my full attention, but the stranger in black kept wandering in and out of my thoughts.

At break time, I helped myself to coffee and donuts at the table near the door. Diane approached me.

"Thank you again for your offer," she said, pouring coffee into a beige mug with the Space Needle sketched in blue. "We'd love to have you, but a new city? New job? Are you sure you're settled in enough to jump into sponsorship?"

"I'm as settled as I'll ever be," I said. "And Seattle's not new. I was born and raised here."

Her eyebrows went up. "I see. And your parents?"

"The ones who kicked me out of the house?" I smiled thinly. "They're close. Down in Beacon Hill."

"Have you seen them since you moved back?"

"Not yet. Still working on that."

Diane put her hand lightly on my arm. "I'll speak to the Service Committee chair about your sponsorship. And with your parents, I wish you the best of luck. I'm here for you if you ever need to talk."

"Thank you," I said. I sipped my coffee, my gaze darting to the door where the guy in black had exited. "Seems like a good group. They been with you a while?"

"All but that hooded fellow in the back. He's new. Or was." She heaved a sigh. "Don't think he's coming back though. Seems like he took one look and decided he's not ready yet."

"I had the same thought."

Adios, Hot Unabomber. Best of luck.

The NA meeting got out at nine, and I headed straight to Virginia Mason Hospital. I'd only been back in the city for two weeks, crashing on my friend Daniel's couch while working the nightshift in the ER. I'd hardly had time to unpack let alone look for a place of my own.

At the hospital's back door, employee entrance, I paused before keying in the code to get in and mentally steeled myself for the night to come. Inside, I strode the relentlessly bright hallways, nodding at faces I knew. The air was sterile and cold, making me shiver.

Or maybe it's just this job.

I'd worked the ER at UCSF and that was hard enough, but the nightshift? A whole other ballgame. There was a sense of ugly danger to a young child being brought in on the nightshift versus that same child coming in the light of day. Broken arms at three in the morning were a lot more sinister than the playground fall at three in the afternoon.

The women too. Battered and bleeding. Brought in by neighbors who'd heard the shouting or sometimes the abuser himself, telling us how she'd fallen. Again.

But the hardest patients for me to tend were the young guys who'd OD'd. Homeless. Desperate. Guys with infections in their arms that I cleaned out, knowing they were just going right back out there to shoot up some more. I had been them.

This was supposed to be my dream—to be on the other side of the fight for life. But it was as if a mirror were being held up to my face, and instead of reflecting back the guy who put himself through school to be here, I saw myself as I'd been after Dad kicked me out of the house. The person I'd sworn I'd never be again.

Tonight was extra brutal. We lost someone.

A teenager was brought in. Not breathing. We did our best, but it was too late. While the kid's mother screamed in the hallway with the social worker, Dr. Figueroa, the attending physician, huddled us over the gurney for what she called The Pause. If we lost someone, she insisted we take forty-five seconds to hold hands, bow our heads, and honor the human being who had passed before us.

I bowed my head and squeezed my eyes shut to keep the mother's screams out and my tears in. Dr. Figueroa saw me wipe my hand over my eyes and pulled me aside.

"Hey. Max. You want to take five?"

I started to shake my head no, then nodded. "Yeah," I said gruffly. "Just give me a sec."

I hurried to the nurse's breakroom. In an ER, it was always empty. Always an emergency and always a shortage of nurses to attend to them. In the empty room, I sat on the bench and cried. I cried on the bus on the way back to Daniel's after work a lot of mornings too. I wondered if I were cut out for this.

You're here to help. This is what you signed up for.

After a few minutes, I pulled my shit together, heaved a breath, and went back to work.

At seven in the morning, shift over, I threw on my black leather jacket and headed out of the nurse's breakroom. Dr. Figueroa was waiting. She reminded me of Holly Hunter: small, smart, with dark eyes and brown hair cut in a razor-straight line at her shoulders and bangs. At 6'1" I towered over her by almost a foot, but she seemed tall and imposing.

"Want to tell me about it?" she asked. "How hard it's been for you?"

"Not really," I said with a rueful smile. "Growing pains. I'll get used to it."

She pursed her lips and we both stopped walking as I realized what I'd said.

"Get used to kids dying in my arms. Jesus." I shook my head and rubbed my burning eyes that stung with new tears.

"Come on," she said. "Let's get a coffee."

Down in the cafeteria, the doctor sat across from me, two steaming cups between us on the table.

"I've worked here for twenty-seven years," she said. "I know your type."

"My type?" I asked, my hackles starting to rise, but I was too tired to be offended.

"Empathetic. Wanting to help everyone to your own detriment."

"No, I—"

"You covered for Nurse Gabrielle on Monday?"

"She had an emergency. And we're shorthanded. That's not news."

"You covered for her this week, Peter last week, and Michaela two nights ago. When was your last day off?"

"I don't know," I said, thinking through a fog of exhaustion and the cacophony of my brain constantly screaming at me that I needed to be asleep when the sun went down, not the other way around.

Dr. Figueroa was staring at me pointedly.

"No, you're right," I said. "I'll take my time off. I need it. It's irresponsible not to."

"It's not just that. You came highly recommended out of UCSF. You're brilliant at your job. I'd hate to lose you."

"Lose me?" My heart slammed against my chest and now I was *awake*. "Are you firing me?"

"No," she said. "But I need you to be honest with me, Max. You can be the best nurse in the world but if it's too much, it's too much." She put a hand on my arm. "And I think, for someone like you, it's too much."

"It's not—"

"You have a huge heart. A genuine kindness. And it's sucking in every bit of misery that comes through those doors every night and not letting go. Right?"

I turned my coffee cup around in circles. "It's hard. There's so much pain."

"There is. But the desire to help alleviate that pain can't generate more pain for you."

I started to protest but then imagined a year in the ER. Five. Ten. Hell, I was already dreading next week.

"I wanted this so bad and now it seems I can't hack it."

"You might," Dr. Figueroa said. "But I think you could use some time to evaluate."

"I can't take time. I have to work. I need to find a place to live. I need to. . ."

Beg my parents to take me back as their son.

"I know you do," Dr. Figueroa said. "Dr. Archie Webb, a neurologist, is a friend of mine. One of his patients is very high profile, if you catch my drift." She rubbed her thumb over the pads of her first and second fingers. "He wants private, first-class care. All very hush-hush."

"Who's the patient?"

"One of our friends at Marsh Pharmaceuticals. Perhaps you've heard of them?"

I smiled wanly. "The name sounds familiar."

Every pen and pad of paper in the hospital had the Marsh name on it, not to mention every major museum from here to Europe. The Marsh's lived on a giant estate just outside the city and were considered royalty. Old world wealth that had ballooned into an empire when Marsh Pharma got the green light from the FDA to produce their most popular product, an opioid-based pain med called OxyPro.

"The patient works for Marsh?" I asked.

"The patient *is* Marsh." Dr. Figueroa lowered her voice and leaned over the table. "Edward Marsh III, president and CEO."

My brows raised. "Shit. He's sick? Something neurological?"

"He has multiple sclerosis," she said. "Primary progressive MS to be exact. Newly diagnosed. He's asked Archie to pick his nursing staff for him. He refuses to work with a hospice outfit or go through any of the other channels. Only the best of the best. Discreet to the point of iron-clad non-disclosure agreements and threats to sue anyone who breathes a word under patient privacy violations and such. Bottom line, Marsh doesn't want a soul to know he's sick. Or more accurately, he doesn't want his shareholders to know he's sick." She gave me an arch look. "I'm allowed to tell you, since you're bound to HIPAA regulations about patient privacy."

"I won't breathe a word," I said slowly. "And I'd be lying if I said I wasn't interested."

"Good. I'll put in a word for you with Archie, and he'll set up the interview with Marsh's team."

"I hate the idea of leaving you even more shorthanded but. . . Yeah, this sounds good."

"I think it is too," she said. "I'm not in the habit of finding my best nurses other places to work, but watching this job eat you alive kills me. Take care of Edward Marsh for a little while and reevaluate. It won't be easy. He's a ballbuster and tyrant. But you'll get more of a breather with him than here. And if the ER is really what you're meant for, you'll come back. Okay?"

"Thank you. I appreciate this a lot." I felt as if a three-thousand-pound weight had been lifted from my back. "When should I expect to hear from Dr. Webb?"

"Sooner rather than later, I'd guess. They're moving fast because the MS is moving faster." She reached across the table and patted my hand. "I'm going to miss you."

"I have to get the job first."

"Like I said, I'm going to miss you."

Outside, I hunched deeper into my jacket. Late August in Seattle brought warmer afternoons, but the mornings already had a bite of winter in them. I caught the 47 bus up Summit Avenue to Boylston, in the Capitol Hill neighborhood where a buddy of mine from high school, Daniel Torres, lived.

Inside, he was just getting ready for work, doing computer graphics at a start-up. Daniel was a small, slender guy, and spoke with a trace of an accent from his Mexican-American heritage. Today, he wore a black blazer, black skinny jeans, white shirt and bolo tie. His hair was dyed silvery-blue and a hoop earring glinted from his left ear, a small bar pierced his eyebrow.

"Hey, man," he said, watching me hang my jacket on the hook by the door. "You look like shit."

"Good morning to you too," I said with a tired laugh.

"I'm serious," Daniel said, pouring me a cup of coffee as I sat on a stool at the counter. His place was a small one-bedroom industrial-chic loft—brick walls, exposed ductwork, chrome fixtures. Prints with bold, wild streaks of paint hung from most walls, and the occasional houseplant added some warmth.

Daniel shook his head at me from across the counter. "I know you wanted this job, but damn."

"It's hard," I admitted, rubbing my eyes. "Harder than I thought."

"You want to talk about it?"

I probably *needed* to talk it out, but I didn't want to pollute Daniel's mind with the grisly images that haunted me. The blood and vomit. The gunshot wounds. The death.

"Thanks, but I'm good. I might be getting out of it, anyway."

I told him about the job offer as a private nurse to a wealthy patient, leaving out Edward Marsh's name.

"If I get the job, I'll have time to look for my own place and get out of your way."

"You're not in the way," Daniel said. "You know you can stay here as long as you need to, so put that out of your mind. When's your interview?"

"Not sure. Waiting for the call. But shit, Danny, I feel like a failure. Quitting already? What the hell did I come back to Seattle for?"

"To make amends with your folks," he said and sipped his coffee. He grinned. "To hang out with me the way we should've done in high school."

"Truth," I said, clinking my mug to his.

In high school, Daniel had been just as closeted as I was, though we'd both been suspicious of one another. *Because* we suspected, we never talked about it or even hung around together. We both feared being friends would somehow broadcast our homosexuality to everyone else, so we avoided each other like the plague.

But when I got the job offer at Virginia Mason, he was the only person—aside from my parents—I knew in Seattle. I reached out on Facebook, which led to phone calls where I confessed my whole sordid story. Our connection—or reconnection—was instant. The day he picked me up at the Sea-Tac airport, it was as if I were being reunited with a long-lost brother.

Daniel had shared his house and his friends with me, and I took it all as a sign that coming back to Seattle was the right thing to do. I hadn't counted on my job breaking me down, but now that was looking up too.

"So how goes it with the parental units?" Daniel asked.

"Slow. Mom keeps 'rescheduling' our dinner dates. I need a game plan with her before I tackle The Dad Situation."

Daniel waggled his brow. "And what about your Sex Situation? Any hot doctors at the hospital who are going to miss you terribly if you go?"

"No and besides, I have too much work to do on myself before I get involved with anyone. And no hookups," I said when Daniel started to speak.

He pouted. "A pity. You have the perfect set up. 'Hey, Hot Doctor. I'm leaving. Who knows when we'll see each other again? Oh look! This x-ray room happens to be empty. . .'"

"X-ray room?" I asked, laughing, then mentally replaced Hot Doctor with Hot Unabomber and nearly choked on my coffee.

"The *where* isn't the point," Daniel said. "The *who* is what counts."

"There is no who," I said. "I've got my hands full with scraping together a relationship with Mom and Dad."

"If you change your mind, you have options. Charlie thinks you're hot, and he's not wrong. You've got that sexy, smoldering, dark James Dean, motorcycle-greaser vibe going on."

I rolled my eyes. "I don't own a motorcycle."

"No, but you know how to accessorize like you do."

I laughed and sipped my coffee. "Aren't you going to be late for work?"

He heaved a dramatic sigh. "Yes. I'll go and let you sleep. Nighty-night. I hope you get the call."

"Thanks. Me too."

Daniel left, and I slumped on the couch. The idea of working for Marsh came over me again like a warm blanket of relief, bundling me against the guilt for leaving the ER already. Because lying to myself was an old habit too and one that I'd vowed never to pick up again. If I stayed in the ER, burnout was inevitable. I wasn't going to be good for anyone or myself. And after years on the streets, protecting myself was now my number one priority.

"The same goes for you, Mom and Dad," I muttered to the empty apartment.

I wanted desperately to rebuild all that was broken between us, but I'd spent the last seven years either in a drug-induced hell or climbing my way out of it. There was no way I'd let them push me back into the long, downward spiral of self-loathing and shame.

My exhaustion overpowered the coffee I'd had that morning, and my eyes started to droop. What felt like a second later, my phone rang. I peered blearily at the unknown number.

"Hello, Max speaking."

"Max Kaufman? This is Dr. Archie Webb."

CHAPTER TWO

Silas

The alarm went off at 5:00 a.m., but I was already awake. Outside the huge windows of my bedroom suite, the morning was gray and drab. I threw off the Egyptian cotton sheets and crossed my room that was minimalist but modern, like a five-star hotel suite. The fireplace was cold.

The immense walk-in closet was nearly empty. I didn't live here; I had my own penthouse in the city, but Dad had gotten sick, and so I moved back home to help get him situated. As soon as he was stable, I was out.

I put on workout clothes and headed through the upper floors of the east wing. My athletic shoes made no sound as I descended the long, curved staircase that led from the east wing to the marble foyer. Its twin curved down from the west wing.

In the kitchen, Ramona was there with her team preparing breakfast.

"Good morning, Mr. Silas," she said. "The usual? Fruit, eggs, coffee, and would you like sausage or bacon?"

"Bacon," I said without stopping. "In my room at seven."

"Very well."

I passed through the butler's kitchen, the formal living room, the dining room, and the "family" living room that was just as cold and unlived-in as the formal one but for the baby grand piano in the corner. I continued down into the basement that had been converted into a rec and workout room.

I lifted weights at fifty reps per arm, did fifty squats with a barbell across my shoulders, three hundred crunches with the medicine ball, and then ran five miles on the tread. At precisely 6:30 a.m., I went back upstairs to my room to shave and shower.

With steam from the running shower filling the cavernous bathroom, I drew the razor over my chin and made the mistake of making eye contact in the mirror.

A mask stared back.

Blue eyes, hard like ice. Blond hair in a two-hundred dollar cut—short on the sides, longer at the top so that a lock fell over my forehead. Tanned skin. Broad mouth. Square jaw. Long, straight nose.

A memory rose up around me, screamed in my ear.

Pretty boy, ain't you? Look at that face. But who's it for, eh? You're a ladies' man; don't tell me different. You were trying to thwart nature. Spit in the face of God with all your gifts. Genetics like yours are meant to be shared. You gotta spread your seed. Put it in a woman's womb and let it bear fruit. Sons. A lineage. You don't want to stray from the path nature intended, do you? Of course not. That's why you're here. To set you straight. Now pick up your tool, pretty boy, and get back to work.

I flinched out of the memory and half-expected to see my breath plume with icy Alaskan air. Instead of a forest of green trees brushed with snow, the bathroom materialized around me; expensive tile and chrome. Instead of an axe in my shivering hands, there was a razor. And instead of Coach Braun screaming in my face, only my reflection stared back.

Holy shit.

I sucked in a breath through my nose and the fear retreated behind the blue of my eyes. Blue like the water at Copper Lake in Alaska. Still and flat and cold.

I picked up my razor and got back to work.

I dressed in a Valentino suit of deep blue with a lighter blue silk tie and slipped on a pair of Ferragamo shoes. As I'd commanded, Ramona had one of the maids bring up my breakfast—fruit, coffee, bacon—on a silver platter and kept warm under silver domes, precisely at 7:00 a.m. I sat at the bay window that overlooked the grounds that were still summer green, the pool not yet covered for winter. I ate the food, hardly tasting it, and read the news on my phone.

Nothing about Dad. Yet.

I set the phone down and stared out over our forest. Beyond the treetops, Seattle still slept; the Space Needle poked out of a blanket of fog.

The lack of news about Dad's condition couldn't hold. Sooner or later, they'd wonder why he wasn't showing up to his offices downtown or why he'd video-conferenced his last board meeting. The shareholders would whisper or a nurse from the team his neurologist was hiring would talk, and then Dad would be forced to retire.

"And then it's mine."

The words came out cold and clipped. My voice had all the emotion of a robot. A shitty actor reciting lines. I was a character in the play of my life. A life that was nothing more than an endless string of days pretending, lying, burying truths and feelings until I was more stone and steel than hot, beating blood.

But as sick as he was—and getting sicker—Dad still had hoops for me to jump through before he'd hand me the keys to an empire *Forbes* said was worth twenty-six billion. Thinking I'd ever cross a finish line was dangerous—and foolish.

I whipped my wrist from under the cuff of my suit to check the time from my Patek Philippe watch. 7:30 a.m. Precisely on schedule.

I'd been careless and worn that eight-hundred-thousand-dollar watch to that shabby room in a dinky community college the other night. What the fuck had I been thinking?

Help. You need help.

I silenced the thought like an axe coming down in the winter forests of my memory, splitting the words into meaningless sounds. Coach Braun taught us that all weakness, including *needing help* belonged in the tight vault of my mind and heart. A vault created in Alaska, and so airtight I'd nearly convinced myself there was nothing in it. No weakness. No need for anything. Not help, not friends, not love. . .

Discipline. Order. Precision. Denial.

That was my life now.

Going to the NA meeting had been a mistake. A sign of weakness, just as it had been weakness to let pain killers disrupt my ordered, disciplined life in the first place.

Being the second son of Marsh Pharma was like carrying around a giant prescription pad. And that had made me a very popular guy at my high school, Benington Boarding Academy.

But I'd never taken them myself until after Alaska.

When I came back—and after they reluctantly released me from the hospital—our company's most popular painkiller, OxyPro, had been my constant companion. My helper through Yale School of Management, then management training at Marsh Pharma. Feeling nothing—keeping the vault locked tight—was fucking exhausting. The pills helped. A false euphoria that was like taking a break from life.

I'd pulled myself—kicking and screaming—out of the addiction on my own, but the pills were whispering to me again. So there I was, slouched in the back room of a community college, because if anyone knew Silas Marsh was at a fucking *Narcotics Anonymous* meeting with a bunch of fucking *drug addicts*.

And then this guy got up to speak.

"Hi, I'm Max."

"Hi, Max."

The Greek chorus had predictably chimed in, but I'd said it too. My mouth had formed the words—his name—without my permission.

Max. Tall, dark-haired, a wide mouth, and brown eyes that were sharp with intelligence and warmth. Kindness. The cut of his clothes—the way he wore his jeans, and how his black leather jacket lay over his broad chest and shoulders—told me he was built. Not as big as me, but he took care of himself, of his body. . .

The fork in my hand clattered to the plate, bringing me back to my room. Coach Braun was up in my face again, screaming so that his spittle flecked my stiff, cold cheeks.

You know what you are? You're a pathetic little pansy who forgot who he is. But I'll make you remember. Oh yes, by the time I'm done with you, you'll remember exactly what you are. And that is nothing. You. Are. Nothing.

I wiped my mouth with the linen napkin and left, leaving Max at the podium in that room where he belonged, telling his story of selling his body—to men—for drugs. That had nothing to do with me. Nothing at all.

Down the hall, in the right wing, I found Cesar Castro, head of household, talking to Dr. Webb outside Dad's suite of rooms. Cesar's smooth face made him look younger than his sixty years. I strode over to them quickly.

"Well?"

"Silas, good morning," Cesar said. "You remember Dr. Webb."

"Of course." We shook hands and then I crossed mine over my chest with a scowl. I hated repeating myself. "*Well?*"

"He's resting today," Dr. Webb said. "I recommend he keep resting. No work. Not even a phone call."

"Of course not," I said. "He can barely speak. How long do these flare-ups last?"

Dr. Webb rubbed his chin. "Multiple sclerosis is an unpredictable disease. In the case of your father, the flare-ups, or active periods of symptoms, are going to be more prolonged and progressive than in other forms of the disease. Remissions might be few and far between."

I stood silent, processing this information. It had only been a few weeks since Dad's hands had begun to shake over his dinner plate. By the next morning, his speech was affected, and he complained of numbness and tingling in his legs. An MRI showed lesions on his spinal cord and brain that led to his diagnosis. I'd immediately begun researching primary progressive MS and my stomach had twisted tighter and tighter the more articles I read. PPMS was the worst form of the disease and the hardest to treat.

"Will he improve?" I asked.

"Again, it's hard to tell. He may have periods of inactive symptomology. We've got him on the best and newest drugs—"

"Of course you do," I snapped. "We make those drugs."

Dr. Webb nodded. "Yes, quite. And we'll schedule another MRI in a week to see if there are any new lesions. That will give us the best indicator of the disease's progression. We'll have to wait and see."

Wait and see wasn't in the Marsh lexicon. Dad had never waited for anything a day in his life. He took action. As he had with me. Swift. Harsh. Unrelenting.

I straightened. "And who's taking care of him today?"

The doctor looked to Cesar uncertainly. "Yes. I have Roberto and Nina with him now—"

"They've been with him for two straight days," I said. "Where's the rest of your team?"

"It's a process," Dr. Webb said, "given the secrecy and legal hoops we have to jump through."

Cesar cleared his throat. "Dr. Webb has assured me that he has two more interviews today."

"Good," I said. "Make sure they won't talk. Get that ink on paper and then get them to work."

Dr. Webb looked miffed. He was a board-certified neurologist who'd pioneered gene sequencing therapy for Alzheimer's patients and was clearly not used to being spoken to like a servant. But you'd be surprised what people would put up with when you had the kind of money we did. The kind of money that made a world-class neurologist's salary look like minimum wage.

"I am interviewing the candidates personally," Dr. Webb said. "Two excellent prospects. One of whom comes especially highly recommended from a friend at Virginia Mason—"

"Fine. Get on it." I turned to Cesar who looked politely embarrassed on my behalf. "I'm going to see him before I head to the office to try to keep the hyenas from barking. Is he awake?"

"He was as of a few minutes ago."

Without a word, I strode through the first door to the sitting room of my father's suite, past a roaring fire, and then to the bedroom that smelled of disinfectant and urine.

A female nurse—Nina, I guessed—was there, making notes on an iPad. She smiled at me warily as I came in.

"I was about to go find you," she said, whispering. "He's been asking for you."

I nodded and approached, still marveling that the figure in the bed was my father. He'd been larger than life only a few short weeks ago. Tall—I'd gotten my height from him—imposing, with a voice that snapped and whipped and sent people scurrying to do his bidding.

Marsh Pharma had started as a tonic and elixir shop at the turn of the twentieth century and had grown over the decades into a family-run corporation, specializing in diabetes meds. But it was Edward Grayson Marsh III who'd taken the company into the stratosphere with its labs' production of OxyPro. Millions of dollars became billions in profit over the course of the last ten years, and Dad became a giant among men.

Now he looks like a scarecrow someone forgot to bring in for the winter.

I pulled up a chair. The chair my mother would have been sitting in had she still been alive. Dad's silver hair was thin and brittle, his beard yellowed around the nose and mouth. Even in sleep, his brows were furrowed, and his lips were drawn down in a scowl.

"I was told he'd be awake," I said irritably to cover my uncertainty about waking him. Even now, even as sick as Dad was, I second-guessed every word that came out of my mouth, every decision, every movement I made in front of him.

I coughed into my fist and Dad stirred. His eyes—clear and blue like mine and still sharp—opened and took me in. On a spasming, jerking neck, he turned his head to me on the pillow.

"Hey, Dad," I said in a quiet voice. "How are you?"

"D-d-don't be a f-fucking idiot," he hissed, each word a challenge to enunciate. "Time is. . . wasting. . ."

I sat up straighter. "I'm going into the office, business as usual. I'll run interference with Bradley and keep Vera off our backs. The latest line is you're taking a few days off—"

He shook his head and spit a word that might've been *bullshit*. Spittle flecked the bedsheets. "I d-don't take d-days off."

"Fine. You're meeting with investors at. . . I don't know. Our Tokyo compound? Or New York? Pick a place, Dad. We can't hide this forever. It's not going away."

"They s-said it c-comes and g-goes," he managed. "It'll g-go. T-Toe the line."

"That's not going to be enough."

"Toe... the... l-line."

"I'll do my best," I said and started to rise.

His hand shot out with surprising strength, and he gripped my wrist. "You l-love this, d-don't you? You love seeing the old man d-down."

"No, Dad, I don't."

He acted as if he hadn't heard me. Or believed me.

"It's not y-yours. N-Not yet. D-Don't f-fuck this up."

"I won't."

I got to my feet just as the door burst open and Edward Grayson Marsh IV came busting in. Eddie was my older brother by two years but looked ten years younger. Skinny, with hair darker blond than mine and greased into a perfect coif. He wore a tweed suit, bowtie, vest, and spats on his shoes. He looked like he was cosplaying at a Charles Dickens festival. Cesar, Nina, and the other nurse piled into the room after him, trying to hush him.

"I say, my good fellow!"

Eddie's high-pitched, reedy voice filled every corner of the huge bedchamber. Dad's hands on the coverlet clenched even as they trembled, and he grimaced at the noise.

"Silas!" Eddie boomed. "What's the news, old chap? Visiting our sweet P*apa*?"

"Hey, Eddie," I said, moving quickly to him and holding him loosely around the shoulders. "Let's tone it down a little. Dad's not feeling well."

"Right-o," Eddie said, just as loudly, pulling quickly out of my embrace. He addressed Dad without making eye contact with him or anyone else. "Father dearest, how are we? Not up to dick, I see. Terribly unfortunate."

I clenched my teeth and put my hand on Eddie's arm, carefully. His Asperger's meant when my brother got on to something, he stayed there. For months. My brother's latest obsession was with the Victorian era: speaking, dressing and behaving as if we were in England, circa 1880.

Eddie was supposed to be Dad's heir. Next in line to inherit the company like a modern-day monarch inherits the throne. But that was impossible and so it fell to me.

But I'd been a disappointment in other ways.

"I daresay it looks like rain," Eddie said to the floor. "We haven't had a good rainfall in a fortnight, I do believe."

Dad's jaw was working, his eyes squeezed shut. I looked in vain for Marjory, Eddie's personal therapist, while trying to gently usher my brother out of the bedroom before the entire situation blew up.

Too late.

"*Get that godforsaken retard out of here*," Dad bellowed without the slightest hitch or stutter.

Eddie froze, then began rocking back and forth. Anger filled me in a rush, and I whirled on my dad. "You don't talk to him like that."

Dad shook his head, beseeching the ceiling. "What have I d-done? Why am I c-cursed? Cursed with two defective sons?"

The anger burnt into humiliation. The nurses had no idea what Dad meant, but Cesar had been with the family since I was a kid. He looked anywhere but at me.

"Come on, Eddie," I said. "Let's go."

Gently, I led him out of the bedroom and down the huge, curving stairs to the family living room, where he began to pace. His hands were twisting together, over and over, around and around.

My phone buzzed a text from my assistant, Sylvia, at the office. **On the way? They're asking a lot of ???**

I muttered a curse and tapped out, **Coming.**

"I have to go to work, Eddie," I said. "Be good. Marj will be here soon."

"I say, old chap," Eddie said, his voice high and trembling. "Stay awhile, can you? There's a good man."

I glanced at my watch again. "I have to get to the office."

"Distressing," Eddie muttered. His hands twisted over and over, and he quickly paced the room, head down, back bent. "Terribly, terribly distressing. . ."

I put my hand lightly on his shoulder so he could move away easily if he wanted.

"Shh, it's okay."

But I could feel Eddie tremble beneath my palm. Dad's insult rattled my brother and he'd stay rattled all day if I didn't do something. I glanced at the piano while the seconds ticked by. I was late. I hated being late, but music was one of the few things that calmed my brother down.

"How about I play for you?"

Eddie nodded, his hands trembling. "M-Marvelous. I do so love a good tune now and then."

"Any requests?" I asked, taking a seat at the bench. Eddie hovered behind me and resumed pacing.

"Something snappy, I daresay," he said. "Perhaps a little 'Rondo'?"

"Sure thing, Eddie."

I laid my fingers over the keys, and after a second to focus, I played Mozart's "Rondo alla Turca." It was snappy for eighteenth century classical but complicated.

My hands moved by rote—I knew the piece backward and forward—while the oil portrait of Mom over the piano smiled down at us. The Rondo was one of the first pieces I'd learned to play when I was a kid, when Mom found out I had a knack for it.

You could be a classical pianist, playing for all of Europe, just like young Mozart, she'd often told me, clapping her hands and smiling. No one in our household smiled the way Mom did. Full of life and light.

I didn't know how I felt about my ability to play. It came naturally, almost uncannily. Like a language I was born knowing how to speak. I read music on the page and it translated to sound in my head and heart, and then was channeled instantly through my fingers. But what it meant to me or what I wanted to do with it. . . I never had a chance to think about it. I was never allowed to think about it.

Dad said playing the piano was a hobby, not a serious profession.

Only soft men twinkle their fingers over a piano for a living. My son will not be soft.

Mom had died before she knew just how serious my father's words were.

I brought the Mozart to its crashing conclusion and looked behind me to see Eddie had ceased his pacing and was smiling at the ground.

"Excellent show, my good man," he said, clapping his hands, though his gaze never met mine. He didn't or couldn't express his emotions the same way as everyone else.

After Alaska, neither could I.

"Yes, quite good. I have no doubts we shall see you bring down the house at Carnegie Hall." Eddie tipped an imaginary cap. "Good day, sir."

"Have a good day, Eddie," I murmured.

I gave the portrait of Mom a final glance. She'd died when I was eleven. Now she lived in oil paintings and photographs, staring and smiling at us from the other side of the film or canvas. I wanted to crawl inside those photos and be wherever she was.

Anything was better than here.

CHAPTER THREE

Max

"I got the job," I said, sliding onto a barstool next to Daniel.

His favorite bar, Smoke & Mirrors, was like his loft—industrial chic with brick walls, ductwork, and with a mirror behind the bottles of booze that enhanced and reflected the light. It was busy for a Wednesday night.

Daniel took up one rounded corner of the bar with his friends, Malcolm Nelson and Charlie Bryant. Over the last few weeks, those guys had become my friends too, though Charlie's eyes always raked me over with a slightly more-than-friendly interest, and his smiles for me were always loaded, as if he had a secret he was itching to tell me.

Charlie gave me one of those knowing smiles now. "Déjà vu. Weren't we just here a month ago, toasting your employment at Virginia Mason?"

"This is how Max gets us to pick up the tab," Daniel said, grinning over his White Russian. "He announces major life events. Next week, he'll come out of the closet. Again."

"Once was plenty, thanks." I turned to the bartender and said over the noise and music, "Soda water with lime."

"I'm happy for you, man," Malcolm said. "You were starting to look a little haggard. I was getting worried."

"Same," Charlie said.

"Thanks," I said. "Though I'm not sure this job is going to be much easier. The interview was brutal."

"But you aced it and now you're. . ." Daniel raised his eyebrows. "Wait, are you allowed to tell us?" He turned to the other guys. "He's hardly said a word to me. Top secret stuff. Very hush-hush."

"It's hardly James Bond-level intrigue. I'm now a personal nurse on a team for a very wealthy individual."

To put it mildly.

I coughed into my drink, thinking of the salary Cesar Castro, the Marsh head of household, had floated at me.

"*A very wealthy individual*," Daniel teased.

"Sounds silly, but I can't say more," I said. "My hand cramped from signing NDAs." I turned to Daniel. "But I can tell you that starting Saturday, I'll be off your couch. It's a live-in position."

"Not a cupboard under the stairs, I hope," Daniel said.

"Not quite. They gave me a room in the mansion."

"Fancy. Are you still in the city, at least?"

"Across the lake, over in Bellevue," I said with a smile and sipped my soda water. "I can still hang out on my days off."

Charlie eyed me over his beer. "Good to hear."

"Cheers," Daniel said, raising his glass. "To Max and his new job, taking care of a Rockefeller or one of Bill Gates' people." He froze, then clutched my arm. "Oh my God, is it? Is it Bill Gates? He lives in Bellevue. It's him, isn't it?"

"If it is, tell him Explorer crashed on my computer," Malcolm mumbled into his beer. "Again."

"It's not Bill Gates."

But in the same billionaire ballpark.

The guys toasted my job, and I smiled back and turned to scan the crowd of men—and a few women—talking at small tables under the '90s' alternative music playing over a sound system.

From the other side of Daniel, I felt Charlie's eyes on me. With blond hair and a beard over pale skin, he wasn't unattractive. His features—close-set eyes, small nose, small mouth—were all bunched in the middle of his face. Had I been looking, Malcolm would be more on my radar. He looked like Michael B. Jordan in a three-piece suit.

But I wasn't looking.

Longing, maybe, but not looking.

"Oh, I see Sheryl and Adnan," Daniel said, waving enthusiastically to some people at the door. He grabbed Malcolm's hand. "Come. You have to meet them. They're fab."

"We'll just stay here then?" I called after him, but Daniel only twiddled his fingers at me over his shoulder. When Charlie scooted onto his vacant seat beside me, I knew it was a setup.

He leaned in, while Chris Cornell sang about falling on black days.

"So, Max."

"So, Charlie," I said with a wry smile. "Something on your mind?"

"Yes, as a matter of fact," he said. "You've been on my mind. Quite a bit."

"If that didn't sound so much like a line, I'd be flattered."

"It's one hundred percent a line." He nudged my arm. "But come on. You haven't thought about it? You and me. Hanging out. Alone. Doesn't have to be serious. In fact, I'm sort of allergic to serious."

I sipped my soda water. "Has Daniel told you about my situation?"

"A little. You grew up here, but your parents kicked you out and now you're back to try to make them see the light. The song of our people."

"That's part of it," I said. "The rest of it has left *me* allergic to being dishonest. With myself. With others."

"I'm about to be shot down, aren't I?"

I smiled to take the sting out of it. "Nothing personal, but I don't do casual. Not now anyway. I've been on shaky ground since I was seventeen, and I'm not. . ." *Letting myself get hurt.* "Getting involved with anyone until I know it's the real deal."

Charlie blew air out his cheeks. "Danny warned me about you."

"How's that?"

"I told him I wanted to hook up with you. He said I could give it a shot but that I'm not worthy."

My eyes flared. "Not *worthy*?"

Charlie waved his hands. "I was peeved at first, but I get it." He tilted his beer bottle my way. "There's something about you, Max Kaufman. You're like. . . I don't know. Too good to be true. Danny's phrase, not mine. But I see it."

"That's so far from the truth," I said, even as a warmth spread in my chest. I hated to admit it, but since I got kicked out of my house, my heart clung to kindness. Tightly.

Charlie shrugged. "You're smart. No, *wise.* I heard that advice you gave Mal about his brother the last time we were here. You got some shit to say."

I shifted on my stool. "If I have any advice worth hearing, it's only because I hit rock bottom a few years back and have some perspective."

"Right. Perspective. And from my utterly shallow and superficial *perspective,* you're hot. And that's my primary focus right now." He sighed dramatically and laughed. "See? Danny was right. I'm not worthy."

"That's ridiculous."

Charlie shrugged. "You have your shit together. Nothing wrong with that, rare though it may be."

I didn't have my shit together. It only looked like I did because I stayed focused on my work and on keeping myself protected, in my job or anywhere else. But that came with drawbacks. I wasn't able to have fun without overthinking everything or letting my time on the streets creep in and fuck it all up.

I'd made a promise to myself that the next time a man touched me, it'd be because he wanted to give as much as take. He'd look at me with more than naked lust in his eyes. He'd see *me*...

"Yeah, Daniel's overstating it," I said. "By a lot. I don't have my shit together and I'm certainly not *wise*. I don't feel wise, anyway. I feel..."

Lonely.

The thought crept in and I kicked it right back out.

"Focused," I said. "I'm just focused."

Charlie smirked. "You know what you want, right? And you're not going to compromise." He clinked his glass to mine. "That, my friend, is having your shit together."

I didn't have anything to say to that. The others came back, Daniel shooting Charlie and me a questioning look. Charlie gave a thumb's down, but after another hour at the bar, he ended up going home with some guy he'd met at a party a week ago. Daniel and his friends went out clubbing.

Me and all my "wisdom" went home alone.

Friday afternoon, I stuffed my meager belongings into a duffel bag and rolling suitcase. Cesar Castro had told me my room in the gigantic house would be ready for move-in the following morning.

Daniel was working late, but when he got back, we'd have a farewell pizza. In the meanwhile, I decided to go back to the community college to talk more with Diane about potentially sponsoring someone. Now that I was out of the ER and not perpetually on the verge of a nervous breakdown, I felt more able to help.

At the college, I sat with mostly the same group. Some I recognized from last time. Some were absent. Some new.

And in the back was Hot Unabomber.

Damn. . .

My heart inexplicably skipped a beat to see him slouched in his chair again, long legs spread out, arms crossed. He wore a different expensive-looking hoodie, jeans, and black boots. The sunglasses over his eyes couldn't disguise how damn beautiful he was. I drank in his chiseled jaw and that mouth. . . Jesus. Daniel liked to drool over Tom Hardy's full lips. Hot Unabomber would've given Tom a run for his money.

The guy caught me staring and cocked his head to the side as if to say, *Can I fucking help you?*

I coughed and faced forward as Diane took the podium to call the meeting to order. A woman came up to share, followed by an older man. I did my best to give them my full attention, but I felt a gravitational pull to the guy in the back.

Get a grip. You're a self-proclaimed monk and everything about him screams "fuck off."

But he'd come back. I'd thought I'd never see him again, and here he was, back to give it another shot.

Good for you, man.

Diane addressed the assembly. "Would anyone else like to share?"

The crowd wasn't talkative that night. Neither was I. The room went quiet.

"Sure."

The word dropped into the silence in a low, deep voice.

Heads turned to the guy in the back. Casually as hell, I turned too, to see Hot Unabomber had leaned forward and rested muscular forearms on his thighs.

"Wonderful," Diane said. "Would you like to come up—?"

"I'm good here."

"Very well."

The guy studied his hands, steepling long fingers together. "My name is. . . Scott."

"Hi, Scott," we all replied.

His shoulders hunched up higher, and for a split second, I thought he was going to bolt. But he inhaled, his broad chest and back expanding. Though he spoke to the ground, his voice carried through the room, deep and strong but flat. Emotionless.

"A few years ago, I went through some rough times, and when I came back—came out of it," he amended quickly, "I was pretty fucked up. And I didn't want to feel that way anymore. I didn't want to feel anything. I had a ready supply of OxyPro at my disposal. You know? The painkiller?"

More than one head in the room nodded. More than half, actually.

And now I'm working for the owner and CEO who created that painkiller.

It occurred to me I knew next to nothing about Marsh Pharma except that they dumped a ton of money into Seattle Medical Center to get the doctors to push their pills.

"I crushed the pills and snorted them," Scott was saying. "They worked faster that way."

More heads nodded.

"I did that on and off for years, and then it got worse. And it stopped helping. I don't mean I built up a tolerance, though I did. I mean that the pills stopped helping because it didn't matter if I took them or not. My life was still my life. I was either going to keep doing more and more drugs and wind up dead, or I could just cut out the middleman and get it over with."

My heart clenched in my chest and I found myself leaning in my chair, wanting to be as close to Scott as I could. His pain was evident in every hard syllable. No tears. No choked throat. Only a stiff, stoic resignation of what was. A soldier doing his duty. I wondered if he were a veteran. Maybe the "rough times" he'd come back from was a deployment.

"But I have responsibilities," he continued. "To my brother, mostly. So, I got myself clean. I weathered the withdrawals on my own, got on Narcan to curb the craving. A few months later, I cut out that too. That was six months ago." He stopped talking and sat back in his chair, arms crossed again. "So. . . that's it. That's my story."

Diane smiled gently. "And what brings you here tonight, Scott?"

He stiffened. "I don't know. Weakness, probably."

"You think it's weakness to need help?"

"I'm not here for help," he said. "No one can help me but me. I'm here because. . ." His lips pressed together, and he waved a hand in a short, curt gesture. "Nothing. Never mind."

Diane nodded. "Okay, then. Well, we're here for you. Always."

Scott said nothing, though it seemed as if his eyes were boring into me from behind the sunglasses.

Your imagination. Your wishful *imagination.*

Another person took a turn at the podium to share. Scott's courage had spurred mine; I planned to finish my story about how I'd gotten clean, but now a lot of people were suddenly ready to talk, so I listened instead. By the end of the meeting, rain was pattering at the high windows and Scott was sitting as if he were waiting for something, arms crossed impatiently. When Diane called the meeting adjourned with a serenity prayer, he got up and left without a word to anyone.

I left too, wanting to get home to hang out with Daniel for as long as possible before I went to the Marsh estate in the morning. I figured I'd give Diane a call about sponsoring after I got settled into my new place.

Outside, the rain was falling in sheets. Other meeting attendees scurried down the college's cement steps and into the night. I huddled against the wall to call an Uber, shielding my phone from the rain that was driving down in hard bullets. The app said a driver was nineteen minutes away.

"Shit."

Stupid to wait in the storm. I pushed the heavy door to get back inside and smacked headlong into Scott.

He was a few inches taller than me—6'3" to my 6'1"—broader across the shoulders. I was a regular gym rat too; we hit like two boulders crashing together and stumbled back.

"Watch it," Scott snarled, then stopped as he eyed me up and down behind his glasses. "Oh. You."

He said it impatiently, as if he'd been waiting for me.

"Yep, it's me," I said. "I thought you'd left."

Scott jerked his chin at the phone in my hand, where the Uber app was visible. "You need a ride?"

I blinked stupidly. This close, his cologne—something clean and undoubtedly expensive—went straight to my head. "Uh. Sure."

"Let's go."

I took two steps and came to my senses. "Wait. Hold up. Despite what I said the other night, I don't get into strange men's cars on the regular."

Scott's stony expression morphed into flustered shock that looked out of place on his features. "I know that. I'm not trying to. . . I mean, that's not why I offered."

"I'm kidding. Rehab humor," I said with a grin. "I'm just saying we don't know each other very well. Or. . . at all."

"Right," he said flatly, nodding at the Uber app. "It would be totally reckless and crazy to get into a complete stranger's car."

I laughed. "Touché. But my Uber driver wouldn't wear sunglasses in a thunderstorm."

Scott started to speak, then cut himself off as Diane and some other people from the meeting went by; the director nodded at us with a small smile. He waited until she was gone.

"It's supposed to be Narcotics *Anonymous*," he said in a low voice.

"You're more conspicuous with them on, honestly."

"Fine." He took the glasses off his face and pushed the hood down on his sweatshirt. "Better?"

I stared, drinking in his chiseled features—a face cut from stone but covered in tanned skin. His eyes were a crystal blue under heavy brows. His hair was metallic blond, thick, shiny and perfect. And his mouth. . .Jesus. Full lips and chin with a cleft you could fit a quarter in.

"Are you an actor?" I blurted and then held up my hands. "Don't answer. It's just that you're so. . ." *Fucking beautiful.* "Hell-bent on secrecy."

"I'm not an actor," he said. "I'm in. . . the family business. You?"

"I'm an ER nurse. Or was. I'm on hiatus. I took a different job to slow down and get my bearings."

The lights in the building started their automatic shutdown, and a man with keys was heading down the hallway to lock up.

Scott glanced down at me. "Satisfied yet? Have we made the requisite amount of small talk to convince you I'm not a serial killer?"

You'll always be Hot Unabomber to me.

A laugh nearly burst out of me, and I corralled my runaway thoughts just as lightning sliced the sky.

"I'll take that ride."

I followed Scott to the parking lot at the side of the college, both of us hurrying through the rain that bounced off my black leather jacket but soaked his hoodie straight through. Scott unlocked a new-model black Range Rover SUV with a key fob, and we dove in. I climbed into the passenger seat, him behind the wheel. The car was immaculately clean and smelled expensive; hints of his cologne hung in the air.

I tried not to stare as Scott peeled off his drenched hoodie, but holy shit. . . He wore a white T-shirt that clung to his broad chest and powerful shoulder muscles. The expensive watch I'd seen the other night highlighted the perfection of his tanned forearms. With effort, I averted my eyes.

My own hair was wet, and I ran my hand through it, pushing it off my face. From my peripheral vision, I saw Scott's eyes widen, taking me in, drinking me up like rainwater.

Then he whipped his gaze away and muttered something to himself. I only caught the word "mistake."

"Sorry?"

"Never mind." He started the car, making the engine roar. "Where am I going?"

I gave him Daniel's address and he punched it into his GPS. Scott began to drive, and the silence was thick and potent. I had the sense of a clock ticking down the seconds of our time together.

Do I want more time with him?

On a purely physical level, the answer was a resounding *yes*. But Scott was a mystery. No ring on his finger. No clue about his sexual preferences. I got the impression he was extremely intelligent, which was almost more of a turn-on than his looks. If, by some miracle, he was gay, I'd have felt cosmically obligated to ask for his number, precautions be damned. But I had no clue. Not even on an instinctual level. Scott was a walking, talking ice cube; I couldn't imagine him looking at anyone—man or woman—with warmth or affection.

Fucking like a racehorse? Yes. That I can imagine.

I shifted in my seat and struggled for something to say that wasn't wildly inappropriate since my brain's normal filter was apparently broken around Scott. But Daniel's loft wasn't far from the community college, and suddenly the SUV was at the curb.

Time's up.

I reached for the door handle, slowly, waiting for Scott's motive for giving me a ride to show itself. His face was stony, but a thousand thoughts played behind his eyes.

"Well. Thanks for the lift. . . ?"

"You never finished your story," he said abruptly.

There it is.

"My story?"

Scott turned the ignition off and faced forward, watching the rain come down. "The other night you said you hit rock bottom, but you never told the rest of it."

"That's why you offered me a ride."

"What was I supposed to do? I fucking came back *to the group* to hear it, but you never talked."

I sat back in my seat. "You came back to hear *my* story?"

"Yes."

"Why?"

"Because what the hell is it all for? You told the shit part. What about the rest? What's on the other side of the misery?"

I faced forward, my brows furrowed. "It's personal. I don't just go spewing it on demand."

"But you'd tell a room full of strangers?"

"Because that's what the group is for. I'm not your personal happily-ever-after ATM. I don't even know you. If you want to hear my story, come to the next meeting."

"I'm not going back."

Anger brewed in him, cold and stony instead of fiery. He sat forward, his hands gripping the wheel, and I got another strong impression that he was used to getting what he wanted.

"Okay, well. . ." I said. "See you around."

I reached for the door handle again, and then Scott's hand was on my arm, hard through the leather of my jacket. My nerve endings lit up and electricity danced across my skin, across my shoulder, and made the hair on the back of my neck stand up.

"Wait."

In one syllable, I heard the crack in his cold shell of armor. When I lifted my gaze to his, I saw it in the blue depths of his eyes. He *needed* to hear that there was "something on the other side of misery."

Hope. He needs hope.

We locked gazes, then both looked to where he touched me. He snatched his hand away.

"Forget it," he said. "Go if you're going."

But I didn't move. For several seconds we sat in silence. The rain streaked the windshield in rivulets, lit from the lone lamp on the darkened, deserted street.

"Where did I leave off?" I asked finally.

"You let go of the lamppost," he said quietly. "You got in the car and. . ."

"I sold myself for the first time."

Scott flinched, and I wondered if he had a similar history. I wondered why the hell I was telling him my story in his car on a darkened street, but the words came out.

"I worked that street corner for six weeks. Doesn't seem like much but it was the worst fucking six weeks of my life. One night, a retired undercover cop pulled up to the curb. I was high as fuck and thought he was a customer. He took me to his place, and I started to unbuckle my pants, but he shook his head and lay me on his couch. He didn't touch me but to cover me with a blanket and sit with me while I talked nonsense. His name was Carl, and I stayed on that couch for days."

Scott nodded, listening, his eyes straight ahead.

"When I puked from the drugs wearing off, Carl held the trashcan. When the sickness became a monster, he held *me* as I fought and screamed and begged him to get me more. I hit him. I called him a pervert and a son of a bitch. I cried on his shoulder. I don't remember him saying much. He was just there. Like a rock, sheltering me from a terrible storm that had been blasting me since my dad kicked me out of the house for the crime of being gay."

Scott's entire body stiffened, and he turned his head to look at me, slowly. "He caught you with someone."

"Yes," I said, remembering I had said that at the meeting the other night.

Scott nodded once. "Continue."

I smiled faintly. "Yes, sir."

He didn't smile back.

"I was sick as hell for days and the cop never left me. When the worst was over, we talked. Or I talked and he listened. He brought me hot meals and water. He took me to the doctor, where, by some miracle, I was given a clean bill of health. He got me into recovery. He drove me to NA meetings. He helped me get my GED and then apply to college. He co-signed on my own place. We went to dinner once a week. He hardly spoke, but I talked until I was sure he was sick of me."

I fought back a wave of emotion that always swelled when I thought of the incredible kindness and sacrifice that man—a stranger—had shown me. More than my own parents had.

"The addiction was still there, of course. I fought it as best I could, but I was slipping. Then Carl didn't show up for our weekly dinner without a text or call, and that wasn't like him. When I went to his place, I found him on the couch where I'd lived for months. Heart attack, they told me later."

"Shit," Scott said.

"Yeah," I said gruffly, tears threatening as the old grief flooded me. "I sat beside him on the couch and said, 'Thank you.' I didn't say it enough in all of our time together. I've been clean ever since."

I heaved a breath, mastered my emotions again.

Scott faced forward, seeming to process all of this. "You kept clean for him."

"At first, yes," I said. "He was dead, and the idea of going back to drugs after all he'd done for me felt like a betrayal. As if he'd died for nothing. But later, I stayed clean for me. And when all is said and done, that's the only way to make it stick."

Scott snorted as if he didn't believe me, and I got the impression he was waiting for something else to happen. Some word or gesture that would let him tell more of his own story that he'd only scratched the surface of in the meeting.

"Hey," I said slowly. "Do you want to go grab a coffee or something?"

For a split second, Scott's chiseled, handsome face softened, and he looked at me as if he were about to say yes. As if he wanted nothing more in this world than to say yes to sitting at a crappy diner over a cup of hot coffee while the rain came down outside. With me.

Then he faced forward, a door slamming shut.

"I have to get home," he said, curt and clipped. "Have a good night."

I stiffened, then stared for a moment, feeling how I used to feel when I'd been high and had made a fool of myself in front of someone sober. Feeling used. My cheeks burned hot, and I reached for the car door handle.

"Yep," I said shortly. "Thanks again."

I slammed the door and hurried through the rain to the awning over Daniel's building.

So what? I thought, fumbling for my keys and fighting that goddamn tired feeling of rejection. *I would have told my story at the NA meeting next week.*

Except telling Scott in the dark of his car, in the rain, wasn't the same. And as the car pulled away from the curb and was swallowed by the night, I knew Scott meant what he said about not going to any more meetings.

He'd taken a piece of me and then driven off, and I was never going to see him again.

CHAPTER FOUR

Silas

"Fuck." I glanced to the empty passenger seat where Max had been sitting. Max. I hadn't even done him the courtesy of saying his name. I used him. Got what I wanted out of him and kicked him out of the damn car. My hands itched to swing the car around and go back and...

What? Just what the hell are you thinking?

I was thinking about Max.

My damned thoughts were full of him and had been since I first saw him the other night at an NA meeting I swore I wouldn't go back to. But I went back. I *shared* for fuck's sake because...

I'm pathetic and riddled with weakness.

Defective.

I pulled the car over. The road in front of me was black, streetlights streaking it with silvery rain. I could go back. Go to the next meeting. Find Max and tell him...

Tell him what? Coach Braun wanted to know. *Just what do you think you'd like to tell your street hustlin' fairy friend?*

An ugly laughed burst out of me. Braun had been a skinny, wiry guy.

Leathery skin, craggy face bitten by cold and wind. Max was no lightweight; he could have taken Braun out in one punch. I'd seen the way Max's black leather jacket hung on his broad shoulders. Lean muscles and with a wide mouth that I couldn't stop staring at while he talked.

We don't think about things like that, a real memory from Alaska whispered. *You get one of those unwanted, unnatural desires, you just lock it up in the vault. Pay it no mind. You do that long enough, and one day you don't feel anything. And feeling nothing is better than feeling the things you shouldn't.*

I rested my head against the steering wheel. Damn, I was tired. So tired of being this. . . creature. Not a real man. Not anything. Stuck permanently between what Dad and Coach Braun wanted me to be and the real me, whatever that was. I didn't know anymore.

It was locked in the vault too.

I sucked in a breath through my nose and pushed it all down. Max too. Especially Max. He'd stayed clean for that guy, Carl. I could stay clean for Eddie. Maybe someday it'd feel like being clean was worth it for me. Maybe Dad finally trusting me to take over the company would be worth it. Maybe controlling how half the nation got its meds and rolling in billions of dollars would make up for living half an existence.

I started the car and kept driving. When I got to my rooms in Dad's house, I turned on the shower, cold bullets like the rain drenching me. Purifying me. Cleansing me of thoughts I shouldn't be having about Max. About a man. My skin broke out in gooseflesh, my chest constricted.

But after a few minutes, the cold settled in.

The next morning, Saturday, I went through my usual routine: workout, breakfast, and then I headed to the office after making sure Eddie was happy. Usually we spent Saturdays together, but I had too much work to catch up on in my new-ish post as Chief Operating Officer.

Eddie sat at the fireplace in the family living room, reading Chaucer with an unlit pipe stuck in the corner of his mouth.

"I have to work today, Eddie," I said. "Raincheck on hanging out?"

He frowned at his book. "I do enjoy our Saturdays," he said. "Your piano talent is a gift from the very gods."

"Don't know about that. I'll make it up to you later this afternoon, I promise."

"Very well, dear brother. If you must go, I shan't keep you."

"Have a good day, Eddie," I said, kissing the top of his head. He didn't like to be touched too much beyond that.

"I say, have a marvelous day, old chap," he said with his teeth clenched on the pipe.

He didn't look up from his book. Eddie was living on the periphery of this world too. Pretending to be something else except he was happy doing it. And his happiness was the only fucking thing that was real. I had to protect him at all costs.

I nodded coldly to Marjory who had just come in. "Make sure no one bothers him."

Especially our dad.

Her smile tilted at my harsh tone. "Of course, Mr. Marsh."

Downtown Seattle. The office was humming even this early on a Saturday morning. There was simply too much work to do and too much money at stake, and Dad's absence had to be explained. Earlier that week, we announced he was "taking a small, temporary step back," and that I would step more fully into my role of COO.

I was met with polite nods or ass-kissing smiles as I strode through the executive floor. A few offered a "Good morning, Silas," which I ignored. I'd spent the last five years—from Yale through management training—practicing the "don't fuck with me" demeanor I'd been taught in Alaska. It left me cold. Unsmiling. "Masculine."

Most of the old-timers at Marsh Pharma knew about Alaska, but the PR line on that—even among my own family—was that I'd been "acting up" and needed discipline. They all thought that Dad had sent me to a character-building wilderness-survival type of extended camp. Hunting, fishing, making lean-tos out of shrubbery and splitting wood. Manly-man activities and nothing but, for six months.

They didn't need to know I'd nearly lost two toes to frostbite after being forced to march all night in a snowstorm with six other boys in the dead of winter.

Or that I spent Christmas huddled around a thin flame in the middle of the icy nowhere, blowing on my fingers and trying not to freeze to death while being screamed at that I was nothing. Worthless. Unnatural.

They didn't want to hear about the "personality reprogramming" happening around the cabins and campfires at night or the generators that powered not space heaters but TVs, a VCR, and electrodes.

"Good morning, Silas," said my assistant, Sylvia Timmons, at her desk outside the COO office. She handed me a black coffee and the morning's briefing as we entered the glass-enclosed corner office that looked down on all of Seattle.

It had only been mine for a month; I was newly promoted. Dad had—not coincidentally—ordered my promotion on the Monday following the weekend Faith Benson and I had made our big announcement. If any of the staff were upset that I'd ousted Howard Bruckheimer from his role after thirty-plus years with Marsh Pharma, they kept their mouths shut about it around me.

I sat in my chair and Sylvia flipped her razor-cut shoulder-length black hair out of her face as she stood behind me, handing me one file after another.

"This is the quarterlies report you asked for. These are the projections. These are the shareholder email inquiries about your dad's whereabouts. I printed them out and did email triage, tabbing them according to which ones I felt needed immediate attention and which would be satisfied with a thinly-veiled, 'Everything is fine; fuck off.'"

"And the distribution reports?"

"Here." She handed me another file. "You have a meeting with Stephen Milton at ten. He'll give you the movements of the sales reps in the field and some ideas on where to take the marketing next quarter."

"Fine. Thanks."

Sylvia left me to study the reports in order to be prepared to meet

Stephen Milton, the head of the marketing department. From what I'd heard, he was sharp, but an oily bastard who'd sell his own mother for a dollar. Because his department had been generating profits in the multi-millions every quarter, our meeting was mostly a routine check-in. The marketing department had a green light to do what it pleased.

As I flipped through the files, last night's NA meeting kept filtering in between the sales figures and profit margins. More than half of the group nodding to say they were quite familiar with OxyPro, the star in our pharmaceutical galaxy.

I pulled up a profit index from the southeastern region of the country. The dollar signs had been my focus, but now I looked more closely. The numbers on the pages in front of me started to align themselves more clearly, like hieroglyphics morphing into English. Profits morphing into people.

Miller's Creek, West Virginia	Pop. 3277	30,000 doses distributed
Havenwood, South Carolina	Pop. 8935	70,000 doses distributed
Marquette, Virginia	Pop. 2502	25,000 doses distributed

One glossy photo at the bottom of the report boasted of the lone pharmacy in Marquette looking like an Apple store on iPhone release day; people in a line that stretched around the corner.

"What the fuck. . .?" Without looking up, I reached my hand to the intercom button on my phone. "Sylvia. Get in here."

She scurried in. "Sir?"

"Are these right? How can they be right?"

She came around to my side of the desk and hovered over my shoulder. "I'm not sure I'm seeing the issue."

"The issue is the dosages," I said. "Why the hell are we dosing a town of less than four thousand people with thirty thousand pills?"

She blinked. "I. . .I don't know. The doctors, I'm sure, know what they're doing. . ."

"Really?" I held up another piece of paper. "This expense report says Marsh Pharma spent more than fifteen million last year in private retreats, incentives, bonuses. . . And if I'm reading between the lines, they even offered favorable ratings to doctors if they pushed OxyPro."

"Okay?"

"Not okay. Something's really *not fucking okay*, and things that are not fucking okay usually turn into *gigantic fucking lawsuits*."

Sylvia blinked then regained her composure. "Shall I see if Mr. Milton can come in sooner?"

"Yes. As in, now."

In the car on the way back to the estate, I tugged at my tie and rubbed my eyes. Stephen Milton had talked a good game, selling me on his department's strategies likely in the same way he sold our painkillers to the nation. The bottom line: we'd become the world's largest and most profitable drug dealer. OxyPro, that was supposed to treat terminal cancer patients and others with chronic, severe pain, was being prescribed for wisdom teeth removal and tennis elbow.

It had taken me all of a week to figure out I'd get a better high from crushing and snorting the pills than from swallowing them to feed my own addiction. I couldn't be the only one.

This is bad.

But the drug's addictive potential for abuse wasn't part of Milton's battle plan. I'd ordered him to show me overdose data for those same counties and he smoothly replied, "Essentially, you're new to the game and need not trouble yourself with all the details just yet."

I *essentially* told him to get the fuck out of my office, ordered Sylvia to pull the data for me by Monday, then went home.

"Christ," I muttered now as the sedan pulled into the circular drive. I didn't have the big picture, but what little I'd seen told me that, at best,

Marsh Pharma was wading through a minefield of potential lawsuits for over-prescription that could bankrupt us. At worst. . .

Heads nodding in a dim room. Misery. Addiction.

At worst, thousands upon thousands of lives ruined.

The car came to a stop and I shook my head. It was too early to be this pessimistic. I'd talk to Dad and let him tell me I was a fucking moron for worrying over matters I knew nothing about. He'd set me straight, and then I'd find Eddie and play piano for him. The rain had stopped—gray sunlight filtering in through the clouds. Maybe we could take a walk and pretend we were strolling through the English moors in 1885, or wherever he imagined us to be.

Inside the expansive foyer, Cesar Castro was speaking to a man in royal blue nurses' scrubs and two doctor-looking types—Dr. Webb, Dad's neurologist, and Dr. Tran, Dad's primary physician.

"Ah, Silas," Cesar said. "The doctors were just explaining that the nursing team for Mr. Marsh is in place, under the command of Mr. Roberto Carrillo, here." He indicated the nurse in royal blue. Cesar had decided that all the hires for Dad would wear a uniform while on duty.

I nodded curtly at the group. "How is he today?"

"Better," Dr. Webb said. "The flare-up seems to be quieting. He—"

"Can he talk? I need to speak with him."

"Yes. Much more clearly today. He's up there with his full nursing team, giving them their marching orders, so to speak."

Poor bastards.

"Roberto will go up with you," Cesar said.

I nodded and we headed up the spiraling staircase. Roberto was a tall guy with a friendly face.

"I was speaking to Cesar just now about the possibility of putting in an electric mobility chair on this staircase to help your father come down when he's ready."

"The back stairs, not these," I said. "He'd hate the spectacle of it here. And it'd be an eyesore."

"Right."

"An elevator would be better. We'd been planning to implement one anyway. I'll have Cesar get in touch with the contractors."

"Uh, great," Roberto said. He laughed lightly. "It's fortunate your father has the means for such care. He must be so grateful to have you."

"Yep," I muttered into my collar. "He's so grateful."

I stepped into Dad's suite of rooms with Roberto behind me. Dad was sitting up in his bed against a mound of pillows with four other nurses standing nearby—three men and one woman—in the new Marsh royal blue scrubs: short sleeves and V-neck collars.

"I may be the patient but that doesn't mean you're in charge," Dad was saying. "Do as you're told, keep your mouths shut, and we'll get along."

I went inside, impatient to clear the room and have a word. The chamber was dim, the curtains drawn closed, and *holy shit*, one of the nurses looked exactly like. . .

Max.

I jerked to a stop. Stared. My heart tried to crawl out of my throat while my stomach dropped to my knees. And for one perfect, incomprehensible second, something light and warm and good flooded the empty spaces in me before being flushed out in a deluge of adrenalized fear.

Max stared back at me, his dark eyes wide with surprise. I thought I saw a smile tug at the corner of his mouth, but it was dim, and I probably imagined it.

Was I imagining him too? How was he here, in my house? The only person on earth who knew I'd been hooked on my family's favorite commodity was standing less than two feet from my father. He knew my dad was sick, too. He knew everything. . .

"Silas," Dad barked. "What the hell is wrong with you?"

I snapped to attention, tore my eyes from Max and inhaled sharply through my nose. I hardened my heart, my muscles, my entire body, until I stood like a statue at the foot of Dad's bed.

"Yeah, hi, Dad. We need to talk. But I can come back."

After I deal with the mole in our ranks.

"Talk now," Dad said. He waved a hand at the nurses. "They aren't anyone."

It took every ounce of will I had not to look at Max. "No," I said in a rare act of defiance. "I'll come back."

I turned on my heel and strode out of the suite, ignoring my father's gruff call. I waited farther down the hall, in a window alcove beside the linen closet, until the nurses filed out some ten minutes later. Max came last, closing the door to Dad's suite softly behind him.

I swept up silently and gripped his arm. "May I speak with you for a moment?" I said through clenched teeth. I shoved Max into the walk-in linen closet, flipped on the light and shut the door behind me, still with him tight in my grip.

Max's face contorted in anger. "The hell—?"

I crowded him against the back wall, seething. "What the fuck is going on?"

He tore out of my arm and gave me a rough shove. "Hey, back off, man. What do you think you're doing?"

We were still nearly chest to chest; up close Max's face was inches from mine, twisted in shock and anger, and I stared at every bit of it. A jawline of granite, cheeks dusted with stubble. Liquid dark eyes met mine fearlessly. But that mouth. . .

Jesus. . .

My body felt suddenly awake like it hadn't been in years. Alert. Waiting. A humming mesh of nerves and heat.

Alarmed, I jerked back. "Who sent you?"

Max blinked. "Who sent. . . ? No one sent me. I got the job through Virginia Mason. Dr. Figueroa—"

"Bullshit," I spat. "You expect me to believe that? The NA meeting and now here? How long have you been following me?"

Fuck, just how much does this guy know? More than the NA meetings? Alaska?

Max held up his hands. "You need to calm down. I haven't been following you."

"This is a coincidence?"

"*Yes*," he said. "Until ten minutes ago your name was Scott and I thought I'd never see you again."

I took a step back, considering. "I don't believe you."

"I hate to break it to you, but I'm not super interested in what you believe."

My eyes flared. "How much?"

"What?"

"How much? This is a shakedown, clearly, so let's get it over with. How much do you need to walk away and not say a word? I know you signed NDAs for Dad, but I'm afraid the *Anonymous* in Narcotics Anonymous isn't legally-binding enough to satisfy me."

"You're unbelievable," Max hissed. "I don't want your money."

"No? You either take mine or the tabloids', right? What's your name? Your full name?"

"Max Kaufman." His lips cocked in a wry tilt. "The first."

"If you're lying. . ."

"I'm not lying, *Scott*."

His eyes were clear. Unflinching. He had nothing to hide, while my entire life was in his hands. I tried to keep the naked fear out of my own eyes, but Max must've seen it since his shoulders dropped and he sighed.

"I'm not going to sell you out," he said. "I swear to God, I'm not. I'm here for the job. I had no idea who you were and now that I know, I'm not going to say a word. It's your business."

I wanted to believe him, but I didn't know how. He read that in my eyes too.

"*You* offered *me* the ride, remember?" Max said. "You wanted to hear my story, and I told you." His voice lowered. "I shouldn't have told you."

I was right. I hurt him.

Max wasn't hard like me. He wasn't made of ice and stone. He was mutable. Flame and water. His pain wasn't crushing the life out of him but fueling him. Making him better. Stronger. And he didn't tolerate anyone—me —taking it lightly. He wouldn't use his story to get close to me for monetary gain. I hardly knew the guy, but I knew that. I *felt* that.

I backed off, paced a small circle in the space. "Fuck. I hate feeling like this."

"Confused, are you?" Max tilted his head up and crossed his arms, corded with lean muscle, over his chest. "Try being shoved into a linen closet by your boss's son on your first day on the job."

The mere mention of my dad brought me around like a slap to the face. "That's right. My father is your boss, and I'm second in command around here, so that makes me your boss too."

"Silas—"

"*Mr. Marsh*," I said. "And if you breathe a word of this, I'll bring the entire legal department down on your head so fast—"

"Yeah, I get it." Max's eyes darkened with anger. "Whatever you say, *Mr. Marsh*. Are we done here?"

I nodded.

He started to push past me, and our bodies brushed together in the small space. I felt him everywhere we touched, and even through his clothes and mine, my body reacted again. A crack in the ice.

Max stopped, a small intake of breath, and his eyes met mine. Dark and deep. He swallowed hard. His Adam's apple bobbed, and I wasn't supposed to be watching so closely. I wasn't supposed to notice how his heartbeat pulsed in the hollow beneath.

I jerked my head back, looked anywhere but at him. I felt Max study me, and I knew he missed nothing. Not one reaction. Not one skipped breath.

"See you later," he said, finally. "Silas."

And God, my name in his mouth sounded both inappropriate and perfect. Sibilant s's broken by a languid l, spoken in a man's deep undertone.

He continued past me and out, leaving me alone in the closet. I rested my hand on a shelf, my head on my arm. Then with a muffled shout, I tore a stack of towels off the shelf. The gold thread with the monogrammed EGM glinted up at me.

I sucked in a breath. Losing control was dangerous. The first step toward losing everything else. I smoothed my hair in place, stepped out of the closet and nearly crashed into one of Dad's maids.

"The closet is a mess," I said. "Clean it up."

Without waiting for an answer, I went to Dad's suite.

"Well? What the hell is wrong with you?" he demanded, holding a newspaper in his trembling hands.

"We need to talk."

"I gathered. What is it?"

I opened my mouth to tell him he had to fire Max Kaufman. Immediately.

"Silas," Dad said, like a warning.

Even bedridden and weak, his blue eyes bored into mine. Mercilessly cold and unforgiving. Like the frigid waters of Copper Lake where he'd sent me for six months in the dead of winter. He'd taken everything from me. Because I was defective.

I pulled a chair beside his bed.

"Dad. . ."

"Yes?"

"I. . . met with Stephen Milton today," I said. "I have some concerns."

CHAPTER FIVE

Max

Holy shit, what just happened?

I strode quickly to the west wing of the estate, to the rooms belonging to the maids and other nurses. My shift with Edward Marsh was over until Sunday morning.

"Time enough to evaluate my questionable employment choices," I muttered.

I unlocked the door with a keycard Cesar had given me. My new room was sparse and neat, like a small but elegant hotel room. It had an en suite bathroom and a window overlooking the sprawling backyard: tennis courts, pool, garden, and an entire forest beyond. I pressed my burning forehead to the glass and shut my eyes, willing my blood to cool.

Scott the Hot Unabomber. Here. Under the same roof.

God, when he strode into his father's chambers, I'd thought I was seeing a mirage or that someone was playing an elaborate prank.

When he cornered me in the closet, anger and surprise warred with a flood of heat. An electricity I hadn't felt with anyone in a long time. I hadn't *let* myself feel for anyone. My breath caught thinking of how our bodies had been briefly pressed together so that I felt the hard angles and planes of him.

And in that moment before I left him, how he'd looked at me, as if he were seeing me for the first time. Or seeing himself.

Like I had with Travis.

The chaos of feelings carried me on a tide to seven years ago. To the summer I had everything and lost everything. To the last time I had felt something for someone and had it ripped away.

Travis was older. Nineteen to my sixteen. I met him when he came to pick up his little sister—my friend Kayla—from a party. Instead of dragging Kayla home, he and I ended up talking until the party ended, until the sun rose on the start of a new day.

After that, Kayla became my new best friend. Travis was home from college for the summer. I'd come over looking for Kayla, when I knew she wasn't home, and Travis would invite me in anyway. "Since you came all this way."

I practically lived at their house during that summer. My last summer, it turns out, in my own home. Travis and I didn't dare touch each other the way we wanted to. We touched how guys do. Little punches on the shoulder, a hand on the back, fist bumps and handshakes.

The pretending finally ended the late summer night when we kissed, and something that had been loose and jangling inside me clicked into place. A wildly spinning compass finally found its true north. The kiss was the first thing that made sense in my long, anguished, and confusing puberty.

I finally made sense.

When Dad kicked Travis out of my life and then kicked me out of mine, the compass needle wobbled and wavered again.

Until today.

Silas Marsh walked straight into that room like the answer to a question I hadn't known I'd been asking. A strange thought had battered itself around my heart: *There he is.*

For a split second, before his own panic took over, Silas had been happy—no, *relieved*—to see me too.

"That's crazy," I said to the empty room.

Silas was an asshole. A bully like his father. A straight, rich guy who'd made a mistake with pills and was now petrified that his privileged lifestyle would be disrupted if the secret got out.

But that summary wouldn't stick. Instead, the sense memory of Silas's power, the solidity of his body and the sheer masculine perfection of him in that expensive suit, stayed with me like the remnants of his cologne. As if I'd worn one of his shirts and now the scent of him clung to my skin.

I can't do this right now.

After seven years, dozens of calls, and a few false starts, I'd finally pinned Mom down for dinner that night. I needed to get my head on straight. If this meeting went to shit, I'd have my world rocked twice in one day.

One emotional crisis at a time, thanks very much.

I took a very long, very cold shower, then dressed in jeans, short boots, a button-down shirt and my leather jacket. Rules of the Marsh household said I needed to wait for any Ubers or taxis on the back access road. My salary was enough that I should probably start shopping for a car but, shit. . . Could I keep this job? As I headed down, I expected to run into Silas around any corner and my stomach clenched in anticipation or dread. Maybe both.

Multiply that by however long I live here.

And yet the idea of bailing on another job so soon left a bad taste in my mouth. I needed to be professional and not throw in the towel over a good-looking guy.

Yeah, Silas is "good-looking," I scoffed at myself. *And Jason Momoa is "slightly attractive."*

I chuckled and felt more sober. The potent hit of Silas Marsh was wearing off and being replaced by a tangle of nerves as the Uber took me across Lake Washington and into the city. In all the chaos of the new work and the move, I hadn't had time to process that Mom had actually agreed to meet with me.

I'd made a reservation at an Italian restaurant near the Pike's Place Market. The little bistro had views overlooking the bay, where the dark of the water was broken by boats glittering with gold lights.

Mom wasn't there.

I sat at the table for two, my heart thudding and my fingers tapping my phone, waiting for the text that said she was canceling. She'd already postponed or rescheduled a dozen times, and my heart cracked a little more with each one. Why should tonight be any different?

And then, there she was, Barbara Kaufman, walking nervously behind the maître d', her purse clutched in both hands in front of her like a shield.

I got to my feet and blinked hard against the sudden sting of tears that came to my eyes. I hadn't seen her in nearly a decade, yet neither the years, nor the circumstances of the past could change the fact that she was my mom.

Her hair was more gray than brown—she was in her early sixties; she and Dad had had me late in the game. She still wore the same style of polyester pantsuits she liked to wear when I was a kid. Big hair, bigger glasses, and red chalky lipstick. An apparition straight out of 1983.

She's beautiful.

"Oh, my boy," Mom said when the maître d' had left. She dropped her purse on the table and held her arms to me. "Look at you. Oh, Max. . ."

I hugged her tightly, fighting the urge to give in completely. I couldn't trust her motherly embrace that should have been safe and unconditional.

She sniffed. "It's been so long."

Not by my choice.

I pulled her chair out to sit. "But we're here now," I said, and took my seat across from her.

"We are," she said, smiling weakly.

I swallowed seven years' worth of rejection, pain and loneliness down my throat. I had to try again or what was the point?

"Mom," I said, taking her hand across the table. "Thank you for coming."

"I. . . of course. Of course, yes." Tears threatened to crumple her face. "You look so handsome. My goodness, you're 'a looker' as they used to say. And healthy. So fit and healthy, aren't you?"

"Yeah, I'm okay, Mom."

She nodded, a tight smile holding back her tears. Finally, she pulled her hand away to grab the menu and held it in front of her face, her shoulders shaking.

"Mom. . ."

"It's okay. I'm fine, really."

A few thick moments passed, and then she cleared her throat and set her menu down and dabbed her eyes with her linen napkin.

"Awfully fancy place you've picked," she said, still sniffling. "You must be doing quite well at the hospital. Isn't that what you're doing?"

"I'm taking a break from ER nursing," I said. "Maybe permanently. Not sure yet. I have a new job."

"Oh?"

"I'm a personal nurse for a wealthy businessman over in Bellevue."

"Bellevue? Is it Bill Gates? He lives over there on the water."

I chuckled. "If I had a dollar. . . But no. Another wealthy someone, though I'm not at liberty to say who without being sued into oblivion."

"Sounds important, whoever he is," Mom said. "That's wonderful. I'm glad you're doing well."

I turned my water glass around. "I wasn't always doing so well."

"I know, and I—"

The waiter appeared and asked for our drink order, crushing the moment before it could take root.

"Soda water and lime," I told the guy.

Mom's eyes widened over the wine list. "Oh, you're not having a drink? Should I not?"

"Order whatever you want."

"A glass of house cabernet," she told the waiter. Then to me, "Are you on call? Is that why?"

Everything my mother didn't know about me hung heavy between us. I spoke slowly, knowing every word I said was going to slap her in the face.

"I don't drink because I'm a recovering drug addict and it's better to keep a clear head."

"Recovering." She took a sip from her water glass. "Yes, I think your sister may have mentioned. . ."

Her words trailed off and she looked like a guilty person being grilled at a congressional hearing. As much as I didn't want to punish her, I owed it to myself to be honest.

"Yes." I smiled grimly. "Being kicked out of your house and family isn't as fun as it sounds."

"God, Max, don't make jokes." She set her water glass down with a deliberate *clunk*. "I knew this would be hard. Things happened so fast back then, and I. . . I wasn't considering the big picture. The ramifications to you.

It was a shock. You and that boy. . . And then you were gone. I blinked and seven years had gone by and here we are."

She shrugged helplessly, as if that explained everything.

I shifted in my chair, marveling at the human ability to justify almost anything rather than admit being wrong. My anger and hurt boiled to the surface. The waiter returned with her wine and my soda water, and I took a long sip to cool down.

"I'm not here to place blame or dig up old pain," I said after a minute, more for my benefit than hers. "But I'm not going to lie or sugarcoat it. It's been hard. Really fucking hard. Those seven years didn't pass in a blink for me. The *ramifications* were that every day was a struggle to survive."

"Stop. Please. I don't think I want to know the rest," Mom said, hardly a whisper. "It would destroy me, I think." She dabbed her eyes under her glasses with a napkin and looked at me. "But you're okay now? You're better?"

My jaw worked from side to side, and I finally nodded. "Yeah. I'm better."

"Wonderful."

"No, not wonderful," I said. "I've been without a family for seven years. I deserve to be in this one, but I'm not going to beg. I shouldn't have to." I bit the inside of my cheek for a second. "A child should not have to beg for a parent's love."

She nodded quickly. "You're right. I've missed you. So much. And so do Morris and Rachel. But you've spoken to them, yes?"

I nodded. My brother and sister were twelve and fourteen years older than me, respectively. I was "a happy accident," Mom used to say, while Morris teased me that was code for "a mistake." Because of our age differences, we'd never been close. They were estranged from me by time and geography; Morris lived in Manhattan and Rachel in North Carolina. I had spoken to them sporadically over the years, usually to ask for money when I was on the streets.

"We text now and then but it's been a while," I said. "How are they?"

"Very good," Mom said. "Morris is working for a big bank in Manhattan. Rachel was just promoted to editor at her magazine. Both married, I think you know that. Rachel's twins are six now, and Amy—Morris's little girl—is two." She coughed and sipped her wine. "What about you? Any significant others?"

"Not at the moment."

Silas Marsh tried to crowd into my thoughts, but I kicked him right back out.

Mom's smile was forced as she said, "I remember. . .in the second grade you told me that you were going to marry Brian Robbins. You said that your friend Holly was going to marry a boy named Justin, so you'd decided to marry Brian."

"I don't remember that."

"I'll never forget it."

An itchy silence fell.

She picked up her menu, then set it down again. "I'm trying, Max."

"I know, Mom. But. . ." I sighed. "Does Dad know you're here?"

"Yes," she said. "I told him."

"And?"

"And he said to pass on his regards."

"Uh-huh," I said, toying with my fork. "How cordial of him."

"He's trying too."

"How? Does he have any idea what it feels like to be rejected by the two people on earth who are—specifically—not supposed to do that?"

"We. . . we didn't know that you were. . ."

"Gay?" I asked. "You can't even say the word."

Mom swallowed hard and smoothed her napkin. "Your father. . . he's not so rigid now. I think he's feeling like he overreacted, though he won't admit it."

I sat back in my seat. "Dad *overreacted* and so I had to squat in a condemned, roach-infested hovel instead of graduate high school."

"Max, please. . ."

Her eyes filled with tears and then *I* felt like shit, and I hadn't even told her how I'd earned a living for six weeks until Carl found me.

"Talk to him for me, okay?" I said after a tense silence. "Just do that."

"Okay."

"Okay and what? Because it's not going to be enough to tell him I'm in the city. You need to advocate for me, Mom."

She nodded vigorously and dabbed her eyes. "I will. I promise. But Max, you know how he is. Old-fashioned. And so am I, honestly. I love you, but this isn't easy for me either."

"I love you, *but. . .*" I said, my lips twisting wryly. "Oh, how I've dreamed of hearing those words."

"Please try to understand, Max. When you're a mother, holding your baby, you have an idea of the kind of life you want that child to have. You never think—"

"That you'd end up kicking that child out of your house because of something he had no control over?"

Her lips pursed, and she shrugged slightly.

I gaped. "You get that it's not a choice, right? I have brown hair, brown eyes, and I'm gay. It's all the same package."

She glanced surreptitiously at the other diners. "Please lower your voice. You *did* have a choice. You didn't have to bring that boy into the house. Flaunt him—"

My eyes flared. "*Flaunt?* We'd been hiding for weeks. *I'd* been in hiding for *years*."

"You could have told us. If you'd told us, instead of it being such a *shock*. . ."

Under the table, I strangled my linen napkin. The waiter reappeared to take our order. Mom ordered the seafood linguini and I muttered the first item on the menu I laid eyes on. When he left, I took another long, bracing drink of cold water.

"We can't rehash the past," I said. "It's done. I asked you here to tell you that I'm sorry. I'm sorry for any hurt I caused you and Dad. And to say that I forgive you. Even if you don't ask for it, I forgive you. That's part of my own healing process. For me. That's why I'm here, no matter what else happens."

"Of course. I understand. Thank you."

Not quite the stirring, emotional reaction I'd been hoping for, but that's the deal with forgiveness. It can't matter what the reaction is. You either forgive or you don't. I had to try or else I'd never heal from the past.

"And Dad," I said, my voice tight. "Tell him to call me. Just start there."

"Yes, I think that's fair."

My hands were choking the napkin again.

"I want us to be a family, but I swear to God, Mom, I did not come this far in my life and rebuild so much of what was wrecked just to have it all torn down again. I don't want to give an ultimatum, but I suppose I am. For my own self-preservation. This is it. *He* calls *me*." I swallowed down the jagged lump in my throat and blinked hard. "I need to know there's hope."

"Yes, okay." She reached tentatively across the table and took my hand. "Okay, I'll tell him. I'll do my best."

"Thank you."

She gave my hand a squeeze and sat back, huffing a sigh that sounded like relief. The hardest part was over. I hadn't thrown a fit or caused a scene. I hadn't cried, though I wanted to.

"Now," she said, settling her napkin smartly in her lap. "Tell me more about this new job."

CHAPTER SIX

Silas

Late Sunday morning and I had jack-shit to do.

I'd talked to Dad yesterday about my concerns over the dosages prescribed to small towns. As predicted, he told me not to be stupid. Stephen Milton's marketing strategies were all above-board, or else the FDA would have put the clamp down on us a long time ago.

But what had we been telling the FDA? I wondered but did not say. I'd nodded my head in agreement like a good little minion, but I hadn't told Sylvia to forget about her data collection either.

Downstairs, Eddie was reading again by the cold fireplace in the family living room. He had on a full suit, a driving cap, and argyle socks pulled up to his knees. A smile tugged at my lips. The world could be crashing down around me, but at least I knew how I felt about Eddie. I wished everything else could be as simple.

I started into the room but stopped and pressed myself against the wall around the corner as Max Kaufman passed through wearing his scrubs, probably on his way to Dad's suite.

"Hi," he said, stopping in front of Eddie. "I don't think we've met. I'm Max."

My stomach tightened. Cesar must have told the new hires about Eddie, but that didn't mean they always treated him the way he deserved to be treated.

"Oh, I say, my good man," Eddie said, his gaze flickering to Max, then back to his book. "A fine morning, isn't it? Yes, indeed."

Max paused for a second, taking in Eddie's attire and the unlit pipe clenched in his teeth. "So it is," he said. "And what are you reading, if I might inquire?"

"Dickens, old chap. Dickens." Eddie held the book so Max could see the cover. "*David Copperfield.*"

"His quintessential work, I daresay," Max said, sitting on the edge of the couch but not near enough to crowd Eddie.

"Bravo," my brother said. "I heartily agree. Though there are factions who have concluded *A Tale of Two Cities* or *Great Expectations* to be his masterpiece. To that I say, hogwash."

"Rubbish," Max agreed. "*David Copperfield* is pure Dickens. I admire how his character names seem to describe their personality."

"Bravo again! I quite agree. Uriah Heep does sound so terribly odious."

"Or Murdstone. And Barkis. Is that not the perfect name for him? A lovable mutt, loyal to Peggotty."

To my utter shock, Eddie reached out and offered his hand to Max. "It does my old heart good to meet a fellow Dickensian connoisseur. And your name again, sir?"

"Max Kaufman."

"Eddie Marsh."

"A pleasure, Eddie," Max said. "But you must excuse me, I'm late for work."

"Right then. I shan't keep you."

Eddie went back to his book, shutting off any affection or connection as if it had never been. I watched Max's face closely for signs of derision, but his smile was real. The warmth in his eyes was genuine.

Max left the room, and I sagged against the wall.

He's a medical professional. That's why he was so good with Eddie. That's all.

But I'd seen medicos come and go by the scores over the years, and few had slid into Eddie's groove so easily and comfortably. As if it were perfectly normal to speak in a hodgepodge of old-timey slang while discussing *David Copperfield*.

My phone chimed a text from the back pocket of my jeans.

Are you coming home tonight?

I stared at the words, irritated at how quickly the few precious seconds of happiness evaporated.

My fingers hovered over the keypad to reply *Yes*. Now that Dad was stable, I supposed I had to go back to my penthouse apartment in the city.

I hadn't wanted to come, and now I didn't want to leave.

We're made stronger by denying ourselves, Coach Braun reminded me. *There's power in abstinence and clarity in starving the body of base lusts and desires.*

I pushed off the wall, scoffing at the memory. I had no lusts or desires. I was hollowed out and empty. Cold. The rush of heat yesterday with Max didn't mean anything. Weakness. It wouldn't happen again, and tonight I'd head back to the city.

But instead of replying to the text, I shoved my phone back in my pocket.

For the next few hours, I ate a leisurely lunch on the back patio since the day was warm enough and procrastinated checking in on Dad.

Why? Because Max is still on duty?

I threw my napkin down in disgust. Why the hell were all my thoughts and actions funneled directly to Max fucking Kaufman? This was *my* house. I wasn't about to be restricted as to where I could and could not go because of some. . . guy.

But I didn't make it to the stairs. Without letting myself think too hard about why, I knew it was safer if Max and I weren't in the same room with my father ever again.

I wandered into the family room. Eddie had gone out with Marjory. The house was quiet. I sat at the piano and opened the lid. Mom's portrait hung above me, smiling.

God, I missed her. I wasn't supposed to admit that; my grief needed to stay in the vault. According to Coach Braun, her love had contributed to my weakness. It had made me soft, and no real man was ever soft.

I laid my hands on the keys. Ravel's *Pavane pour une Infante défunte* slipped out from under my fingers. One of Mom's favorites. I hadn't played it since she died.

Unbeknownst to my father, I'd taken piano classes in college. The professors had immediately wanted to ship me over to the Yale School of Music for a fellowship and every major program under the sun, but Dad would've lost his shit.

Now, I only played piano on Saturdays for Eddie.

The tune wasn't particularly difficult but haunting and melodic. I closed my eyes and I soon lost myself in notes that carried me back to a time before Mom was dead. Before *I* was deadened inside by ice and cold and the lessons —beaten and shocked into me—that I was worth nothing as I was.

When the last note dissipated, the warmth of the music faded, and my blood turned icy again. I knew before I opened my eyes, I wasn't alone.

"Holy shit, man. That was incredible," Max said in a low voice. He was at the door on the north side that led to the kitchens. "I didn't mean to eavesdrop," he said, answering my cold stare.

"What are you doing?" I asked. "Aren't you on duty?"

"Lunch break," he said. "You're very good. Hell, more than *good*. Professional-level. Have you been playing your whole life?"

"Most Marsh employees don't ask such personal questions of the family."

Max smiled wryly and crossed his arms. "We know more about each other than most employees and employers, I reckon."

My eyes flared. "Is that some sort of threat?"

He sighed and came into the room and sat on the arm of the couch as he'd done with Eddie earlier. "I was merely pointing out the obvious."

"I don't know how to make myself more clear or *obvious* that everything we discussed previously needs to be kept between us."

"It will," Max said. "I've sworn to that."

I ran my fingers along the piano keys. "I don't like relying on others."

Understatement of the century.

"I noticed," Max said with a small grin. "What was the name of the piece?"

"*Pavane pour une Infante défunte*," I said. "Ravel."

"What does it mean?"

"Dance for a dead princess." I jerked my head at Mom's portrait. "Her favorite, even though there was nothing sad or morbid about her. She just liked the way it sounded, not what it meant."

"She was very beautiful," Max said. "I'm sorry for your loss."

I glanced up at him sharply.

"Cesar told me she passed away some time ago," Max said.

"What else did Cesar tell you?"

Alaska? Did Cesar tell him about Alaska?

"Not much," Max said. "He was only explaining why there was no wife in the picture to help care for your father."

"My father never remarried, and he never will. MS or not."

"He loved her."

"I think so. And when she died, something in him died too. She was compassionate. Kind. She took it all with her when she left." I waved a hand. "Never mind."

Jesus. What is it about this guy that makes me so goddamn talkative?

"Okay," Max said, letting it go. Because he was kind and compassionate too. He nodded at the piano. "When did you learn to play?"

"When I was a kid," I said. "I don't remember learning. I remember doing. My mother said I was born with it."

"You don't want to do it professionally?"

"I'm the COO of Marsh Pharmaceuticals. One day, I'll be the CEO."

"That didn't answer my question."

I cocked my head. "Are you always this direct?"

Max shrugged. "Short answer: life's too short to play games. Long answer, I spent a lot of years lying to myself about who I was. When I got clean, I made a No Bullshit policy. I don't dish it out and I don't take it from anyone, including myself. *Especially* myself."

Jealousy swept through me. To be that free. . .

I sat up straighter. "My job duties for the family mean I have no time to pursue idle follies like piano."

"That's too bad," he said and then chuckled. "Wait, how old are you?"

"Twenty-four. Why?"

"You sure about that? No twenty-four-year-old I know would use the phrase 'idle follies.'"

"A Yale-educated twenty-four-year-old might," I said, unable to keep the smile off my lips.

Max laughed, full and throaty, and waved his hands in front of him. "Oh, excuse me, Mr. Yale. I stand corrected."

I chuckled, gears creaking inside me with ice and rust.

"Anyway, you play like a master," Max said. "I wish I could. I took lessons as a kid, but they didn't stick."

"There's something Mighty Max can't do?"

His eyebrows shot up. "Mighty Max?"

"ER nurse, NA sponsor, taking care of a tyrant, connecting with my brother." I widened my eyes at him. "I'm trying to pay you a compliment."

"*Obviously.*" He started to laugh, then his brows furrowed. "Hold up, how did you know I met Eddie?"

"I was eavesdropping."

"And you feel *so* bad about it."

"*Obviously.*"

He laughed again, his mouth wide, showing perfect white teeth. "Careful, Silas," Max said, "or the world will know you have a sense of humor. Your cover will be blown."

I stiffened. "My cover?"

"Yep. The world may learn you're a flesh and blood mortal after all and not a demigod of industry."

If only that were true.

Our eyes met and Max's face softened as if he sensed the longing in my thoughts. I swear to God, the guy could read me like a billboard. I schooled my expression back to neutral. After a short silence, he nodded his head at the piano.

"Have you really never thought about performing?"

"Where? At an airport lounge? Department store?"

"Carnegie Hall?" Max said. "Scoff all you want," he said when I scoffed, "but you're good enough."

"There's no time to play. I have responsibilities. To my father. To Eddie."

"Your brother is awesome, by the way."

"He is, though not everyone feels the same."

"Who doesn't? I'll kick his ass."

God, don't say that, Max. Don't be this fucking good.

I cleared my throat. "My father, for one."

Max frowned and moved to sit on the couch cushions, resting his forearms on his thighs.

"Yeah, I'm familiar with that old father-rejection song and dance." He cocked his head at me. "But you knew that already."

I didn't want to talk about that night in the car or about anything personal ever again. It would only draw us closer—closer than it had already—and I couldn't allow that. But after what he'd said about defending Eddie, he could've asked me for a million dollars and I'd have written the check, no questions asked.

"How are things with your family now?"

Max smiled thinly. "It's a process."

I nodded. "I'm sorry about the scene in the closet."

"You are?"

"*Yes*. Is that impossible to believe?"

"Demigods don't apologize," Max said, that teasing smile on his lips again. "Now your cover is truly blown."

"Stop saying that." I shut the piano lid down—hard—and stood up. "I have no cover."

Max got to his feet too. "Hey. I'm kidding."

"I don't have time for jokes. I need to see my father before I go back to the city. Is he awake?"

"Oh, you're not. . . staying here?" Max said, and the naked disappointment in his words hung between us like an open door.

Does he want me to stay?

I slammed that door shut too.

"What possible difference does it make to you where I go?"

Max met my stare unflinching. "I guess it doesn't," he said. "To answer your question, your father was awake last I was with him, where I gave him twenty-five milligrams of Orvale, which reduces disease activity but comes with a more significant side effect profile—"

I waved my hands in front of me. "Whoa. I didn't ask for a medical report."

"I'm being the employee," Max said, crossing his arms. "Keeping things strictly professional. Isn't that what you want?"

"What I want. . ." My words trailed off into the unknown. Everything I wanted was locked in the vault.

"Friends, Silas," Max said into the silence. "We could be friends. It seems sort of weird not to at least give it a shot after all the personal shit we've shared."

I glanced at him hesitantly. His quiet smile was back, forgiving me for being cold to him. A smile that made his dark eyes warm. To stay in their reflection would be too good.

Too dangerous.

Temptation is the devil's game, Coach Braun said. *The only way to beat him is to not play.*

"I have enough friends."

I strode out of the room without looking back, my entire body feeling leaden and heavier with each step up the stairs, away from Max. Outside of my dad's suite, I rested my head on the door, Max's words floating across my vision like skywriting.

I spent a lot of years lying to myself about who I was.

I squeezed my eyes shut. That wasn't me. I didn't suffer what I did in Alaska for nothing. Christ, I nearly died. . .

I pulled out my phone to reply to the text from earlier: **Are you coming home tonight?**

The autofill *Yes* was waiting.

My fingers typed, **Not yet. Another day or two.**

A response bubbled up almost immediately. **Why?**

I put the phone away without replying. I had no answer.

CHAPTER SEVEN

Max

S ilas walked away from me for the second time in two days.
That's called a hint. Take it.

I'd been on my way to my lunch break when I'd heard piano music—haunting and melodic—coming from one of the Marsh's ten different living areas. At first, I thought it was an audio recording of a professional player. I could hardly believe what I was seeing when I peeked around the corner and there was Silas, sitting at the baby grand. I had to blink twice; he looked so different. His usually impassive-yet-perfect face was softened by the music, and his elegant, long-fingered hands flowed like water over the keys.

I should've slunk away but I'd have been fascinated by anyone who could play an instrument as Silas did that piano. It took a kind of genius, I thought, to be able to speak the language of music so fluently.

And I hadn't wanted to stop looking at him.

Not that anyone could blame me. I'd teased him about being a demigod, but holy hell, Silas Marsh was simply a stunningly handsome man. The kind you found in magazine ads for expensive cars or clothes or cologne.

Worse, he was smart, funny when he wanted to be, talented. But with a vein of ice running through him. Just when I thought we'd taken a step closer, he snapped back, cruel as ever. Why did I bother? I was like the little kid who kept putting his hand on the stove, thinking *this* time it wouldn't get burned.

Not burned. Frostbitten.

The next day, I wasn't on duty until three p.m. I decided to get out of the house and into the city. I needed some new clothes, maybe pick up a book. . .

Maybe stop thinking about Silas every minute of my life.

After years of talking about my drug abuse in recovery meetings, nothing felt truly honest until I said it out loud to someone else. I showered, put on my other uniform—jeans, T-shirt, leather jacket—but before heading out, I called Darlene.

In San Francisco, I'd been a sponsor to a vivacious dancer and recovering addict. I was only supposed to be her sponsor, but Darlene Montgomery was impossible not to love and our relationship instantly morphed into a deep friendship.

"Maximilian!" she said, picking up on the first ring. "I am so happy to hear your voice. Or I will be once you say something."

I laughed. "Hey, Dar. How are you?"

"I'm fabulous," she said. "What are you doing?"

"I'm pacing my room in a huge manor house, having an existential crisis. You know, the usual."

"Yikes, sounds serious."

"First tell me about you."

We chatted for a few minutes about her latest dance gig and how she was still clean, going on two years now.

"I'm so proud of you," I said.

"Yeah, well, you're a huge part of why I'm doing well," Darlene said. "Sometimes, if I'm having a really bad day, I just think of you waiting for me at the bus depot that day I arrived in San Francisco and I instantly feel better."

"Thank you, Darlene," I said, blinking hard. "I needed that."

"What's wrong?" she asked, her voice downshifting to concern. "What's this about a crisis? Are you okay? Boy trouble?"

"No, not really. Sort of. Yes."

"Spill it."

I leaned against the window and stared down at the grounds that were green and white under a brilliant sun. I told her about Silas, how we met, and our coincidental living arrangement, leaving out his last name and the particulars of the family business.

"So let me get this straight," Darlene said. "You're living at Downton Abbey with a tortured billionaire you met at an NA meeting. A likely story."

"Too much?" I asked. "If someone at a party asks what I do, should I scale it back?"

"No, embellish. Tell people you're working for Bill Gates." Darlene gasped. "Oh my God, Max—?"

"*No*," I said, chuckling. "There are other billionaires in the Seattle area, you know."

"Tell me, he's good-looking, this Silas?"

"He's not. . . unattractive. He's fucking perfect, actually. No embellishment needed. Hell, I called him a demigod. To his face."

"You *did*?"

"A demigod of industry, though I meant *actual* demigod."

"Do you think he's gay? Bi? Curious? Bi-curious?"

"Don't know, but sometimes, the way he looks at me, I could swear. . ." I stared at the blank white ceiling. "Nah. Wishful thinking."

"Maybe not," Darlene said. "Maybe he's repressed."

"It's possible," I said. "God knows everything about him is stiff and cold and locked down. And he's kind of a dick, if I'm being honest. Though to be fair, he thought what he shared at the NA meeting was going to stay there, not stare him in the face in his own house." I waved a hand. "Anyway, I'm just crushing on him because he's unbelievably hot. I'll get over it."

"If you say so," Darlene said. "But you don't sound happy. That makes me not happy. Are you sure everything's okay?"

I smiled against the phone. "I love you, you know that?"

"I love you too. What else? What's happening with the parents?"

"Achievement unlocked: dinner with Mom."

Darlene made a sound and I could envision her bolting upright and brushing her long dark hair out of her face. "Holy shit, she finally showed up? So? How did it go?"

"Okay," I said. "Not as well as I'd hoped but it didn't crash and burn, either. She tried to rationalize seven years of estrangement with the it-all-happened-so-fast defense."

"And what about your dad?"

"She's going to talk to him. I told her he has to call me. I'm not going to beg."

My throat started to close. I coughed, but Darlene heard it anyway.

"Oh, honey," she said. "I swear to God, anyone who can't see how unbelievably amazing you are—demigods included—can suck it. Truly. I know that doesn't really help at all, but. . ."

"I'll take it."

"I wish I could hug you right now."

"Me too, but damn, when it comes to getting people to cry, you're worse than Oprah." I heaved a breath. "How are things with Sawyer the Lawyer?"

Darlene lived in a Victorian and was neighbors with a single dad who was fighting for custody of his little girl. In typical Darlene fashion, she'd given her entire self—heart and soul—to both of them.

"You don't want to know," she said.

"Because you're deliriously happy?" I said. "I *do* want to know that. You being happy is never going to make me feel worse."

"I am, Max," she said. "But literally nothing could make life better than knowing you found someone worthy of you."

I leaned my forehead against the window. "I'm not built like you, Dar. I wish I could put myself out there, but how many times can my heart get demolished before I throw in the towel?"

"Sixteen," Darlene said.

A laugh burst out of me. "Say that again?"

"You can get your heart stomped on sixteen times before things get truly bad."

"Is that so?"

"Yep. It's science. So, you're at. . . what? Three?"

"Three big ones. Travis, Carl's death, my parents."

"By my calculations, you have thirteen to go before you have to worry about slipping."

"How many is a demigod worth?"

"Five," she said with authority. "So be careful with that one."

I laughed, even as my heart skipped a beat at the thought of putting Silas on my roster of potential heartbreaks.

"The math is solid, huh?"

"I don't make up the rules to science."

I laughed harder.

"Welp, I can hear my job here is done," she said. "Shit, I'm late for rehearsal. I gotta go but only if you're really okay. I can cancel. Or tell them I'm running late?"

"No way. Go. They can't start without their lead."

"Okay. I love you, Maximilian. Take care and call me again soon."

"I will. Love you too."

I hung up and smiled to myself. If things didn't work out with my dad, I had Darlene. I had Daniel. And Malcolm. I had friends whom I loved and who loved me. I wanted to rejoin my flesh-and-blood family, but I had another family, made of friends who accepted me just as I was.

I headed down to the kitchen. Ramona was there with her staff of three, as usual. She had a soft, mom-like quality that I liked, and she seemed to be the only staff member who wasn't afraid of the Marshes. I'd heard from Cesar that she'd been with the family for nearly thirty years, hired by Mrs. Marsh herself.

"Good morning, Max," she said with a smile. "How are you settling in? Finding your way around?"

"Better, thanks," I said. "I only got lost ten times yesterday. Aiming to cut it by half today."

She laughed. "Well, if it happens again, you can always find me right here. Let me know if you need anything."

"Thanks."

"What are your plans for the day?"

"I'm heading to the city before my shift. Can I pick you up anything?"

"Aren't you sweet? No, thank you."

Silas Marsh strode into the kitchen wearing a sharp tweed suit, vest, coppery silk tie, his gold hair still wet from the shower.

"Ramona, I need—" He stopped when he saw me, and his eyes widened. For one brief second, the icy blue in them melted into something warmer, then froze up again. "Oh. Hey."

"Mr. Silas, have you met Max?" Ramona asked, her sharp-eyed gaze going between us.

"Yes," he said, not looking at me. "Where the hell is Jerome?"

"It's Labor Day," Ramona said. "He's off."

"Shit. Fine. I'll drive myself."

"Max was saying he was going to the city too," Ramona said. "Perhaps you can give him a ride?"

Silas froze in the act of picking up an apple from a glass bowl on the counter.

The back of my neck was suddenly on fire. "No, it's fine. I was going to call an Uber."

Silas glanced at Ramona who was watching everything, missing nothing.

"I'll take you," Silas said. "But I'm leaving now. Are you ready?"

"Sure, but you don't have to—"

"Let's go."

He strode out and I followed, Ramona giving me a small wave and a knowing, mom-like smile.

I caught up with Silas as his long-legged stride carried him through the rooms, toward the garage. He walked as if the house were on fire.

He doesn't want anyone to see us leave together.

"Hey, if it's too much trouble or you'd rather not—"

"I'm heading there already. Why would it be trouble?"

"You don't like me very much, for starters."

He stopped at the back door that led to the outside of the estate. "I don't like or dislike you. I hardly know you."

"You know a hell of a lot more than most." I held up my hands. "Look, it's fine. I get it. You don't want to be friends, but we don't have to be at war either. Fate—and Ramona—keep conspiring to put us together—"

Silas held up a hand and we went silent, listening as footsteps sounded down the hall. They passed and he gave me a hard look.

"We're not together," he said and shoved open the door that let outside.

"Jesus, that's not. . . Never mind."

My face hot, I followed him along a paved walk that led to a dozen garages at the side of the estate. The morning was overcast and cool, a thin layer of mist hanging over the foliage that lined the drive.

Silas hit a clicker on his key fob and one of the garage doors opened revealing his shiny black Range Rover with a silver grill in the front. I climbed in, and déjà vu of the night after the NA meeting washed over me along with the scents of cologne, new leather, and Silas himself.

He took the wheel and sat for a second without moving.

"Max. . ."

"Forget it," I said.

A muscle in his jaw ticked as his eyes locked on the curved driveway ahead of him.

"I'm sorry," he said, finally. "For that night in the car."

"Christ, you didn't hold a gun to my head," I snapped. "And you already apologized—"

"Well, I'm doing it again," he snapped back. "Look. That night, I asked about your personal shit thinking we'd never see each other again. Hell, I *said* some personal shit in that meeting that no one here can ever know. And now. . ." He bit off his words in frustration. "I don't know what to do about it. We shouldn't know this stuff about each other."

"Yeah, I get it, Silas," I said. "You don't want to be connected to a stranger like that. But we can't put the cat back in the bag, so you're going to have to trust me."

"That's not. . ." His jaw clenched again in frustration. "Why did you tell me? I'm not blaming you—"

"Great, thanks very much."

"—I just want to know why."

"You asked," I said. "You needed to know there was hope."

"And that was enough? Because I asked?"

"Yeah, man. It's not rocket science. I wanted to help if I could. I still do."

The surprise in his eyes was heartbreaking. As if he couldn't imagine someone wanting to help *him*. He'd built himself into a monolith—rich, powerful, impervious to pain. His handsome features could have been chiseled out of stone, but in the early morning light, I saw his humanity. My own physical attraction for him felt shallow. There was so much more to him, most of which he kept locked away. Flashes of pain escaped him now and then, like SOS flares from a deserted island.

I turned in my seat to face him.

He glanced at me suspiciously. "What?"

"I'm going to be an NA sponsor for a minute and ask you how you're doing. Because no one else knows about the addiction you've been fighting, and it's important. Are you ready?"

He sniffed a laugh and glanced away, looking almost shy. "Sure. Yeah, I'm ready."

"How are you doing, Silas?"

"I don't know. That's the wrong answer, isn't it? I should know how the fuck I am."

"That's an honest answer," I said. "Talking it out can help you get somewhere."

"I doubt it. What's the point? It's all still there."

"True," I said. "But the sieve needs to be turned now and then to let the pressure out. Give you some clarity."

He was silent for a moment.

"I don't want to go back," he said finally, then glanced at me. "I don't want to relive all that old shit. Not ever again."

I nodded. "Once, I told a friend that the best way to get over a traumatic event was to remember it over and over again, so it loses its power. I was wrong."

Silas arched a brow. "Mighty Max was wrong?"

"It happens," I said with a wry smile. "Rarely, mind you, but it happens."

He grinned that Silas Marsh grin of his. The blink-and-you-missed-it tilt to one side of his mouth that hinted a full smile was possible but wasn't going to happen anytime soon. I silently vowed I would make it happen. Someday.

"So what is your new solution to getting over traumatic events?" Silas asked. His voice was casual but something in his eyes begged to hear the answer.

"You try to let it go," I said. "Live for right now."

Silas shook his head, his gaze sweeping the grounds in front of him. "What if you can't let go? What if it's too late?"

"No such thing," I said. "Every minute you're alive is a second chance to start over. I honor my past, but I don't live in it. I choose this moment instead. Right here."

With you...

Silas's mouth made a grim line. "And what if there is no honor in your past? What then?"

Now it was my turn to silently beg him to tell me what had happened to him that made it seem as though he were filled with hardened concrete instead of blood and bone.

"The honor is that you survived, Silas," I said softly. "That you're here now too."

With me...

A short silence descended, then he smiled grimly. "Tell me, Max," he said, pressing the ignition button. "What's so great about here?"

He didn't let me answer but started the car with a roar that drowned out anything else I could've said and drove with speed—yet perfect control—out of the estate. He turned on a news radio station, precluding further conversation, and I let him have his quiet.

Fifteen minutes later, he pulled the car to the curb in front of a huge indoor mall and hit the hazard button.

"Is this okay?"

"Yep, perfect."

"I'd give you a lift back, but I don't know how long I'll be at the office."

"I can manage." I reached for the door. "Thanks for the ride."

I climbed out reluctantly. What I really wanted to do was climb back in and talk to him more. Be in his space a little longer. Just before I shut the door, he called my name.

"Hey, Max."

I leaned an arm on the doorframe. "Yeah?"

"On the drive over, I've been thinking about what you said. About trusting you."

"You can, Silas. You can trust me."

He watched me a moment longer, then held out his hand stiffly. "Okay, then. I'm taking you up on your offer," he said to my questioning look. "To be friends."

"Okay."

I reached in and took his hand in mine. He held on tightly then gave a hard, firm shake and let go.

And now we're friends. We shook on it, after all. Sealed the deal.

"Have a good one," he said.

"You too."

I shut the door and watched Silas drive away—a powerful businessman with billions at his fingertips who believed every relationship was transactional. I wanted to be friends and he wanted me to keep his pill addiction secret, so he offered me one for the other. It probably wasn't real to him.

Sadness sunk heavy in my heart and feeling anything for Silas left me exposed. Naked. I was standing on another street corner, leaning against yet another lamppost. I had to proceed with extreme caution. Be his friend and nothing more.

"Nothing more," I muttered and wished I could put barbed wire around my heart just by thinking it.

CHAPTER EIGHT

Max

Days came and went, and I didn't see Silas, though I felt his presence in the house like a ghost haunting its huge rooms and corridors. A whiff of cologne. The echo of the piano drifting on the air.

I concentrated on my job, taking care of Edward Marsh, who I'd come to think of as a mighty oak felled before its time and reduced to lying in bed all day. The MS had weakened him, and given its progressive nature, most days if he wanted to take more than three steps, he needed a wheelchair.

"Here you are, my dear," Ramona said one morning, handing me a plate of eggs Benedict and sliced avocado.

"This looks amazing," I said.

"Has to be," she said with a knowing smile. "Have to take care of Mr. Marsh's favorite nurse."

I snorted. "Hardly."

Her eyebrows raised. "You haven't noticed? The ones he doesn't like get the night shift. He wants you on all day shifts because that's when he's awake. He likes your company."

"He tolerates me, you mean," I said. "I don't think he likes anyone. Not that I blame him. His entire world has been upheaved."

"True. But I've been here for thirty years. You don't think I can read the weather around here? The mood in the house?" She patted my cheek. "He likes you. He won't ever *tell* you that, but that doesn't make it untrue."

"If you say so."

Edward's bedchamber was dim when I stepped in at the start of an afternoon shift. The curtains were drawn when they shouldn't have been. I shot a questioning look at Dale, whom I was relieving. Dale shook his head then inclined it at Edward who was watching a cable news channel on the giant flat-screen across from the bed.

They were all scared of him, but I'd worked in an ER. Being snapped at by Edward Marsh was child's play.

"Mr. Marsh," I said as Dale slipped out of the room. "You know what Dr. Webb said. You need sunlight. Vitamin D. It's just as important as the meds."

"Fuck off."

Yep. He loves me the most. Obviously.

I concealed a smile as I reached for the curtains.

"Sorry, sir, but doctor's orders."

"I'm not stupid, you know," he said without stammering, though his hands resting on his stomach trembled. "I'm weak as a kitten. A ray of sunshine isn't going to make me better, so you can shut those damn things."

"You need the sun." I finished drawing the curtains. "Besides, it's Seattle. Take what you can get."

I turned around, and Edward Marsh's wrath was all over his face, lit by the sunshine that filled the room. When I didn't back down from his cold stare, he gave up and returned to the news.

I went about my business, prepping his Orvale shot, taking his blood pressure and temperature. When I went to lift him up to settle him against the pillows better, he motioned at the TV screen.

"Look at this," he said. "Some faggot actor claiming he was the victim of a hate crime."

I froze. My stomach became a ball of ice, and I nearly dropped Edward's head against the headboard.

"Hate crime?" He snorted. "Bullshit. He had a drink thrown at him. That's not a crime. I'd wager it's a hoax, anyway. He faked the whole thing to get attention. No one attacks homosexuals in broad daylight. Not anymore."

I still hadn't moved. Confusion warred with the gut-punch of the slur flung around so casually.

"What's with you?" Edward demanded, jarring me from my thoughts.

I coughed and stood up straight. "Nothing."

His words stung, but if I let every ignorant comment sink into my heart, I wouldn't be able to get out of bed in the morning. I usually spoke up for myself but at that moment, something instinctual told me to keep quiet. And not only to protect my job.

I glanced down at Edward, his cold eyes were watching me closely, his shrewd glance that oversaw a multi-billion-dollar empire, sizing me up.

"Are you a *fan* of this actor, Maxwell?" Edward asked, and I heard the question beneath the question.

Before I could answer—or correct him on my name—the door opened and Roberto, the head nurse, came in.

"Time for some fresh air and sunshine, Mr. Marsh," he said. "We're going to have you sit by the pool for a few hours."

"I can't get out of bed to take a shit," Edward said. "But yes, let's have a frolic in the pool."

"Doctor's orders," Roberto said. He looked to me. "Help me get him ready?"

"Yeah, of course."

I held my breath for a second, wondering if Edward had anything more to ask me, but he only muttered curses as Roberto and I prepped him for the journey to the backyard. We dressed him in a polo shirt and shorts and a white baseball cap with MP emblazoned on the front in red thread.

I bent over him in his wheelchair with a bottle of sunscreen.

"I'll do it myself," he groused.

I handed him the bottle, but he fumbled it into his lap, then struggled to pick it up, his fingers trembling.

"Goddammit." He slumped in the wheelchair, his eyes closed.

"I got it, Mr. Marsh," I said quietly and brushed sunscreen over his nose and cheeks.

This "fag" doesn't want you to get burned.

I thought of the sponge baths and the times I changed his soiled sheets and wondered what Edward would do if his suspicions about me were confirmed.

Nothing. He can't do anything without me suing his ass for discrimination.

Except now I had to be careful. If he found out I was gay, he might manufacture a story of me behaving inappropriately.

Shit.

We wheeled Edward to the chair lift on the back stairs and then down to the backyard—if you could call something that had its own forest a "backyard." A pristine expanse of cement stretched around a firepit and state-of-the-art grill, and stuffed patio loungers edged a huge pool.

Eddie Marsh, wearing an old-fashioned bathing suit that looked like a black and white striped onesie, was swimming in the deep end. On the side of the pool near where we were coming out was Silas lying on one of the many cushy loungers.

Yep, there he is. My good buddy. My old pal, Silas.

Outwardly, I kept my face impassive. Inwardly, I was reduced to the GIF of Leonardo DiCaprio biting his knuckles.

Silas wore long black swim shorts with a white drawstring, sunglasses and nothing else. A bottle of expensive water sat beside him on a table. As if to torture me further, he was reading a book. *Crime and Punishment* by Dostoyevsky. He was more than halfway done.

Because being ungodly attractive isn't enough.

The sunlight bathed him, filled in the lines of him, made his skin glow—bronzed and perfect. It glinted in his hair and made that gold too; he was blindingly beautiful. I wrenched my eyes away, but it was too late. The promises I'd made to myself were falling apart like ash. My stupid, lonely heart was already in trouble.

I wheeled Edward under an umbrella a few feet from his son. Roberto, seeing us settled, abandoned me to go inside and answer a call on his cell.

"Greetings, Papa," Eddie called from the deep end, waving. "Marvelous day for a swim. Ah, cheerio, Mr. Kaufman. A pleasure to see you, sir."

"Hey, Eddie." I coughed. "Silas."

Silas nodded his head, once.

Edward ignored his eldest son splashing in the deep end and fixated on the younger. "Why aren't you at the office?"

"It's Saturday," he said. "I spend every Saturday with Eddie."

"How are the shareholders?"

"I had to tell them you're taking a rest. Since profits are steady, so are they." Silas shifted on the lounger. The cut lines of his perfect abs grew stark below the planes of his pecs. "There are some things we need to discuss later."

"What is that? The marketing tactics? I told you to leave all that alone."

"We'll talk about it *later*."

"Oh, will we? Now you're giving the orders? We can talk *now*."

"I can leave if you'd like privacy," I said.

Edward stared up at me, then at his son. Then back to me. "Are you asking me? Or my son?"

Silas's jaw clenched, and I thought I saw his head shake *no* once. Almost imperceptibly.

"Either. Both. Whoever. . ."

"Uh huh," Edward said. "You don't ask *him* for permission. You ask me."

"Of course."

Edward was still watching me. Then he turned back around and said loudly, "Silas, did you hear the latest news? A Hollywood fairy claims he was the victim of a hate crime. Someone threw a red drink. . . what do you call those? A slushy. They threw a slushy all over his pretty little outfit."

It had to have been eighty-five degrees out, but my skin broke out in gooseflesh.

"Oh yeah?" Silas said flatly, his face impassive and unreadable behind his sunglasses.

"Yes. What do you think of that?"

"I don't," he said, retreating behind his book.

"It's all over the news," Edward said. "Ridiculous. That's the kind of press we don't have to worry about anymore, thankfully."

Silas's hands clutched his book, the cover of which depicted a sketch of a shadowy man locked in a prison.

"Your brother on the other hand. . ." Edward shook his head, his gaze sweeping across the vast horizon of his wealth and to Eddie diving in the deep end. "A shame. So much potential. Gone."

"Okay, Dad," Silas said. "Drop it."

"We've done well to keep him out of the public eye. And you. . ." He motioned vaguely at Silas. "Dodged a bullet, didn't we?"

"*Dad*," Silas said, sitting up.

They stared each other down; the father fixing the son with a cold look that made my skin crawl. I suddenly felt like a soldier on a battlefield, missiles whizzing past me, right and left.

"How is Faith?" Edward asked suddenly. Pleasantly. "It's been quite awhile since you've brought her over."

"She's fine," Silas said, lying back down.

Faith, I thought, wincing at the small stab to the gut. *Okay.*

"We must have her to dinner soon," Edward said. "Seeing as she'll soon be a part of the family. Decency. Morals. Family values. That's who we are. Always."

A short silence fell. Silas, despite his bronzed glory under a blazing sun, may as well have been a statue.

"It's hot," I said to Edward. "I'll get you some water."

I left before he could order me back. Inside the butler's kitchen, I opened the refrigerator and let the cool air waft over me.

What the hell was that all about? Dodged a bullet?

And there was a woman in the picture. Why that surprised me, I couldn't guess. Between his looks, smarts, and money, Silas probably had scores of women's phone numbers in his contacts. My chest ached a little as if I'd been punched.

You knew he was off-limits. Now it's official and you can stop drooling over him.

I lifted my head and blew out a breath, grabbed a bottle of water and headed out. When I came back to the patio, Silas had put on a T-shirt and was gathering his things. Eddie stood beside him with a towel over his skinny shoulders. He had his head down, intent on making the water dripping from his bathing suit splatter the cement in a straight line.

"I think Dad's had enough sun for the day," Silas told me, his voice heavy and apologetic. "It's going to his head. Making him say things he doesn't mean. Could you please take him back to his room to rest?"

"Sure."

He stopped as he passed me, shoulder to shoulder, both of us looking straight ahead in opposite directions.

"Thank you," he said, and then he and Eddie went inside without another word.

Edward was waiting in his chair, staring out over his vast property, a grimace worn into the lines of his face. Did he appreciate what he had? Not his sons, that was clear. Eddie was anything but a "lost cause"; the guy was smart in ways no one else could touch, and instead of giving him a position somewhere to make use of his talents, Edward kept him locked up as if he were an eyesore. An embarrassment.

And Silas. . .

I didn't understand their strange exchange, but it was likely Silas had disappointed his tyrant of a father at some point in his twenty-four years. Hell, none of the nurses could please Edward while he was bedridden and weak. It had to have been a million times worse growing up with the man when he'd been powerful and strong.

A headache was starting to pound between my temples. Roberto reappeared and I relayed Silas's orders to take Edward back to his room. I told him I would meet him upstairs after I grabbed an Advil.

Back in my room, I noticed I'd left my phone on the bed. It showed a text from Darlene.

How's the existential crisis going?

I texted back. **Bad to worse. I think the demigod has a GF. A fiancée, probably.**

A few seconds later, the reply came. **Booo! Want me to make her disappear? I'm from Queens. I know people.**

I smiled but it faded fast. **Even more fun, my boss is a homophobe.**

Oh honey get out of there. Not worth it. Too much pain 4U.

Can't quit. My resume will look like chopped liver. I'll figure it out.

The words looked so solid in black and white. I wished I felt as confident. Worse, I'd been a hypocrite. My *No Bullshit* policy called bullshit: I talked up friendship with Silas, when the truth was that I was undeniably attracted to everything about him. I wanted dates in dark restaurants and long hours talking about books or music or anything—like his childhood or his addictions that were so like mine.

Impossible. He has a fiancée. Be happy for him.

My own happiness would just have to wait a little longer.

Later that afternoon, when my shift had ended, I changed out of my uniform into jeans and a plain black V-neck T-shirt and searched the gigantic estate for Cesar Castro to talk to him about my situation with Edward. Instead of Cesar, I found Eddie, pacing the living room, head down, hands twisting in front of him.

"Hey, Eddie," I said, reaching out a hand. "You okay?"

He danced out of reach and I backed off.

"Distressing," he said. "Terribly, terribly distressing." He glanced up at me sharply, his face blank of expression but his eyes meeting mine, forging a connection that lasted a second, then gone again. "Mr. Kaufman, my good man. I do but wonder, have you seen my brother?"

"Not since the pool."

Eddie shook his head, eyes on the floor, still pacing. "Distressing. I last found him arguing with Papa after the pool. I couldn't ascertain the subject of their disagreement. Something to do with appropriate language around the staff. I do hope he hasn't been sent away again."

"Sent away?"

I remembered Silas at the NA meeting, talking about how he'd gone away for a while. Again, I wondered if it had been on a deployment for the military. Eddie only paced in a tighter circle, his hands twisting over and over.

"Eddie—?"

"Do you play the piano?"

"A little. I took lessons as a kid, but I'm rusty as hell."

"I shan't mind in the slightest. Not at all."

I cocked my head at him. "Would it make you feel better if I played?"

"Silas plays for me when I'm in a bit of a state."

"I'm nowhere near as good as Silas, but I can give it a shot."

"Please do," he said. "I would be much obliged."

He continued wringing his hands and pacing, while I sat at the baby grand and lifted the lid. I felt like someone who'd driven a Pinto all his life and was now given the keys to a Maserati.

"Fair warning, it's been ages."

"No need to dilly-dally," Eddie said. "Give it the old college try. There's a good man."

I tried to remember one single thing I could play and sounded out the theme to *Star Wars* on one hand.

"Ah yes, John Williams," Eddie said after I'd finished. "Born February 8, 1932, composer and pianist who has scored more than one hundred films, including *E.T.*, *Jaws*, and *Star Wars*. But perhaps you have something a little more classic in your repertoire?"

I bit my lip. The highlight of my "repertoire" was "Chopsticks". The most complicated, two-handed piece I ever played was "The Entertainer" and not very well. For Eddie's sake, I plunked out the song, wincing at every error. Which was frequently.

"Oh dear," Eddie said. "Not very good, I'm afraid."

I burst out laughing. "You can say that again."

But Eddie was no longer pacing, and his hands were still. I considered that a victory.

"'The Entertainer' was composed by Scott Joplin in 1902. Silas can play it most marvelously."

"I believe it." I turned on the bench to face Eddie. "You're quite the music historian."

"I have memorized and cataloged every song that Silas has performed on the piano, from the earliest days of his youth, through his teen years, through his extended stays at boarding school and Yale, all the way up to the present day, with only the one unfortunate gap."

"What gap?"

"When he was sent away."

"What do you mean by that? Was he in the Armed Services?"

Eddie shook his head, eyes always on the ground. "No, my good man.

Between September 1st through March 1st, at the age of seventeen years and three months, Silas Alexander Marsh was sent away for sexual and disciplinary reprogramming."

I stared. "Say that again?"

"Between September 1st through March 1st, at the age of seventeen years—"

"No, sorry, I heard you the first time. I meant. . . where was he sent?"

"Chisana," Eddie said.

"Chisana. What is that?"

"Situated in the southeastern quadrant of the U.S. state of Alaska, Chisana was settled in 1920 at the shores of Copper Lake. Abandoned as of 1977, its current population is zero. It is, in common parlance, a ghost town."

"Silas was sent to a ghost town? In Alaska?"

For fucking reprogramming?

Eddie nodded. "Followed by a brief stint in the hospital afterward for exhaustion, malnutrition, frostbite, pneumonia, and attempted self-harm."

He listed all of this without emotion, while each word pummeled me in head and heart.

"*Self-harm*? Why? Why was he sent to. . . that place?"

"Per our father, on August 15th, two weeks prior to Silas's departure. . ." Eddie stood still and recited, "In the Marsh household, there are certain expectations that must be met. Deviant behavior is not tolerated—nor accepted—and must be seen for what it is: an outlier that can and will be dealt with swiftly. I know you are confused, son, but there is help. And I am going to help you, for this cannot stand. It *cannot*."

Eddie dropped his head and paced a little again. "That's what Papa said that night. I was most distraught and removed from the room once the shouting began. I had never seen Silas weep before and have not seen it since. Then a man came and he. . .he took Silas away."

"He took him away. . ."

He nodded his head, his hands twisted. "Terribly, terribly distressing."

I swallowed down an ugly lump in my throat and forced a smile for Eddie's sake.

"I'm sure Silas hasn't gone away again. Doesn't he live somewhere in the city?"

"Quite right, quite right," Eddie said. "That is most likely. He had been arguing with Father after the pool this afternoon, and it brought to mind that terrible night, seven years ago."

"I understand," I said hoarsely. My throat had gone dry.

Reprogramming. Jesus, what does that mean?

Whatever had happened, it had hurt Silas. Badly. Enough that he hurt himself. Maybe tried to end his own life.

I gave a start as Cesar Castro stepped into the room. He was a mild-mannered man in his late fifties, with a polished, refined demeanor that said everything is fine while he juggled the entirety of the Marsh estate.

His glance went between Eddie and me. "All is well, here?"

"Quite better now," Eddie said. "Mr. Kaufman was soothing my nerves with his terrible piano-playing."

Cesar grinned. "I'm happy to hear it helped," he said with a nod of thanks for me. "And what was so distressing, Mr. Eddie?"

"I feared Silas might've been sent away again."

Cesar's smiled collapsed and his dark eyes widened slightly, the only sign of alarm.

"No, of course Mr. Silas has not been sent away," he said, smiling thinly. "Eddie, I do believe Ramona was looking for you. The silver cutlery has been polished, and she knows how much you love to arrange them in their proper place."

Eddie's eyes lit up for a split second. "I do, indeed. A task of utmost importance." He tipped an imaginary cap to me. "Mr. Kaufman, always a pleasure. Perhaps a few piano lessons from my brother are in order? He has quite the talent and I daresay you need them."

He left the room, and Cesar turned to me, his hands clasped behind his back.

"Eddie is often given to wild flights of imagination," he said.

I crossed my arms. "In my experience, people with Asperger's are more inclined to be extremely fact-oriented."

"Be that as it may, I would ask that for the sake of the family's privacy, you disregard anything he might've divulged to you."

"You mean about Silas's sexual reprogramming?"

God, the words tasted ugly.

Cesar's eyes flared again, then he stiffened. "An exaggeration," he said, though his tone was heavy. "I'm assuming you are speaking of his time in Alaska? Mr. Marsh was sent to a boy's camp for disciplinary issues."

"For six months? To an Alaskan ghost town in winter, over the holidays? And then a hospital after?" I stopped and waved my hands. "I'm sorry. Never mind. It's wrong to be discussing this behind his back, but Jesus. . ."

"Discussing it to his face would be worse, I'm afraid." Cesar's voice was heavy. "It is. . . quite a painful subject."

I'm sure it is, I thought, my chest tightening as puzzle pieces fell into place. Edward's homophobia. The strange conversation by the pool. The strained, strange dynamic between father and son. And Silas himself who seemed so stiff and careful with his emotions.

God, Silas. What did they do to you?

I sucked in a shaky breath and sat straighter, even as the blood in my veins felt sluggish and cold.

"I'd been looking for you, actually," I said. "There is something I need to discuss."

"Which is?"

"Edward Marsh doesn't know I'm gay, does he?"

Cesar's eyes flared again. "I had not known myself until this very moment."

"Given some of his recent remarks, I'd have thought there was a policy against hiring someone like me."

"That would be illegal, wouldn't it?" He sighed. "I'm very sorry, Max, if he's said anything to offend you. Had I known, I would have spared you—"

I waved him off. "I can handle myself."

"If you wish to terminate the contract, I understand and will arrange for a glowing letter of recommendation and comfortable severance."

"A payoff, you mean."

He stiffened. "You are under NDA contract not to disclose anything that occurs under this roof."

"As it applies to Edward Marsh's health," I said. "It doesn't indemnify him against employee harassment." I shook my head when he started to speak. "I'm not after money. I don't even know that I want to quit. The only reason I told you about Marsh is to protect myself." I cocked my head. "In case he tries to send me to Alaska too."

Cesar's shoulders dropped, and the regret was etched in the lines of his brown skin. He was a good man. I felt that about him during my job interview. I felt it now.

"That's what happened, didn't it, Cesar?" I asked, my heart in my throat. "That's why Silas was sent away?"

Cesar stiffened. "Mr. Marsh was sent to a boy's camp for disciplinary issues."

"You said that already."

"And that is all I am permitted to ever say." He started to go. "Please let me know what you decide with regards to your employment. It's understandable, given the circumstances, if you were to leave. But for my part, I hope you stay."

"Cesar."

"Yes?"

"Is he... okay?"

"He's as well as can be expected." He smiled sadly. "All things considered."

CHAPTER NINE

Silas

"Holy fucking shit," I murmured to my empty office at Marsh Pharma, my coffee untouched and growing cold on my desk.

My assistant was superb at her job. The best. Her research into the devastation our company had wrought lay spewed from a file folder in front of me like a bloated corpse, leaking blood and secrets all over my immaculate mahogany desk.

Not one corpse. Hundreds.

OxyPro had swept like a wildfire across Appalachia and down the Eastern Seaboard, from Baltimore to Jacksonville, leaving devastation in its wake. In the last ten years, overdose deaths were up by astronomical numbers, and a wave of petty and not-so-petty crime had swelled as addicts struggled to pay for their pills. When the pills ran out, they turned to heroin.

I rubbed my eyes; a headache was starting to form behind them.

On top of the human toll—soul-sickening enough—there were legal ramifications to consider. Everything Sylvia had found was available online. My having it wasn't illegal, but me asking her specifically to dig it up was probably a really stupid thing to do. My brain conjured a mental image of me on the stand in a courtroom, a lawyer pacing in front of me. *"Silas Marsh, what did you know and when did you know it?"*

I glanced around my office with its wall-to-wall windows. I felt like a fish in a bowl, and that bowl was sinking fathoms' deep into a black ocean, the pressure squeezing in on all sides.

So get out.

It would be so easy. Tender my resignation to Dad as COO and throw away any chance of becoming CEO. Dad's entire legacy rested on keeping the empire he'd built in the family. He'd ruthlessly dictated every minute of my life—including my detour to Alaska—to ensure it happened. Taking a wife would complete the pretty picture. I wasn't a human, I was Frankenstein's monster, built on a slab and molded to fit Dad's idea of the perfect son.

And I'd gone along with all of it. To make him proud of me just for one fucking second in his life. An elusive high I'd been chasing for years, like the addict I was.

And I stayed for the memory of Mom who'd want me to take care of Dad.

And for Eddie, whom I wanted to give the entire fucking world.

If I walked away...

If I walked away, I'd have nothing. Dad had threatened that a hundred times. He'd disown me completely and cut me off from my brother who deserved to have a real life.

My fingers toyed with the edge of the manila folder. If I quit, the damage our drug was doing would continue unchecked. If I stayed to help—kept playing the part—I could try to put some of this right.

A harsh laugh erupted out of me. It was like trying to clean up a flood with a single mop.

I need someone I can trust to talk about this shit.

Max.

Something in my chest, in my heart, shifted just to think his name. A soft ache that had no business being there. *He* had no business being there. He was trespassing. Again. I couldn't keep him out.

If he knew what was happening here, he'd probably hate me. He'd quit working for Dad and I'd never see him again. Because he had principles. Integrity. He was true to himself, while I could hardly look in a mirror.

The sun sank outside my windows, and I shoved the manila folder into the safe in my office, locked it up, and left.

Sylvia Timmons, my assistant and potential future key-witness in *People v. Marsh Pharma,* was at her desk.

"Sylvia. . ."

"Yes, Mr. Marsh?"

Sentences piled up in my mind like a traffic jam.

Thanks for the data. There sure are a bunch of losers who abused our product, eh? Not our fault, though. Goodnight!

Let's keep this between you and me. How's three million sound?

You're fired.

"Mr. Marsh?" Her face was contorted in concern.

"Have a good night," I said tiredly and went out.

I drove my Range Rover out of the Marsh Pharma skyscraping towers and into the underground parking lot at the prism-shaped luxury condo complex called the Spire. A cherry red Mini Cooper was in the space next to mine.

My fiancée was home.

She hadn't moved in with me yet but came and went between her place and mine. . . and whoever else's bed she happened to be sharing.

I walked my rolling suitcase through the cavernous lot, past rows of BMWs, Mercedes, and Jaguars, and keyed in a security code at the elevators. It took me up to one of three penthouse suites.

At 3P, I keyed another code to get into my place, dropped my suitcase by the door, and crossed the expansive living room to the huge windows. All of Seattle lay below in a glittering panorama of lights against the night and the darker expanse of Elliott Bay beyond.

"Silas?" came a call from the bedroom. "Is that you?"

"There is no me," I said softly to the city. "I don't exist."

"Silas? Or is it an intruder come to ravage me?"

"It's me, for Christ sakes," I called.

God, I want a drink.

I limited my alcohol intake to nursing one glass of wine at social events, mostly because people would notice if I abstained and ask why. Getting drunk or even buzzed was a bad idea— the altered-state of drunkenness touched too close to the altered-state of being high.

But fuck it, learning your father's company had destroyed hundreds of lives called for a drink. I could have one glass of wine like an adult.

I went to the wine rack that Faith kept well-stocked and opened a bottle of Chateau Lafite Rothschild. I poured a glass and tossed it back like a shot of whiskey.

Then I poured another.

Don't...

I drowned the word in wine and set the glass down hard. My tolerance was shit; already my skin was warmer, my limbs looser, as I headed through my modern condo that was decorated in sparse, masculine lines and dark colors. It was still a bachelor pad, for now. In the master bedroom, I sat slumped on the edge of the king-sized bed.

Faith Benson was at the bathroom mirror, smearing cold cream on her face. She wore a bathrobe over her slender form, and her blonde hair was tied up in a towel.

"Howdy, stranger." She watched me with her sharp green eyes through the mirror still steamed from her shower. "I was beginning to wonder if you'd decided to move in with Daddy. How is it over there?"

"Same as ever," I said. "Dad's illness has yet to give him a new perspective on life."

Faith scoffed. "Not surprising. And how are you? You look tired."

I'm exhausted down to my soul.

"I'm fine."

"You always say that. Talk to me. Bad news?"

Why not tell Faith everything? She was smart and the closest thing I had to a friend—handshake deals with Max aside. Then I noticed the small reddish mark on her neck.

"Jesus, Faith, you could at least try to be discreet. Dad wants you over to dinner."

"When?"

"Sometime. I don't know. It's been too long. You need to be prepared."

She angled her neck to better examine the hickey in the mirror. "It'll be long gone by *sometime*. And if not, that's what concealer is for." She smeared her six-hundred-and-fifty-dollar-per-bottle cream on her neck, a gift from me for her birthday. "You're right though. It has been too long. We have appearances to keep up. Hoops to jump through."

Faith went to the nightstand, opened the drawer and removed her six-carat diamond engagement ring that she took off before her sleepovers at other men's apartments and slipped it on her finger. The bed dipped as she knelt behind me and she wrapped her arms around my neck.

"Whenever I'm summoned, I shall put on the best of *appearances*. Loving girlfriend-turned-excited fiancée."

I closed my eyes, inhaling her warm scent, the expensive cream, and tried to let myself sink into her embrace. Tried to let the wine I'd chugged lure me into her arms.

I didn't move.

Even years later, the vault I'd built in Alaska was indestructible. Coach Braun and his counselors broke something in me; ground me down to the basement of my soul. Taught me to hate all that I was and all that I wanted, then made that hate survival. Lust or desire for *anyone* was dangerous. Like a glass or two of wine that woke up the addiction in me, letting my body feel anything would only wake it up to what I truly wanted.

Feel nothing, Coach Braun whispered, *because you are nothing.*

"Marsh Senior is going to want updates on our engagement party," Faith was saying, resting her chin on my shoulder. "Shouldn't we get on that?"

I shrugged and her arms shrugged with me. "I suppose."

"Any sign he's closer to naming you the big cheese?"

"No. I know him. At death's door or not, he's not handing me the keys to the kingdom until we're married."

Until I've proven my worth.

"Try to be *a little* excited," Faith said, giving me a squeeze. "Youngest CEO in the history of business, probably. Billions at your fingertips. . ."

. . . and in our soon-to-be joint bank account.

I felt her watching me and turned to meet her gaze, so close to mine.

Faith was beautiful. Intelligent. Ambitious. And without a romantic bone in her body. The perfect business partner for my purposes.

"You look sad," she said and ran her fingers through my hair. "And stressed. Are you sure you don't want a little something? Some oral stimulation? To ease the tension?" She slunk off the bed and knelt in front of me to run her hands up my thighs. "I mean, it's the least I can do."

I caught her hands before they could reach the fly on my slacks.

She pouted. "Really? Nothing?"

"It's not you, Faith. You know this. I don't feel anything for anyone."

Faith sighed. "I can't imagine it. For the rest of your life? I still think you should see a shrink. It's unnatural."

I flinched at the word. "I'm not having this conversation again."

"It just doesn't make any sense to me, to be honest."

I pushed her hands away and stood up. "It doesn't have to make sense. You only need to uphold your end of the deal."

"And what if dear old Daddy has more hoops to jump through, even after the wedding? A grandchild, perhaps? To ensure the family lineage?"

"That won't happen," I said, moving to the door.

I'll never let that happen. I'll never let some poor kid get dragged into this farce.

"Lucky for you," Faith said. "That would require actual sex on your part."

"Goodnight, Faith," I said darkly and made to go to my bedroom, the guest bedroom.

"Wait, Silas. . ." She sidled up to me, toyed with the lapels of my jacket, her eyes demure and downcast. "I'm out of my little helpers. Be a love and grab me a sample tomorrow?"

I removed her hands. "I told you, they're not lying around the office like Halloween candy."

"Then have your guy give me a call?"

She wanted sleeping pills and our company's version of Xanax. But not OxyPro. Thank God.

"I'm not your dealer, Faith."

"It's part of our arrangement, *Silas*." She gave me a parting shot over her shoulder. "And honey, you're the entire world's dealer."

I shut the door behind me. "Tell me about it."

In the plain guest bedroom, I lay flat on my back on the bed in the dark and stared at the pristine white ceiling. I imagined it was keeping the world out, keeping it from crushing me under the weight of what Marsh Pharma had done. For now. Tomorrow, I'd have to get up and do something. But how in the hell could I ever hope to fix all that had been broken?

The wine muted my thoughts, blunted the edges and let them wander without stabbing me with guilt.

Max Kaufman. I could tell him everything. He would tell me what to do. He'd know what was right. WWMD? I should put that on a bumper sticker.

I chuckled to myself, my eyes drifting closed. In my mind's eye, I saw Max leaning against a wall, arms crossed, wearing that quiet smile of his that was so damn distracting. Max was a good man. Too good for me to drag into this ugliness. Too fucking beautiful, inside and out. . .

We don't describe men with pretty words, Coach Braun reminded me. *Real men are ugly, rough brutes who take what they want—including women—because that is the way nature designed us. Men are hard. Women are soft. Yin and yang. That's how it's supposed to be. . . You live like that, or nothing at all. Your choice.*

I sank deeper into the bed and behind my closed lids, the white ceiling above me became the pale sky of Alaska in September. White and flat and endless. I didn't want to go back, but it's what happened when I had inappropriate thoughts about men. My 'training' came to get me and drag me back into the cold. . .

There were seven of us. I guessed them all to be about my age—late teens or even a little younger—lined up on the deserted road in the middle of nowhere. If you could call it a road. A vague track of rocks and packed dirt overgrown with scrubby plants ran between a dozen rotting log cabins that had been new at the turn of the century. We exchanged glances, our breaths pluming in front of us. Winter was still months away and it was already so damn cold.

The guy who'd come to our house in Seattle—the guy Dad had introduced me to as Coach Braun—was conferring with his counselors. Three big guys who reminded me of orderlies in movies about scary mental hospitals or bouncers at biker bars. Nothing about them screamed "counselor"—someone you'd want to talk your problems over with.

Compared to them, Coach Braun was downright scrawny, but he scared me the most. He looked like a snake, with dark eyes in a huge skull and a high forehead. In our living room, he'd made Chisana sound like a summer camp. The boys I'd be bunking up with formed "a team" whose goal was to defeat our "opponent" and repair what was broken in us. He was going to coach us through it, and we wouldn't be allowed to leave until victory was achieved.

Three weeks later, I was standing on this road in a deserted mining town, freezing my ass off with six other guys. Except for a whistling wind, Chisana was eerily silent. Hushed. I thought that if I screamed, the sound wouldn't travel farther than a few feet before being swallowed up in the cold, dry air.

I sort of wanted to scream.

Coach finished conferring, and his henchmen left. They'd driven a U-Haul behind Coach's camper on the thirty-six-hour drive up and were now going to move stuff out of it and into one of the main buildings that still had a roof. Coach told us the U-Haul was filled with supplies for our trip: food, bottled water, and electrical equipment.

"Like TVs?" one of the boys had asked on the drive from the back seat. He was young, maybe fourteen. His name was Toby.

"Exactly," Coach had said. "And a generator, VCR, and. . . other things."

"What's a VCR?" a guy named Holden had asked.

"It's what there was before DVDs. You watch videos on them."

"We get to watch movies?" Toby asked, his eyes lighting up.

"Yep, sure do," Coach had said, smiling to show small teeth. "That's part of the program. Special kinds of movies. And we'll make sure your body does what it's supposed to do while you watch. Like training."

"What kind of training?" I'd asked from the passenger seat. Coach had put me up front to keep me close. He'd picked me out as his trouble-maker already.

"The body is stimulated by all kinds of inputs," Coach said. "The smell of warm pie might make your stomach growl or your mouth water. The sound of running water can make you want to take a piss. And certain visual images can make your manly parts stand at attention. But only certain kinds of images should make that happen. If your body likes other kinds. . ." He shook his head gravely, his eyes on the road in front of him. "Well, we can't have that, now can we? A little rewiring of the circuits, and you'll be all set."

A cold ball of fear had settled into my stomach at those words and seemed to lodge there permanently after Coach Braun's friendly smile vanished the second we crossed the Yukon/Alaska border.

Now, standing on that empty road, surrounded by a handful of crumbling buildings that were wind and weather-beaten, that icy fear spread like a virus into my veins.

Coach Braun turned to face us, pacing the line like a drill sergeant.

"This is it, boys. This is the beginning of your new life. Your best life. You've gotten off the straight and narrow and ventured into the crooked path of deviancy. Unnatural urges have taken hold, and we are going to pry them loose. Free you from the confusion, because it's not too late. It's not too late to rejoin society and take your proper place. We are here to help. To teach you how to walk and talk and behave like the men you truly are."

He stopped and addressed all of us.

"Are you not tired of feeling like you don't belong? Like you don't fit in? Aren't you tired of hiding the flaw in yourself from the world?"

More than one head nodded. Mine nearly did. I had to bite the inside of my cheek to keep tears from forming. Tears of hope because Dad hated me how I was and maybe he'd love me when this was over.

But a small voice whispered that I was betraying something inherent in me that wasn't broken at all. Coming here was to sacrifice the truth of who I was in exchange for love and acceptance. In the warmth and safety of my living room, it had felt worth it.

Now. . .

"We're going to take care of you," Coach Braun said. "Fix you right up. When we're done, you'll have nothing to hide."

He stopped in front of me.

"Only then can you go home again."

CHAPTER TEN

Max

"What do you guys know about conversion therapy?"

Daniel and Malcolm froze, while Charlie choked on his beer. The three men stared at me while the pulsing music of the drag show blared behind us. It would've been funny had the circumstances not felt so damn dire.

"Cue record scratch," Daniel said over the loud music. He batted his eyes at me. "Something on your mind, Maximilian?"

"In my defense, I told you I wasn't in the right headspace for a drag show tonight."

"You weren't kidding," Daniel said. "What on earth is bringing this up?"

I shrugged, hunched over my soda water. "I. . . read an article. Got me thinking, that's all."

"Conversion therapy." Malcolm shivered. "Ugh. The Dark Ages called."

Charlie rolled his eyes. "Pray the gay away? Does that still happen? Are we still burning witches at the stake, too?"

"Oh honey, it still happens," said the bartender, a drag queen named Sure Jan who dressed like Marcia Brady on acid—full '70s dress and bright blue eyeshadow. She leaned an arm on the bar. "My cousin was sent to conversion therapy when he was a teenager. Messed him up for a long time."

"Shit," I said, my heart sinking. "How long is long?"

"For *years*. They broke him down, the poor thing. In a nutshell, they spent six months telling him he was worthless, then six more months teaching him how to 'be a man.'" Her long, lacquered-nail fingers made air quotes around the words. "He tried to commit suicide when it was over. To this day, he's on meds for depression and hasn't been able to keep a real relationship, poor baby."

"Jesus."

"They're all bad, but some are worse than others. They dig in and bury their filth deep. The one Lenny did was intense."

"Where was he sent?"

Chisana, Alaska?

Jan shrugged. "Someplace in Mississippi. He'll never step foot in that state again."

Silence fell between us at the bar, while onstage, a trio of drag queens in gold sequins lip-synced to Lady Gaga's "Born This Way."

"Are we done talking about this pleasant subject?" Charlie asked. "Or is now a good time to bring up how my childhood cat was run over by a car?"

"I'd like to discuss the ongoing conflict in the Middle East," Malcolm said. "As one does. In the middle of a drag revue."

"You heard the *Lady*," Charlie said, jerking a thumb at the stage. "Don't be a drag, Max, just be a queen."

I rolled my eyes. "Yeah, yeah, I'll shut up now."

Daniel frowned. "You okay? For real."

"I'm okay," I said.

If what I suspect is true, Silas isn't okay. Not by a mile.

"Not thinking of going back in the closet, are you?" Daniel teased lightly. "Because that ship has sailed, honey. Those 'therapies' are bullshit. There's no going back."

"I never had to come out in the first place," Charlie said. "Mom said I burst from the womb waving a Pride flag."

"I didn't come out either," Sure Jan said from behind the bar, shooting us a wink from under her ten-pound eyelashes. "I leaped like a gazelle in a feather boa and Jimmy Choos."

I smiled faintly and nursed my soda water while the others resumed talking and laughing. My thoughts went to the moment I came out. Or rather, how Dad had yanked me out by the scruff of my neck, thanks to my own carelessness. There was no kitchen table talk. No calm sit-down where I got to reintroduce myself to my parents as I truly was and hope they'd be happy to know the real me. Instead, the shock split the family like a continental fault line, separating me from them by a wide chasm I was still trying to bridge.

Later that night, as the Marsh estate drew nearer and nearer—a glittering castle on the water—I itched to tell my Uber driver to turn around.

"Goddammit, Eddie," I murmured.

The driver glanced at me in the rearview. "Sorry?"

"Nothing."

Eddie shouldn't have told me about Silas and Alaska. The word "reprogramming" polluted my thoughts and it wasn't my business. Something this personal and of this magnitude belonged with Silas. He should be able to tell me if he wanted to tell me. Or not.

But I didn't know how long I'd be able to keep quiet, either. When I was deep in the shit, it never occurred to me to ask anyone for help. Carl's help came out of thin air, like a ladder lowered from a helicopter, pulling me out of the whirlpool of misery.

Maybe Silas needed a lifeline too.

Or maybe you've got this all wrong. You don't actually know what happened to him.

I climbed into bed in my room in the Marsh house and stared at the ceiling.

"Don't ask, don't tell," I muttered.

As sleep reached for me, I decided the best way to be there for Silas was to do just that. Just be there for him, if he needed me.

That's what friends were for.

The following Saturday, I was off work and debating my options on how to spend the day. The sounds of expert piano playing drifted on the air from the family room, and I remembered that Silas spent Saturdays with Eddie.

I drifted toward the family room too. I didn't want to interrupt the brothers, but goddamn, Silas was insanely talented. I couldn't *not* listen but leaned against the door as he finished a highly complicated piece I didn't recognize.

He belongs on the stage.

"Mr. Kaufman!"

I gave a jolt to see Eddie beaming at the floor but facing my direction. Silas arched a brow at me, the faintest flicker of amusement in his cold blue eyes.

Shit.

Eddie swept his hands to indicate the room. "Please, join us, my good man."

"No, no I'm sorry. I didn't mean to interrupt. . ."

"You're not interrupting, is he, brother dearest?"

Silas and I held gazes for a second, then he turned back to the piano. "No. He's not."

"And since you're here. . ." Eddie said. "No time like the present, grab the bull by the horns and so forth." He drew close to me without touching and gestured grandly at the piano. "If you please, sir. Your piano lesson awaits."

Silas swung around. "Come again?"

"The other day, Mr. Kaufman had hinted to me that he was rusty at the piano," Eddie said, "and then his performance left no doubt."

I snorted a laugh, but Silas frowned.

"Don't be rude," he said to his brother, then turned to me, his expression softening. "You played for Eddie?"

"I don't think 'played' is the exact word," I said. "I banged on the keys a little."

Eddie steepled his fingers together. "Ergo, a lesson or two is in order?"

Silas glared at his brother, which made me grin.

"I'm sure Silas has better things to do than give piano lessons to a hopeless case like me."

"My dear brother has left our Saturday activities to my discretion," Eddie said. "And it is my sincerest wish that he shares his gift with you, Mr. Kaufman."

I coughed and felt the back of my neck redden. Silence fell, and I was sure Silas was going to kick me out of the room. But for a split second he looked almost shy again, as he had in the car the other day.

"Well?" he said finally.

"Well. . . what?"

"You heard the man." He jerked his chin at his brother. "Saturdays are up to him. If you want to play. . ."

"I don't want to intrude. . ."

"You're not, but if you don't want to—"

"My word, but there is quite a lot of dilly-dallying," Eddie remarked.

Silas and I exchanged glances, and we both chuckled.

"It's not going to be pretty," I said, "but I'm game if you are."

Silas surrendered the bench and I felt a twinge of disappointment that I wasn't going to be sitting next to him. I put my hands on the keys where I swear I felt the residual heat of Silas's touch.

Get a hold of yourself, man.

"What do I do?"

"Hell if I know," Silas said with a short laugh. "It's my first lesson too. I guess. . .play something. Give me an idea of where you're at."

I banged out "The Entertainer" and then looked up to see Silas's nose wrinkled like he was smelling something sour. Another laugh burst out of me.

"I warned you."

Silas gave his head a shake. "Now I'm being rude. Okay, let's see what you remember. Can you read music?"

"No. 'The Entertainer' is from memory."

"Can you find Middle C?"

I shot him a look and plucked the key. "This is humiliating."

"I was there once, too."

"When? When you were a toddler?"

"Maybe."

"So modest. Are you going to teach or bask in your own genius?"

"Both."

Now he grinned showing perfect white teeth, and holy shit, Silas Marsh *grinning*...

I'm in so much trouble.

"Let's start with hand position," he said. "Curl your fingers. But loosely. Not like that. Those look like claws. Keep your hands light. And Jesus, don't rest your wrists on the piano."

I leaned back on the bench. "Eddie, is your brother always this bossy?"

"Yes."

I shot Silas a look. "Busted."

He rolled his eyes. "Shove over."

Silas slid onto the bench next to me with a wave of cologne and whatever gel he put in his hair to make it gleam. He looked nearly as sexy in a tight black T-shirt and jeans as he had in a bathing suit. Nearly. I felt the solidity of his presence beside me. Sitting this close to me, in profile, I could trace the line of his jaw and the sharp angle of his cheekbones, both leading to the soft perfection of his mouth...

With effort, I concentrated on the lesson, our elbows brushing now and then as he corrected my hand position and reacquainted me with the simple C and G7 chords.

Twenty minutes later, I was able to play a kiddie version of Beethoven's "Ode to Joy."

"Not bad, old chap," Eddie said. "Not good either, but give it another few weeks, and you'll be up to snuff."

"A few weeks?" The notion of spending every Saturday with Silas made my head light with possibilities, but I grounded them all before they could take flight. "No, no, I think I've tested the limits of Silas's patience. And I can't intrude on your Saturdays."

"And I'm sure Max has better things to do than hang with us," Silas added, and that shy look came over him again, the one that made my heart crash in my chest. "I don't mind. But, I mean, it's up to you, obviously."

I grinned. "Obviously."

"Splendid." Eddie clapped his hands together, beaming now. "We'll have tea and finger sandwiches, Silas will play for us, and then you shall have a lesson, Mr. Kaufman. We'll make a jolly-good show of it."

"Slow down, Eddie," Silas said. "Let's take it one Saturday at a time."

I elbowed him in the side. "Don't you mean, *we'll play it by ear*?"

He groaned and elbowed me back, and our eyes met again, laughter on the surface, mellowing into something deeper the longer we looked. And I didn't want to stop looking. Silas didn't stop either but scanned my face that way he always did, as is if searching for something. An answer to a question he couldn't bring himself to ask.

"Puns, Mr. Kaufman, are the lowest form of humor," Eddie intoned from the couch.

"True." I got up from the bench. "Your turn, Si. Cleanse the air of my terrible jokes and my even worse Beethoven."

Another flush of heat ripped through me as Silas regarded me curiously.

Oh shit, I called him Si.

"Sorry, it just. . . popped out."

"No, it's. . . whatever." He cleared his throat. "What am I playing, Eddie?"

"Something rather difficult, perhaps. Show Mr. Kaufman what you're capable of. Rachmaninoff. The Prelude, I daresay. You must hear my dear Silas's Rachmaninoff."

"Indeed," I said and sat on the couch beside Eddie. "Hold on. Let me get prepared to bask in your genius."

"Shut up," Silas said with a nervous cough, and holy shit, flustered Silas was fucking adorable.

He closed his eyes for a moment and laid his fingers to the keys. Inhale, exhale, and then the room was saturated with music. The piece began slowly, almost somber, and then took off, sending Silas's fingers into a flurry of speed. A piece that seemed designed specifically to challenge anyone who tried to play it.

Starstruck and with my blood running hot—and due south—I watched Silas master the piano. Command it. Bend it to his will. He coaxed out every sound with light touches, or he banged at them with precision and strength, the muscles in his forearms tensed and striated with the effort. He sat with his back hunched, fingers flying over the keys. The music was an electric current, and he was the conduit.

Silas's talent was pure seduction, and my fevered imagination conjured him in the bedroom, in control, orchestrating every move, drawing out every note and sound he wanted from whomever lay beneath him. And then relinquishing that control, letting his own body be played like the perfect instrument it was—honed and taut, the sounds of his release better than any music. . .

Casually as possible, I crossed my leg over my thigh to conceal how hard I was, but it felt futile. I had to be broadcasting how turned on I was; it was coming off my skin in waves of pheromones and heat. Any second now, Eddie—sitting next to me—would pick up on it and ask me why I was blatantly lusting after his brother.

Silas brought the piece to a crescendo and the sudden silence was thick.

Eddie clapped his hands together. "Bravo, my good man." He turned his head my way, though never looking at me. "He's a miracle, isn't he?"

In every way.

Silas caught me staring, his sharp eyes taking me in, missing nothing.

"Yeah. . . wow, Silas." I blew air out my cheeks and laughed nervously. "I'm never playing in front of you again."

"Nonsense," Eddie said. "We have agreed on next Saturday."

Silas gave his brother a small, confused smile. "Why are you so insistent I give Max lessons?"

Eddie shrugged, his gaze on the floor. "Mr. Kaufman is pleasant company. Don't you agree?"

Silas and I exchanged glances again, and then he looked away. "Yeah, he is."

"Marvelous," Eddie said. "Next Saturday then."

I inhaled deeply to calm my still-heated blood. "The weather is supposed to be nice next week. You might want a trip to the city or go out on the lake instead of listening to me suck at piano."

Eddie shook his head quickly, curling in on himself like a threatened animal. "Oh no, no. Papa says to stay home. It's safer for me here. That's what he says. He's always said so."

Silas's lips twisted in a scowl. "We've talked about this, Eddie. Dad is. . . overprotective. If you want to go somewhere—anywhere—I'll take you."

"No, my good man. I am quite content here with you and Mr. Kaufman."

He started to rock back and forth from his seat on the couch.

"That's fine, Eddie," Silas said, his voice low. "It's okay. Whatever you want."

"It's cool, my good man," I said to Eddie. "I'll see you around but next Saturday for sure."

"Very good, yes," Eddie said. "Thank you."

In the hallway on my way out, Silas pulled me aside and leaned in, his voice low.

"Do what you want on Saturdays. It's your day off."

"I might not make it to every lesson, but I'll do my best."

He nodded. "I appreciate it. For Eddie's sake. He needs a change of scenery, but Dad's got him thinking all kinds of bullshit, and I can't convince him he'll be okay out in the world."

"He's capable enough for a job," I said slowly. "Responsibilities."

I braced myself for Silas's wrath that I was butting into family business, but he nodded, his brows furrowed. "I think so too. Dad hates anyone knowing he's got Asperger's, never mind give him a job at the company. When I'm CEO, that'll change. If Eddie wants it to."

"You're a good brother to him," I said. "Not that you need me to tell you that, but I know how it is when your own father doesn't believe in you." I smiled dryly. "I'm living proof."

I'd opened the door and waited for Silas to venture a step toward it. He didn't quite smile but his eyes softened, and I saw the depth lurking beneath their icy surface.

"Right, well. . . Thanks," he said. "Thanks for putting up with the piano lesson. It makes Eddie happy. Next Saturday?"

"Yep. See you then."

Silas turned and walked away, stopped, then turned back around.

"Are you free for lunch sometime this week?" he asked. "There're some issues at work that I think, with your medical background, you might be able to help me with. If you wouldn't mind. . .?"

"No," I said. "I don't mind. But don't you have teams of lab techs and pharmacists that could probably help you better?"

Silas arched a brow. "If I thought they could help, I would've asked one of them." He shot me a brief smile. "Besides, the nature of the issue isn't exactly common knowledge. I'd rather keep it to myself until I know what I'm dealing with."

"Sure. Yeah, I'll do my best."

"Thank you." He pulled out his cell phone from the back pocket of his jeans. "Phone number?"

I stared dumbly. "What?"

"Can I have your phone number? To text you the info on date, time, restaurant?"

"Oh, right. Sure."

I gave Silas Marsh my phone number. He jabbed a text; I felt it chime in my jacket pocket.

"Now you have mine," he said. "Please don't share it."

"No, never."

He nodded once. "I'll be in touch."

"Yep."

When he'd rounded the corner, I grabbed my phone to see the text Silas had sent.

Because I'm back in middle school, apparently.

This is Si

Si. My stupid heart thudded in my chest.

"Yep. Middle school."

Monday morning, I got the text from Silas to meet me downtown at The Ginger Garden at precisely noon. He was already there, waiting for me in a booth when I walked into the swanky restaurant wearing my usual jeans, boots, and black leather jacket over a T-shirt. Silas looked like a movie star in a three-piece suit in silvery gray with a white shirt and narrow gray tie. He got to his feet and offered a handshake as I approached.

"I should've Googled this place before I headed over," I said. "Now everyone's looking at me like this is a job interview and I've already blown it."

"They don't think that," Silas said, a smile pulling at his lips.

"Look at the poor schmuck, they're saying," I said, sliding into the booth across from Silas. "Came all this way. . . The least the nicely-dressed one can do is buy him lunch."

Silas was chuckling now. "Since you came all this way. . . Tell me about yourself, Mr. Koofman, is it?"

"My greatest weakness is that I'm *too* much of a perfectionist."

Silas burst out laughing.

My job is done. Whatever else happens today. . .

The waitress arrived, and Silas was all business again. "Are you ready to order? I only have an hour."

"Uh, yeah. What's good?"

"All of it," Silas said. "You like spring rolls?"

"Definitely."

He turned to the waitress. "We'll take spring rolls, an order of chicken potstickers. . ." He nodded at me. "You good with seafood?"

"Uh, sure."

"Two lobster and prawn dumpling soups and two orders of Mongolian beef with noodles."

We handed the menus back and the waitress left.

"That's a lot of food," I said.

"I need leftovers," Silas said. "Cold chow mein for breakfast is the best."

"Hell yes, it is. Nothing better than greasy, cold-ass noodles straight out of the box."

I offered my hand for a high five, and he returned it, looking less like a Wall Street venture capitalist and more like the young guy he actually was.

I folded my arms on the table. "Can I ask you a question?"

"Shoot."

"How are you poised to be CEO of a multi-billion-dollar company when you're only. . . what? Twenty-four?"

"I got a head start," he said.

"Meaning?"

"I tested high on certain exams designed to measure intelligence."

"Is that the long way around to saying you aced the IQ test?"

"I don't want to sound like an ass about it."

"How high? Genius high? Einstein high?"

"Damn, you're a nosy bastard," he said with a laugh.

"Guilty. But after the way you played the piano the other day. . . it's fascinating."

And a turn on, but we're not going there. We're being friends.

Silas rested his left arm over the back of the booth, crossed his leg, ankle on thigh. "It is what it is."

"Uh-huh," I said, grinning. "The picture of modesty. Then what? You graduated high school at ten?"

"Sixteen. I did half a year at boarding school. . ." He cleared his throat. "Took some time off. . .then Yale. Compacted course schedule, graduated in three years, then management training." He shrugged. "Here I am."

The waitress dropped off a pot of tea, two small cups, and a plate of spring rolls drizzled with pink sweet and sour sauce.

"What about you?" he asked. "You told me you were an ER nurse before working for Dad."

"Yep. After Carl found me on the streets and saved my ass, he got me to take the GED, SAT, and ACT. Not quite Einstein, but I did all right. Then I did four years at San Francisco State's nursing program. Passed the national test to be an RN and was doing my two years before certification when I got the job working for your father."

Silas frowned. "After the ER, taking care of Dad has to be pretty easy."

"I needed the break. You see a lot of shit in the ER. Not sure if I have the stomach for it anymore."

"My father isn't the easiest person in the world to take. He's scared off more staff than I can count."

"He's all right," I said. "Random homophobic comments aside. And he's scared too. The MS knocked him flat."

"Some might call that karma," Silas said. He waved a hand at my expression. "It's no secret he's a bastard. That doesn't mean I don't. . .love him, or whatever. But it's. . .complicated."

"I know how that is," I said.

"How's it going with your family? You ever reconcile with them?"

"Had dinner with my mom not long ago."

"They're local?"

I nodded. "It's why I moved back to Seattle from San Francisco. Still waiting on the call from Dad."

He nodded, toyed with his fork, his brow furrowed almost in anger. "That's bullshit," he said in a low voice.

"Come again?"

"That you have to wait for him to come around. He's the one who kicked you out, right? And despite that, you got your shit together, went to school, worked in an ER. Like that's the easiest thing in the world to do?"

Silas's consideration, bristly as it was, sank deep into my chest, making me warm. "Fathers have expectations for their sons," I said. "They can handle disappointment in really shitty ways."

You know that better than I do, don't you, Silas?

But Silas didn't go there. A silence fell, and I cleared my throat.

"So," I said, "you want to get into whatever it is you wanted to discuss?"

"Let's eat first," he said. "You may not have an appetite later. In fact, you might not want anything to do with the Marsh name after today."

The waitress arrived with our food, setting plates of steaming soup and piles of noodles in front of us.

"Can I get a set of chopsticks?" I asked her.

"Make that two," Silas said.

She pulled two sets from her apron pocket and departed.

"I can't eat any kind of Asian food without chopsticks," I said. "It just feels wrong."

"I can't either, but that's because of my mother," Silas said, as we piled food from the main dishes onto our plates. "She insisted we learn how to use them. But Eddie is—" A pot sticker jumped out of Silas's chopstick grasp and plopped into his soup. "Much better than I am."

"If you don't mind me asking, how did she pass away?"

"She had a blood clotting disorder. She was on meds, but a clot traveled to her brain and that was it."

"How old were you?"

"Ten. Eddie was twelve. That was. . . rough."

"I'm sorry, Silas."

He shrugged. "That's life, right? Though I wonder how things would've turned out had she lived. She was kind. She made Dad kind. I think she'd have insisted Eddie have a fuller life. A job if he wanted it. Groups to hang with. Friends. And she wouldn't have let me. . ."

I found myself leaning forward, wondering if he were going to tell me about Chisana. Wondering if I had the guts to ask him.

He waved a hand. "Never mind. Too late now."

I smiled gently. "You know my thoughts on 'too late.'"

"About starting over? Having a second chance?" He didn't smile back. "Some things just happen. Disasters of epic proportions. . . Like the bomb on Hiroshima or when the planes hit the Twin Towers. Shit like that changes things so profoundly, there's no coming back from them. Not the same as before."

I nodded, remembering what he'd said to me when he'd given me a lift into the city. That there was no honor in his past. I heaved a breath and mustered the nerve to tell him that Eddie had told me about Alaska; it suddenly felt wrong—dishonorable—that he didn't know I knew.

But Silas's shrewd eyes and his Einstein IQ watched me and cut me off at the pass by changing the subject.

"So how long are you planning to work with Dad before going back to the ER?"

"Not sure. Through the holidays, at least."

"Just don't let him make you work Christmas. Because he will. 'Personal time' means nothing to him."

"Well, I'm Jewish, so. . ." I grinned. "Think I can get the first day of Hanukkah off?"

"Shit, sorry. I should've known or. . ."

"Come on, Marsh. *Kaufman* was a dead giveaway."

He laughed. "I feel like a tool."

"You should. It doesn't get any more Jewish than Max Kaufman. Actually, it does. My full name is Maximilian Kalonymus Kaufman."

"Kalonymus? Is that Hebrew for 'smart ass?'"

"Yes," I deadpanned, taking a bite of Mongolian beef. "It means beautiful. Beautiful smart ass."

I was busy with my food and didn't catch at first that Silas had stopped eating and was watching me. When I looked up, his eyes darted away.

We finished the lunch and the waitress packed up two sets of to-go boxes. When the plates were cleared, we drank tea and Silas blew air out of his cheeks.

"All right, I guess it's time." He hauled his briefcase onto the table. "What I'm about to show you doesn't leave this restaurant. Okay?"

"Okay. I promise. It's safe with me."

Silas's icy blue eyes warmed and his expression softened. "I believe you."

He glanced around muttering something about paparazzi and opened the latches on his briefcase.

"My assistant pulled this together for me a few weeks ago and I've been pretending it doesn't exist ever since," he said, his voice heavy. "But I can't ignore it anymore. It's eating at me. I hate to even bother you with it, but you're an NA sponsor. And with your medical background. . . I don't know, maybe you have some bright ideas about what the fuck I should do."

He handed me a folder that was thick with statistics, graphs, police reports, arrest records, obituaries, newspaper articles. There was a testimonial from a small-town newspaper in Virginia about a lone doctor operating out of a mobile clinic who said he was seeing more than two hundred heroin-addicted patients per month.

"What am I looking at?" I asked, my heart aching as I read the obituary of a high school athlete who OD'd on heroin three days before graduation.

"You're looking at some unexpected side-effects of OxyPro," Silas said grimly. "Thanks to our uber-efficient sales team, these people in these little towns were prescribed our drugs for minor shit it was never intended for, and they got hooked on it. When they couldn't get ahold of the pills, they went to the next best thing—heroin."

"Holy shit," I murmured. "But wait, most opioids have safeguards for that. Time-release pain relief."

"True," Silas said. "But if you recall my NA meeting how-to, crushing and snorting the pills gets you around that pesky time-release, straight to the high."

He scooted around the booth to sit beside me, so that his cologne and all that was *him* wafted over me. Intoxicating as hell. No time-release, straight to the high.

Focus, dude. This is serious.

"In the last ten years," Silas said, pointing at the stats on the page in my hand, "Marsh Pharma has been responsible for nearly eight hundred overdose deaths in the Appalachia region alone. Of course, you didn't hear that kind of lawsuit-baiting confession from me."

I glanced over at him, his face was so close to mine I could see the depth of regret in his eyes under the sarcasm. He met my gaze and abruptly scooted back, putting a little more maroon leather between us.

"This is bad, right?" he said. "I mean, shit, I *know* it's bad but we're not the only company selling this kind of product. And the FDA gave us green light after green light, so it's not like we did anything illegal." Silas's voice dripped with disdain. "We merely incentivized doctors to prescribe a *morphine-based* pain pill for muscle strains and toothaches and started an addiction epidemic." He scrubbed his hands over his face. "Fuck. I mean. . . *fuck*."

I glanced down at the stats and graphs in front of me. Pages of loss and suffering; people sent to jail for petty crimes to feed their addictions, lives ruined, families torn apart.

"Silas. . . I don't know what to say," I said quietly. "Why are you showing me this?"

"I don't know," he said. "Because you're smart. And honorable. And we're *friends*, right? You can advise me." He gestured at the paperwork, his shoulders slumping. "I can't fix this. It's too much. But I have to do something."

"Marsh Pharma has to stop making OxyPro," I said. "Yesterday."

"Sure," Silas said darkly. "Convince my dad and the board to stop selling our most profitable commodity. The one that pays for their yachts and trips to the Maldives and their kids' tuition at Exeter."

He sighed and turned his face to the window. The afternoon sun cast a glow in his hair, making it glint gold. In his suit, with that light falling over him, he was the demigod I'd told Darlene he was.

"I have to talk to Dad about this," Silas said. "To warn him. I doubt his people have told him that Marsh Pharma is sitting on a time bomb. It's only a matter of time before the lawsuits start to pile up."

"You're worried about the financial fallout for the company?" I asked in a low tone.

"As the future CEO, hell yes. We stand to lose hundreds of millions, if not more. That's my angle, anyway, to convince Dad and the Board that we have to act. If I approach it from the 'Hey, we're destroying lives' angle, they'll never listen to me. I have to hit them with the financials."

That Silas Marsh, the paragon of a wealthy, entitled young son of a dynasty couldn't care less about the bottom line, only that his family's company was hurting people, sent a flush of warmth through my chest. He must've read it in my expression because his face twisted in anger that couldn't conceal the hurt.

"Shocking, is it? That I give a shit about something besides money?"

"No, Silas," I said. "It's not shocking. It's a miracle that you would still want to take on being CEO knowing this."

The fight went out of him and he just looked so damn tired. His long fingers flicked a piece of rice off the table.

"Yeah, well, I don't want the company to go under. We have other divisions with other drugs that actually help people. I need the labs to come up with something that will make the OxyPro impervious to manipulation. I need more research. I don't know enough about anything." He carved a hand through his hair in frustration. "In the meantime, I have to get the marketing to cease and desist without signaling we're at fault, and I need to help these people."

He waved a hand at the paperwork, and I felt the weight of what his family's company had done settle on his shoulders, and the horror of it sink into his soul. Doing one thing, no matter how small it felt, would help.

"There's a doctor here," I said, holding up a document. "The one who first started seeing those addicted patients. He's operating out of a mobile office. Maybe there's a way to help him?"

Silas straightened. "I could give him an influx of capital. Say. . . five million?"

I coughed. "Uh, wow. Okay. . ."

"Not enough? Ten?"

"You have ten million dollars to give away?" I waved my hands. "Don't answer that. The real question is, how could you give him that much without anyone knowing it came from you?"

"Not an issue. I can create shell companies on top of shell companies. I'll figure it out, but that's a good start, yeah?"

"Yeah, it's a start. But your dad. . . Do you think he'll listen?"

"I don't know, honestly. If he'd just make me CEO instead of insisting that Faith and I. . ." He stiffened and looked away. "It'd be simpler."

"For him," I said quietly. "But then the weight of this is all on you. Are you sure you want that?"

"Hell no," he said. "But it might be the only way to get shit done. It's not enough anyway. Whatever I do, it's not enough. And too late for a lot of people."

"It might be too late for many, but you'll also save countless others that would be hurt if your company continued unchecked. I'm not going to lie, this is a horrorshow. But the fact you're trying to turn it around—"

"Means I must be fucking crazy."

"You're not crazy. You're doing what's right."

He gave me a wry smile. "Funny how often the two are the same damn thing."

I held his gaze for a second more and then looked away before the moment grew too long. We both started stuffing the papers back in his briefcase.

"Anyway," he said. "I've been going to work, pretending like it's business as usual, but it's caught up to me. I haven't slept in three days. I keep seeing this line of people around a dinky pharmacy in a dinky town, waiting for their fix." He looked at me, and the icy façade cracked further to reveal the man beneath. "I was the same as them, you know? I don't have to tell you. You know how strong that shit is."

I nodded. "I know it."

"It fucks with your brain so that nothing else in the world matters but the next high. It makes you think you'll die without it. Hell, you *feel* like you're dying when you stop. Your body revolts. You get sick, puking and shivering. You sink into a depression so deep. . . " His head bowed, and his voice dropped to the floor. "To think we did that to so many people. Poor people who don't have the resources like I did to pull themselves out."

"You pulled yourself out on your own," I said. "You suffered in silence and you triumphed in silence. Don't forget that."

He raised his head and the gratitude in his eyes broke my heart. I saw it, even if he could never voice it.

"Yeah, well. . ." He put the file back in his briefcase and snapped it shut.

"Thanks for listening."

"That's what friends do," I said.

"Right. Friends."

Another thick moment fell, and I realized he was sitting close to me again. Half of the booth was empty, and the other half was Silas and me, together. Our thighs nearly touching, his face, with its axeblade cheekbones and perfect fucking lips, was close enough I could see a faint scar on his eyebrow. And there was nothing friendly about the way he was looking at me in return. As if he were standing at a ledge, mustering the nerve to take the plunge.

The waitress, with an epic sense of timing, came by and dropped the bill.

I reached for it, but Silas knocked my hand away. "No way."

"Just because you could buy this whole restaurant with your pocket change doesn't mean I assume you're picking up the check."

"That's exactly what it means," Silas said. "Besides, I asked you here to help me out. I got this."

I held up my hands, laughing. "Fine. I'll get it next time."

The words *next time* hung in the air, and another thick silence descended. Then something caught Silas's eye and he glared over my head. I looked to see a woman holding up her phone, snapping photos.

Silas slid to his side of the booth as if I'd burned him, muttering a curse.

"Who's that?" I asked.

"*A vulture*," he said loud enough for the woman to hear and she scurried out the door. "People with nothing better to do than get in other people's business."

He paid the bill, but the atmosphere of the meal was ruined.

"Hey, man. Thanks for lunch," I said outside on the street.

"Yeah, sure. Thanks for helping me out with this stuff." He hefted his briefcase absently, his gaze darting around the busy corner. I noticed he was standing as far away as he possibly could and still be considered with me.

"You gotta ride back?"

"I'm good."

He nodded. "Yeah. Okay, so. . . thanks again." He gave my hand a hard, sharp shake and let go. "See you."

"Yep," I said, watching him go with a sigh. "See you."

CHAPTER ELEVEN

Silas

On the way back to the office, my phone chimed a text from Faith.

I'm not coming home tonight. Behave. Not that I need to worry...

I breathed a sigh of relief and typed out a text to Sylvia.

I'm done for the day. Be in tomorrow as usual.

I didn't wait for a response but reversed course. Instead of heading back to Marsh Pharma, I went to my mercifully empty apartment and headed straight to the shower. But the water wasn't cold enough. The shivers that danced over my skin couldn't defeat the heat that burned in my veins.

Goddamn you, Max.

I bent my head into the spray and waited for my body to forget how Max looked at me. How it felt to sit so close to him—close enough for the scent of his shower soap to mingle with the warmth of his skin. I watched his mouth eat, his hands use the chopsticks, and I wished. . .

What? Coach Braun demanded. *Just what do you wish those hands and mouth would do?*

"Nothing," I muttered.

Nothing was the correct answer. Max was my friend, that's all. I could have that. I could fucking have a guy friend and not make it. . . more.

The damn paparazzo made it more.

"I think you should see this," Sylvia said the next day in my office. "I emailed you the link."

She stood behind me as I opened the link to *Seattle Society*, a blog whose stories were often reprinted in online newspapers and media sites.

Shit.

I shifted in my chair, feeling Sylvia hovering over me. Thank God she was behind me and couldn't see my face.

There were ten photos sprinkled throughout the article of Max and me at the Ginger Garden. The headline blared, *Billionaire Bachelor Cozies up to Mystery Man.*

"Fuck's sake," I breathed.

In every photo, I was practically sitting in Max's lap as I showed him the file folder of opioid data, or as we fought over the bill, laughing or talking, our faces inches apart. I scanned the article, looking for something that said the paparazzo had an idea of what we'd been discussing. Or a close-up of the file. Nothing. Only salacious gossip and insinuation.

And where is Faith Benson? Silas Marsh hasn't been seen with his fiancée in weeks. Has the beautiful ad exec decided to call it off? Perhaps seeing her man looking so friendly with someone else might make her think twice before committing to a china pattern.

"It's bullshit," I said, shutting my laptop. "Max is an employee. And a friend. That's it."

"Do we have a response?" Sylvia asked.

I craned around to glare up at her. "Why would we ever respond to tabloid gossip, Sylvia?"

She recoiled. "No, of course. Got it."

Sylvia departed and the cold ice in my veins turned hot.

Fucking hell, this is bad.

I opened the laptop again and scanned the photos. Max was mostly in profile, looking like a dark James Dean in black leather. My eyes went from one photo to another, drinking him in, as he laughed, his smile wide and perfect. And another. . .

Oh fuck. . .

The one that jumped off the screen and clawed into my heart was one in which Max had just told me that I triumphed over my addictions in silence. I recognized the moment because I recognized the look on my face. Gratitude that someone was acknowledging the battle I'd fought for so long, alone, was written all over it. Max hadn't been there when I was puking my guts out, and the depression was so bad, I thought—more than once—about giving up. But in that moment, when he had said those words, it had felt like I'd been seen.

That I wasn't alone anymore.

And if Dad sees this?

But my father was a newspaper-and-TV man when it came to getting his news. If he were back at the MP offices, he'd have seen it. But at home, bedridden, it'd pass him by.

I shut my laptop. At least I hoped.

Over the next few weeks, I found myself slogging through the days to get to Saturday, and the piano lessons with Max. It was the only day of the week I laughed, or even cracked a smile. We joked and talked, and he was so fucking good with Eddie—treating him like one of the guys without overstepping the social boundaries Eddie put around himself. I gave Max a lesson, which mostly consisted of more of his bad jokes and messing around, so that I sometimes got the impression he was trying to make me laugh. As if that were a goal of his, and the lesson was a success when it happened.

You're getting too close.

Like having a bottle of OxyPro in my hand. All I had to do was twist the lid and pop a few. . .

Except there was nothing poisonous about Max Kaufman. He was everything good that had been missing from my life for what felt like years.

And it scared the shit out of me.

One Saturday, a rainstorm battered the bay windows as Max struggled through "Für Elise" while Eddie sat behind us on the couch, reading *East of Eden*.

Max sat hunched over the piano, his brow knit in concentration, and for a few moments, I forgot where I was—who I was—and just watched.

He wore a tight-fitting, long-sleeved shirt that highlighted the muscle definition in his arms and across his broad chest. It was dark blue which made the dark of his eyes stand out, and his hair was rich and thick; a lock fell over his eyes as he played. My hand itched to brush the hair away, because then I'd be touching him.

Shit.

My eyes fell shut as Alaska roared up around me. The cabin where the icy wind whistled between the broken slats. The dirt floor and us huddled in thin blankets, watching a video Coach Braun said would test our fortitude. . .

I tore my gaze away from Max and faced forward, angry. Angry at my weakness. Ashamed that the same old physical need was still there, in hibernation, waiting for me to let my guard down.

"Hey, Si?" Max's voice was laden with concern. "You okay?"

"Yeah, sure."

I raised my eyes to him, and when I did, the anger in me fled. The cabin vanished, taking the cold with it and leaving only the feeling of safety. Which made no damn sense.

"Lesson concluded?" Eddie said, closing his book. "Time for dear Silas to play for us."

I blinked and wrenched my gaze away from Max. "Uh, sure. Any requests? But not classical," I said. "Something more modern for a change."

Eddie frowned at the lush carpet. "There are very few 'modern classics' I daresay."

"Oh, I don't know," Max said, still at the bench beside me. "I can think of a bunch that I'd consider classic."

Lightning flashed outside the window and his face lit up with it.

"Thunderbolt and lightning, very, very frightening me. . . " He knocked my arm with his hand. "Tell me you know 'Bohemian Rhapsody.'"

Mom had had a songbook of her favorite band's songs set to piano specifically so I could play them for her. I pretended to look confused, then began the melody to the first, softer verses.

"Yes! Love this song," Max said, and his happiness made me happy.

I played through the slower verses, and the first staccato notes that led into verse three, the most famous.

"That was your cue," I said.

"My cue?" Max frowned, then his eyes widened. "Oh hell no."

I kept playing the notes. "I'm waiting. Here it comes. . . Nope. You missed it again."

Max leaned over to my brother. "Eddie, do you know this song? Have you seen *Wayne's World* at least? Please say yes."

"I believe I've seen that film, yes," Eddie said. "Quite a long time ago. A rare treat, indeed. And Silas played this song for Mother on more than one occasion."

"The scene in the car, Eddie," Max said, laughing. "I know you remember it. Don't let me do this alone. . ."

"Here it comes again," I warned.

"God, I can't believe I'm doing this," Max said and then, as I cued him again, began to sing. "*I see a little silhouetto of a man. . .*"

My smile was so wide, my damn cheeks ached. Muscles I hadn't used in years were put in motion. After a few lines, Max lost his inhibitions and got into the song so much that I couldn't leave him hanging. I joined in, my hands banging the keys with a different kind of abandon than when I played the classical pieces.

A tiny voice whispered that this was *Queen,* and reminded me who Freddie Mercury was, and what this song meant, and I told that tiny voice to shut the fuck up. I drowned it out in the music and my own—bad—singing, and then laughter that nearly toppled me from the piano when Eddie joined in and hit the high notes right before the head-banging. And hell yes, we all head-banged like morons, while my hands moved over the keys, feeling the music instead of thinking about it.

We were damn loud, and then I turned the guitar solo into a piano solo that led into the quieter, last verse. The music slowed, and I softened my fingers on the keys, and Max's eyes were warm on mine as Eddie, in a surprisingly beautiful soprano voice, sang the outro.

"Nothing really matters to me. . ."

The last note hung in the air and wavered. . . and then shattered as a voice warbled at the door, weak but full of venom.

"What on God's green earth is this?"

The mood in the room—the sheer joy—popped like a balloon and deflated. I broke my gaze from Max's, snatched my hands from the piano, and turned to see Dad in his wheelchair, one of the nurses behind him, looking chagrined.

Max got up from the bench and I gave him credit for not jumping up like a guilty person. Because we weren't guilty. We weren't teenagers caught in the rec room after curfew, for Chrissakes.

"Mr. Marsh," Max said. "Turns out both of your sons are musically gifted."

Dad's stare seemed to tear right through him and then went to me. Then back to Max. Bouncing back and forth, putting us together. I felt flayed open, like I had that night when Coach Braun was in our living room and Dad was listing all the ways I was defective.

"Silas," Dad said, his voice dangerously casual. "Next Saturday. I would like your fiancée to come to dinner. It's been too long." His gaze flickered to Max again. "Much too long."

"Yeah, sure," I said, keeping my eyes steadfastly off of Max, hating the word "fiancée" floating in the air between us.

Why does it matter? It shouldn't. It can't.

The self-hatred poured in, cold and icy instead of fiery hot. Shame never burned me; it sat like a cold, dead lump in the center of me. That addictive need to see admiration and pride in my dad's eyes instead of disdain, distrust, *disgust*. I'd come so close, I'd suffered through so much, and now that suspicion was back.

I can do better. . .

"Good," Dad said. "I look forward to it."

He waved a hand and the nurse turned him around to wheel him out. A silence fell, and the old rebellion—an echo of the guy I was before Alaska—flared.

Fuck him. Fuck all of this. He's the one that needs to do better. . .

I started for the door to follow Dad, not even sure what the hell I'd say to him when Eddie's voice—small and scared—arrested me.

"Silas. Is he going to send you away again?"

"What? No."

My gaze darted to Max, his face a portrait of concern. Care. Empathy. But not confusion. He knew exactly what Eddie was talking about.

"What's going on?" I demanded of Eddie. "You haven't been talking about... things you shouldn't, have you?"

Eddie rocked slightly on the couch. "After your confrontation with Papa the other day, I expressed to Mr. Kaufman my concern that you might be sent back—"

"*Stop saying that*," I thundered, fear squeezing my stomach.

"It was nothing," Max said quickly. "He was just worried about you."

"Anytime you and Papa have a disagreement, the fear of another Chisana situation returns."

The blood drained from my face to hear that name spoken aloud. Out in the open. In front of Max...

My gaze snapped to him. "He told you about... that place?"

"I don't think he meant to—"

"What did he tell you? *When* did he tell you?"

"A while ago. I should have told you I knew. But it's your business and I—"

"That's right, it's my business. Not yours. Not anyone else's." I rounded on Eddie. "You shouldn't be talking about that. *Ever*."

Eddie flinched and went quiet, his eyes on the ground, his shoulders hunched to his ears. "I was merely explaining—"

"Don't explain. Don't say *a goddamn word*."

"It's not his fault," Max said. "I was asking too many questions. I'm a nosy bastard, remember?"

"He shouldn't have brought it up at all," I said. "Eddie, I think you should go to your room now."

Eddie nodded, his hands twisting again. "Yes, yes of course. I shall leave you to it."

He left and Max and I were alone, the air between us tense like a wire about to snap. I should've left too, but I didn't. Didn't move.

"Silas. . ."

"Forget it."

"I don't want to forget it. I. . . care about you. I want to know that you're okay." He swallowed hard. "What happened?"

"Nothing happened."

"Eddie said—"

"Eddie doesn't know what the fuck he's talking about."

"Eddie *always* knows what the fuck he's talking about," he said. "He uses his words precisely, and the word he used was '*reprogramming.*'"

I flinched which only made me angrier. "I was a teenager acting up and my father sent me to a wilderness survival camp. That's it."

"I don't think that's it," Max said thickly. "I don't think that's it at all."

I tried to stare him down. He stared right back.

The urge to let it out, let it go, and fall at his feet and tell him everything nearly undid me. Of everyone on the planet, Max would understand.

He'd make me feel like I wasn't alone.

Max saw me waver and took a step toward me. "Talk to me, Si. Please."

Si. Familiar. Intimate. I could sink back into that intimacy created on the piano bench. In the restaurant. In the car on that rainy night when we first met. The air between us trembled. The edifice of stone and ice around me started to crack. And that couldn't happen. I'd come too far, endured too much. . .

"There's nothing more to say," I said, moving to the door. "This conversation is over. And I think it's better if we cease the piano lessons. You've learned enough."

CHAPTER TWELVE

Max

The week dragged to the next Saturday where there was no piano lesson. Instead, the house buzzed in prep for the dinner for Faith.

Silas's fiancée.

The words slugged me in the chest, because it wasn't real. Had it been real, I'd have sucked it up and dealt with the fact that the man I cared about was marrying someone else. But it hurt more to think that Silas wasn't marrying for love but to fulfill some sort of twisted obligation to his father. The horror of the idea defeated any hope or gladness that he might be attracted to men.

"I think," Ramona told me in low tones the morning of the Big Dinner, "that Mr. Marsh might tell Silas the CEO job is his. Tonight." She nodded at the buckets of ice on the counter. "He's having us prepare three bottles of Roederer Cristal champagne," she said. "There must be something to celebrate."

I nodded vaguely. Silas shouldn't drink champagne, but then no one knew he was a recovering addict. No one knew the real reason he'd been sent to Alaska either, except me.

You don't know that for sure.

But while the conversation with Eddie grew fainter as time passed, the same words kept coming up like warning flares. Reprogramming. Deviant. Self-harm.

"Max?"

I blinked and smiled faintly. "Sorry, what?"

"I was just saying that it's been quite some time since we've seen Miss Benson," Ramona said. "Faith. Lovely girl—a little wild, though. Mr. Marsh adores her."

"How long have she and Silas been together?" I asked as casually as possible.

"Three months? Since he finished management training this last June. Mr. Marsh made it a stipulation of his trust that Silas be married before he turned over the company to him. And voilà. Two weeks later, there she was."

I frowned, wondering why Ramona was sharing this with me, and she read my expression with a laugh.

"Just getting you up to speed on goings-on around here. We've all signed the paperwork to keep mum outside these walls and it gets tedious, honestly. It wasn't the same when Marilyn was alive, God rest her soul."

"Marilyn? Their mom?"

Ramona nodded. "A different era, that was. So much laughter and Silas playing the piano for the sheer joy of it. Sort of like he did last week. With you."

The back of my neck reddened. "You heard about that?"

She laughed. "The entire household heard it. Marvelous. Marilyn would have been so happy. She wanted him to be a concert pianist. I think Mr. Silas did too, at one time. But. . ." She sighed. "Anyway, I think she would have liked hearing him play like that. I think she would have liked you, Max. Very much."

Before I could speak, Ramona continued, sprinkling orange zest on the duck she was preparing.

"She also would've wanted to see her son married to a person he loves, though perhaps not in such a hasty manner." She glanced at me sideways. "I don't believe Faith is quite right for Silas. In fact, I think it would be extremely difficult to find the right woman for him. Impossible, even."

I still struggled to find something to say, when Ramona brightened and the knowing tone in her voice vanished.

"In any event, Mr. Marsh's recent health issues make me suspect he's giving the CEO post to Silas tonight. No marriage required." She looked up at me and beamed. "Wouldn't that be nice?"

I'd finished the day shift. All week, Edward had barely spoken to me and when he did, it was pleasant, without the usual barking or swearing, which made me suspicious. I had the night off and Daniel had texted about a party in the city. I'd jumped at the chance to get out of the house. There was no need to torture myself with visions of Silas with his fiancée.

Before I got to my room, I went to the library for a new book. Cesar had told me I could take whatever I wanted as long as I returned it to the exact same spot.

Inside, I gaped at the wall-to-wall bookshelves, each stuffed with leather-bound tomes, most of which were encyclopedias and reference books. The rest were old hardbacks of titles from the '70s and '80s. The centerpiece was an enormous desk under tall windows, with a green Tiffany lamp at one corner.

And Silas sat at the desk.

He looked like he'd stepped off the pages of *GQ*, wearing a sharp suit in deep blue with a lighter blue tie, a briefcase beside him. His hair was still wet and gleaming from a shower, and the scent of cologne and soap wafted off of him.

He was alone.

My heart quickened at the sight of him and then crashed against my ribs. After what I suspected now to be true, his beauty was somehow painful to look at. The model of masculine perfection and yet, in his dad's eyes, he hadn't been good enough.

"Hey," I said.

He lifted his head and for a split second, his face lit up, then collapsed again. There were dark circles under his eyes, and his jaw was tense and tight.

"Hey."

"Everything okay?"

Silas hesitated, a hundred thoughts—none of them good, judging by his grim expression—clouded his eyes.

"Fine." He indicated his briefcase on the desk. "All that shit I showed you at the restaurant? I've finally worked up the balls to tell Dad about it. After the dinner is as good a time as any, I guess." He glanced me up and down. "Are you working tonight?"

"No, I'm done. Going out to a party with friends."

"Sounds good," he said, and I caught the longing in his eyes. He looked like he was about to walk down death row instead of attend a family dinner. I wondered if instead of brokering deals he ever went to parties for the hell of it.

Come with me. . .

But it was impossible, because Silas believed it was impossible.

"What you're doing. . . It's noble, Silas. Honorable. You could walk away and instead you're trying to help."

He smiled thinly. "I feel like I'm about to take over captaining the *Titanic*. Thanks for listening the other day."

"That's what friends do."

"Right. Friends. Well, I'd better get going." He got up from the desk and started past me.

"To dinner with your fiancée."

He stopped, his jaw tightened. "Yes."

I met his eye. "I realized I never congratulated you on your engagement."

Silas froze and then stiffened. "Thank you."

"I hope. . ." I shook my head, my voice low. "Nothing."

"Nothing?" He crossed his arms. "I doubt that. Spit it out."

"I hope you're happy, Si. I do."

"But . . ? What's the catch?"

"No catch."

"That's bullshit. I can see it in your eyes. The nonsense Eddie told you is messing with your head. Forget it."

"I can't," I said

We stared at one another, a thousand more thoughts and emotions traveling on waves across the short distance between us.

Silas's shoulders slumped and he looked so tired. Down to his soul.

"What do you want me to say?" he asked, his voice hoarse. "Just what is it you want from me, Max?"

"I don't want anything from you. Except. . . I don't know. You could talk about it."

"There's nothing to talk about. How many times do I have to say it? It's over."

"It's not over if they made you do things you didn't want to do. If you're still doing things you don't want to do."

"What I *want*? How the fuck do you know what I want?"

"Silas. . ."

"It's done," he said. "Alaska made a man out of me, as advertised. End of story."

"Then why aren't you walking out the door?" I said. "Why aren't you telling me to mind my own fucking business? I'll tell you why. For the same reason you came to the NA meeting. For help."

"Help?" He barked the word. "What possible help is there?"

"You can tell me. You can get it out so it doesn't keep poisoning you." I sucked in a breath. "Why were you sent to Chisana?"

"Disciplinary measures needed to be taken. I was acting up."

"Bullshit."

"It was survival camp."

"It was conversion therapy."

God, the words tasted sour in my mouth. They hung in the air between us like a noxious cloud. Silas stared.

"No," he said. "It wasn't. . . that. You don't know what the fuck you're talking about."

"Really? Tell me what sexual reprogramming meant. Why Eddie said your dad thought you were deviant and confused."

"Leave me alone," Silas said. He started to shove past me, then changed his mind and got in my face. "I know what this is. I see how you look at me. You want so badly for it to be true. That I might want to fuck men because *you* want to fuck *me*. Right?"

I stiffened. "I'm attracted to you. I admit it, and I'm sorry if I've been really damn obvious about it. But I also care about you, Si. I care about you a lot. More than I should."

Silas's eyes softened, and I felt him want to let go.

"But what I feel doesn't matter," I said. "I don't have an agenda here. I don't want anything, except to tell you that what happened to you? It was wrong, Silas. Wrong and evil."

"It wasn't. . . evil. It wasn't anything. It's over and—"

"Silas—"

"*No.* It's over, Max," Silas shouted, stepping back. "Don't you get it? It's over and I survived. Barely. I did not go through all that shit for nothing. I was confused and so tired of feeling ashamed."

"And did they make you feel better about yourself? Or worse?" I asked. "From what I heard, it's torture and it *doesn't work.* No one can force you to be what you're not."

He stared, his jaw working. "They showed me how to be. How to act. So I wouldn't be confused anymore." He raised his eyes to mine and I saw the scared shitless boy inside the stony edifice of the man in front of me. "So I could go home again. I did what they said. . . I let them do things to me. . . So I could go home."

"God, Silas. . ."

He started to go and without thinking, I reached out and grabbed his arm to stop him, as he had done with me in the car the night we met. My hand closed over his expensive suit; I felt his muscles tight and strong beneath and pulled him into my space. He turned and then we were face-to-face.

"What did they do to you?"

Silas didn't answer. His eyes roamed my face, studying me with his strange kind of curiosity that made my skin hot. His arm slid out of my grasp and I expected him to walk away. I did not expect him to slip his hand in mine and hold it tightly, palm to palm.

"I knew you'd be like this," he said gruffly. "I knew if you knew. . . you wouldn't let it go. You wouldn't ignore it or pretend the lies are true like everyone else in this damn house."

I held him tightly, our fingers lacing together. "I'm here," I said thickly. "You can tell me anything. You can tell me what happened."

"What happened, Max, is that my father's investment paid off." His lips twisted in a terrible smile, anger over agony. "I'm the acceptable son now."

Fucking hell, my heart cracked right down the middle. Tears filled my eyes and Silas's own clear blue eyes widened in surprise to see it.

"Max," he whispered. "Don't. . . "

I could smell his skin and feel the power in his body that was awakening mine, drawing us closer without moving. A gravitational pull. But more than any physical need, I just wanted him to be okay. To not hurt anymore.

A feminine voice came from the library door. "There you are!"

Silas and I let go of each other's hands and stepped apart. I blinked hard, as if coming out of a warm bath and into cold reality.

"Oh poo, I interrupted something, didn't I?"

"No," Silas said, not looking at me. "Nothing."

A woman in her mid-twenties strode through the room. Tall, slender, in a red dress that hugged her feminine curves and highlighted her long legs. Her blond hair was loose and almost wild around her shoulders. Her eyes were full of laughter but took in Silas and me standing so close to one another with shrewd intelligence. Her wide, red-lipstick smile didn't falter as she sidled up and looped her arm through Silas's. Her hand—sporting an enormous, glittering diamond ring—slid into his palm where mine had been only seconds ago.

"They're looking for you," she said to Silas, planting a kiss on his cheek. "The huge production known as *dinner* is about to begin." She turned to me and held out a red-lacquered nailed hand. "Since my fiancé has gone mute, I'll introduce myself. Faith Benson."

"Max Kaufman," I said, trying not to wince at the word 'fiancé ' that felt even more wrong in my ears and heart.

Silas stiffened and I watched whatever vulnerability he'd shown me ice over into cold formality. "My apologies. Max is part of Dad's nursing team."

"I guessed that by the uniform, sweetie," Faith said, reaching out to pluck the sleeve of my scrubs on which the Marsh Pharma insignia was embroidered. "The Marshes like to put their name on stuff the same way dogs pee all over everything—to mark their territory."

Silas's jaw stiffened.

"Hell, I'm in the same boat." She held up her hand with the heavy engagement ring glinting in the light. "I've been marked. Though I'm the first to admit a ring like this is slightly nicer than being peed on." She shot me a wink. "Save that for the bedroom fun, am I right?"

"Jesus, Faith."

"I'm *kidding*. Nothing goes on in the bedroom, isn't that right, dear?" She gave him an adoring look, then said to me, "Silas has decided to save himself for our wedding night."

"Faith likes to make inappropriate jokes," Silas said. "It's her defining characteristic."

"And you love me for it," she said, cuddling closer to him. "If there's one thing Silas Marsh loves, it's a good laugh. Always laughing and joking around. . ." She smirked and turned to me. "If only. Tell me, Max, don't you find him unbearably *stiff*? Or just the right amount?"

Silas stared past her, while I fumbled for something to say.

A soft bell chimed from the hidden sound system that ran through the house.

"Dinner's ready," Silas said in frigid tones. "It's time to go in."

Faith heaved a sigh. "The bell tolls for thee and me. A pleasure to meet you, Mr. Max. Will I see you again?"

Her smile was bright, her tone light and fun, and yet the shrewdness in her eyes was impossible to miss.

"No," Silas answered. "You won't."

My stomach tightened at the finality in his words. "I'm not on duty tonight."

"That's too bad," Faith said. "To be honest, you two looked quite cozy together, and Silas rarely talks about his friends." She put her hand on mine. "If you ever want to hang out at our place, feel free. Open invitation. I'm not one of those girlfriends who nag about her man having the guys over. Being loud. Carrying on. Boys will be boys, right?"

"Faith," Silas warned.

"I'm just saying, in our future married life, I will *never* mind when you have friends stay over." Her brows went up meaningfully. "Isn't that what the *guest bedroom* is for?"

Silas's neck reddened and he fumbled for a response when Cesar appeared at the door.

"Dinner is waiting."

Faith sighed, then turned on a Julia Roberts smile. "Time to go play family."

"Enjoy," I said grimly.

"Oh, I'm sure it'll be delightful," Faith said. "Let me guess. We're having duck again? I never ate so much waterfowl in my life till I met you, Silas, my darling."

He grunted a response, but I found myself liking Faith against my will. She was kind of wild, witty, filterless.

"Mr. Kaufman," Cesar said. "Mr. Marsh has requested that you attend him at dinner."

Silas's and my gaze darted to each other, causing Faith to glance between us again.

"I thought I was done for the day," I said, though it was futile to plead my case to Cesar and we both knew it.

"He's in the sitting room," he said and went out.

"You hear that, Silas?" Faith said happily into the silence. "We aren't saying goodbye to Mr. Max after all."

CHAPTER THIRTEEN

Silas

Eddie was already at the dining room table, head bowed, aligning his silverware—three forks, two spoons, and a knife—perfectly at the edge of the tablecloth. I noted the table was set for five, Dad at the head and two on either side of him.

Dad's having Max eat with us?

The notion filled me with suspicious dread and a twisted kind of happiness at the same time—or whatever passed for happiness in the vast wasteland of my heart.

One of the servants—Andrew—offered a tray with two tumblers of cognac on ice. Faith took hers and waited for me to do the same, then clinked her glass to mine.

"Bottom's up."

I put the glass to my lips.

Don't...

But the wine I'd had a while back had reminded me how good it felt to take a step or two back from reality. To live life with a little bit of a buffer so that everything wasn't so goddamn painful.

That "buffer" turned into an addiction.

I shut off the thought and swigged my five-hundred-dollar-per-glass Louis XIII like it was a shot of Jager at a frat party. The alcohol bit the back of my throat as it went down and then mellowed into smooth warmth. I nodded at Andrew to pour another.

When Max wheeled Dad in and set him up at the head of the table, I did my absolute best to look anywhere else. I could still feel the touch of Max's hand in mine and ran my fingertips over my palm. Touching him, feeling the strength in his grip. . . I'd felt anchored to something real and solid for the first time in years.

The texture of my skin changed under my thumb where Coach Braun had made me pick a burning ember out of a campfire one night.

Max knows about Alaska.

The shame/relief battle began again, and this time the shame brought reinforcements: memories of snow and endless cold. Of hunger and forced marches through dead forests with bare trees like skeletal fingers scraping a leaden sky. Of Coach Braun's words hammering into our heads how worthless we were. Unacceptable. Unlovable. Of being submerged in the flat, frigid water of Copper Lake when I spoke out. When I spoke up. When I fought back. For me and the other boys.

And yet Chisana still happened.

I put my cognac glass in my left hand, the ice and alcohol killing whatever was left of Max's touch. Because it was too late for me. I had a company to take over and a huge wrong to try to set right. Everything that happened in Alaska had to stay there. All the humiliation, the shame. Those scars and ugliness needed to stay buried forever.

What I felt for Max. . . that needed to stay buried too.

"Hello, Edward," Faith said, bending to kiss Dad's cheek. "You look dashing as ever."

He gave her hand a pat. "Don't bullshit me, dear. I can take it from anyone but you."

"Well in that case, you look terrible. Someone get him a drink."

"Only one," Max said to the servant as he poured the cognac from a crystal decanter. "It'll interact badly with his medications."

"You heard the doc," Faith said. "Only one."

"He's not a doctor," Dad grumbled. "A nurse. A *male* nurse. I'm surrounded by them."

"Halloween is coming," Faith said. "I'll dress up as a candy striper and fluff your pillows."

Dad chuckled—the first time I'd seen him so much as crack a smile since his diagnosis. I grew careless and caught Max's eye. He watched me take a long pull from my drink.

I raised my eyebrows at him. *Is there a problem?*

He raised his right back. *Isn't there?*

I shook my head, once, looked away.

Eddie was turning his water glass to align it with his empty wine glass. Guilt wracked me, but I couldn't apologize for being angry with him and risk him telling the entire room what was said. I drank my booze and watched Max sit on his heels beside my brother.

"Good evening, Eddie. How are you?"

His gaze slid to Max and then back to the glasses. "Ah, Mr. Kaufman. We meet again," he said listlessly.

"I haven't seen you all week," Max said. "What are you reading these days? Steinbeck, was it?"

"David Copperfield," Eddie said.

"Again?"

Eddie nodded.

"We had quite a lively discussion about that one," Max said.

"I quite fondly remember."

"A bit of trivia for you. What is the full title of Mr. Dickens' masterpiece?"

"The Personal History, Adventures, Experience and Observation of David Copperfield the Younger of Blunderstone Rookery," Eddie said without hesitation. "Quite the mouthful, I daresay."

"I knew it would be fruitless to try to stump you," Max said. "But I won't give up."

Eddie smiled at his dinner plate. "I eagerly await your next attempt. Emphasis on attempt."

Max laughed. "Challenge accepted, my friend."

My friend...

I had to clench my jaw to keep the damn tears out of my eyes. The way he smiled at my brother... There wasn't enough alcohol or frigid lakes in the world to dim what I felt for him in that moment. Max stood up and froze to see the rest of us watching him. Our gazes locked and—typical Max—he read the gratitude on my face like a billboard and smiled softly in return.

"What are you two blithering about?" Edward asked.

"A book," Faith interjected. "Some old classic. Silas has read it too, haven't you, my darling?"

"Yeah, I read it."

"He's always got his nose in a book," Faith said. "Both your sons are bookworms, Edward."

"Goody—*wait*. Don't sit yet," he bellowed suddenly, as we moved to take our seats. "Only the infirm"—he waved a hand to encompass Eddie and himself—"can sit before all the guests arrive."

"Eddie isn't infirm," I said darkly.

"Quite right, my good man," Eddie said, his voice low and wavering. "I am ever so afternoonified and up to any task one might lay before me."

"Afternoonified," Dad muttered. "Whatever the hell that means."

Eddie stared down at his place setting. "Smart. Intelligent. Up to snuff."

"Ridiculous—"

"What guests?" I asked loudly. "There are five place settings. There are five of us."

"*He's* not eating with us," Dad said, indicating Max, then cocked his head, studying me. "Is that all right with you? Are you disappointed, Silas?"

I felt my neck redden. "At your atrocious manners? Yes. Who are we waiting for?"

"Stephen is coming."

I gaped. "Stephen Milton?"

"The same."

"Who is Stephen Milton?" Faith asked in a loud whisper intended for everyone to hear.

"Head of Marsh Pharma marketing," I said, my glare fixed on Dad. "Why?"

"Because I invited him," Dad said. "You're awfully dense for a *bookworm*."

I inhaled through my nose and then jerked my chin at Andrew to pour me another drink.

Faith nudged my arm. "Slow down, my lover. The night is just getting started."

Max was staring and I could practically hear his thoughts. *Yeah, Silas. Slow the fuck down.*

But I was already tipsy on the way to drunk and running out of fucks to give. I had no clue why on earth Dad invited that slimy worm Stephen to dinner, but it wasn't going to be good.

The double doors opened, and Cesar stepped aside to let a man through. "Stephen Milton, Mr. Marsh," he announced.

"Sorry I'm late," Stephen said. "Wrapping a few things up at the office. Edward. So pleased to see you looking so well, sir."

Stephen Milton didn't look any less like a scumbag since last we met. Middle-aged, he was almost entirely bald but for a narrow band of dark hair above his ears and the back of his head. His expensive suit hung on his thin body like a coat on a hanger. His dark eyes were sleepy-looking but sharp over a beak nose and a mouth that hung down with a heavy lower lip. He moved like an oil slick to Dad and shook his hand.

"Stephen," Dad said in a grateful tone that I'd yet to hear him take with me. "Thank you for coming."

"I'm immensely humbled and honored to be invited." He straightened and turned to Faith. "You must be the future Mrs. Silas Marsh. A pleasure."

He briefly grasped Faith's hand, his smile smug.

"I'm not sucked into the Marsh yet," she said, wiping her fingers on her dress. "Until then, you can call me Faith."

Stephen tossed his head back and something like a laugh shuddered out of it. "Such wit and beauty. Silas, you are one lucky man. Congratulations to you both."

"Thanks," I said into my cocktail.

"Sit, everyone," Dad said. "Eddie. Move down. You're in Stephen's chair."

"*Dad*," I said, glaring.

"I have more to say to Stephen, and I don't want to be shouting down the table. Eddie. Move."

Eddie flinched and hunched into his shoulders. "The cutlery is arranged just so," he said in a trembling voice, pushing back from the table. "Be mindful. I have taken great pains with it."

The silence was thick as Eddie moved seats so that Stephen Milton could sit at Dad's right hand. Faith and I sat on the other side, me on Dad's left.

"Go," Edward said to Max. "But stay close. I'll need you later."

Max hesitated, reading clearly that I had no intention of slowing down with the booze—and then his concerned glance enveloped Eddie too.

"I'll be in the kitchen," he said, and reluctantly left.

Faith pouted and gave him a little wave. "Bye, Max."

I turned my gaze on my cocktail and when Max had gone, I poured another.

Dinner flowed around me to a soundtrack of clinking cutlery on china, Faith's loud laugh, ice cubes rattling in cocktail glasses—mine, mostly—and the unctuous susurrations of Stephen Milton's voice dripping into Dad's ear. By the time dessert was served—German chocolate mousse—I was a hair shy of flat out drunk.

I loosened my tie and slouched in my seat that was spinning a little under me. When Dad sent Andrew to fetch the champagne and bring Max back in, a jolt of nerves sobered me up for a second.

What the hell are you up to, Dad?

Andrew came in with Max behind him. The servant set out the glasses and popped the cork. When he tried to pour, Dad held up a hand.

"Max will do it."

My face burned. "What? Why? Andrew can do it."

"I want Max to do it."

"Why?"

"It's fine," Max interjected with a thin smile. "I waited on my share of tables in college." He filled our glasses. "Eddie? You okay?"

Eddie shook his head miserably. "Terribly distressing. I would very much like to be excused."

"No one leaves until I say what I want to say," Dad said. "Done? Good. Max, to me."

"Jesus Christ, he's not a dog," I muttered but Max made a negating motion with his hand and took up an awkward position, standing slightly behind Dad's wheelchair.

"I have an announcement," Dad said. "Given my aggressive affliction, it has become necessary to take equally aggressive action. I have met with my attorneys and Clay Horton—"

"When?" I said, cutting in inelegantly, the name making me sit up. Clay Horton was general counsel for Marsh Pharma. Nothing happened within the company until it went through him. "When did you have this meeting with the attorneys? And Clay?"

"This morning."

"Clay Horton was in this house? This morning?"

"Do I stutter?"

"Sometimes, yes," Eddie said, staring at his plate. "Due to the unfortunate nature of the multiple sclerosis—"

"Christ almighty, be silent, you imbecile!" Edward bellowed.

Eddie flinched and retreated like a crab scuttling back in its shell.

Anger flashed across Max's face.

"He's not an imbecile," I snapped back. "He's a fucking genius and he needs to be doing more than wandering around this house, cosplaying Dickens."

"Okay, okay. Getting loud." Faith put a hand on my arm.

"What do you know? You're drunk," Dad growled. "My sons, the drunkard and the moron. My decision now seems more appropriate than ever. Thank God for you, Faith. If not for you, I'd have lost all hope for my youngest."

"What decision?" I asked, locking eyes with Dad. Something was wrong, and I'd drunk too much to deal with it or talk to him about the company's immoral practices.

"Oh, yes please," Stephen Milton said pleasantly. "Please tell us the big announcement. I'd hate for this undoubtedly delicious champagne to go untasted."

"I'm announcing that I've made changes to my trust with regards to my stepping down from Marsh Pharma. I will still sit on the board. I am still majority shareholder with controlling stake. But this godforsaken illness is forcing my hand. It's been generally known that Silas will take over as CEO after his nuptials, but as I no longer have the energy or health to run the company, the new CEO must be named now."

My heart dropped into my stomach. I wanted this and I didn't want it. I wanted to run as fucking far from Marsh Pharma as I could, and yet, I needed to take it. To fix what we'd done.

"It is now my wish," Dad said, "now laid forth in legal decree in my trust —that you, Stephen, shall be made acting-CEO of Marsh Pharmaceuticals."

His words swept through the room, leaving various reactions in its wake.

"Oh damn," Faith breathed.

"My word, this is an unexpected honor. . ." Stephen began.

"Distressing," Eddie said, rocking in his chair. "Terribly distressing. . ."

"What the ever-loving fuck, Dad?" I said, my voice hollow in my ears.

"A temporary place-holder," Dad said, "for three years, or until such time as you and Faith have produced a child."

Silence gripped the room in a fist, and then Faith burst out laughing.

"Hear that, honey? We're going to have a baby."

I ignored her and glared at my father, icy and wrathful, while a tempest of emotions stewed in alcohol broiled beneath.

Three years? God knew how bad the opioid crisis would be by then. And a baby?

No way. No fucking way.

"This illness," Dad said, "has shown me the fragility of life. The importance of legacy. This company has been in the Marsh family since its inception in 1852. I want you, Silas, to demonstrate your commitment to our legacy. To stability. To strong family values and to carrying on the Marsh name. No distractions. No mistakes." He leaned back in his chair and glanced up at Max and then to me. "No exceptions."

He knows. . .

I don't know what that even meant. Knew what? Max was a friend. Nothing more. Nothing else. He was... nothing to me.

I lifted my bleary eyes to Max, and we stared at one another across oceans of impossibilities.

Then I wrenched my gaze away and leveled a finger at Dad.

"No. Wait. I need to talk to you," I said, starting to slur. The drunkenness turned my words petulant and scattered. "There are *concerns* about the marketing strategies, potential lawsuits... And for fuck's sake, now you're demanding a *kid*? This isn't a monarchy."

Faith, a little more than tipsy herself, giggled. "What happens if I fail to produce a male child? Divorce? Beheading?"

"You were already going to wed," Dad said. "A child is the next logical step for you and the family. That's all."

"That's all," I repeated, staring at Dad. "Just dictating the course of our lives, as usual."

"Faith is no dummy," Dad said. "She knows the score. You don't marry into this much wealth without there being expectations." He snorted a laugh. "What, you think she's marrying you for *love*?"

The words slapped me across the face. Faith coughed into her champagne. Max gritted his teeth and excused himself.

"This is personal, family business," he said. "I shouldn't be here. I shouldn't have been here in the first place."

Dad didn't notice his departure; his usefulness having run out. He only wanted to send me a message and have Max witness my humiliation.

Another silence descended, Dad and I locked in a battle of wills and years' worth of rules, hoops to jump through, me jumping through everyone, and him moving the goalposts again and again.

"I have to say, this comes at quite an auspicious time," Stephen said, his whispering words sliding into the silence. "I have made great headway with the Indonesian government, laying the groundwork for expanded distribution. Millions of untapped potential customers."

I felt sick. Indonesia? Millions of people—not customers—about to have their lives ruined. "What... no. Dad. Wait. I have data... something you should know..."

He ignored me. "Excellent. Well done." Dad raised his glass in a toast. "Cheers."

"Cheers," Stephen said heartily.

"Sure, why not? Cheers!" Faith said, still giggling as she took a long pull from her glass.

There was nothing left for me to do but toss back the champagne too and pour another. And another after that.

"Distressing," Eddie muttered to no one. "Terribly, terribly distressing."

CHAPTER FOURTEEN

Max

A soft knock came at my door as I finished changing into flannel sleep pants and an undershirt. Faith Benson was there, her eyes glassy but sharp, wearing a dark coat over her red dress.

"Hey," she said. "Wild night, eh? And that's not even the worst dinner I've been to at Chez Marsh."

"How did you find me?"

"I have my ways," she said with a coy smile. "I asked Ramona. We'd better be careful, or they'll think we're having an affair."

"I doubt it."

"No, that would be impossible, wouldn't it?"

"What do you want, Faith? It's late."

"Indeed. The others have gone to bed. Stephen Miller or Milton or whatever his name is has oozed home, but Silas is in the sitting room. I can't get him to come with me and I don't want to stay the night."

"What do you want me to do? He has a room here."

"He's drunk as hell, and I've never seen him like that. He's usually so careful, and lately he hasn't been." She looked at me pointedly. "I'm worried about him, but I don't think I'm necessarily the person he wants to see right now."

I stiffened, folded my arms tightly across my chest. "What makes you think—?"

"Come on, Max," Faith huffed and sagged against the doorframe. "Neither of us are stupid, so let's not play pretend. Just check on him, would you? Make sure he gets to bed okay without drinking himself sick or burning the house down."

"Yeah. Sure. Is someone driving you?" I asked after I grabbed my key and closed the door behind me.

"Is that your subtle way of telling me I've had a little too much of the bubbly myself?"

"Yes."

She grinned. "My escape vehicle awaits, thank you for asking. And I'm sorry for all of this. I know I'm not the person you want to hear that from either."

The house was quiet but for Faith's soft humming as we made our way to the foyer. She craned up to give my cheek a champagne-tinged kiss in the dark.

"Thank you."

While she went out to the waiting sedan at the drive, I went to the sitting room, my heart pounding louder with every step that brought me closer to Silas.

He sat in front of a low fire in the gas fireplace. It cast the only light, making long shadows dance. A bottle of vodka sat at his feet, a glass dangling from his long fingers.

"Silas," I said, moving in front of him. "Hey, man. Let's call it a night."

He peered blearily up at me. His eyes traced the lines of me, down the V-neck of my shirt, and then he looked away.

"Come on," I said, taking the vodka bottle and setting it on the nearest table. "It's late. You're done. Time for bed."

"Leave me alone."

"To drink yourself sick? Nope. Let's go."

I took his hand and tugged him to his feet. He yanked free of my grip and stumbled back.

"I think you've gotten the wrong impression of me, *my friend*," he snarled. "I'm engaged. To a woman."

My neck and ears burned, and my heart felt as if it had been punched.

"I'm aware." I lifted my chin. "You need to sleep this off and tomorrow we'll go to an NA meeting—"

"*We* aren't going anywhere," he said, jostling into me. "You heard my father. No exceptions. He meant you. Dad doesn't want you to be my exception to his rule."

Silas staggered away from me and fell back into the chair.

"He sees everything," he said darkly. "Always has. At the pool he saw how I looked at you."

"How you looked at *me*?"

I was the one who'd been gaping at Silas like a spectator at a strip club.

Silas waved a hand. "If he thought it was you. . . If he saw something after we played 'Bohemian Rhapsody,' or if he'd seen the photos. . ."

"Photos?"

"From our lunch the other day. They're out there now but if he's seen them, you'd have been fired the same instant. Or maybe not." He shrugged and pursed his lips. "Maybe he does know and he's keeping you to test me. To torture me."

I sat on my heels next to him. "Silas, you don't have to live in these lies. You don't have to keep hiding—"

"Hiding? Are you trying to get a confession out of me? Admit that I'm. . . what? Like you?" He chuckled into his drink. "I'm *nothing* like you."

Heat climbed up my face, anger and embarrassment, both.

"That's a compliment, by the way. *Obviously.*" He downed the last dregs of his liquor and set the glass on the table. "I wish I were like you. You're not a sellout. A fraud. You're real. . . made of flesh and bone." He barked a hateful laugh. "You're a real boy, Maximilian. Not a puppet. Someday, I hope to be a real boy, too. Someday. . ."

God, Silas.

What I'd learned about the horrible effects of conversion therapy was on display right in front of me—Silas, drunk and miserable, with lies ingrained in him by pain and fear. The basic human need to be loved was strong in all of us, and he'd been told to change who he was to get it. When

I first heard he'd been sent away, I thought it meant deployment to battle. Silas *had* gone to battle; he'd fought for himself and lost. The scars the enemies inflicted were miles deep, and what had been done to him, still had power.

No. He's not done fighting yet.

I took him by the arm and pulled him to his feet. He slung his arm around my neck, and I hauled him by the waist. Even then, in that moment, his nearness, his body pressed to mine and the scents of him, infiltrated my senses. Expensive booze and cologne and clothes, everything expensive and meaningless. Unbelievable wealth that was used to cover secrets. To put on a show for the rest of the world while hiding the truth.

I started for the door, half-dragging him.

"Where we going?" he slurred. "To my room? So someone can catch us on the way? Great idea. Let's do that."

I paused. He was right. Silas's room was clear on the other side of the estate, past kitchen staff that might still be working and near his father's suite where other nurses went in and out.

"Is there a guest room on this side?"

"Nope," he said and looked to me, his face inches from mine, his eyes sleepy with booze but unguarded too. "What are you going to do with me, Maximilian?"

"Put you to bed."

"Oh, really?"

"I mean. . . You know what I mean."

I took him to my room, sure that someone was going to walk around every corner. But the house was heavy and dark. Quiet. I keyed into my room and shoved the door open. Silas regained his footing and disentangled himself from me while I shut the door behind me.

"This is your room, eh? Your *servant's* quarters."

"Sure is," I said, not taking his bait. His attempt to put distance between us. I turned on the lamp by the bed, keeping the room dim but for the amber light.

He staggered to the small bookshelf I'd set up near the window. He pulled my copy of *David Copperfield* and flipped it open, though it was too dark to read.

"*Will I be the hero of my own life?*" he murmured. "Isn't that how it goes? The very first sentence."

"Something like that," I said, moving to him.

"I'm not, Max," he whispered, suddenly defeated. In the dimness, his eyes were pale blue and shining with moonlight and tears. "I never will be."

"You will." I took the book out of his hand. "Come on. Time to sleep."

He took a shambling step and flopped to sit on the edge of my bed, his shoulders hunched, his head down.

I knelt in front of him and took off his shoes. I helped him slip out of his suit jacket and then stood in front of him, undoing his tie.

He looked up at me, a slant of light falling over his face that was too beautiful, too heartbreaking for the pain imbedded in every perfect detail.

"Max. . ." His hands came up and held mine.

"It's okay, Si," I said.

My breath caught as he pressed his forehead against my chest. My arms went around his shoulders, and I ran my fingers through his hair, soaking in the feel of him.

"I'm so tired," he whispered. "But this. . .You. . ." He shook his head miserably. "It was beaten into me. Frozen into my bones, how wrong I was. How I shouldn't be. . . this."

Tears stung my eyes, and my heart damn near cracked in two when he sat back and looked up at me.

"What am I going to do?" he begged. "Tell me what to do."

"Sleep, Silas. That's all you have to do right now."

I leaned him back to the pillows and he stretched out on top of the covers. I took the other pillow and a throw blanket and tossed them both on the floor.

"What are you doing?"

"I'm giving you space," I said. "It's been a crazy night and I think it's best—"

"Come here."

I froze and then my blood went up in flames, heat flushing through me at the raspy, bedroom-y quality of his voice. But it was washed in liquor and that killed any sexual feelings in me as fast as they'd come.

"You've had a lot to drink. . ."

"I know," he said. "I can't. . . I don't know what the fuck I'm doing. I haven't had an authentic thought or feeling in years. But right now, I just don't want to be alone."

And in that moment, with pain saturating his every word, I couldn't leave him. Couldn't fucking stand the thought.

"Yeah, of course, Si. I'm here."

I went to the other side of the bed and lay flat, unmoving, staring at the ceiling. Silas was turned to the window, his broad back to me.

For a few seconds, the only sounds were his breathing and my heart pounding in my ears. I thought he'd fallen asleep, and then he rolled over to his other side, facing me.

"Max."

I rolled to face him. "Silas."

He smiled tiredly, his eyes lidded and heavy. His hand came up and brushed clumsily against my face.

"Ow," I said with a small laugh.

His touch turned soft, and he slid his palm over my cheek, then trailed his fingertips over my lips.

Oh Christ...

"Are you going to kiss me?" he asked. "With that mouth of yours... I can't fucking stop staring at?"

I wanted to laugh. Cry. Throw caution and my ethics to the wind and fall into him. I shook my head against the pillow and took his hand in mine between us.

"Nope. Not tonight."

His brows came together. "Now's the time. Tomorrow..." His shoulders rose and fell in a helpless shrug.

"I know. Get some sleep."

I think he fell under even before I finished the sentence. I brushed a lock of burnished gold hair off of his brow and smiled. It was all wrong. Too much lay between us, but in those moments, the weight of him in my bed and the sound of his breathing in my space was enough. It was perfect.

"Goodnight, Silas."

And then sleep took me too.

CHAPTER FIFTEEN

Silas

Dawn's icy, silver light slanted into the room, falling over my eyes. I blinked and stifled a moan. My head pounded in time to my heartbeat, and my stomach warned me that if I moved too fast—or thought about food—there would be consequences.

I turned my head slowly to look at the man in bed with me.

Max slept on his stomach, his face half-buried in his pillow. One arm curled over his head, muscles sharp and defined, even in sleep.

I shouldn't have been noticing his strength. His masculinity. His thin beard on his jaw or his thick eyebrows. The way his hand between us looked like it was reaching for me. . .

And I was hard.

Fucking hell, I was hard.

My cock strained against my slacks, aching and seeking relief. There was no denying or pretending it was merely morning wood. I wanted Max. The vault lid was blown off, and there was no putting it back on.

No. . . I can do better.

My eyes fell shut as the headache raged. The hangover echoed withdrawals from the OxyPro. A reminder of how weak I'd been, and now I was weak again.

Alaska raged too, awakened and roaring in my memory because I was hard for a man.

In the thudding darkness behind my eyes, Coach Braun held the controls in his hand, delivering the electricity without mercy but with a promise: fix the one little flaw in ourselves, and it would all stop. To avoid the shock and cold and the beatings and the forced submersions in the lake, all we had to be was anyone besides who we were. We could go home again.

And now, years later, with Max Kaufman lying in bed next to me, when my rational mind wanted to speak up and call Chisana what it was—madness and torture—my body remembered the pain and the cold. My soul remembered the shame and the fear. It had all burrowed down deep, maybe embedded in me forever.

A sliver of a memory cut through my thoughts: the hospital after Chisana. I was half-dead with pneumonia and screaming at anyone who tried to touch me. The doctor diagnosed me with PTSD.

"The effects of what was done to this young man could last years. A lifetime."

My father frowned, confused at the doctor's anger.

"That's the entire point."

I sat up in the bed, carefully, so as not to anger my headache further, determined not to wake up Max. I sucked in deep breaths until my stomach felt settled. My erection was long gone.

Carefully, I stood up, trying not to let the bed creak. Bits and pieces of last night came back to me as I put on my shoes and reached for my coat. I'd held onto Max. Clung to him. I'd been at his mercy. He could have done whatever he wanted, and I'd have surrendered. But I was drunk, so he hadn't touched me.

I was relieved he hadn't.

I wished he had.

No, I can do better...

I crept out of the room and shut the door behind me. The corridors were empty. The house slept but for Ramona—the faint sounds of her preparing breakfast clanged distantly from the kitchen.

Faith had likely taken the car service home. Feeling like a burglar in my own house, I made my way to the ten-car garage without being seen. From the lockbox, I grabbed the first set of keys I touched—to the Aston Martin—and drove back into the city. Twice, I had to pull over to puke my guts out.

As the vodka, champagne, cognac and approximately three bites of actual food poured out of me, I tried to imagine I was puking out Chisana. Purging myself of the poison so I could start over.

But both times I got back in the car, my hands were shivering with cold, and flashes of endless, black winter nights assaulted me.

Please, stop. I can do better.

At the penthouse, I keyed the front door. Faith, wearing a silky bathrobe, was curled up on the settee by the window, flipping through a magazine. A mug of something hot curled tendrils of steam beside her. She watched me drop my briefcase and kick off my shoes at the door. I slipped out of my jacket and let that fall to the floor, too.

"Well, look at you. I hope this is a walk of shame I'm witnessing."

I tore off my tie I'd slung loosely around my neck and strode down the hall.

"Silas?" she called after me. "Where are you going?"

In the bathroom, I turned on the shower, stripped off my belt, peeled off my socks. Over the noise of the shower, I heard Faith calling my name. Still in my slacks and dress shirt, I stepped in. The water found my skin in cold patches as it soaked through my clothes, and I bowed my head into the spray.

Faith appeared at the door, her eyes wide with alarm.

"No," she said. "*No,* Silas. I don't know what's happening but... no."

She opened the shower door and reached for the handle. I tried to push her away, but she slapped at my hand and shut the water off.

"Jesus, you're shivering." She undid the buttons on my shirt, one at a time. "Take them off. Your pants. Now."

I was too tired, too sick, too fucking done to argue.

I stepped out of my sodden pants leaving me in my boxers. Faith wrapped a towel around me and dragged me out of the bathroom, to the living room. She pushed me to sit on the floor in front of the fireplace.

"No more," she muttered to herself and grabbed the fireplace remote. She hit a button and the gas lit, the flames blue. "No more, Silas."

"Faith, please. We don't have to have a baby. I'll talk to him. . ."

She laughed, dry and bitter. "Oh, we are most definitely not having a baby." She knelt in front of me on the carpet and rubbed the towel vigorously over my chest, face, and hair. "We're not getting married, either. It's over."

My headache ratcheted up ten notches and I covered my eyes with my hand. "Christ. . ."

"Hey." Her hand was gentle as she pulled mine away to look at her. "I'm still here. I'm not going to abandon you. But last night. . . God, Silas."

To my utter shock, tears filled her eyes. To her shock too, since she fumed and swiped them away.

"This is messed up." Faith tossed the towel aside and flumped onto her ass next to me. "What happened?"

"Nothing. I was drunk. Max put me in his bed. We slept."

She was already shaking her head. "Not last night. I mean. . . What *happened,* Silas? I love your dad because I pretend he's a rich old curmudgeon who needs indulging. Even before he got sick, when he was big and powerful, I played Daddy's girl, and it worked. For both of us. But I'm not stupid. I see how he treats Eddie. And you. . . I know something happened to you. That disciplinary camp I heard about? Was that it? Or when your mom died?"

"The camp," I said, staring at the flames in the fireplace. "It was the camp. That's what happened."

"Okay," Faith said slowly. "Do you want to talk about it?"

I heard the reluctance in her voice. She wasn't a talk-about-serious-shit kind of person, but in that moment, she was willing, and I sort of loved her for that.

"No."

She nodded and gave my hand a squeeze.

"Last night was a real eye-opener," she said. "You'd always told me you felt nothing for anyone, man or woman. I believed you. I didn't get it, and I was probably rude about it, but I believed you. Until last night. Seeing you and Max in the library, and how you looked at each other at dinner. . . It was like a light coming on, and I was so relieved. And so happy for you."

"Why?" I asked miserably.

"Because it means you don't feel nothing, honey. You do have feelings under this big strong man-body. To be honest, I was hoping you'd come back this morning to tell me the engagement was off because you and Max had been fucking like rabbits all night."

A flush of heat swept through me, warming me faster than the fire.

"We just slept," I said.

"Figures. Max doesn't strike me as the kind of guy to take advantage of sexually confused drunk people."

"I'm not. . . confused."

"In denial, then." She moved to kneel in front of me and held my face in both hands. "This isn't you. You can't spend the rest of your life taking cold showers. I was willing to play the game when I thought there wasn't anything at stake. But I see now that there is. I can't watch you be miserable, married to me and in love with someone else."

"I'm not. . . in love with anyone. I don't know what that is."

"Well, you have a shot at finding out. At being happy. But not with me."

Happy. God, that felt so far away. The people Marsh Pharma had hurt weren't happy. Many of them were dead. I had a job to do and that depended on Dad thinking the reprogramming had worked. Maybe it had. I tried to imagine being with Max without the fear or shame poisoning us and couldn't do it.

"You can't quit, Faith. Please. I have to be named CEO. Not for the money. . . God, no. It's a long story, but I have to take control of the company. I need you."

She shook her head. "Your dad put that on hold for three years. That's a long time, even if I did marry you and we had a baby." She shuddered dramatically. "Can you spend three more years on the end of his leash?"

"No," I admitted. "I can't."

I can't spend one more fucking second.

Faith made a face and shrugged. "You'll have to get it from him some other way, honey. I'll be here. Not *here*, in this apartment. I'll go back to my own dinky, tiny, claustrophobic little place," she said, arching her brows expectantly. "But I won't bail on you. If you need me for a dinner or a grand-opening or public appearance, I'll do it. I won't like it, but I'll do it. To give you time."

"Thank you, Faith," I said and put my arms around her. She stiffened in surprise and then hugged me back.

"Gah. I've been waiting to have your naked chest pressed to my body for months and when it finally happens, we're breaking up."

I smiled against her hair. "I'll buy you a better apartment."

"Yeah? Isn't that sweet of you," she said, purring like a contented cat. "Well, since you're offering. . . in Queen Anne? Big but not too big."

"Whatever you want."

"Oh, sweetie." She held me tighter. "Have something that *you* want, too. He's a good guy, that Max. And hot. I know you've noticed that. Impossible not to."

"I'm not. . . I haven't figured anything out."

"Maybe you don't have to figure anything out. Maybe you just have to go and be with him. Let things figure themselves out." She put her lips to my ear and whispered, "But don't let him get away."

She patted my cheek and climbed to her feet.

"Gotta go pack now. I don't want to be here when you bring Max home and the sexcapades begin. Unless you let me watch?" She waggled her eyebrows.

I rolled my eyes with a tired laugh, even as my body tried to react again.

Faith headed to the bedroom, humming. "Oh, and speaking of Max, I wouldn't let dear old Daddy see the latest *Seattle Society*."

"Don't remind me," I muttered to the fire.

I sat for a few more minutes. My head, heart and body were all clamoring for different things, and it was making me fucking exhausted. It was Sunday. No one was expecting me anywhere. I could sleep for a little while. Vanish.

I hauled myself to the guest bedroom, stripped out of my still-wet boxers and climbed into bed. Sleep hauled me down almost immediately.

Night had fallen when I woke next. The penthouse was silent. I put on clean underwear, soft pants, and a T-shirt from my dresser and went to the master bedroom. Hangers hung empty in the closet. The drawers would be empty too, if I looked. The bed—my bed now—was a barge of rumpled silk sheets that smelled of women's perfume.

I went back to the living room and dug my phone out of my jacket pocket. There was a text from Max.

Hope you're okay. -M

I closed my eyes at the warmth that spread through my chest. But I couldn't reply. Not yet. I had to talk to him about Alaska, my past, last night. . . All of it. But it had to be in person. Max was a face-to-face kind of guy. Probably from his time as an NA sponsor. Another wash of warmth spread through me to think of how committed he was to helping people.

Even poor, confused jerks like me.

I went to my contacts and found my cleaning service. I called them and left a message that I needed the master bedroom cleaned and the bedding laundered tomorrow. Then I Googled the number for the Steinway Gallery. It was after hours, so I left a message with them that I wanted a Classic Grand delivered as soon as possible and to call me immediately to sort out the details.

I don't know what the hell prompted me to order a piano, but it no longer made sense why I didn't already own one.

Last on my list, I texted Sylvia to say I wasn't coming in the next day. The reply was immediate.

I've been debating whether to text you, not sure if you wanted privacy. WTF? Milton??? He's already sent an internal memo about his 'promotion.'

I stifled a groan and texted, **We'll talk on Tues. If the new boss asks where I am, tell him he can fuck right off.**

A pause and then, **Silas, I'm sorry.**

A smile pulled at my lips. Sylvia never called me Silas. Probably because I'd been a cold-blooded asshole to her since forever.

Thank you. For everything. CU Tues.

My stomach was no longer pissed at me, so I ordered Chinese from my favorite place around the corner. Extra chow mein. I sat on the couch and watched the news, sports, whatever was on. When the food came, I ate it, fumbling with the chopsticks but not giving up and grabbing a fork, even though no one was watching.

I slept in the next morning and felt better than I had in months—years, maybe. I dressed in jeans, a blue Henley, and dark gray Ferragamo sneakers. I ate cold leftovers out of the box, leaning against the fridge, and ignored the stupid, fluttering feeling in my chest for what I was about to do. It got worse as I drove back to Dad's estate—my stomach felt as queasy as it had when I was hungover.

From nerves.

Shit, I was nervous. About a guy.

Don't go there.

Chisana lurked at the edges of my consciousness, ready to pounce.

As I parked by the garages and headed in, I realized I had no idea if Max was on duty. I couldn't wander around the house looking for him, broadcasting that I was there just for him. I went to the only person I could trust.

"Ramona, is Max working? I need to speak with him."

She beamed at me from her side of the kitchen counter. "Why, no. He's off. Said he was going into the city for the day."

"Shit, has he left yet?"

"I have no idea. He could still be in his room."

"Right. I'll check, thanks," I said stiffly. All business. "And Eddie?"

"Out with Marjory. In the yard. She brought him a very fine walking stick. He's taking a stroll for 'the good of his constitution.'"

"Great, thanks."

I left and headed to the east wing, and now my heart wasn't just fluttery, it was slamming against my ribs like a prisoner throwing himself against the bars, wanting to be free.

Jesus, calm down.

I knocked on his door.

"Just a sec," came the muffled reply. Then, "Come in."

I opened the door to see Max hunched over in a chair by the window wearing jeans and a black T-shirt. He looked up as I came in and quickly wiped his eyes on the crook of his arm.

"Hey," he said, his voice a croak. "You okay?"

"I'm okay. Are *you* okay? What's going on?"

I saw a cell phone in his hand, and for a second, my enormous ego told me he was upset because I hadn't texted him back.

"Just got off the phone with my sister," he said. He tossed the cell onto the desk and rubbed both hands over his face. "My father is. . . I don't know. He's not ready to talk to me, apparently. So. . . yeah. Fuck him, right?"

He turned back to the window, his eyes shining.

I'm a selfish dick.

All of my nerves and confusion and turmoil evaporated. Max, I stupidly realized, was a human being with a life that had nothing to do with me. And right then, he didn't need me dumping years' worth of my pain and abuse and my own confused feelings in his lap.

I crossed the room and put my hand on his shoulder. My eyes fell shut at how good it felt when he leaned into me, took comfort from me.

"It's stupid, right?" he said. "I shouldn't care, but I can't stop caring. And I'm right here, in the same city again and he can't even. . ."

He shook his head and I pressed my fingers into his shoulder, feeling the muscle beneath, now tight with tension. My fingers wanted to touch the bare skin of his neck above the collar of his shirt, then slip into his hair. . .

"Come on," I said, snatching my hand away. "Let's go."

"Where?"

"I don't know. Anywhere. You name the place."

"Right now?"

"Right now. Anything you want to do, we'll do it. I have a fleet of helicopters, a yacht, and a private jet at our disposal."

I want to take you somewhere that'll make you happy.

He laughed now, waving his hands. "I don't need all that. Maybe just walk around Pike's Place? Grab lunch?"

"Boring. Think big, Maximilian."

He smiled that quiet, unassuming smile of his that made my damn heart melt.

"I wouldn't mind just hanging out. I don't need to do something that requires a helicopter."

Max didn't get it. I wanted to spend money on him. I wanted to spoil him and buy him stuff. Anything he wanted. I wanted to thank him for just existing.

And bonus, it was a hell of a lot easier to go out than talk about last night or the rest of the horrible shit in my past I'd wanted to tell him.

I frowned. "You sure?"

He nodded. "I want to wander around Pike's, maybe get something to eat and just not worry about anything for a couple of hours."

"Actually, that sounds kind of perfect," I said. "But if you change your mind about the helicopter, I know a guy."

Max chuckled.

"Just let me grab something," I said. "Meet me at the garages? We're taking the Aston."

His smile thinned out; he knew I didn't want us to be seen together. But, Christ, he had no idea what it meant that I was standing in his room in broad daylight.

"Max, I can't give my father any more ammunition. I have to somehow get the company back from Stephen Milton. You get that, right?"

"I get it, Si. It's fine. I'll meet you there."

I nodded, feeling shitty but it couldn't be helped. In the west wing, on my way to my room, I ran into Dale, one of Dad's nurses.

"Sorry, Mr. Marsh. He's sleeping."

"Oh. Right," I said. A little smokescreen never hurt. "Damn. Could you let him know I was here to see him?"

"Of course."

I continued to my room, grabbed a baseball cap, sunglasses, and threw on a black hoodie.

Max was outside the garage, leaning against the black Aston Martin Vanquish in his black leather jacket and boots, his arms crossed. I became acutely conscious that my body had begun a deep thaw; every part of it was coming back to life. Nerve endings waking up and blood heating. And every sensation grew stronger the closer I got to Max.

When he looked over at me and gave me one of his trademark smart ass grins, my first urge was to kiss it off of his face. My body made the demand before my brain had time to tell me it was wrong.

Holy shit, calm down.

I put on my sunglasses and baseball cap.

"The Hot Unabomber returns. . ."

"Say again?"

"When I first saw you at the NA meeting you were wearing this get up. I had no name for you but Hot Unabomber."

"That's. . . dumb."

"I call it like I see it, pal."

I chuckled and started up the car. We drove into downtown Seattle and I parked at an underground garage near Pike's Place.

"You're okay with leaving an Aston Martin in a public garage?" Max asked as we stepped out onto the sidewalk. "I feel like the attendants from *Ferris Bueller's Day Off* are going to take it joyriding all over the city."

"Not worried."

"Really?"

I shrugged. "I'm not careless. I hate waste and throwing money around. But I also don't worry about losing something I could replace with a snap of my fingers."

Max smirked. "No comment."

I couldn't tell Max that the kind of money we had in the Marsh family meant we could buy a fleet of three-hundred-thousand-dollar cars; it would sound like boasting. Most people understood that billions was a lot of money but couldn't wrap their brains around exactly how much. Like knowing the universe was "big" didn't make it possible to grasp its enormity. Our money was like outer space. There was always more of it.

"And anyway, I've never seen that movie."

He gaped. "You've never seen *Ferris Bueller?* How is that possible?"

"We weren't allowed to watch too much TV or movies growing up. Dad had me studying night and day. For free time, Mom wanted me to learn an instrument and read. So that's what I did. I made up for it in boarding school and college a little, but generally, if a movie was made before the year 2000, there's a good chance I haven't seen it."

"Your mom's probably very proud of you."

I smiled thinly. "That remains to be seen."

We walked through the crowded shops and markets of Pike's Place. The scent of crab wafted over us, mingled with the fishy boiling water smell. I felt like everyone with a cellphone in their hand was going to snap a photo, and I itched to pull the hood over my head.

Max caught me tugging at the hood for the tenth time and looked straight ahead. "Wear it, Si, if you're so concerned."

"It's not. . . you," I said. "It's the paparazzi. I don't want a repeat of our lunch. I hate the invasion of privacy. And it's. . ."

"What?"

I tore off my sunglasses and waved them at the crab shack. "Don't you wish like hell you could have a bucket of crab legs and wash it down with a bucket of beer like a normal person? No addictions. No thinking twice. Just. . . life?"

Max looked out over the marketplace, at the candy shops with barrels of taffy on the sidewalk. The scents of coffee and chocolate laced the air, mingling with the salt of the Sound; tourists clogged the walkways while seagulls screeched overhead.

"This is life," he said. He turned his gaze to me. "This is it."

Our locked gazes deepened and fell into each other. My breath felt trapped in my chest. I wasn't a romantic guy, but the way the sunlight beamed through the clouds to fall over Max, turning strands of his dark brown hair coppery. . .

Another urge came, to fist my hand in that hair and haul him to me. Roughly. Demanding. And those muscles under his jacket would feel as hard as I imagined they were. He'd grip me just as tightly, and we'd kiss like it was a battle of wills, of who would conquer who; and wouldn't end until we were both naked somewhere, sated, sweaty, and spent. . .

Jesus fucking Christ. . .

"Si?"

I blinked and mentally submerged myself in Copper Lake. But goddamn, I was unraveling so fast. It was as if Chisana had kept its power so long as it stayed in the dark. A dirty secret. A sham that I had needed to endure to purify myself for my father. Once the light came on, its true nature was obvious.

And so was mine.

"Nothing, sorry. What?"

"I was saying normal is overrated." Max cocked his head and that sharp gaze took inventory of my dilated pupils, my shortened breath. "You want to talk about the other night?"

"The other night?" I wondered if he was remembering me in his bed.

"The drinking," he said. "You want to talk about it?"

"No. We're here to forget about shit for a few hours, remember?"

"Okay," he said, letting it go. "You hungry? I'm hungry. Let's eat. But no beer."

"Sure," I said, smiling grimly as we resumed walking. "Let's get some juice boxes and peanut butter sandwiches."

Max laughed and jerked his chin at a pizza joint where the smell of pepperoni was drawing in tourists. "How about pizza and a Coke?"

"If that's what you want."

"Works for me but what about you?"

"What about me?"

"What do you want?"

"I just said. . ." I fumed in frustration. "Jesus, will you shut up already and let me take care of you?"

The words burst out of me before I could snatch them back. Max's eyes widened and I cursed.

"Take care of lunch, I meant," I said. He kept smiling and I rolled my eyes. "Shut up. Let's go eat pizza."

We shared a pepperoni pizza and washed it down with soda. Max told me about his life in San Francisco and his best friend there, a dancer named Darlene. In exchange, I told him about Holden.

"He was a guy in Alaska," I said slowly. "Early on, when I was still fighting back, he was. . . a friend."

"Okay." Max leaned over the small, high table that was hardly bigger than the tray the pizza came on. He listened with his full attention, his entire self.

"But I'm not going to go into all that," I said. "Not here."

"You don't have to, Si," Max said. "But I'd love to know that you had something good there. Even just one thing. That it wasn't all a nightmare."

I turned my gaze to the sun-lit street. "It was a nightmare. Being caught with Holden made it worse. We didn't do anything," I added quickly. "We were trying to get warm. He was shivering so fucking badly. . . They made us sleep in the same cabin, but we weren't allowed to touch. A test of our willpower, they called it."

The marketplace dissolved, and I was huddled under a scrap of blanket, while Holden, a few feet over, was shaking and moaning softly.

"I said 'fuck it' and moved next to him and tried to warm him up. I swore I'd stay awake and keep watch, but it felt good. Not just the warmth but being touched by someone that wasn't a beating or. . . " I closed my eyes as the memories assaulted me with fists and clubs and icy water. "But I fell asleep and they caught us. And there were consequences."

I blinked to see Max's expression cycling through pain, horror, anger.

"Christ, never mind. I'm ruining the day."

"*No*." Max reached over and took hold of my wrist. "I'm sorry, Silas. I'm so sorry that happened to you."

I stared. No one had said that to me before.

His fingers curled around mine, and I held on. "It was so much worse. Whatever you're thinking. . .it was worse. How do I. . .?" I swallowed. "How do I come back from something like that?"

A muscle in his jaw ticked. He started to answer when a guy jostled me from behind. The place was getting crowded. With sudden panic twisting my stomach, I realized I was holding Max's hand. In public.

I snatched mine away and glanced around. "You done? We should go."

Max's face went blank. "Sure."

Back out in the market, we wandered past shops, Max walking with his hands tucked in the pockets of his jacket.

"What next?" I asked after the tension between us had unraveled a little. "You change your mind about the helicopter?"

"Nope," he said. He jerked his chin at something ahead, a slow smile spreading over his lips. "There."

I looked. "The arcade? What, are we ten?"

"Who says you need to be a kid to love an arcade? Come on. I have the sudden need to kick your ass at *Galaga*. Which I will."

I snorted. "You wish."

We entered the dark confines of the arcade where blue-ish white light, loud music, and video game sound effects of firing guns and thrown punches surrounded us. Max found *Galaga* as if drawn by a homing beacon.

"Shit, I haven't played this in years," I said.

"The old school games are the best. *Galaga, Frogger, Centipede*. . ." He dropped two quarters into the slot. "Prepare to be destroyed, Marsh."

"Bring it."

Max wasn't kidding about his mad *Galaga* skills. He made it to stage seven before losing his first life and giving my fighter jet the chance to shoot the bug-like dive-bombing aliens against a starry expanse of space.

I made it to stage three before blowing up in a red and white explosion.

"Tough break," Max said, taking over the controls. "You might want to find a lawn chair or maybe a hammock."

"Oh yeah?"

"Get comfortable is what I'm saying. Because—"

"Because you're going to be playing a long time. Yeah, I got that." I laughed. "Who knew you were such a tremendous shit-talker, Maximilian?"

"I told you, I tell it like it is."

The glow of the game washed over his face. I leaned against the tall console and watched him. His high score earned him a free fighter jet which he promptly gave up to an alien tractor beam. When he shot that alien, he got the fighter back and now had double the firepower.

I made a big show of yawning and checking my watch.

Max's eyes slid to me for a second, then back to the game, laughter shining in their dark depths. "Can you get me a bottle of water or something? With a straw?"

"So I can hold it to your mouth while you play?" I laughed. "Fuck off."

"Being this awesome is thirsty work. . . Aw shit." Onscreen, his fighters blew up and he shook out his fingers. "Only stage eighteen. I must be having an off-day."

I rolled my eyes. "Must be."

"Your turn."

"Nope, I know when I'm beat. You're the best *Galaga* player in all of humanity. There. I said it. Can we do something else now?"

He laughed. "If it makes you feel better, yes."

We played pinball, Skee-Ball, and then air hockey, the plastic disc ricocheting back and forth between us on the table. We laughed, talked more shit, and when we got hungry again—or just because we felt like it—we ate hotdogs and popcorn, stuffing our faces and generally making asses of ourselves.

As we headed back to the parking garage when the sun began to sink, it occurred to me that both of us had interrupted childhoods. I'd spent very few Saturdays at an arcade with friends, being carefree and young. And Max's happy childhood memories were probably tainted by the violence of his parents' kicking him out of his house and onto the streets. As we climbed into the Aston, we wore identical expressions of fullness. Not for food—though we were stuffed too. But we'd filled up on the day; gorged on it and reclaimed something we'd lost.

I pulled up to the garage, and we sat in the falling twilight. My heart had pounded a heavy beat on the drive back and grew louder in the quiet of the car. I was sure Max could hear it.

"Well," he said slowly. "Thanks. That was pretty fucking perfect. Just what I needed."

"Me too," I said stiffly. I felt frozen to the seat, my hands stuck to the steering wheel, my gaze glued to the blank white garage door in front of me.

"Okay, well. See you later?"

"Yep."

Max started to say something, and I wished he had. Something to break me out of my stasis and that would tear apart the bonds of shame and confusion that still wanted to wrap around me, squeeze the life out of me.

But he changed his mind—probably feeling like he was doing me a favor by giving me the space.

"Later, Si," he said and climbed out of the car.

His wallet that had been tucked in the back pocket of his jeans fell out and slid between the passenger seat and door. He shut the door without noticing and headed to the side of the house.

"Shit," I said. "Shit, shit, shit."

I lunged to grab the wallet, then got out of the car.

"Max," I called, my voice sounding gruff and thick. "You left this."

He stopped at the side door and turned while I strode to him, my legs carrying me to him in three long steps

"Oh shit, thanks," he said. "I would've been in a world of suck if I—"

I gripped him by the lapels of his jacket, hauled him to me, and the rest of his sentence was lost when I crushed my mouth to his and kissed him.

CHAPTER SIXTEEN

Max

In one sudden, delirious moment, my entire reality became Silas Marsh.

I froze in shock and then the sensations of him bombarded me and sunk in, heating every inch of my skin. Liquid fire surged in my veins instead of blood, nerve-endings vibrated with electricity. My arms went around him, grasping and then roaming, needing to feel his hair, his muscle, the power and strength in him humming under my palms. I fell back against the wall, and he came with me, his body slamming against mine, while he gripped the front of my leather jacket. And his mouth. . .

Jesus Christ, yes. . .

Never in my life had I felt anything so goddamn perfect as that kiss. His tongue invaded my mouth in ferocious, greedy sweeps. I let him in, gave him everything he wanted while taking at the same time. We devoured each other with teeth and tongues, heads angling for better access, consuming with raw, relentless need.

And Jesus, the taste of Silas. . . Like fine wine or the richest food, all saturated in the masculine essence of him. Our hands grabbed and grasped, made fists in clothing, gripping and pulling, trying to bring the other closer, trying to climb in each other's skin. His hand raked my hair at the back of my head; the tingling pain shot down my spine, to my groin, and I moaned as it felt as though nearly every drop of blood in my body went straight to my cock so that it strained against my jeans, hard as steel.

I ventured to open my eyes and moaned again at the sight of Silas, beautiful but pained—eyes squeezed shut, brows drawn. Silas kissed me as if he were suffocating and I was his breath, his life. As if he only had a few seconds of us before it was taken from him.

He pressed me against the wall, and I let it prop me up while my hands slid down the hard contours of his torso, to his waist. My fumbling fingers found the belt loops on his jeans, hooked into them and hauled him to me. His erection, hard and stiff beneath the denim, met mine and Silas groaned into my mouth, a rumble from deep in his chest.

"Fuck, Max. . ." he managed and attacked me with renewed lust; with hard, biting kisses. I gripped the front of his shirt in two fists, pushing him back, like holding a wild animal at bay.

"Shit, sorry," he breathed.

"No, just. . ."

. . . slow down a little so I don't fucking drown in you.

But the two words were all I could manage. I needed to kiss him again. He'd become *my* lifeline and stopping was like death.

My hands slipped up his chest, into his hair, as I slowed us down. He relented and gripped my jaw with one hand, deepening the kiss until it stole my breath, making me dizzy. I slid my tongue against his, sucked on his lower lip, then moved down, to his chin, his throat. I planted heated kisses against his neck, until his arms went around me and held me still.

I didn't move. My face was buried in his neck, inhaling his warm skin, his scent, living there in that perfect darkness while he clung to me. Slowly, I lifted my head. The shame and uncertainty in his eyes broke my damn heart. He'd been tortured not to feel anything; to mistrust his own feelings and desires. To think of them as wrong or bad or unnatural.

Fuck those assholes and everything they did to him.

"Hey, it's okay."

He gripped me by the back of my neck, pressed his forehead to mine, his face a mask of pain. We breathed together as one for a few short moments, rasping breaths. . . and then he pushed away.

His gaze was everywhere but on me as he stumbled back, wiping his mouth with the back of his hand. He looked like the survivor of a bomb blast, staggering through the aftermath, lost and confused.

"Si. . ."

He walked back toward the car, still not looking at me, swallowing gulps of air. Without a word, he climbed into the Aston. The engine roared, gravel spit from under the tires, and he was gone.

"So that happened," I murmured to the darkening sky.

I slumped against the wall, still feeling Silas all over me. Stubble-burn chafed my lips and chin. The sensations of heat and the pressure of his body crushed against me faded. My erection, which had never felt more urgent or desperate, subsided slowly. A few brutal kisses were everything and yet not enough. His sudden departure was like coming down from the highest high, leaving me craving more.

When my blood had cooled, I straightened my clothes and adjusted my crotch. Inside the house, the scents of dinner wafted on the air. Something fancy and complex, probably. Not pizza or popcorn. The luxury surrounding me tried to undo the simple perfection of the day, and I went straight to my room, hoping not to run into anyone.

"Mr. Kaufman, my good man!"

I stopped at the stairwell to the east wing, my shoulders hunching. I turned slowly. "Hey, Eddie."

He bowed with a flourish. "Good to see you, sir," he began, then cocked his head, his gaze rising to study the lower half of my face before dropping back to his feet. "I say. . . Your skin looks a tad crimson around the mouth, there. Are you quite well?"

My hand flew to my chin. "Fine. I'm. . . fine."

"Very good. And have you seen my brother? Since we missed Saturday's piano lesson, I have been most aggrieved and hoping to make up for it."

"I haven't seen him."

Silas was all over me and Eddie's perceptions were preternatural—like a lightning rod that sensed electricity in the air. I braced myself for his loud voice to share with the house that his brother and I had been mauling each other as if our lives depended on it.

And I hated that I had to lie. I hated how Silas had been overwhelmed by the shame the conversion therapy had drilled into him. His words haunted me.

Whatever you think it was. . . it was worse than that.

"I'm tired, Eddie. Going to bed early."

"Very well, then," he said, disappointment lacing his words. "I shall leave you to it."

I hated too, how trapped he was in this house and how bored he must be. So bored, he'd adopted another era to live in, maybe just to give himself something to do.

"Hey, Eddie," I called before he could go. "How about tomorrow after my shift, we hang out? I can practice the piano and you could sing?"

"Sing?" He chuckled like a kid playing Santa Claus—grabbing a rotund belly that didn't exist and rocking back on his heels. "You must be mistaken. . ."

"I heard your 'Bohemian Rhapsody.' You're quite good."

"We shall see, we shall see," he said and tipped an imaginary cap. But his smile was wide and at least that was something.

I started up the stairs, and Cesar appeared at the foot.

"Mr. Kaufman," he said, his hands behind his back. "My apologies. I realize you are not on duty until tomorrow, but Mr. Marsh is having a rather rough time. He is refusing to have his medicine injection from anyone but you."

"Why me?"

"He says that you are the only nurse who quote, 'Knows what the fuck he's doing.'" He smiled sadly. "I believe that's his way of saying that he likes you."

Oh, the irony.

"I'll do it," I said.

"Thank you, Max. I appreciate it and he does too, even if he can never articulate it."

Outside Edward's suite, I hesitated, dread sitting like a jagged rock in my guts. It was my first time seeing him since The Dinner. Outside his door, I mentally rehearsed being casual.

Hello, Mr. Marsh, how are you feeling? My tongue was in your son's mouth a few minutes ago.

I stifled a laugh and felt better. . .until I remembered Edward was the architect of so much of Silas's pain.

My fear evaporated, leaving me to wonder why I was still working here.

Inside, Dale and Nina were trying in vain to convince Edward to let them administer the shot of Orvale.

"Oh, thank God," Nina said, seeing me come in.

Dale nodded. "It's been a rough day."

That was clear. Edward moaned miserably, trapped in a body that shook and trembled as if he were cold.

As if he were lying in a cabin in Alaska, in the middle of winter. . .

"M-M-Max," he managed, the tremors so bad he could hardly speak. "Help m-m-me. . . "

"Be right there, Mr. Marsh." I slipped out of my jacket and went to the bathroom to wash my hands. When I came out, Dale handed me a pair of latex gloves.

"Have you called Dr. Webb?" I asked.

Nina nodded. "He says if the meds don't seem effective within an hour of injection to call him again. But as our patient won't let us administer it at all. . ."

I took the syringe out of her hand and leaned over Edward. "Mr. Marsh," I said loudly over his moans. "You have to let us give you the shot. It'll make you feel better."

"B-Better," he spat. "There is n-n-no such thing. . ."

But he didn't fight Nina as she swabbed his upper arm or when I depressed the needle into his loose skin. He moaned louder at the pressure, then fell back against the pillows, breathing hard.

"Note the time of dosage," I told the other two. "Call Webb immediately if he spikes a fever."

They bobbed their heads and I turned back to Edward. "Try to get some sleep, Mr. Marsh."

He shook his head from side to side, and already I could see the meds were working. His tremors lost a little of their violence.

"M-M-Maxwell. . . S-S-Stay." His flailing hand reached for me. It looked like a dying bird with broken wings, flapping on the sheet. I tried to harden my heart, but I sat down in the chair beside him and put my hand in his, lending him my strength.

His tremors traveled from me to him like an electric current and his eyes were watery as they locked on me. They were the only part of him that was still.

"Just for a minute," I said and nodded at Dale and Nina.

"Amateurs," he snarled weakly as they retreated to the anteroom. "Licksss. . .spittles with n-no backbone."

"Lickspittles," I said. "Now that's a word. An Eddie kind of word."

He ignored that. "I r-respect only b-backbone. Strength. . . not weakness. And m-me. . . Weak n-now."

I nodded. "I know."

"H-Has it all come to this? W-Worked so h-hard. . .for what? To d-die like this?"

"No," I said. "This isn't all. You have two sons."

His tremors were releasing their hold on his jaw, slowly.

"My s-s-sons. . . I have no sons. I have placebos. Placeholders. But then their m-mother died and so there's no more."

His words slugged me in the chest. "That's not true. They're so much more than that. Both of them."

He acted as if he didn't hear me. "I've given them everything. They haven't had t-to work for one damn thing."

"Yes, they have. Their entire lives, they've worked for one thing. The one thing that you could give, and it would cost you nothing."

He snorted. "Nothing is free. Nothing was free for me and I'm glad. I'm not s-s-soft. Weak, maybe. Now. But not soft. They're soft." He turned his watery gaze to me. "You have a backbone. You're n-not soft."

"No, I'm not," I said, heaving a breath. "But Mr. Marsh—"

He gripped my hand with surprising strength.

"Sshhh." Saliva speckled his lips. "Don't say anything else. I like you. I want to k-k-keep liking you. You're the only one who hasn't disappointed me yet. Don't s-s-start now."

I should've let go of his hand. It felt like a betrayal to Silas not to. It felt like betraying myself.

But at that moment, he was the only father around, holding my hand.

An hour later, in my room, I shut the door and went to my bathroom. I splashed cold water on my face, over the fading redness around my mouth where Silas's kiss had burned right through me.

"You have to give him space," I told my reflection.

I dried my face and went back to the bedroom. I kicked off my shoes and lay flat on my back to stare at the ceiling.

My new mantra. *Give Silas his space.*

More irony. I wanted no space between us. No clothes. No air but what we shared, sweat mingling like our groans as we came hard together, our bodies tangled until there was no distinguishing where mine left off and his began...

God...

I shifted on the bed as another erection began to make my jeans tight.

But I didn't have the full story of Chisana; only little hints of atrocities that he'd endured. For seven years, he'd been living with its repercussions. Kissing a man had obviously rocked him hard. I prayed it would crack him open and not send him back into whatever barren wasteland he'd been living in. And I'd be there for him, however he needed me to be.

And if he's drunk right now? If he's using his name to score some pills? How much space do you give him then?

The NA sponsor in me had to ditch the mantra.

I reached over the side of the bed to fish my phone out of my jacket pocket, then rolled onto my back to text Silas. It rang in my hand, startling the shit out of me, and I dropped it on my chin.

"Dammit."

I peered at the screen. My sister. Her phone call earlier—to tell me Dad was unwilling to talk to me—had set this rollercoaster of a day in motion. Maybe he'd had a change of heart.

"Hey, Rachel."

"Hi, Max," she said, her voice laced with regret like it always was lately. "I just got off the phone with Morris. We're coming to Seattle."

"You are?" My brother, sister and I hadn't been in the same state for nearly a decade. "When?"

"Soon. Next week, maybe."

"Okay." I shifted the phone to my other ear. "Why?"

"We want to see you, dummy," she said with a forced, watery laugh. "We miss you."

My teeth clenched hard, but tears stung my eyes anyway. Instead of pretending I'd just been "far away" and "doing my own thing" for the last seven years, they were now all forced to contend with the reality of me.

"Max?"

"Sorry. Yeah, that would be good."

"God, I hate this." Rachel's voice became muffled as she told one of her two children—nephews I'd never met—to "Be quiet, Mommy's on the phone." She came back on. "What was I saying?"

"You hate this."

"I do. I hate that things happened the way they did. Mo does too. We both moved far away, got busy with our own lives and just. . ." She sighed. "It was really easy to take your word for it when you said you were fine."

I covered my eyes with my hand. "I know. I told everyone I was fine."

Even when I was high out of my mind and squatting in abandoned buildings.

"I still hate it," my sister said. "And I don't want it to be too late."

"It's not," I said without much energy. "But I don't want to talk about it on the phone."

"No, right. You're right. So. . . next week? I'll text you when we're there. We're staying at Mom and Dad's, so I can. . ." Her words trailed into a curse. "Shit. I'm sorry."

"It's fine," I said, the tears threatening again. "I have to go, Rach. I'll talk to you soon."

I hung up before the emotion in my voice bled over the phone. The last fucking thing I wanted was for my sister—or anyone else—to feel sorry for me.

I sat with my phone on my chest for a few moments, composing an opening text to Silas.

I rejected a bunch of long-winded speeches about how I wasn't going to pressure him and decided they all sounded condescending.

He doesn't want anyone feeling sorry for him either.

I decided to go with casual as fuck.

U OK?

The reply came a few minutes later.

Yes.

I smiled. **Care to elaborate?**

The rolling dots of a reply came and went, came and went. Then, nothing.

My thumbs flew. **You're prob thinking: Stage 5 clinger, texting mere minutes after a date but my motives are pure, I swear.**

I hit *send* a split second before the word "date" jumped up, sticking its tongue out at me from inside the safety of the blue bubble.

Shit.

Date, huh?

I fumbled for a witty backtrack, but my mind was blank.

Mighty Max is at a loss for words? Silas texted. **I'm so impressed with myself rn.**

Shut up, I sent, smiling like a dork. **I *meant* I don't want to be That Guy. But you got drunk the other night when you were upset, and you seemed upset when you left. . .**

After we kissed like wild animals. . .

I'm clean. Pinky swear, came the reply. **Who is That Guy?**

The guy who gets all up in your business.

That ship has sailed, dude.

My smile widened, and the NA Sponsor in me was given the boot by That Guy who was completely losing his heart to the man on the other end of the line.

But thanks, Silas added. **For checking in.**

Of course. It's kinda my thing.

A pause followed. I started to type a goodnight when Silas texted again.

I'm beat. Up early for work tmrw.

Yep, same. I wrote. **Have a good one.**

After today—and that fucking unreal kiss—I wanted to say more, but the mantra was back. Then another text came through.

I don't know what I'm doing, Silas wrote. **I have a lot of shit to figure out. A lot of old garbage to deal with.**

I know you do.

Alaska comes at me at all times. Flashbacks, I guess. Fucking brutal.

My heart felt heavy in my chest. **I'm here if you ever want to talk about it.**

I know.

A pause.

Doesn't have to be me, I wrote. **A professional. It'll help.**

Maybe. I'm signing off.

OK Goodnight, Si.

Goodnight.

I started to put the phone away.

Max

Y?

Another pause. Then. . .

It was a date.

I didn't reply. I knew that was Silas's last text of the night. I could practically see him hit *send* before he could change his mind and then toss his phone across the room. I'd have bet money on it, and it made me smile that I knew him so well.

And that he was okay.

And that it was a date.

My body felt light all over, but the promise I'd made to protect myself from heartache reminded me that being involved with Silas was a lot more complicated than Boy Meets Boy.

My hand dropped to the side and the phone dangled from my fingers off the edge of the bed. I debated calling Darlene—or Daniel to see if he was free that night. I needed advice too, but how could I talk about us without betraying Silas's confidence? The phone fell from my hand and I let it stay on the floor.

It was early, but I fell asleep anyway and dreamt of a shabby log cabin. Icy wind whistled through the broken slats, and drifts of snow slanted through a hole in the roof. My breath plumed in front of me as I stepped between young men lying on the floor, but the cold didn't touch me. Daniel was one of the boys. And Joey, who'd started me on my path as a street hustler. And Eddie.

And Silas.

The other boys had sleeping bags, but Silas lay on the dirt floor under a thin, ratty blanket. He was shivering. Badly. I put a blanket on him. And another. And another. I piled so many blankets on him I couldn't see anything of him but one pale hand, still trembling.

"Max, don't," he said, his voice in tatters. "There will be consequences. . ."

I woke up with my skin broken out in gooseflesh, shivering on top of the covers. I pulled the blanket around me but didn't sleep again that night.

And it was more than a week before I heard from Silas again.

CHAPTER SEVENTEEN

Silas

It was a date.

I hit *send,* turned the cellphone to silent, and chucked it onto the couch where I stared at it for a solid minute like a dope.

"I can do this," I said to the empty apartment.

What *this* was, I had no clue. Right up until Max's text had come in, I was anything but okay.

Kissing him had been fucking everything. Like a reward for surviving Alaska. And then my time there roared in to freeze over the heat of Max's kiss and the feel of his hard body pressed to mine. The infinite fucking goodness of knowing how badly he wanted me and the miracle of finally touching him, his hair, that mouth. . . all of it had been blasted away by shame and guilt and the echoes of harsh voices that told me I was worthless.

I'd driven home from that kiss with a storm of emotions and memories ruining the perfection of the day. PTSD flashbacks of being forcibly dunked in Copper Lake, of being shocked and beaten and berated, nearly drove me off the road. Alaska attacked me with a ferocity I could hardly believe. As if the emotionless zombie they'd created in me was now fighting for its life.

Just die already. . . I'd begged.

Somehow, I'd made it to my apartment without killing anyone. I started a cold shower but didn't get in it. Faith had left some wine behind, but I didn't drink it. It took all I had to not pop a cork and guzzle it straight from the bottle. Instead, I'd sat on the chair opposite the couch, trying to hold on to today and feeling it slip through my shivering fingers.

Then Max's text had come in.

I did a pretty damn good job of pulling my shit together so I wouldn't worry him. When we signed off, I was actually proud of myself. And I did feel better, because that's what he did for me. He made things better in every way. Max's compassion and honesty were first on the growing list of everything I loved about him.

Love. . . ?

I sucked in a breath. The idea of having something as good as what I felt with Max seemed impossible. Out of reach. But maybe. . .

Maybe we have something. Maybe it'll be okay.

I poured every bottle of wine down the sink and went to bed, warmed by the memory of Max and full of something I hadn't felt in a long time: hope.

Then I went into work the next morning.

"Sylvia," I said, passing her desk outside my office. "Can you come in here, please?"

She followed me in, and I tossed my briefcase on the settee near the window while she shut the door.

"What the hell is going on?" I demanded.

"I'm not sure I know what you mean," she said in a small voice that told me she knew exactly what I meant.

"All conversations stop when I get close. No one's making eye contact. Is it because of that dickhead Milton being named acting CEO instead of me?"

"Possibly," she said. "But I think, honestly. . . it's a combo of that and the *Seattle Society* photos."

An icy lump formed in my stomach and my ears suddenly felt stuffed with cotton.

They know. . .

I clenched my teeth in anger or maybe it was to keep them from shivering.

"That's fucking ridiculous. They're all so backward and ignorant that two guys having lunch is something to gossip about?"

"No, it's the juxtaposition. Optics. The photos come out and then Milton is named acting CEO. The word around the water cooler, so to speak, is that the photos are why your father gave it to Milton." She looked anywhere but at me. "There are rumors. . ."

No, I can do better. . .

"My father hasn't seen any photos. And it wouldn't matter if he did," I lied. "They're nothing."

Sylvia nodded. "Of course, sir."

She doesn't believe they're nothing because she knows they're not nothing.

I glanced up at her with a sneer. "Get out."

Sylvia flinched, and I felt like an asshole but couldn't bring myself to apologize. I was naked. Exposed. Paranoia gripped me. They were asking questions about my father and me. If they asked enough, they'd learn about Chisana and the humiliation of it. . . It would all come out, and the entire world would think they knew who I was before I did. Before I could break free of what Alaska had done to me.

"They don't know shit about me," I muttered.

To prove it, when Max texted me to check in, I didn't reply. I forced myself to put him, our date, our kiss out of my mind and concentrated on my work. I had a company to take back, lives to save, and communities to rebuild. What was more important than that?

That's what I told myself as one day slid by after another, until an entire week had gone by and I hadn't said a word to Max.

Not one.

On Friday morning, Sylvia wasn't at her desk. I wondered if she'd grown sick of my shit and quit, but no sooner had I sat down then she hurried in.

"It's started," she said. "Click on CNN."

I opened my laptop and pulled up CNN's website.

"There," Sylvia said, leaning over my shoulder. "The first lawsuit against Marsh Pharma has been given the green light to proceed by a local judge in Virginia."

I scanned the article. "This is bad."

A group of grieving moms who'd lost their kids to overdoses had teamed up with the sheriff of their small town and the local doctor to contest that their children weren't turned into junkies out of thin air. OxyPro had been too pervasive, too powerful, and Marsh Pharma was negligent in its prescription practices.

"They need to be held accountable," the article quoted one mother, whose photo showed her holding a picture of her deceased daughter.

I agree, one hundred percent.

But I'd been hoping for more time. Only two days ago, under my authority as Chief Operating Officer, I'd sent a memo to the head of Labs, demanding that an abuse-deterrent be added to OxyPro to make crushing the pills useless, and to draw up stricter prescription guidelines.

I'd sent another to Marketing, ordering them to immediately review all distribution practices.

A third went to Finance to allot more funds for more clinical trials of Orvale. The drug was actually extremely effective for patients with MS. Early trials—not to mention my own father—were proof of that.

I wanted something to be proud of; to show that our company was good for something besides lining our pockets with the misery of OxyPro addicts.

Sylvia's cell phone chimed. Her eyes widened as she read it.

"It's Milton. He wants you upstairs immediately."

I shut my laptop. "I'm sure he does."

I took the executive elevator up one floor to what had been my father's office—and what should've been my office. Like all executive suites, it was glass-walled but twice as large. I saw six suits sitting around on the couch and lounging in the overstuffed chairs, drinking cognac and laughing. They looked self-satisfied. Celebratory.

"Ah, Silas. Come. Sit, sit," Milton said. "Drink?"

"No, thanks," I said and remained standing outside the circle.

"You know the boys," Milton said. He made introductions of men from various divisions in the company. I hadn't been there long enough to know any of them.

"What's the occasion?" I asked coldly, my hands in my slacks pockets. "It's not even nine in the morning."

"My promotion, of course," Milton said. "Shareholders are sympathetic to your father's plight but pleased with the announcement. Stocks are up. Profits are up." He nudged my arm before taking a seat in a plush chair. "Bonuses all around."

I nodded absently, my eyes drawn to the giant flat-screen TV—muted—on the wall. It showed a CNN newsroom. Below whatever political interview was happening was a running scroll of other news. The lawsuit against us was among the bites.

"Ah that," Milton said. "A few white trash villagers have taken up their pitchforks and torches. How cute."

A rumble of laughter rippled through the men. I stared. Milton met my gaze with his own flat, emotionless eyes. Like a snake or shark.

"Leave us, boys," he said. "Mr. Marsh and I have a few things to discuss."

The men tossed down the rest of their drinks and left, patting each other on the back. When the door closed, Milton pursed his lips.

"You've been quite busy this week, passing out executive orders here, there, and everywhere."

I jabbed a finger at the TV. "This isn't cute. It's an epidemic. And we created it."

He steepled his fingers together. "And you feel the best way to serve the company is to shoot off a bunch of memos that leave a black and white paper trail of our guilt?"

"I'm not stupid. It's proactive," I shot back. "The data is already out there. And it's probably too fucking late anyway. This lawsuit? It's going to be the first of many."

"Agreed," Milton said. "But I've already spoken to General Counsel, and he feels the plaintiffs have very little legal standing beyond sentiment and finger-pointing. We can crush any litigation by stalling with our infinite resources. However, your actions make us *look* like we're doing something wrong and we're most certainly *not doing anything wrong*."

"A lot of broken families beg to differ."

He snorted. "It's our fault a bunch of weak-willed people abused our product? We make the best possible medications for patients in severe pain. That's all."

"It's blood money," I said. "We need to give it back. We shouldn't fight them. We should settle—"

"Settle? Ha! No greater guilty plea than a settlement," he said. "No, the policy is to bring the hammer down on the abusers—criminals, really—in every possible way. They are the problem. Not us." Milton set his cocktail down and cocked his head at me. "And you, Silas. You're becoming a problem."

I started to speak but he cut me off.

"I know you want this company. To 'keep it in the family.' Or maybe it's for the multi-billion-dollar paycheck that comes with being CEO. But I'm beginning to see you want to share the wealth with a bunch of degenerates who couldn't control themselves. You can't have this company. It's mine for three years. And a lot can happen in three years. How's Faith, by the way?"

I crossed my arms over my chest. "She's fine."

"Mmm. You must be getting excited about the wedding. And yet you haven't had a formal engagement party. I've been absolutely *scouring* the pages of *Seattle Society,* and there's not one peep about you and Miss Benson. On the contrary, I found a curious spread of you and a young gentleman. You looked quite. . . comfortable with each other."

My jaw stiffened. I couldn't speak.

"We're working you too hard, is what I think. No time to plan your engagement party if you're here at all hours." He sat up and rested his elbows on his knees. "You're going to take a leave of absence. Starting now."

I clenched my teeth. "That won't be necessary."

"I believe it is." Milton's voice turned low and sinister. "Don't fight me on this, Silas. I've been a friend of your father's for a long time. I know more than you think about your unfortunate time in Alaska. Your sickness."

My heart thudded in my chest, the blood in my veins having turned to ice. He smiled smugly at my expression.

"Take your leave, Silas. I'd hate to have to show your father that you've had a relapse."

"Well?" Sylvia asked when I came back. "How did it go?"

"I'm on a leave of absence," I said, gathering my suit coat from off the back of my chair.

"A leave? For how long?"

I shrugged and took up my briefcase. "Don't know. Maybe it's for the best. There's not a lot I can do, anyway. Milton will just reverse my executive orders and override any decisions I make on how to handle the litigation."

"You're giving up?"

"What am I supposed to do? He's acting CEO."

"Appeal to Mr. Marsh."

I barked a harsh laugh. "Have you met *Mr. Marsh?* Besides, I tried that already. He doesn't care about the victims."

"What if you presented him with legal and financial risks. I can put together the data on distribution versus population."

"I don't know. Maybe," I said, thinking. "In charts and graphs. He needs to visualize how fucked up it is. It's worth a shot."

"Got it. I'll put together a mini-presentation and bring it to you tomorrow morning."

"Tomorrow is Saturday."

She raised her brows at me. "Can it wait?"

I smiled grimly. "No. It can't."

Back at my place, I changed out of my suit and into sleep pants and a T-shirt. A shiny black Steinway piano had been delivered a few days ago and sat untouched in the corner of the apartment. I had yet to try it out. I still didn't know why I bought it.

Because of Max. He's bringing you back to life.

I sat at the bench and rested my fingers on the keys, but nothing came out.

Again, dumbass, because of Max. You ghosted him and now there's no music in you.

"That's some fluffy romantic bullshit right there," I said to the empty apartment, but the words had no bite. The truth was that I wanted to hear his voice more than I wanted to hear any other sound on the damn planet.

But I fucked it up.

And I was scared.

The flashbacks from the last time we spoke and touched and kissed. . .they felt like they were lurking at the edges of consciousness, ready to pounce. So I did what I figured any red-blooded American male would do in my position: I ignored my feelings, put *The Big Lebowski* on my enormous flat screen, poured myself a bowl of cold cereal and wallowed on the couch.

As it turns out, for someone who typically worked sixty hours a week, I was pretty good at wallowing. I wallowed until the day bled into twilight. After *Lebowski* I watched two *Fast and Furious* movies and was about to start a third when my phone chimed a text from Max.

You don't have to call me back or explain anything. Just fucking tell me you're OK. Do that and I won't text again.

I shut off the TV and scrubbed my hands over my face. I started to text him that I was okay, but my thumbs had a mind of their own.

Come over.

I blinked at what I had written but no part of me wanted to take it back. His reply came quick and angry.

RU fucking kidding me right now?

Shit. I hit *call*.

"Si. . ."

"Come over."

"Why? Are you okay? At least tell me that much."

"I'm okay. And I've been a dick. I should've texted or called you—"

"That would've been the adult thing to do, yes."

I growled irritably. "I'm saying I'm sorry, okay? I should've talked to you. You deserve that and. . . Christ, just come over. Please."

A silence. "Is Faith there? Because I realize I don't know shit about that situation. Or much else about your past or. . . or any of it."

"I know," I said. "We need to talk. *I* need to talk. I need to tell you everything, but Max . . It's a lot."

His voice grew quiet. "Okay."

"It's going to be a lot to hear, but it's also going to be a lot for me to say."

"I understand," he said, and in those four syllables I heard how much he cared and that he'd take everything I had. No matter how ugly or raw or hellish, he'd take it. He wouldn't leave me to deal with it alone.

"But Si," he said. "Before anything else happens between us, I need to know about you and Faith. I don't want to get in the middle."

"You won't. There's nothing between us. What she and I had was a business deal and nothing more."

"Had? You're not engaged?"

"Not anymore. Not since the night I passed out drunk in your room. She knew there was something happening between you and me, and that was a deal-breaker. She moved out the next morning."

"She was the one who sent me to you," Max said. "One last question."

"You want to know if I slept with her?"

"No, I want to know if you have feelings for her. Present tense."

"As a friend, yes. That's all. And because I don't believe you about the sex part: no. We never slept together." I inhaled a breath. "I'm not attracted to women." I exhaled. "Holy shit. I've never said that out loud before in my life. I'm half-expecting Coach Braun to pop out of a closet with a stick and start wailing on me."

"Who's Coach Braun?"

I scrubbed my hand over my face. "Jesus Christ, Maximilian, should I send a car? The helicopter? What's it going to take? I'll tell you everything when you *get over here."*

"Okay, okay," he said, laughing, and his next words sent my stupid heart into fits. "I'm on my way."

CHAPTER EIGHTEEN

Silas

Max arrived forty-five minutes later. I opened the door to see him in his usual get up—jeans, jacket, boots. My first instinct was to haul him to me and smash my mouth against his, but I heroically restrained myself.

"Security is tight around this joint," Max said. "I'm amazed I got in without a strip search."

He slipped out of his jacket to reveal a plain white T-shirt that was almost worse than him wearing nothing, given how it clung to his skin and highlighted his lean muscle definition.

Fucking hell, Max, don't talk about being strip-searched.

I coughed and hung up his jacket for him in the entry closet. "Make yourself at home. You want something to eat? Drink?"

"Maybe later," he said, wandering my apartment, his hands jammed in the front pockets of his jeans. "This place is huge," he said. He gave a low whistle at the piano. "I thought you said you only played for Eddie." He shot me a trademark Max Kaufman know-it-all glance. "Looks new."

"Yeah, it's new," I said. "I don't know why I bought it. Felt like it."

"I can relate. My impulse buys usually involve grand pianos. Sometimes I'll throw a BMW into the cart, if I'm in the mood."

"Don't wealth-shame me, Kaufman."

He smirked. "That's not a thing."

I sat on the couch, watching Max go to the wall-to-wall windows that revealed all of Seattle falling under the amber twilight.

"Not a bad view, Marsh. Not bad at all." He turned with that other smile of his I loved, the quiet one that was reflected in his deep brown eyes. "So. How're you doing?"

I frowned. "Why aren't you pissed at me for going radio silent for a whole week?"

"I was. Kinda hurt, if I'm being honest, but mostly worried. I had to eavesdrop on Cesar to know you were at the Pharma offices and not drinking yourself into a stupor."

"I chucked all the booze in the house. And I've stopped taking the cold showers."

"What does that mean?"

"It's..." I shook my head. "It's fucking humiliating, is what it is."

Max crossed the living room and sat on the leather chair opposite me. "It's what happened, Si."

Somehow, the simplicity of those words helped to loosen the shame's hold on me.

"So what do I do? Just start talking? Just...vomit all my horrible shit into your lap?"

"Yes," he said. "If you're ready."

"And if I'm not?"

He shrugged. "Then we order takeout and watch the Mariners *not* make the World Series. Again."

"That works for me, actually."

Max waited.

I sighed.

"I don't know where to start."

"The cold showers?" he asked gently. "Does that mean more than what it usually means?"

"It's not all that far off the mark. Eddie probably told you, but where we lived was a ghost town. No running water, just a lake nearby. We were often forced to submerge ourselves naked. Keep in mind it was Alaska, late fall through winter. That water was a few degrees above freezing."

Max sat back in his seat. "Why the hell did they make you do that?"

"Sometimes as punishment. Sometimes as a tool to help curb our 'unnatural' urges. Coach Braun—the ringleader asshole fuckwad—taught us to use the concept of the cold shower when we got out of Alaska for the same reason."

Max stared at me.

"What?"

"This is going to be bad, isn't it?"

I smiled grimly. "You throwing in the towel already?"

"No way." He wasn't smiling. "I'm not going anywhere, Si."

I closed my eyes a second, overwhelmed by the emotion that flowed through me on a warm wave across my chest and heated the tears that stung my eyes. I sucked in a breath and started from the beginning.

I told him how my mom's death changed my dad, bringing out the worst in him. He'd always been intolerant of everyone: women who weren't my mother, the poor, people of color. He thought being gay was a choice—a slap in the face to nature and a threat to the family legacy. It was perfectly clear, even before I hit puberty, that relations with boys beyond friendship was unacceptable. And how, consequently, my teen years were full of confusion and fear when it turned out it was boys I liked after all.

I explained how Eddie got our father's name and the mantle that came with it and how his autism diagnosis devastated my father. How he shifted the entire weight of our family's business and legacy onto me.

I told Max about Benington Boarding school and fictional girlfriends I claimed to have, while in truth, I was getting drunk at parties and hooking up with guys in dark hallways or empty parking lots any chance I got. I told him how I did everything but sex, because that felt like going too far.

"I thought if I only messed around, it wouldn't be such a travesty in the eyes of my dad if he found out."

"But he found out," Max said.

I nodded. "I was already mentally beating myself up about what he'd think. I was fifteen hundred miles away from him and still living under his rules. So I drank a lot. Drank to allow myself to hook up with the guys and I drank to cover the shame afterward. But the drinking made me careless."

Max sat back in his chair, as if bracing himself.

"My grades started slipping and my drinking got worse. Everyone at Benington came from wealthy families but our money was a different story. One of my regular hookups told his sister he'd been trading blowjobs with Silas Marsh. She told their father, who happened to be on a federal regulatory committee that worked with Marsh Pharma. They played golf together and the guy casually told my dad that if I came near his son again, he'd call the police."

"Oh shit," Max said.

"Dad sent for me to come home immediately," I said. "I met Coach Braun a month later. Two weeks after that, I was in Alaska."

Max nodded, his mouth tight. "Okay."

"Six months," I said. "Over the dead of winter, with hardly anything to eat. They made us hunt squirrels and rabbits with traps, or fish in ice holes. The cold was constant. Jesus, it was so cold, I'd forget what warm felt like."

I swallowed hard over a throat that had gone dry. I'd never told anyone what I was about to say. Not in seven years.

"They made us watch movies of guys. . . To see if we'd get aroused, and then they'd shock us. Negative reinforcement, they said. To 'repair' something in our bodies that had gone haywire somewhere along the way."

"Wait, wait. . . They fucking *shocked* you?" Max's voice cracked, and he covered his mouth with his hand.

"Jesus, Max, don't fucking cry or I'll never get through this."

He shook his head, anger—no, rage—burning behind the tears in his eyes. "Go on," he gritted out.

I continued, telling him about the beatings and the insults and the forced midnight marches through the woods with Coach and the counselors shouting at us the entire time how worthless we were.

"Why?" Max demanded suddenly, literally shaking with anger. "Why the marching?"

"Commands sink deeper into the psyche when you're sick, cold, tired. We were all three. Half-delirious. Almost hypothermic. It was like being in a dream state where all the horrible shit they told us slid right in. We were too exhausted, too beat down, too ready for it all to just *stop* to hold on to our own sense of self. Believing what they told us was easier than fighting it. And many of us didn't want to fight it. They promised us. . ." My throat started to close. "They promised that if we changed, we'd be loved. That we could go home."

Max shook his head again, his eyes falling shut. "God, Si. . ."

"That's how they got us," I said, and shit, my chest felt heavy, my hands were shaking. "The seven of us. . .we were all sent to Chisana by our families. They somehow found Braun's program and they all signed us up *voluntarily*. No one put a gun to their head. They *wanted* that torture for us. We were there, in that fucking cold. . ." I clenched my jaw, but it was useless against the flood that was welling up in me. "One kid. . . Toby. Jesus, he was maybe thirteen. Cried every night. He nearly died. We all got sick. . . because our *families* put us there."

Max moved wordlessly from his chair to sit beside me. He put his left arm around me, held my hand in his right. I gripped him hard. Max. My goddamn anchor, while the storm that had been raging somewhere in me for years finally broke.

"What the fuck else were we supposed to think?" I demanded, tears streaming out of my eyes. "Braun had to be right. Why else would our own parents put us through this shit if they didn't think it was for our own good?"

The enormity of it—six months, one hundred and eighty days—all came at me, surged through me, and finally came out in a howling torrent of stomach-clenching pain. It wracked me like a snowstorm, and through it all, Max didn't let go. He held on, saying nothing except, *I'm here. I'm here. I'm here.*

I cried like a goddamn baby till I felt like my guts were going to literally fall in Max's lap just as I'd predicted.

"I can't fucking. . . stop," I managed through gasping breaths.

"You don't have to," Max said. "You shouldn't. Let it go."

It felt as if I'd never be done purging Chisana from me, but the sobs finally ceased. I felt turned inside out but better. The wound lanced open and the poison spewed out.

"Come on," Max said, helping me to my feet. "Where's the bathroom in this high-rise mansion?"

I jerked my chin down the hallway and he led me to the guest bathroom. He turned on the faucet in the sink and I splashed handfuls of water over my face.

"Christ, I'm a mess. Snot everywhere. . ."

"You're in luck," Max said. "As a nurse, snot is one of my stocks-in-trade."

I sniffed a laugh and saw myself in the mirror. The robot, the Frankenstein's monster that had always stared back at me, was gone. What remained looked like shit, with puffy red eyes that were bloodshot and still shining with tears, but I was fucking alive. For the first time in years, it was me staring back.

And standing next to me in the reflection was Max. He was busy rinsing out a washcloth and then reached up to wipe my face. I caught his hand and turned my gaze from the mirror to his.

A thousand words piled up in my mouth, most of them variations of *thank you* and *I owe you everything* and *please stay with me forever.* But I was wrung out and afraid of losing my shit all over again.

Because it was Max, I didn't have to say a word. "Come on," he said. "I don't know about you, but I'm starving."

I introduced Max to my favorite Chinese place by ordering take-out, and we put on the baseball game. Max sat on the couch at one end and I stretched out against him. My back to his chest, my head on his shoulder, his arm slung around me. Protectively. We ate and watched and didn't talk much about anything. And I'd never felt so comfortable. As if I were sinking into my own skin.

The game ended, and the leftovers were stowed in the fridge.

"Do you want me to stay or get the hell out of here?" Max said. "It's been a lot for you, so tell me what you're up for."

"What happens if you stay?"

"We sleep," Max said.

I tried to come up with a joke or a come-on, but I was too damn tired. "That's it?"

"That's it, Si," he said. "We don't have to cram everything into one night. We have time and you *need* time. And sleep. You can barely keep your eyes open."

"I want you to stay."

He smiled. "Then I'll stay."

I gave Max a pair of my pajama pants with a drawstring. He wore them with his white T-shirt, and we climbed into the master bedroom's king-sized bed. Like we had the other night, we lay side by side, facing each other.

"I don't know what I'm doing," I said tiredly. "I don't know how to be with anyone. I told Faith I was asexual, but that was a lie. Asexuals aren't repressing every last fucking desire and pretending they don't exist. That's what they taught us to do in Chisana. If we don't want to fuck women, fuck no one."

"I'm astounded those people haven't been arrested for kidnapping, abuse. . ." Max's brows drew down in anger. "There's nothing they did that has any basis in real science. They can't change anyone with torture."

"They did their best," I said grimly. "And now I don't know what comes next. I've been living as nothing. A robot. I don't know what's expected of me as a gay man. Or as. . . anyone."

"Nothing's expected," Max said. "Except I don't want another week to go by without knowing you're okay."

"It won't. I promise. Christ, I'm tired." I looked at him, his face so close to mine. "We've been here before. And I was too wasted to do anything then, too."

"Yep. Though you did manage to clock me in the face."

"Did not."

"Like you remember better than me?" He grinned. "It's okay. I can take it."

"You can. All my shit tonight. . . Just like you said you would."

Max's expression turned deadly earnest, his eyes soft. He propped his head on one hand, leaning on his elbow. With the other, he took my jaw against his palm and ran his thumb along my lower lip.

"Last time you were too drunk to kiss," he said.

"I'm not drunk now."

"Nope. Goodnight, Si." He leaned over and kissed me.

It was soft, but I felt that scrape of stubble against my lips. It was gentle, but I felt the masculine power in him, and I wanted it. I wanted all of him. . .

"Dammit, I really wish I wasn't about to pass out," I said.

"So do I, but I think everything happens exactly the way it's supposed to happen."

Max kissed me again and rolled me over onto my side. He wrapped his arms around me spooning me. "Go to sleep. It's been a day."

"Truth. I didn't even tell you I got laid off."

"How do you get laid off from your own company?"

"Not laid off. . . a leave." I shook my head against the pillow. "Tomorrow. I'll tell you tomorrow."

After a few minutes, I felt Max melt against me. But despite the exhaustion dragging me down, sleep wouldn't come.

"Max."

"Hm."

"Something's not right."

"Feels pretty alright to me," he murmured.

I rolled over and pushed Max onto *his* side, so his back was against me. I wrapped my arms around him and held him against my chest.

"Better," I said.

I needed to hold him. I couldn't say it, so I did it. I needed to fucking gather him against me and hold on because something this good couldn't possibly last. Or it was a dream, and I was going to wake up in a broken-down cabin with an icy wind blowing over me. . .

I woke up in the middle of the night, not shivering with imagined cold but wrapped in real warmth. Wrapped around Max. The room was dark but for a beam of silvery light slanting in from the window

Max and I had hardly changed positions. Or maybe I hadn't let him. His head was in front of me on the pillow, his neck inches from my mouth. I smelled remnants of his cologne, shower soap, and the warm scent of his skin. I nuzzled my face against his neck, scraped his skin with my stubble. I wanted to sink my teeth into his flesh. Devour him.

He stirred awake and shifted against me, pressing into me. He rubbed his ass against my erection. I cursed and felt him chuckle.

"It's not funny," I growled and bit the slope of muscle between his neck and shoulder, soothing it with my tongue after.

His breath hissed through his teeth, and his hand reached between us to stroke me over the flannel material of my pants. "You want to. . .?"

"Yes," I breathed onto his neck and nipped him again. "Fuck, yes."

Max rolled over to face me, and we kissed with sudden, desperate hunger that was wide awake. Within moments, I'd hauled him on top of me, gripping his hips and grinding our erections together through the material of our pants. He raked his fingers through my hair, while his hand stroking me squeezed harder, moved faster, and I fell back against the pillow.

"Fuck, it's been too long. This is too good. I'm completely. . ."

"Useless to me?" Max smiled. "You don't have to do a thing. I got you."

He straddled me, sitting on my thighs, while he stripped out of his T-shirt.

Holy shit. . .

The last time I messed around with a guy had been in high school, the early years. Max was a man, hard and lean, the cut of his abs thrown into stark relief by the dim light and shadows in the room. His chest was smooth and fucking perfect, and my eyes drank it in, then moved to his rounded shoulder muscles, down to lean biceps and forearms. The sight of him made me harder, if that were possible, but sent a current of tension running through me.

Max picked up on it instantly.

"You okay?"

"Yes, but. . . it's been a while."

"I know," he said softly. "I want to make this good for you."

"It is already," I said, my heart pounding. "But Jesus, Max don't stop."

He nodded and braced himself on all fours over me and bent his head to kiss me. Softly and first, then deeply, leaving no part of my mouth untouched by his tongue's soft exploration. I knew what he was doing—drowning me in the sensations of him, taking me out of my thoughts, and it was working.

He moved his mouth to my neck, nibbled at my earlobe. "I'll go slow," he whispered hotly against my skin.

I didn't reply and he didn't ask me to. He was going to let me tell him what I could handle without making an issue of it, and that consideration burnt up any hesitation left in me.

He trailed biting kisses along my neck, and I sucked a breath between my teeth.

"I swear to God, Maximilian, if you don't quit messing around and do something. . ."

He laughed lightly and then—like a bastard—he took his sweet time lifting my shirt up enough to slide his tongue between the ridges of my abdomen. I dug my heels into the sheets, gritted my teeth, a part of me fighting how good this felt. Lower and lower he moved down my torso, his mouth blazing a maddeningly slow trail. He pushed my pants and underwear off my hips, releasing my cock that was hard as steel. My heart was rampaging in my chest as he touched me for the first time, wrapping his hand around me, stroking slowly.

"God, Si," he said with something between a growl and a moan. "You're fucking perfect."

Then he dragged his tongue from the base of my cock to the tip in one worshipful lick.

"Oh fuck. . ."

He did it again, then his hand took a turn, squeezing and releasing. Just when I thought I was going to lose my goddamn mind, he took me entirely into his mouth, and that warmth felt like everything I'd been wanting since Alaska. It was everything they'd told us was wrong and yet nothing had ever in my life felt so perfectly right.

Using his hands and mouth in conjunction, squeezing, sucking, Max drew me closer and closer to the most perfect oblivion.

I inhaled through my nose. My hand made a fist in his hair.

"Max," I gritted out. "I'm going to come."

It was a warning, but Max didn't heed it. If anything, it spurred him on. And as if he were attuned to every part of me, he knew exactly when to take me as deep as he could, to the back of his throat just as I came harder than I'd ever come in my life.

"Holy shit," I said, panting, as the orgasm throbbed and hummed through me.

Max straddled my thighs again, running his hands up and down my quads. That Cheshire cat grin was all over his face.

"Was it good?" he asked. "Because you deserve something good."

You, Max. You're everything good.

"Get over here," I growled.

He braced himself over me again, while I roughly pushed his pants down enough to get at his erection that was hard and huge in my hand. I kissed him, tasting vestiges of myself on his tongue. I took his mouth like a fucking madman while stroking his cock faster and faster.

"Silas. . ." he said against my lips, our teeth and tongues biting and licking in desperate, raw kisses. "I'm close."

"On me," I said, hardly believing what I was saying. "I want you to come on me."

"Jesus, Si. . . " he managed, his hands making fists in the sheets on either side of me.

My hand shot up and gripped his hair so I could hold him in my kiss while his release rocketed through him. He came in hot spurts that landed on my chest and stomach.

Max groaned and I swallowed it down, then released my hold on him. He collapsed beside me, and we lay side-by-side, panting and listening to our breaths in the silence and the dark of the night.

After a few minutes, Max hauled himself up and went into the bathroom.

From my post-orgasm stupor, I heard running water and then he came back with a warm washcloth and wiped my chest and stomach clean.

"You're a boy scout."

He shot me a dry look. "Not quite."

When he was done, he climbed into bed, climbed straight into my arms, and we tangled up, so I couldn't tell who was holding who.

"You still okay?" he asked.

"No," I said with a tired laugh. "I'm somewhere way beyond 'okay.'"

I was with Max, and with him, the cold couldn't touch me.

CHAPTER NINETEEN

Max

I blinked awake. Silvery, predawn light filtered in through the windows in a room I didn't recognize. Silas stirred beside me, and all of last night returned to me in a rush. Every kiss, every moan; the taste of him on my tongue, the sounds he made when he came, the heat and power in his body...

My own body started to wake up with me, but I inhaled deep to cool my blood.

Calm down. Let the man sleep.

Silas lay on his side, facing me, his face still and beautiful. No trace of the anguish that had rocked him as he recounted the nightmare of his time in Alaska. He'd been wrung out by it, and my heart had been wrung out along with him.

Because I'm falling.

In the dark of night, I'd flung every part of myself at him—heart, body, and soul. My promises to keep myself from being hurt were torn apart by biting kisses and grasping hands. They were silenced by my insatiable want of his body and my heart's lonely need to be with a guy—*this* guy—and no other. I was reckless, with no thought about what might happen in the stark light of morning.

And now it was morning.

My friend Darlene was fearless. Her philosophy was that it was better to be deliriously happy, even for a little bit, than to feel nothing at all. I wished she were here to tell me what to do.

And then—like a download from the ether—I heard her voice in my head.

Be happy, Max. Grab it with both hands and run like hell. That's what we're here for.

A smile touched my lips as I turned to look at Silas again. When you jumped off a cliff, the flight was awesome, but a fall could leave you smashed into a thousand pieces. Was it worth it?

He opened his blue eyes, a lock of metal blond hair falling over his brow.

Silas Marsh is worth it.

A guy like him came around once in a million years. And who knew? Maybe it wouldn't come to utter annihilation. We could be happy. We could grab it and run like hell.

"What are you grinning about?" Silas said sleepily.

"You."

He smiled but it melted off his face as last night returned to him too. Remembering how he'd torn himself open and let everything fall out in front of me. He was coming back to himself but slowly; he needed a light touch and all the dumb jokes he could handle.

"I was thinking how you're reacclimating to life as a gay man with tremendous gusto and technical prowess, and I, for one, look forward to seeing what you do next." I clapped my hand on the warm skin of his shoulder. "Well done."

He snorted a laugh, though his smile was almost shy. "Whatever."

"I'm hungry and there's chow mein in the fridge. You want?"

"I want."

In the kitchen, we leaned against the marble countertops, drinking bottled water and eating cold noodles out of boxes with chopsticks. I teased Silas that he dropped more than he ate. Between mouthfuls, he told me about the first lawsuit being filed against Marsh Pharma and Stephen Milton kicking him out of the office.

"It's blackmail," he said. "Those stupid *Seattle Society* photos. He's threatened to show my father if I don't back down."

I poked at my food. "Would it be so terrible if he saw them?"

Silas's sharp eyes met mine. "Part of me would love nothing more than to waltz into Dad's room and tell him that his torture therapy failed. Or, we could suck each other's faces in front of him and call it a day."

"Subtle."

"But if I do that, he cuts me off from the company. And from Eddie. I can't let that happen."

I nodded, though I didn't quite believe him that there'd be any waltzing in front of his dad anytime soon. Silas was strong—he'd endured a nightmare and had come out the other side. But PTSD wasn't magically cured with one cryfest and a blowjob. He'd come a long way last night toward reclaiming himself, and I was so fucking proud of him. But here, in his kitchen with no prying eyes, we were safe. He was safe. The Marsh estate, however, was filled with bad memories that would haunt him the second he crossed the threshold.

Maybe not. Maybe try not to be such a pessimist for once.

"You could petition the state for conservatorship over Eddie," I said. "It's not telling you something you don't know when I say there's evidence enough of verbal and emotional abuse to sway a judge, right?"

"There is," he said darkly. "I think Dad would only fight it to spite me."

"So let's say you get Eddie safe and happy somewhere. Why the hell would you want the company back? It's not the money. . .?"

"I don't give a shit about the money."

"Then why not just walk away?"

Silas poked at his food for a moment, chewing. Thinking. Finally, he set his carton on the counter. "Have you ever heard of the Winchester Mystery House?"

"Sounds vaguely familiar."

"It's a mansion in Northern California, outside San Francisco. It was built in the 1800s by the widow of the guy who invented the Winchester rifle."

"Okay."

"When Winchester died, his wife inherited a shit-ton of money from the rifle company. The story goes, that a psychic told her to move out west and build a house. So she did. And she kept building and building, continuously. For decades. In forty years, construction didn't stop for longer than a month."

I raised my water bottle to my lips. "That's a big house."

"Huge. But a lot of the additions and add-ons don't make sense. There are stairs that go nowhere and doors that open on brick walls instead of rooms. It's a tourist trap now, but for that woman, it was a house of guilt. She thought the ghosts of everyone who'd ever died by a Winchester rifle were haunting her, so she kept building the house to appease them. Or maybe confuse them. Point is, her incredible wealth was bought and paid for by tragedy. And she knew it."

I set my water aside.

"Silas, no. That data you showed me? You can't take that all on yourself. It's too much, and it's not your fault."

"Being at fault and taking responsibility aren't the same thing."

"Very true," I said, and I couldn't help my smile. "But it's a lot to take all the same."

"I know," Silas said. "But I'll go fucking crazy if I think about all those people who died so I can live like I do. With yachts and cars and a private jet that can take me to any one of our *six* houses around the world. Our family—*one* family—uses up more resources than entire villages in some countries. It's too much. And as nice as it all looks, it's bloodstained. That's what I see. People suffering like how I suffered." He gestured to encompass his penthouse apartment. "Except they don't get to come home to this. Hundreds of them never came home at all."

Admiration for Silas washed over me so quick and fast, my mouth was on his before I realized what I was doing. My hand cupped the back of his neck as I kissed him hard, tasting the salt of the chow mein and the heat of the chili sauce.

Silas returned the kiss with a moan that sounded like relief, then made a fist in my shirt and pushed me back.

"I'm hanging by a thread, Maximilian, trying not to do exactly this," he said and pulled me back in close. "But I have shit to do. I can't spend all morning..."

"Reacclimating?" I gripped his hips and ground mine against him, talking between kisses. "You're laid off—"

"On leave."

"You're on leave. What could you possibly have to do this morning that's not this?"

As if to answer my question, the doorbell rang, and Silas jerked away from me so instantly, I thought he'd been electrocuted. His body stiffened like a soldier coming to attention, and I stepped back, my cheeks burning.

"It's my assistant," he mumbled. "She's bringing me some stuff. Didn't think she'd be this early. . ." He stood stiffly, his eyes anywhere but on me, and not making a move.

"Right," I said. "I'll just go get dressed."

I didn't need to look back to know that Silas waited until I was safely out of sight before answering the door.

After pulling on my jeans and boots—and after listening to hear when his assistant had gone—I came back to the living room. Silas had a file folder on the glass coffee table in front of him and was parsing through charts and graphs.

He looked up at me when I came in. "Hey."

"Hey. I'm going to head out. My brother and sister flew in last night. We're going to have lunch."

His eyes widened. "Wait. . . what? That's big, right?"

I shrugged. "We'll see."

"It *is* big, and I didn't know. I didn't know because I didn't call you for a week and then I got wrapped up in my shit. . ." He got to his feet and hugged me. "I'm sorry," he said against my neck.

"It's okay."

"About earlier too, when Sylvia came. It's. . . ingrained in me. To hide. To pretend. I trust Sylvia, but she's from the company."

I pulled away, hating the feeling that sat in my gut like a lump. That unsettled mix of hurt that felt justified and selfish at the same time.

"That didn't feel good, to be honest," I said. "I hate hiding. I promised myself I was done. I wasn't prepared for the reality of our... situation."

Whatever that is.

"But I'm trying not to be That Other Guy," I added.

"There's *another* guy?"

"The one who gets needy and clingy after one roll in the sack. It's not about that."

Silas didn't smile. "I don't want to be That Asshole who makes you feel like shit. But Max..." He shook his head. "Like I said, I don't know what the fuck I'm doing." He slipped his hand to cup my jaw. "Just give me some time, okay?"

"I will." I kissed him lightly. "Talk to you later."

"Good luck with the lunch," he said. "Text me if shit gets rough. Or... for any reason."

"Same."

I grabbed my jacket and left with another unsettling mix of emotions swirling in me: a euphoria over everything that happened last night—that I could still smell Silas on my skin—while at the same time, a small voice wondered if I did text him, how long it would be before he replied.

I could practically see Darlene again, shaking her head at me.

Give him a chance, Max. Don't let your old hurts scare you away.

A smile touched my lips, as I thought again how my best friend—even as an imaginary voice in my head—was so much braver than me.

My brother and sister had set up a reservation for noon at a swanky Italian restaurant that had Lake Union views and made all its own pasta on site.

I'd been cavalier to Silas about how momentous—or not—this reunion was, but the second I saw my brother and sister waiting for me, something inside cracked and a flood of pain, regret, and love flooded through me.

They both stood when they saw me, and Rachel's brown eyes filled with tears. She looked exactly as I'd remembered her—tall, lanky, with large eyes and a broad mouth. She wore dark jeans and a deep brown turtleneck that matched the color of her shoulder-length hair.

Morris had put on some bulk around the middle, but his face was unlined and almost boyish. His hair—lighter brown than Rachel's or mine—looked unbrushed and his shirt a little rumpled, as if he'd just woken up. *He hadn't changed a bit*, I thought with a pang of nostalgia. If the President invited my brother to the White House, Morris would show up slightly disheveled and blinking like a mole just come up from underground.

For both my siblings, the age difference between us was so stark it looked as if we came from entirely different branches of the family tree.

"Max." Rachel hugged me and I smelled her perfume, hairspray. . .all foreign. Her hands came up as if to hold my face, then fluttered away. "You look amazing. All grown up."

Morris gave my hand a hearty shake. "Lookin' good, little bro."

"You both look great," I said as we took our seats, Morris and I on either side of the booth, Rachel in the middle. "I wasn't expecting you until next week."

Morris jerked a thumb at our sister. "Her idea."

Rachel shot him a look. "And Mo agreed immediately, because we both felt we couldn't wait one more day."

Your guilty conscience couldn't wait. . .

I shelved the unkind thought. "I'm glad. It's good to see you."

We fell into superficial chitchat about their jobs—Rachel was editor for a *Town & Country*-type magazine in Raleigh, and Mo ran a division of a bank in Manhattan, despite looking like he couldn't manage a Little League team.

They asked about my move back to Seattle and current employment, apparently deciding it was safer to go no further in my history than last month.

Once the food arrived, Morris dug in, while Rachel and I both picked at our plates.

"I wish I was better at this," Rachel said after a while. "Instead of coming here, I wish I'd invited you back to my house, bundled us up on the couch to talk and cry and let you yell at me, if you needed to."

I eased a sigh as something in my heart unclenched. "I would've liked that too. No yelling required."

Rachel shook her head, pushed linguine around in garlic butter. "I deserve it." She whipped her fork at Morris who was stuffing his face. "So does he."

"Huh?" Morris's glance went between us. "Oh, yelling. Right." He jerked his chin in Rachel's direction. "We picked this place because you were afraid of a scene, remember?"

"I'm not going to make a scene, for God's sake," I muttered, and the good feeling of a second ago evaporated.

"I knew you wouldn't," Rachel said, glaring at Mo. She turned to me. "I was afraid *I'd* make a scene." She sniffed and dabbed a napkin to the corner of her eyes.

"Dad's thinking the same way, I bet," Morris said, intent on his food. "That's the vibe I got from him when he told us. . . what he told us."

I frowned. "What did he tell you?"

"Dad's asked us to pass on to you an invitation," Rachel said.

My stomached tightened and I set my fork down. *This is it. Here it comes. What I've been waiting for, all these years. . .*

I swallowed hard. "What invitation?"

"To Thanksgiving dinner."

The words hit me in the chest and a lightness filled me with hope tinged with pain. I hadn't had Thanksgiving dinner with my family since I was fifteen. A mental photograph of all of us at the table brought tears to my eyes, but it was charred at the edges, damaged and faded by my exile.

"Thanksgiving. . ." I said, hating how thick my voice sounded.

It was a month away, but still. . .

"I would like that. That would be. . . nice."

That would be everything.

"Great! He's made reservations already at that new restaurant in Pike's. The Harvest Inn."

My heart deflated in my chest, and I sagged in my chair. "Not at home?"

Rachel shook her head. "Not this year. Can you bring someone?"

I blinked. "*Bring* someone?"

"I think it'll help."

"He kicked me out because I had a guy in my room. Who does he think I'll bring to dinner? Not to mention, the first time I see him in nearly seven years and he wants it public? At a restaurant?"

"The restaurant is because—"

"Let me guess, to avoid a scene," I said, anger burning through me, burning the mental image of us together to ash. "This is fucking ridiculous. And to wait a whole month? What the hell?"

Rachel covered my hand with hers. "It's the best he can do."

I ripped my hand back. "It's not good enough. He's too chickenshit to see me but when he does, I should bring *a date*?"

"He wants to pick up and carry on. If you bring someone, that person—"

"A guy, Rachel. I'd bring a guy."

"That *guy* would be welcome."

"And that's supposed to make everything better? Dad's willing to let another human being I care about sit at a dinner table with him?" I rolled my eyes. "What a hero. What a champion of the LGBTQ."

"Max. . ."

"This is fucked up. All of it."

"The question you have to ask yourself," Morris cut in, in his droning, practical tone, "is do you want to fix things with Dad or not? Because this is your best shot."

"It's bullshit," I said. "We need to sit down. Talk. Not just carry on like nothing happened."

Rachel held up her hands. "Have you ever seen Dad sit down and talk? To anyone? Ever?" She turned to Morris. "Have you?"

"Nope," he said, rolling a mountain of spaghetti onto his fork.

"Not with me," Rachel said. "Not even with Mom. It's not his thing. He's not an emotional person and never has been. To ask that he suddenly become someone who shares his feelings isn't realistic."

I crossed my arms, while under the table my leg jounced with nervous anger and that fucking desperate need that just wouldn't quit.

"And if I show up alone?" I gritted out through clenched teeth.

They exchanged glances.

"That works too, of course," Rachel said. "But I'm bringing Ted and the boys. And Mo's bringing Angela and the baby, aren't you? It would be kind of perfect if you brought someone too. To balance your side out."

"My *side*?"

"You know what I mean. It would be good for Dad to see you in a... stable situation."

"Right. To show it's possible that former homeless gay drug addicts can be loved too."

Rachel's eyes filled with tears. "That's not what we mean and you know it."

I unclenched my arms and raked both hands through my hair. "I feel like I'm being asked to give him a lot more leeway than I should, given the circumstances. But I don't have a choice, do I?"

"Don't think so." Morris chewed a bit of breadstick. "Do you have someone you could bring?"

"Maybe."

My sister brightened, clearly desperate to salvage the lunch. "Do you? Are you seeing someone?"

Yes, a beautiful billionaire with a heart of gold and a huge cock.

I bit back a sudden, crazy laugh that threatened to break free. "Sort of. It's... new."

"Well, Thanksgiving is weeks away."

"I'll ask. But... Dad really won't see me before that?"

Rachel tried again, putting her hand on mine, and this time I let her.

"After the dinner," she said, "when the ice is broken and you two have been in each other's spaces for a bit... that's the time to try for a sit-down."

Morris nodded in the affirmative as he finished the last bite on his plate. He wiped his mouth with a napkin and clapped his meaty hand on my arm, so that they both had a hold on me.

"I think it'll be great, little bro. And it's really damn good to see you again."

Rachel's head nodded vigorously. "It really is. And Max..." She inhaled a shaky sigh. "No matter what happens with Dad, we're not going to vanish on you, I promise." Her tears started again, drawing my own out. "We want you to be in our lives and I hope you do too."

I nodded, unable to speak for a moment. They were doing their best, and so was my dad. That's all anyone could ask, even if it felt like you deserved a lot more, with no terms or conditions. Even if it felt like surrender.

This is your family. Do you want them or not?

"Yeah," I said to my sister, my voice gruff. "I'd like that."

After lunch, Morris and Rachel hugged me goodbye. They were only staying the weekend and were going to hang out with our parents for most of it. I tried not to let that hurt, but I felt the stab of it in my gut the entire Uber ride to the Marsh estate. I was no more than two steps in the door when Marjory, Eddie's assistant, found me in the back mudroom.

"Just the person I wanted to see," she said brightly as we moved into the kitchen. Marjory was a middle-aged woman with blond hair and a friendly kindness ingrained in her. As if she'd been born to be a caretaker.

"Max," Ramona said from usual post at the stove, stirring a huge pot of something that smelled meaty. "How are you, love? You look like you could use something warm and comfy to eat."

"Yeah, it's been a day."

"We can talk here," Marjory said. "Ramona knows what I'm about to ask anyway."

Ramona nodded and set a bowl of beef stew in front of me. "You look a little pale, love. Eat up while she talks."

"Thanks," I said. I'd hardly touched my food at lunch and was suddenly starving. "What's up?"

"It's Eddie."

I glanced up sharply. "What's wrong?"

"Nothing. He's fine. But this. . ." Marjory gestured to indicate the house. "It's not enough for him. His level of independence is such that he can't and shouldn't live alone, but he still needs gentle but varied stimulus. I feel he could hold a part-time job and be social with a group. He's expressed interest in meeting people who, as he calls it, 'share my particular personality quirks.'"

"You think he can handle that? Like a group home?"

"I do," she said. "I think he would thrive in a safe, supportive environment. He needs friendships and to experience the world, little bits at a time. Being locked up in here. . ." She shook her head. "It's not helping him. In fact, I think it's hurting. His make-believe world is sweet, but I feel like it's closing in on him. If he keeps it up, he's going to get stuck."

"What can I do?"

Marj and Ramona exchanged knowing smiles.

"Well, seeing as how you're Mr. Marsh's favorite. . ." Marjory began.

I nearly dropped my spoon. "God, not this again. I'm really, truly not his favorite. Trust me."

Ramona sniffed, brushed some pepper off her palms and into the pot. "He respects you. And he's doing better."

"That's the Orvale meds, not me."

"Perhaps," Marjory said. "But the fact is, you're a medical professional *and his favorite*. He might listen to you."

I frowned. "Marj, *you're* Eddie's companion and a medical professional. Why the hell would he take my word over yours?"

"Because you're a man," Marjory said with a resigned shrug. "In his eyes, I'll never be anything more than Eddie's nursemaid. A glorified babysitter."

There was no sense in arguing, and I sure as shit couldn't tell them that Edward suspected there was something about me he didn't want to look at. Why he kept me on, I couldn't guess. True, we had a strange, comfortable rapport and I wasn't afraid of him. Maybe that's what Ramona meant about him respecting me. In a world where everyone scurried to do his bidding, maybe he appreciated the people who didn't swallow his shit on a silver spoon and ask for more.

Maybe it'd change things if Silas didn't take his shit, either.

The women were waiting for a reply.

"I'll talk to him, but I can't promise anything."

"Thank you, Max." Marjory took my face in her hands and pecked a kiss on my cheek. "You're a keeper."

I smiled thinly over the steam of Ramona's home-cooked stew, holding on to the compliment with both hands.

The back door that led to the garages slammed, and Silas strode through the kitchen, a file folder in his hand. He jerked to a stop to see me but recovered quickly.

I inwardly cursed as my body stood at attention, my skin heating and every nerve-ending attuning directly to Silas; a magnetic energy that wanted only to draw him straight to me.

"Hey," he said, not looking at me. "Smells good, Ramona."

"Are you staying for dinner, Mr. Silas?"

"Maybe." His gaze flickered to me, studying me, his sharp eyes likely reading my afternoon on my face, then away. "No. I'm busy tonight."

"It's Saturday," Marjory said. "Eddie is looking forward to you playing piano for him."

"Right," Silas said, his expression hardening. "Yeah, sure. I'll be there after I talk to Dad." He smiled grimly and gave a sharp nod in parting. "Ladies. Max."

And then he left without another word.

"That one," Marjory said with a sigh and fanned herself with her hand. "Sorry to subject you to girl-talk, Max, but that Faith is one lucky lady."

Ramona's eyes met mine, and then she took up the paprika. "Not really our business, is it?" she scolded lightly. "Besides. Who knows what the future brings?"

I pushed the stool out and stood up. "Thanks for the stew, Ramona."

"Anytime, my dear," she said. "And if you need anything ever. . . food, drink, a friendly ear. I'm here."

Marjory smiled. "Ramona is the Mama Hen, and we're all her chicks."

I'll take it, I thought. *I'll take whatever I can get.*

I met Ramona's eye and nodded in gratitude. She nodded back, satisfied, and I went upstairs, to my room. No sooner had I shut the door than a text from Daniel came in.

Hey boo, we need to hang. U free?

I thought about Silas saying he was busy tonight and the meaningful glance he'd shot me and nearly told Daniel no. But then again, I'd been feeling dicked around all day and decided I wasn't going to be That Other, Other Guy. The one who waited around for a text or phone call from someone to determine how his night was going to go.

I'm free, I said. **Usual spot?**

Yasss! 8pm. CU then bb.

CHAPTER TWENTY

Silas

"Dammit," I muttered.
In the hallway outside Dad's rooms, I ducked into the linen closet. The one where I'd cornered Max on his first day. I sucked in deep breaths, because *holy shit*, being in this house after everything Max and I had said and done felt like returning to the scene of a crime I hadn't committed but had been convicted of anyway. Max was freedom from a prison of lies, and yet I was walking right back in it.

Just a little longer. I only have to do this a little longer...

But Christ, my skin was broken out in gooseflesh, and that old familiar numbness wanted to creep back in. Worse, my old baggage was hurting Max too. Twice in one day, I'd hidden or ignored him.

I tucked the file folder of data Sylvia had given me under my arm and tore out my phone to shoot Max a text. The irony of texting the guy I wanted from inside the same fucking house—and *in a closet* no less—was not lost on me, but there I was.

U OK?

No reply. I waited with mounting anxiety, and then finally a text popped up.

Been better. Lunch w/sibs was rough, tbh.

My thumbs flew. **I saw UR face in the kitchen. Want to C U tonight.**

I need to make it up to you. I need to touch you, to be seen by you...

Made plans with friends.

I sagged against the shelves with disappointment while jealousy stabbed me in the gut.

Another text followed. **I'd invite U to come but not sure UR up for that.**

Where?

Smoke & Mirrors in Capitol Hill. A pause, then: **It's a gay bar.**

I blew air out my cheeks. It was like walking a tightrope to wrangle control back from Milton while not fucking things up with Max. While I pondered how to take my next tentative step, he texted again.

Gay bars are safe spaces, but if it's too big of a step, I get that.

Too big of a step. Christ. As if he were reading my mind.

And of course, he understood. That's what Max did. He was the only person on the planet who saw me as I was. Living in that reflection was the best thing that had ever happened to me. But he was only going to put up with my shit for so long before his integrity told him I wasn't worth it.

I can't. I want to but if I'm recognized, game over w/ Dad.

I know, he replied, which was almost worse than him chewing me out.

I'll call U later, I wrote.

OK

I hated 'OK' but I had to leave it for now. I heaved a breath, tucked my phone away, and put on my game face. I slipped on the mask of a cold, calculating asshole whose only concern was the bottom line and went to Dad's room.

The curtains were open and gray, watery light filled the room. Dad was sitting up in his bed, reading a newspaper while his favorite news channel blared from the flat screen across from him. His hands holding the paper hardly trembled at all.

He peered at me from behind half-moon reading glasses as I approached, and it was as if everything I felt about Max were scrawled all over me in black Sharpie.

"Give us a minute?" I said to Roberto, the nurse on duty. He got up from a chair by the window where he'd been filling out a chart and left us alone.

"Well?" Dad said.

"You look good," I said. "Better."

"They tell me it's the Orvale. Our Orvale. Some sort of breakthrough drug."

I sat in the chair beside him, elbows resting on knees. "That's great. Could be our next big thing."

Dad's gaze slid to me. "Indeed."

I heaved a breath. "Your new acting CEO put me on a leave of absence."

He went back to his paper, unperturbed. Which meant he already knew. "Why would he do that?"

"Because we're getting sued, Dad. The first lawsuit of many has been filed. That overdose data I was trying to tell you about? It's coming to bite us in the ass just as I predicted."

I opened the file folder on my lap, but Dad waved a dismissive hand.

"I'm not interested in your little pie charts, Silas."

My cheeks burned. "Dad, you need to listen to me. This shit is bad—"

"And Stephen is aware and handling it." He peered at me. "You don't approve?"

"He's going to try to squash the plaintiffs and draw out the litigation for years."

"Sounds about right. It's what I'd do."

I tossed the file folder onto the side table. "You trusted my judgment enough to make me COO. Someday, CEO. Is that bullshit or not?"

Dad let his paper fall flat on his lap to pierce me with his own icy blue gaze. "Very well, I'll bite. What do you think?"

"I think it makes us look like a soulless fucking corporation that cares less about helping people than it does the bottom line," I said. "But we don't have to be. You said it yourself, Orvale is a breakthrough. We have a chance to do some real good here, but our reputation or legacy that you want to preserve so badly? It's not going to be worth shit if we don't help clean up this mess we made."

Dad's gaze turned even icier. "I see. You think *we* made a mess. That we're responsible for the weakness of a bunch of criminal addicts who abused our product."

God, it was Milton's words exactly.

I swallowed hard. "I think the marketing department, under Milton's direction, got extremely overzealous and made access to OxyPro as easy as buying a packet of Tic Tacs at the 7-Eleven."

"Interesting theory," Dad said. "I also find it very interesting that you believe Stephen took any action whatsoever without my knowledge or direction."

"Fuck, Dad. . ." I scrubbed my hands over my face. "You knew?"

"I knew the numbers, Silas. I knew the profits. I knew that doctors were prescribing our drug as needed. *As needed.* They are *doctors,* after all."

"Doctors who'd been misled and incentivized all to hell." I shook my head. "This is bad. This is really fucking bad."

Dad narrowed his eyes at me. "And if I indulge your whimsy that this is 'really fucking bad,' what do you propose we do?"

"Get rid of Milton, for one."

"Ah. The man to whom I gave temporary custody of *your* job and who put you on leave. He's the culprit."

"No, shit, that's not why. . ." I said, gritting my teeth. "He may have shown you some great numbers, Dad, but not how we got there. The company needs to cease and desist his marketing practices and help make amends. Start rehab centers, give money back to community—"

"Where is Faith?"

I blinked and sat back in the chair as Dad hit the brakes on the conversation and veered onto another. "She's. . . at home. Or shopping. I don't know where she is. I don't keep tabs. She's free to do what she wants."

Stop talking stop talking stop talking. . .

"Our annual company Halloween party is fast approaching," Dad said, going back to his newspaper. "I was thinking this year, we'd hold it here."

"Here."

"Yes, I know it's short notice, but I have confidence in our team to transfer all preparations to the house. I'm feeling better and the employees enjoy it so much." He glanced at me again. "Since our *numbers are so good,* there is much to celebrate. You'll bring Faith, of course."

"Yeah, sure. . ." I said absently while my mind raced. *Something's up. This isn't normal.* "You hate parties. You never go to any of them, and you want to hold one here?"

"My illness has given me a different perspective on life, Silas," he said. "I'm looking forward to it."

He held the paper up as a barrier between us, my cue that the conversation was over. I wanted to argue further, but I knew it was useless so long as Milton was pouring poison in his ear.

"I'll just leave my 'little pie charts' here," I muttered and got up to go.

Dad's voice floated to me from across the room. "And Silas?"

I turned.

"Your leave of absence is rather embarrassing. Please do your best to make amends with Stephen. Before the party, preferably, where every executive in the company will be present, eh?"

I clenched my teeth and headed out. In the hallway, I immediately called Sylvia.

"Well?" she asked.

"No go," I replied, heading down the curving stairs. "We have to get rid of that fucker, Milton. I need you to dig up some dirt on him, Syl."

"Business or personal? Or both?"

I nearly said "both" but prying into that bastard's personal life was unethical. Tempting but unethical. *Imagine explaining that one to Max.*

A small smile touched my lips.

"Silas?"

"Business only," I said. "Get in touch with IT and tell them the Chief Operating Officer wants every email and internal memo that's come in or out of Milton's company account in the last ten years."

"That's a lot of email," Sylvia said. "Is it. . . legal?"

"Company emails are company property," I said. "And COO is high enough on the food chain to have clearance. Hell, the guy before me, Bruckheimer, was probably cc'd on all of them. I want his shit too."

"How do I keep IT from spilling to Milton?"

"Tell them I'm doing a full review of every department in the company *including* IT. Hint that cutbacks are on the horizon, but if they do what I ask without alerting the other departments, they'll have nothing to worry about."

"That's perfect," Sylvia said. "Not to mention, everyone hates Milton. I've been hearing a lot of complaints about him being made the big boss."

"*Acting* big boss," I said with a grim smile. "Let me know when IT comes through."

"You got it."

We hung up and I headed to the living room where Eddie was waiting for me.

"Ah, Silas, my good man," he said, rocking slightly, eyes on the floor. "I'm so very pleased to see you."

"Me too." I smiled and sat at the piano. "Any requests?"

"But are we not waiting for Mr. Kaufman?"

I stiffened and turned to face him. He was frowning at the carpet.

"I explained this to you. We're not doing lessons with Max anymore."

"I do remember, though I must admit, I don't recall being given a satisfactory explanation."

"You're too pure for this world, Eddie," I said. "Max can't have lessons with us anymore because Dad doesn't approve of staff members hanging out with family."

"That's quite odd," Eddie said, "given that Mr. Kaufman is quite more than a staff member, is he not?"

"What. . . ?" I cleared my throat and tried again. "What do you think he is?"

My brother cocked his head, confused. "Do you not recall your *David Copperfield,* dear brother?" He clasped his hands and recited: "*New thoughts and hopes were whirling through my mind, and all the colors of my life were changing.*"

"Yeah," I said gruffly. "I remember." The line was from the scene in which David finally confesses to Agnes that she's the love of his life.

"If you'll forgive my personal observations," Eddie said, "but during the course of our afternoons here with Mr. Kaufman, I have rather felt that sentiment in you."

"You have?" Why the fuck I suddenly felt on the verge of tears, I had no idea.

Yes, you do. You know exactly why.

Eddie smiled, met my eye for one quick second, then looked away. "Mr. Kaufman is quite more than a staff member, is he not?"

"You're right, Eddie," I said and laid my fingers on the piano keys, symphonies of emotion rising in me, each drenched in colors I'd never seen before. "He's so much more than that."

CHAPTER TWENTY-ONE

Max

In my room, I lay down for a quick nap before I headed out to meet Daniel and the guys. From below, the sounds of the piano rumbled like musical thunder. Silas playing for Eddie. The piece was unlike anything I'd ever heard—pounding and intense and stunningly complicated. A storm of sound that shuddered and rampaged, as if Silas were trying to bring the house crashing down to its foundation.

Maybe he was. He and I were under the same roof and yet miles away, me lying up here on a bed and wanting him and him taking out his feelings on the instrument below. Silas had all of that in him, and only I knew it.

Give him time. You promised.

The music stopped. I drifted to sleep.

"Hey, man." Daniel gave my arm a nudge and jerked his chin at my empty glass. "You're hitting the soda water pretty hard. You okay?"

"Yep. Fine."

It was just the two of us at Smoke & Mirrors so far—Charlie was running late, and Malcolm had canceled, wanting to avoid a huge rainstorm that was set to hit that night.

Daniel had rolled his eyes at that text, saying, "If we stayed in every time it rained—in *Seattle*—we'd turn into mole men."

Now, I sat hunched over my drink facing the bar while Daniel sat resting his back against it to scope out the crowd that was thin for a Saturday night.

"You sure you're all right?" Daniel asked. "Because you blew off that party I told you about, and the last time we hung out, you wanted to discuss conversion therapy, of all things."

"I told you, I couldn't make the party because I got called to work that night."

"Uh huh. And speaking of your work, since you took the job with Billionaire Who Shall Not Be Named, you either vanish or you show up looking like a sad boy."

"I'm not sad," I said. "I'm. . .conflicted."

Daniel raised a pierced eyebrow.

I sighed. "Okay, so there's a guy."

"I knew it!" He slapped his hand on the thigh of his stylishly ripped jeans. "Oh, honey, I get it. When I don't hear from you, you're in the bliss, right? And then shit happens, and you reemerge into the real world."

"I guess." I turned my glass around, thinking of what Silas had been put through and what it was doing to us. "The real world can be a really shitty place."

"Indeed," Daniel said. "So tell me about him."

"I can't."

"I'm your friend. You can tell me anything."

"No, I literally can't."

Daniel's eyebrows shot up to his silvery hairline. "A fellow nurse? The butler? The billionaire himself?"

I chuckled. "You're out of guesses."

"Is it serious?"

"I. . . Yeah," I said. I couldn't tell him everything, but I wanted to be honest wherever I could. "Yeah, I think it's serious. Or it could be."

"How serious?"

I promised to protect my heart and instead I ripped it out of my chest and handed it to Silas Marsh.

"Uh oh," Daniel said. "That look on your face. . . It's mega serious. So what's the issue?"

"There's some family stuff on his side, and all the shit in my past is making me overthink like a motherfucker."

My friend nodded. "Maybe. But you went through all that stuff and survived, honey. You deserve not to be yanked around. If that's what's happening. Which I don't know. Since you can't tell me."

"I will. Someday. He—I just need a little bit of time."

"Mmkay. Well, just remember: Someday isn't a day of the week. It doesn't come around automatically. You gotta go out there and get it."

I arched a brow at him. "Since when did you get so wise?"

"I'm not." He sipped his cocktail. "I just watch a lot of Wendy Williams."

Charlie showed up shaking water out of his hair, and he and Daniel chatted about their jobs, guys, the current scene in the bar, which wasn't much; the place was dead. Malcolm wasn't the only one who stayed home to avoid the rain.

It wasn't my scene either, I realized. I wasn't up for superficial talk, and the guy making eyes at me from the end of the bar was irritating for his lack of being Silas.

I wanted out but didn't want to go home either. The Marsh estate wasn't a home. It was a fancy hotel—not a destination but a stop on a journey, and I was beginning to think it was time to check-out.

I told Charlie and Daniel goodnight, and Daniel gave me a hug. "I'm here whenever, okay? In the bliss or the shit. I'm here for you."

"Thanks, man. I appreciate it."

Outside, the storm was only rain, but it was coming down in sheets. It had washed the streets clean of people but for one. A guy in a hooded, waterproof jacket leaned against a lamppost at the corner. The amber light fell over him in a cone while bullets of rain splattered around him, unheeded.

He was a good twenty feet away, in a downpour, and yet I recognized every line of him, every detail.

A smile spread over my face as my heart jackrabbited in my chest. "Hot Unabomber strikes again," I murmured.

Silas pushed himself off the lamppost with his shoulder when he saw me, and I left the protection of the awning to stand under the light and rain with him.

"How long have you been out here?" I asked.

"Can't go inside," he said in a low voice, his blue eyes glittering from inside the dark of his hood. "This is the best I could do."

I heard the unspoken question, *Is it enough?*

I nodded, because it was. He was here. He'd been waiting for me in the rain.

"I'm glad you're here."

My words sank into him and his crossed arms came down, a lowering of defenses. Silas's eyes scanned the empty street.

"I'm parked over there," he said, jerking his head at a side street behind the bar.

We ducked into the side street where his Aston waited but we didn't make it to the car. The moment the darkness fell over us, Silas gripped me by the lapels of my jacket at the same time I reached for him. I fell back against the wall and took him with me.

Silas's body pressed against mine. His mouth hovered over my lips but didn't touch. Our eyes roamed each other's faces, drinking the other in, as if it'd been years since we'd been together. For a few trembling, halting moments, we basked in the nearness and electricity of each other, shivering with unleashed want instead of cold.

His hand reached up and gripped me at the back of my head, his fingers sinking and then making a fist in my hair. The slight pain zipped down my spine, straight to my cock, and I prepared myself for the onslaught of his kiss. But I was drenched, and Silas's gaze took in the raindrops that rolled like mercury off my leather jacket.

His brows furrowed, concern tempering the heat in his eyes. "We should go..."

I reached up and pushed the hood off of his head. He smirked and blinked as the rain came down. It dampened his gold hair and streaked down his cheeks.

"Now we're even."

I watched, mesmerized by a raindrop that journeyed down the sharp angle of Silas's cheekbone to his mouth where it hung suspended off his lower lip.

Mine...

I tilted my chin up, licked that drop of water with a swipe of my tongue and swallowed it down.

Silas's eyes widened and then darkened with an almost feral look that was empty of everything but want. The tension snapped, and our mouths came together in a crushing kiss that obliterated everything around me until there was just him.

Silas Marsh was a delirium. A fever of sensation, and I lost myself in the kiss that was instantly deep and hard, raw and open. We crammed ourselves into each other, taking and taking with long sweeps of our tongues and biting clacks of our teeth. Our hands grasped and pulled at whatever we could get a hold of. Our mouths bit and sucked, nearly violent as if the energy surging between us couldn't be contained—fuck or fight, kiss or kill. The mindless need was taking over, desperate for release, ready to combust until there was nothing left of us but smoldering debris in a pile of shredded clothing.

"Want you so bad," Silas growled. "All day... every fucking minute."

"I'm here," I managed, shifting my hips against his, grinding. Offering.

Silas's kisses never stopped as his hands dropped to the fly on my jeans, tore open the button, yanked the zipper down. My eyes rolled back in my head as his hand found me, hard and aching.

"Today was bad," he said, his voice husky as he sucked at my neck, bit my ear. "Going to make it up to you..."

Before I knew what was happening, he was on his knees, freeing me from my jeans. The cold air and rain were instantly replaced by the impossible heat and wetness of his mouth and I moaned, wondering how anything could feel this fucking good.

This. Always this. Always him...

I turned my face to the sky, succumbing to Silas as he worked me over. He was merciless with his mouth, devouring my cock deep or sucking with long, reverent swirls of his tongue; his hands stroking and pumping all the while. I scrabbled for something to hold onto as every nerve-ending in my body converged where his tongue touched flesh.

My flailing hand found his head, fingers fumbling weakly in his damp hair.

"Don't get shy on me now, Kaufman," Silas growled.

I raked my fingers over his scalp and then made a tight fist in his hair while my hips rocked back and forth. He grunted his approval, moving harder and faster to get me over the edge.

"Oh God, oh shit, Si. . ." I moaned mindlessly, using every bit of will I had not to fuck his mouth as hard as my body wanted.

"Yes," Silas hissed, catching his breath. "Come for me. Want it. Want all of it. . ."

He took my cock back in his mouth with a deep, long suck, and I released a harsh cry into the night as the orgasm flared through me. It ignited the tight knot of aching pleasure at the base of my spine, turning me inside out. Silas took all of it, coaxed it out of me, sucked it down and then used his tongue in long, slow strokes to finish me off.

I sagged against the wall, ragged and limp; putting myself back together breath by shuddering breath.

"Holy. . . fucking. . . shit," I managed while Silas tucked me back into my jeans and got to his feet.

"Good?" he asked, a proud, rakish grin on his face.

I gave him a weak shove on the shoulder. "Shut up. You know it was good. Fucking epic."

He glanced around the still-deserted street. "Shit, that was dumb."

"You think we're the first guys to hook up behind that bar?" I laughed tiredly, but it faded quick. "But we shouldn't press our luck."

That's what I said, but what I meant was that if we stayed out here a second longer, I was going to attack him.

We drove back to Silas's apartment and went straight to his shower, shedding sodden clothes on the way. Under the hot, steaming downpour, I went on my knees and took my turn worshipping his cock while stroking myself at the same time. After what he'd done to me in the alley, I didn't think I'd get hard again for a year, but his nakedness, the cut perfection of his body, and the huge, hard length of him in my mouth had my blood surging.

We came nearly together, the sounds of his orgasm coming from deep in his chest and echoing in the cavernous bathroom.

After, we dried off, hardly saying anything, but not moving further than a few feet from each other either—too tired, too spent, not needing words, only wanting to be in each other's space, breathing the same air.

Silas put on a pair of sleep pants and tossed me a spare. I wanted to sleep skin to skin, but I followed his lead, let him have whatever boundaries he needed. We climbed into his bed, and he wrapped his arms around me, my back to his chest, falling into our perfect places like puzzle pieces.

We slept almost at once, heavy and satiated, while the storm outside relented and gave way to the dawn.

CHAPTER TWENTY-TWO

Max

Sunlight blasted in from the windows, playing over Silas's smooth, bronzed skin, and filled in the sleek lines and planes of his muscled back. He lay on his stomach, head turned away, toward the window where the only traces of last night's storm were the pebbles of water on the glass.

It looked like his lazy ass was going to sleep until noon, so I sunk my teeth into his bicep, then sucked the skin and ran my tongue over its salty warmth.

Silas grumbled deep in his chest and turned his head my way. His eyes, fringed by dark lashes, opened and the beautiful smile that came over his lips when he saw me lying beside him was everything, because it was automatic; before thought or self-consciousness.

Holy shit, I'm in trouble.

He brushed his thumb over my lower lip. "Hey," he said, sleepily. A lock of his tousled hair fell over his eyes.

"Hey, yourself." I reached over and brushed the hair away. "You're doing that on purpose."

"Doing what?"

"Looking like. . . how you look."

He laughed. "What poetry, Maximilian. You're gonna make a guy blush."

"Bumbling compliments are my specialty."

He leaned over and kissed me, and my body started to wake up. But before it went too deep, Silas broke the kiss and climbed out of bed to go to the window.

Disappointment tried to nip at me, but I brushed it off. There was a slight undercurrent of unease running through Silas, and I got the immediate impression that he was taking things as fast as his fucked up time in Chisana would allow: bursts of heated, potent desire tamped down by cold memories and insidious lies that no doubt still whispered in his head.

Giving him his space wasn't just the right thing to do, it was imperative for his healing.

"So, you have the day off, right?" Silas said from the window, shirtless, wearing only sleep pants. "It's looking like we're going to have decent weather out there."

"You have a plan?"

His expression darkened as he regarded the city below. "I want to get Eddie out of that fucking house."

I sat up and yawned. "Marjory was telling me he's ready for a group home. He can socialize, make friends, and maybe even work."

Silas turned. "She told you that?"

I nodded. "Wants me to bring it up with your dad."

"My father will never go for it. And Eddie can't be yanked out of the house and dropped into a new place. He needs a gradual transition. Hell, getting him out of the front door might be a challenge."

"Might not," I said. "Only one way to find out."

He glanced at me. "That's not the stuff of dates, hanging out with my autistic brother. . ."

"Shut it, Marsh. I love Eddie."

Silas stared at me for a moment. "Goddammit, Maximilian."

He crossed the room and crawled on hands and knees on the bed to lean over me. His lips brushed mine as he spoke. "You're doing that on purpose."

"Doing what?"

"Being like. . . how you are."

Dressed in Silas's sleep pants, T-shirt, and my jacket, I took a Walk of Shame that nobody witnessed, as I snuck into the Marsh estate to change. Silas's mission was to coax Eddie out with the promise of a boat ride on Lake Union. I hated all the sneaking around, but Silas had told me in the car on the way over that he had a plan for taking back the company.

"I'm not sitting on my ass," he'd said, weaving the Aston through light Sunday morning traffic. "Trust me, okay?"

"I do," I'd said.

Of course, I did. But that didn't make me feel less of a fraud as I ducked into a bathroom to avoid talking to Dale on my way out. I felt like the sixteen-year-old me again, sneaking around my parents' house. And if I got caught. . .

They'll kick me out of here too.

I made it back to the car and waited in the front seat. Time ticked by from five minutes to ten, then twenty. I was about to give up and text Silas when he and Eddie emerged from the side of the house. Eddie was hunched over, hands twisting, head down as he followed Silas to the car.

Maybe this is a bad idea.

But Eddie's face brightened when he saw me. "I say, Mr. Kaufman, my good man," he said, climbing into the backseat. "This is quite the pleasant surprise."

"How are you doing, Eddie?" I asked, shooting Silas a questioning glance. He shrugged as if to say, 'so far, so good.'

"I confess, I'm a tad jumbly in the nerves. . ."

"Yeah? You want to talk about it?"

Eddie rocked slightly in his seat. "I. . . rather. Well. . . Perhaps we might do this another time?"

Silas turned around in his seat to face him. "Hey. We're here. We're not going to let anything bad happen to you. I promise."

Eddie pondered this, still rocking. Silas glanced at me, gave his head a little shake. I turned in my seat to give it a try.

"I say, my good man, if we thought for even a moment that your constitution wasn't hardy enough for such an excursion, we would never undertake it."

Eddie ceased rocking and he tilted his chin up, though his eyes never met mine.

"Is that so?"

"Indeed," I said. "I propose that we venture out, and if you find it to your displeasure, we shall return at once."

The idea of returning to the house made Eddie's nose wrinkle.

"I must remind myself that betwixt you and my dear brother, I am in good hands." He motioned for Silas to drive as if he were a chauffeur. "Sally forth, then, there's a good man."

Silas grinned at me and put on his sunglasses. "Let's roll."

We arrived at the Lake Union marina, and after conferring with the harbormaster for a few minutes, we were given the go-ahead to take out the Marsh's speedboat. We grabbed sandwiches and drinks from the minimart and headed to the docks.

"I wanted to sail but the wind's too rough for me to go it alone," Silas said as we climbed aboard the sleek boat that looked like a red and white arrow with twin outboard motors.

Eddie had grown more apprehensive since getting out of the car at the marina parking lot, and now his hands were twisting around one another again as we prepared to embark.

"If I might request that you do not take the vessel to the pinnacle of her velocity," Eddie said as Silas helped him step in.

Silas frowned, but I shot him a look and shook my head.

"No, of course not," Silas said, while I helped his brother into a life vest. "We'll take it easy, Eddie."

Silas expertly maneuvered the boat through the marina and onto open water. Whitecaps bearded the waves, and the spray on our faces was cold. But the sun—likely the last real sun before winter set in—was metallic and bright.

Eddie held on tight to the rail and I stayed close while Silas drove the boat with restraint; I could see how he was itching to gun it. He looked like he'd stepped out of a magazine, with the sun glinting off his hair and warming his tanned skin. Now and then, we exchanged glances and small smiles, each loaded with memories of last night. The storm seemed a million years ago, but everything we'd done in the rain was right there, on the surface, and ready to surge again.

We hit a patch of smooth water and Silas killed the engine to let us drift.

"How you doing, Eddie?" I asked, as Silas passed around the drinks and turkey sandwiches he'd stowed in a cooler built into the seat.

"Quite well," he replied, and I saw it in his hands that sat in his lap, relaxed. "I do wonder why Papa has been so adamant that I remain indoors. I admit to a great deal of hesitation on my part, though I have long felt a growing dissatisfaction with the monotony of the house."

I took a sip of bottled lemonade. "On that note, what would you think about living elsewhere?"

Silas lowered his sandwich and pushed his sunglasses up onto his head.

"Move out of the estate?" Eddie tapped his chin thoughtfully, his gaze in his lap. "Where might I reside?"

"You would live in a home with other people who also have Asperger's," Silas said slowly.

"Is that so?" He brightened at this, then his hands reached for each other again. "But there are quite many times where I feel overwhelmed by the magnitude of my environs."

"There would be people there to help," I said. "People like Marjory. But because you're capable of a lot more than what you're doing now, we think—and Marjory thinks—it would be kind of perfect for you."

Eddie pursed his lips. "Will there be book lovers among the denizens of this house?"

"Could be," Silas said.

"And connoisseurs of the finer things in life?"

"Unknown," I said, "But perhaps they could share something of their likes and interests with you, and you can share with them your encyclopedic knowledge of *Charles Dickens?*"

"And everything else under the sun," Silas added.

Eddie frowned. "Would you live there as well, brother?"

"No, but I would come and visit as often as you wanted. And we'd take trips like this, into the city. Or anywhere in the world, really. Whatever you feel like you're up for. I'd work at my job and you could work at your job."

"A job?" Eddie tasted the word. "Are there such places of employment for those with my particular skill set?"

"Hell, yes," Silas said. "There are a ton of places that would be thrilled to have you; you're so damn smart. And if you don't like any of them, you can come work with me."

I turned to hide my eyes that stung at the kindness in Silas's heart—a heart that lay concealed beneath a beautiful exterior.

"I'd work with you in the same office?" Eddie asked.

"Absolutely."

He tapped his chin thoughtfully, then turned his head in my direction, gaze on the floor of the boat. "Mr. Kaufman, my good man. Would I ever see you if I were to vacate the Marsh premises and inhabit my own domicile?"

"Eddie," I said, "you wouldn't be able to get rid of me."

Silas looked my way, shaking his head at me with a small smile on his lips.

Eddie looked very pleased. Happy. "I had thought I was far too craven to entertain such notions—"

"You're not craven," Silas said darkly. "Dad's just been telling you a bunch of bull—"

"Your father is concerned about your well-being," I cut in. "Overprotective."

Filling Eddie's head with negative shit about his dad wasn't going to make him feel good, even if it was all true, and Silas knew it.

He frowned. "Yeah, that. Overprotective."

"Well, I must say, I am in quite a kerfuffle over such a prospect."

"It sounds good?"

"Indeed, Mr. Kaufman," Eddie said. "It sounds rather marvelous."

Silas and I exchanged smiles and the day felt even warmer and more golden than before.

"Now can I let her rip?" Silas asked, starting the engine.

"I should say not, brother," Eddie said. "I am not as bricky as all that. Take it slow, if you please."

Silas laughed and knocked his sunglasses down over his eyes. "Whatever you say, Eddie."

After the boat ride, Eddie wasn't ready to go home yet. A place crammed with people was too steep a step, so we went to Volunteer Park where he strolled over the grass, pointing out the differences in foliage between the park and the Marsh backyard while Silas and I sat on a bench. Close enough to touch but not touching.

Twice, our hands brushed, wanting to hold on, but Silas pulled away when someone walked close to us.

"Sorry," he muttered.

"Don't be," I said. "Even if you weren't trying to keep things on the down-low, it's not like it's always comfortable showing affection in public. You never know if some asshole is going to make a comment or if a mom is going to shoot you a dirty look for existing in front of her kids."

Silas's face twisted. "That happens a lot?"

I shrugged. "How much is a lot? Once is too many."

He nodded, thinking. "I keep wanting to touch you, Max, out here on this bench, but this memory from Alaska keeps jumping out at me, whacking me in the face. Literally."

"Tell me."

Silas had his sunglasses off and his eyes were clouded and heavy.

"We were outside, gathered around a pitiful campfire. It was January, I think, cold as fuck. I was cleaning a fish, hardly able to hold the little knife, my hands were so numb. I started thinking about Eddie and how I was so fucking glad he wasn't there to see me go through all this shit." He nodded his head in his brother's direction. "Then I *kept* thinking about Eddie, because he was something good, you know? Something good and far away from the misery."

I nodded, listening, feeling a tightness in my stomach for what must be coming next.

"Out of nowhere, pain exploded across my cheek, knocking me flat."

Silas turned his gaze to me. "Coach Braun had whacked me across the face with a log."

I ground my teeth. "Why?"

"He said it was written all over my face that I'd been thinking 'soft thoughts.'"

"Goddamn," I breathed. "Goddammit, that asshole. That's awful."

"And now I'm sitting here, with you, watching Eddie be out in the world, definitely having what Braun would consider 'soft thoughts.'"

"No one is going to hit you, Si," I said quietly.

"No, but if I were holding your hand, or if we kissed, we might get a snide comment or a dirty look, right?" he asked. "How is that different? Seems to me that that's almost as fucking awful. You're just. . . minding your own business, being happy, and you get whacked." He shrugged. "Doesn't seem all that different to me."

I turned facing forward because if I looked at Silas for one more second, I was going to grab him and hold him; *I* wanted to grab a log and beat away anyone who'd even think about hurting him.

"Where is Braun now?" I asked. "Please tell me some parent came to his damn senses when his kid came back and had him arrested."

"Some parents from my group were pissed, I heard. Their boys were in the hospital with me. There was talk of hauling him in. Not from my father, of course. But Braun vanished."

Vanished, without paying for what he'd done. Vanished after leaving a trail of broken boys behind him.

I glanced over at Silas. He had his left leg crossed so that his ankle rested on his right knee. I did the same, crossing my right leg, so that our thighs made a barrier from prying eyes, and I took his hand.

He stiffened for a second, then relaxed. His fingers entwined with mine, and we sat like that for a long time.

We drove back to the Marsh estate at twilight so that Silas could drop Eddie back into Marjory's care.

"Are you coming in, Mr. Kaufman?" Eddie inquired, stepping out of the car and looking brighter and more relaxed than I'd seen in a long time.

I traded glances with Silas, not wanting the day to be over.

"I'm dropping Max off in the city," Silas said. "But let's keep it to ourselves, okay, Eddie? Remember what I said about Dad not liking us to hang out with... staff."

He said it as if every word tasted sour, but Eddie nodded. "Right-o." He gave me a small salute. "Much obliged, my good man, for such a splendid day."

"Anytime, Eddie."

Silas walked his brother in and returned a few minutes later. He climbed into the driver's seat and sat for a minute.

"He did great," he said. "Right?"

"Amazing."

Silas had his glasses off and his blue eyes pierced mine with a familiar want, but there was something deeper behind them. The air between us felt different, charged with electricity—a low hum now, but that promised wild, sparking live wires.

"You want to go out?" Silas asked. "Grab dinner or...?"

"Stay in," I said. "Maybe order a pizza."

He nodded. "That's what I was thinking too."

The air thickened further. A heavy clang started in my chest, and my skin tingled with nerves.

Back at Silas's, he ordered a pizza from a local place.

"It'll be forty-five minutes," he said, setting down his cell on the kitchen counter.

"Cool," I said and jammed my hands into the front of my jeans.

A silence fell. We were confronted with not just the next forty-five minutes, but the entire night that was waiting, its breath held.

Silas ran a hand through his hair, looking halfway between frustrated and ready to jump out of his skin. "Yeah, so, you want to watch TV or...?"

"Nah." I jerked my chin at the piano. "I want you to play."

"Now?"

"Have you played at all since you got it? That's got to be a crime in some musical lawbook."

"Sure it is," he said with an eye-roll, but I thought he took the bench with

257

no small amount of relief. Something to do with his hands, some outlet for the energy that was swirling between us like slow winds that gradually took up speed to become a tornado.

Silas began a classical piece that sounded like the one he'd played for Eddie the day before. I listened from the couch, mesmerized by this man, wrapped in a package of bronze skin and muscle, with blue eyes that were fathoms deep beneath their icy surface. As his fingers flew across the keys, I marveled at how he was so filled with talent and intelligence, spiced with a hot temper and impatience.

The pizza came early. Silas was still playing, not noticing that I practically threw money at the delivery guy to get rid of him and tossed the pizza on the counter.

When the piece came to its end, Silas scowled at my applause.

"Cut it out."

"Nope, you're going to take my compliments, Marsh. Because if you think I can sit here and not say anything after hearing that. . ."

He smirked. "I told you. It's just something I can do. As if the wiring was already laid down for me. I don't think about it."

"I think it's fucking amazing," I said. "I can't imagine playing like that. I'd sprain my fingers if they moved that fast."

Silas thought for a second. "Come here." He got up and turned the bench so that it was perpendicular to the piano. "Sit."

I sat on the end of the bench in front of the keys. "All this time, I didn't realize if I wanted to play like you, I only needed to turn the bench."

"Yes," Silas said dryly. "That's the secret of the masters. Now shut up and let me try something."

He sat behind me, straddling the bench like a horse. His legs went to either side of my thighs and his chest was flush with my back. My body reacted; electricity between us hummed louder, and I felt him everywhere.

Silas reached around me and put his hands on the keys, his chin over my shoulder. "Put your hands on mine."

I laid my hands on his, lightly.

"Harder than that, Maximilian, or you're going to get bucked off."

I gently pressed my fingertips between his knuckles. "Here?"

"We'll see. I've never done this before."

Silas inhaled; I felt his chest expand against me, hard and strong against my back. His chin was on my shoulder, the stubble of his cheek brushing mine. I turned slightly to see his eyes were closed. He exhaled and opened them, caught me watching him.

That shy look of his that always undid me came over his face again.

"Eyes on the keys, Kaufman," he said, his voice low and throaty.

And then he began to play, and his fingers—our fingers—moved slowly over the keys.

It took some false starts to keep my hands on his, but after a few moments, we fell into a rhythm. A harmony. His hands became extensions of myself. I felt him under me and around me, sensed the music and his intentions; his heartbeat against my back, a metronome I kept time to.

"What are we playing?" I asked.

"*Moonlight Sonata,*" he said. "Beethoven." Without missing a note, he brushed his mouth against my ear. "You're very good."

I was completely out of smart-ass things to say, awestruck at the skill he possessed that had become a tangible thing, right there under my palms, as if I were holding the brush while Picasso moved my hand over the canvas.

"It's going to get faster," he warned.

And holy hell, did it. Silas's fingers danced over the keys, stunningly agile and precise, even with the weight of mine over them. I closed my eyes and could almost pretend the incredible music that filled the room was mine.

Because it was. Because Silas gave it to me. He shared the music in him with me, made me a part of it, and I never wanted anything so bad in my life as I wanted this moment and thousands more just like it. A lifetime of that communion. . . starting with this night.

I slid my fingers down, twining them with his, so that he ceased playing, and the apartment was suddenly quiet. The quiet before the storm. I wrapped myself in his arms, and leaned into him, melted against him.

"Max. . ." he whispered gruffly, then pressed his forehead to my back. I felt the heat of his breath on my skin, through my shirt.

I closed my eyes, relishing the feel of that electric hum, that moment right before the spark ignites.

Those few delicious seconds between the striking of the match and when the flame bursts to life.

CHAPTER TWENTY-THREE

Silas

Max stilled my hands and wrapped my arms around him. I buried my face in the hard muscles of his back, relishing the solidity of him. That such a guy existed in the world and he wanted anything to do with me. . . it was a fucking miracle.

We sat in silence for a moment, while a need that was a thousand times more potent than any physical desire coiled and tensed in me, drawing tighter and tighter. Its intensity scared the shit out of me. I realized how badly I wanted Max—in my space, my bed, my house, my life. . . As if I'd crossed a threshold and the thought of going on without him was torture.

He stood up, moving away from the piano, and I stood with him. I don't know who reached for who first, but in the next instant, we were kissing. Not the mauling, animalistic kisses of last night but deep, intense kisses with promises embedded within each bite and lick and sucking pull.

More. Now.

"Right now," I whispered, and I searched Max's rich brown eyes.

He nodded. "Yeah, Si. God, yes. . ."

We made it to the bedroom on stumbling legs, kicking off shoes and stripping out of shirts. I pressed him to the wall, our mouths crashing together while our hands fumbled at our waists, tearing at buttons and zippers.

"I don't want to. . . hurt you," I said, my heart pounding between my words. "But I want to fuck you so bad, I can hardly see straight."

He arched a brow. "See *straight*? I should hope not."

"Christ, you and your dumb jokes."

I love you and your dumb jokes.

"We have some. . . technicalities to deal with," Max said, nipping at my ear. "I have condoms, but do you have lube?"

I reared back. "Shit, no."

"Aloe?"

"Maybe."

"Go check."

I went to the bathroom and found that Faith had left behind a bunch of bottles and creams, and one of them—thank fuck—had a picture of the spiky plant on the front.

"This do?"

"It works."

"Good, because I'm fucking dying."

Dying for you. To have you. Be in you. . .

Max's smile faded, and he hauled me back to him and kissed me, raw and deep, leaving me no doubt as to his intentions. I felt it in the way his tongue swept across mine and in the heavy hardness of his erection pressing between us. My own cock ached with need, and I bit back a curse as he reached into my pants to stroke me.

"Fuck, Silas," he gritted out. "You might just break me."

His words brought me around to reality, and I pulled back and searched his eyes again. "We never. . . I mean, we didn't talk about who. . ."

"I know what you want, Si," he said, and I could see his pulse pounding in the hollow of his throat beneath his Adam's apple. "And I know what I want. Jesus, I've never wanted anything more."

My eyes fell shut and I kissed him softly for the first and last time that night. After that gentle kiss, our clothes seemed to melt off our bodies in a frenzy of heated kisses and touches that left me dizzy and delirious. Max lay back on the bed and I settled my weight over him, needing for there to be no space between us, no part of our skin that didn't touch. When our hips aligned, my heart crashed against my chest at what he was offering me.

"Max. . ." I growled, his name a plea because I was begging and desperate for him.

"Get me ready. Make it good. That's the deal."

I nodded, understanding flooding me over the heat that raged in my blood. He was letting me in and I had to make it as good for him as possible. To give and not just take. To ensure that he felt safe with me. Because it was going to hurt at first, and my job was to make sure that pain was as short-lived as possible.

"Stop thinking," Max said, reaching to kiss me. His short beard scratched my lips before his hard, hot mouth took mine. "I want this. And I trust you."

I did as he said and stopped thinking and calculating, assessing and weighing. The tools of my cold, perfect life weren't needed here. I succumbed to the night, and to Max, and to being naked with him; touching and kissing him, my hands roaming his body, then finding the condom, the lube. I never stopped kissing him as my fingers prepared him for me. His trust loosened him more than I did, and I could've fucking wept when we were joined, him inhaling the pain and exhaling it out, so that there was nothing left but how good it was.

"You okay?" I breathed.

"Perfect," he whispered back. "But go slow. . . Slow."

I nodded, pressing him on his back and sinking in deep. "Jesus, Max. . ."

"Breathe, baby, breathe."

Baby. God, this guy. It caught me off guard to hear him say it, and even more to discover how much I liked the word in his mouth. I wanted to hear it again and again. . .

But the sensation of being inside him was breaking my thoughts further apart with every thrust of my hips and every tight pull of his body around me.

"Holy shit," I ground out. "You. . .Max. This. . . It's. . ."

It's everything.

It was a thousand wishes coming true. A thousand broken promises to myself becoming whole. A hundred black nights of ice and shock, fear and shame, followed by hundreds more of self-denial and starvation, all washed away under the perfection of this moment with him.

It took all of my control, but I moved slow. The incredible tightness of him around my cock was drawing years of pent up need and want and desire out of me—a fault line finally ready to slip and release. My world became Max. Max's hands pulling at me. Drawing me in deeper. Max's breath, ragged and raw.

"Harder," he gritted out.

I didn't waste breath asking if he was ready for harder. Max knew what he wanted and who he was and I fucking loved that about him. My hips obeyed, and I moved faster, my hands braced on either side of him, propping me up under an onslaught of sensation. The heat of skin and muscle beneath me, the taste of my sweat and tears because—fuck—this was really happening. Not only a completion of us but of something in myself becoming whole at long last.

"God, Max," I breathed between thrusts. "Is this real? Is this fucking real?"

He nodded, his neck corded with the strain of taking all of me, his abs hard and defined. I coaxed a groan out of him with my cock that seesawed faster and harder in him. He craned up to kiss me, hard and biting before falling back against the pillow, his liquid brown eyes dilated with want and shining with love, both for me.

This. This is what wealth feels like. This is privilege. Being here. With him. . .

"Max. . ."

"I'm here," he said, reaching for me. "I'm here, Si. Give it to me. Now. Hard. I want you. Want you so bad."

Christ.

His words were sending me over the edge. He reached between us for his cock, but I knocked his hand away and took him myself. I wanted to give him everything, anything in the fucking world. I braced myself on my right elbow, lowering myself down. Aloe still coated my fingers and I used my left hand to stroke him.

"Ah fuck," Max rasped. "So good. . ."

God yes, it was good. I stroked him as hard and as fast as my thrusts inside him, a rhythm. A harmony. Within seconds, he was arching into me, tensing with a climax that I created in him. With a grunt that morphed into a short, harsh cry, he came on his stomach and over my fingers, and it was mine. *He* was mine. All of him. I owned his release and watched it happen, felt it in his body that shuddered beneath me and tightened around my cock, heard it in his voice and breath that turned ragged.

I kissed him because I wanted to taste it too, but it was too much. My orgasm followed like an explosion of light and heat in a sky that had been dark and cold for so fucking long. I came, shuddering and moaning, my body suddenly at the mercy of Max's that had allowed me in and took my release. *He* took all of it, watching me now with eyes that shone with unshed tears.

"Yes, Si," he said gruffly, his hands roaming my back, my waist, gripping my ass and pressing me into him as my thrusts turned erratic. "Come for me. Fuck, yes. . ."

I floundered and drowned in the delirium of pleasure, heat, and the perfect rightness of us. He brought me down against him where his own sticky release sealed our skin. His arms went around me and held me in their strong embrace, and I collapsed into them, utterly spent. I buried my face in the crook of his shoulder, our chests rising and falling together, while my body hummed and vibrated with the climax that left no nerve-ending untouched.

I'm alive. . .

Gently and slowly, I pulled out of him, raised my head to see him. Max. *My* Max. He was mine and I was his. Fuck yes, I was his. He owned me.

But as the raw heat and intensity of the orgasm mellowed into a warm wave that bathed me after years of cold nothing, reality began to whisper again, stealing little pieces of my happiness.

He doesn't own you. You *don't own you. You are the property of your father, and if you break with him, the souls of all who have been destroyed by addiction. . . they will own you too.*

"Hey," Max said, his eyes searching mine. "Stay with me. Okay?"

I nodded and let him hold me. He wrapped me in his arms and just let me be, exactly as I was. His fingers trailed lazily in my hair. His heartbeat slowed under my hand.

"You okay?"

I nodded. "You?"

He gave a short laugh. "Uh, yeah. I'm a lot more than okay. Holy shit. . ."

"It was good?"

"You couldn't tell?"

"Don't be a smartass, I'm new at this."

"It didn't show." He held my jaw in one hand and kissed me, then met my gaze, unwavering. "Silas, it was fucking perfect. I've never. . ." He swallowed. "In the past, I've never felt like it was. . . mutual, you know?" He shook his head when my eyes widened in anger and alarm. "I consented. I gave the okay. But it wasn't what it should've been. Ever. Until tonight."

I didn't have the words for the emotion that roared in me, making my eyes sting and my throat close. Instead, I kissed Max, hard and deep, and grasped him tightly. Protectively. I vowed to end the next person who tried to hurt him.

I should've known that person would be me.

CHAPTER TWENTY-FOUR

Silas

"Some people will trot out that childish phrase, love is love, as if there are no differences at all." Coach Braun said, the campfire casting dancing shadows over his narrow face.

The seven boys huddle close around the fire, looking attentive to his words, but were mostly trying to keep warm. Behind us, somewhere in the dark, the counselors loomed. It was our first night after being settled in, and the utter mistake of coming here—of agreeing *to come here—was sinking in with the cold and filling me with dread.*

"But there are differences, aren't there?" Coach said. "The very fact a woman conceives a child after the physical act of sexual intercourse in order to propagate our species tells you that's what the act is for. No other reason."

I withheld a snort. What bullshit. I sincerely doubted the porn industry existed to help "propagate the species." This guy, Braun, was a lot dumber than he had been in our living room, explaining his program.

"What about love?" I asked.

The others snickered but I held my chin up, my gaze unwavering from Coach's.

"You have thoughts you'd like to share, young Silas?" he asked, studying me.

"Mom told me when two people love each other, they screw. And not just to make babies."

A gasp went around, followed by more snickers. No one was afraid. Yet.

Coach smiled with condescension, unrattled. "I've no doubt she was speaking of the love between a man and a woman—"

"What if I love someone?" I asked. "A boy. What if I love a boy?"

The other guys in the ring froze; only their eyes moving as they darted glances at one another.

Coach Braun's black gaze held mine. "Go on."

I felt the promise of danger in those two words and the emptiness of his eyes. The first sliver of real fear slid into my gut, but I couldn't—wouldn't—stop myself.

"What if I love how he laughs, or the funny things he says, or how he's polite to little old ladies, or how he loves dogs, or how he recycles religiously because he cares about the environment?" I stared defiantly. "What about that?"

Coach Braun never blinked. "Those are only reasons your mind gives in order to make the physical act seem justified. But it isn't."

"You're saying—"

"I'm saying, young Silas," Coach's voice rose up in the night, hard and stony, like a preacher on Sunday morning. "That in your present state, there is no love. Only lust that will twist all reasoning to make the unnatural seem natural."

Booted footsteps crunched the dead leaves behind me.

Braun addressed the group. "I'm grateful to young Silas for advancing our lessons with these thoughtful questions. Because the first lesson you're here to learn, boys, is that you have sinned. You are sinners in the eyes of God. Only if you get that, feel it, and know it to be true, can your path be clear. Do you know that to be true?"

Heads nodded.

"Time will tell. But it's clear Silas does not know that to be true. We're going to help him."

The two counselors yanked me to my feet and started stripping off my *jacket, my hat. . .I fought back like a wild animal until a fist knocked me senseless. Then I was marched, naked and barefoot across the rocky shore of the lake, a dozen feet from the campfire.*

Coach Braun had stood up, instructed the other boys to do the same. "The first step on the path of every sinner begins with purification."

The water touched my foot, and a deep ache filled my bones and traveled up my legs. The counselors, gripping my upper arms painfully, shoved me out farther and the water came up higher, stealing my breath and making me shiver until my teeth rattled and my skin turned a pale, blue-ish white in the moonlight.

"A baptism to purify you," Coach Braun said from somewhere in the darkness behind me. "The first of many."

I could hardly breathe, or move, or think except for one thought that went around and around my aching, panicked head.

I'm going to die, I'm going to die, I'm going to die. . .

"And after purification, comes atonement. . ."

I gasped awake, my chest constricted, my skin broken in gooseflesh, because that cold. . .that goddamn cold was all over me.

"Si. . .?"

My bedroom materialized around me in the dimness, and the icy fingers of the lake slid away from me to be replaced by warm, strong hands. Max.

He reached for me and tried to pull me back into the safety and perfection of last night. I lay on my side, Max wrapped around me, his face buried in the back of my neck. I felt the heat of his breath against my skin.

"Nightmare?" he murmured, hugging me tighter. It wasn't yet light out.

"Yeah."

But it wasn't a nightmare. It was a memory. It had happened. And it was still happening. I left Chisana years ago, but it was in my blood and bones. I carried it with me. I could smell the brackish water on my skin. Couldn't he?

Max's arms tightened around me, protectively. "Goddamn that place. I wish I could erase it for you. Take it from you." He kissed my neck, my shoulder. "I would if I could."

My eyes fell shut as a thousand emotions swamped me, every one with his name on it. I lay still, stiff, trying to contain them as last night warred with Alaska.

Because I haven't gone anywhere, I'm still right there. It's right here...

Disgust at myself flooded me, and I tore away from Max.

"Fuck," I snarled, sitting up. "*Fuck.*"

"Hey, Si," Max said, his voice low and calm. "Talk to me."

"This is bullshit. I thought I was done, Max. I thought it was *over.*" I pulled out of the warmth of the bed, my back to him, yanked on my boxers with shaking hands.

I heard a rustling of bedsheets behind me and the lamp clicked on. Max had pushed himself up against the headboard, his hands in his lap. God, he was so fucking beautiful, watching me with love written in every line of him. Love for me.

He can't love me. I can't love him. Not like this. Because this poison... this icy poison is going to follow me forever.

"Si," Max said, concern thickening his voice as he watched the anguish play over my face. "Please... tell me what you're thinking."

"Why?" I demanded, hearing the crazed desperation in my own voice. I was on the verge of freaking the fuck out and couldn't stop myself. "Why, Max?"

"Because I'm here for you," he said. "Tell me and—"

"No, I mean, why isn't it just sex? Just fucking? Because that I can control. Why does there have to be so many...?"

"So many what?"

"*Feelings*. Emotions. Where the hell is it all coming from? I feel like I'm drowning. Why does my heart...?" My words choked off; tears stung my eyes. "Why does my damn heart have to feel so full—no, *saturated* with you, Max? It's so goddamn full of you, I'm petrified it's going to spill over or shatter into a million different pieces."

Max came to me, and his hand shot out to grip the back of my neck, his fingers sinking into my hair. He met my gaze unblinking.

"Hey. Look at me. It won't," he rasped out. "Because the last thing in this world I want to do is break your heart. You're safe with me, Silas. I've told you that and I mean it."

"They said it wasn't possible," I gritted out. "To feel this way..."

"They lied," Max said, his voice trembling. "They lied, Silas. You have to know that."

"Yeah, I know that. But the sick part, Max, is that it doesn't make a damn bit of difference. I think I am free and then the nightmares come, and everything that was tortured into us comes back up. Is that a life? Is that *my* life? Forever?"

Max's eyes swam with anger and agony. He held me to him, his warm skin seeking to erase the icy nightmare. But it would only come again. I could lose myself in him a thousand times; I could be *happy*. . .but it wouldn't last. The cold nightmare of Alaska would take it all away. Beat me down again and again.

Max felt my shoulders slump in defeat. His grip loosened and then slid away. "Maybe we're moving too fast. You've been through a lot and I. . ." He swallowed. "I should've thought of that."

It wasn't too soon. It's been perfect, but I ruined it. I'm ruining it

"Right," I snarled, disgust at myself giving me new energy. "You should have thought of that while I was attacking you, kissing you, trying to get inside you as fast as possible."

Max gathered his clothes, pulled on his jeans. "PTSD isn't simple. It doesn't follow rules. Even if it leaves you alone for a little while, trauma like you experienced isn't going to vanish overnight. But Si, don't."

"Don't what?"

"Don't let them take from you what we have."

The nakedness of his feelings; it was all over him. In his words, his eyes and the way they looked at me. It tore a rift in me. Everything that had been beaten into me in Chisana tried to freeze over what I was feeling for him. The cold was a shield. Armor. That's what they taught us. Max was stripping it away, leaving me weak and defenseless.

"It's not. . .that," I said. "I told you, I have shit to do. There's a lot at stake if I don't stop Milton and our company from bulldozing thousands more lives. It's happening every minute. Every hour that I'm sitting here with you."

Max closed his eyes for a second, absorbing that, and I hated myself more for hurting him.

When he opened his eyes, he spoke in a low, controlled voice.

"If you want to be free of Alaska, Silas, you need to take your life back from your father. If you're ever going to be free of the shame and the guilt and the violence that haunts you, that's where you start. With the man who put you through it all in the first place."

He finished dressing and made to go, and I came to my goddamn senses. I grabbed him, held him, inhaled him.

"I'm sorry," I whispered against his neck. "I'm so fucking sorry. Please. Don't go. I'm sorry. . ."

My mouth sought his, desperate to reclaim these last few days. To put it all back the way it had been—real and perfect and good. Max kissed me, and the spark started to ignite, but then he pulled back. Pushed me away.

"I can't. . .I have to get to work. And I think we should. . .take a little breather. It's better. For both of us."

My own stubborn pride had me tilting my chin up. "Yeah, okay."

He ignored my false bravado and reached up to cup my jaw. He kissed me softly, melting the hard smirk off my lips and suddenly I was on the verge of begging at his feet again to stay.

"I'm here for you, Silas," he said. "I truly am. What they did to you was unspeakable and I will stand by you every step of the way as you come back from it. But you have to fight."

"What do you think I'm doing? I'm fighting to take back—"

"Not the company. You. Fight for you." He swallowed hard. "And for us."

Max went to the door and hesitated, his hand on the knob.

"You're not the only one of us who's scared shitless. Your heart isn't the only one that's. . ." He bit off his words, his jaw working. "Do what you have to do, but don't break mine, Silas. I'm fucking begging you. Don't do it."

Then he was gone.

A day later, I'd hardly moved from my couch, waiting for Sylvia to get back to me with the data from IT. I'd lied to Max about that too. There was no work for me to do until I heard from her. I had nothing to do but feel Max's absence in every damn corner of my apartment.

On the second day, I found my backbone and called him.

"Hey," he answered, sounding sad. And wary.

Afraid of how I'm going to hurt him next.

"I'm sorry," I said immediately. "I'm so fucking sorry."

He sighed. "It's okay, Si. . ."

"No, it's not okay. I just. . ." I scrubbed my hand over my eyes. "It's so much bigger than me, what I'm trying to do. I just need a little bit of time. I'm waiting on some stuff that might help and then. . . We can go from there. Okay?"

I held my breath.

"Yeah, of course," he said. "I know it's a lot. What you're trying to do. I don't want to stand in the way of that. I've been there. Those people need help."

Hot tears stung my eyes. *He's too good. Too good for the world. For me.*

"Yeah, okay, thanks," I said, my throat thick.

A silence.

"Okay, Si. Well. . . Talk to you later?"

Jesus, I had no words. Nothing to say that would bridge the gap I'd created between us by freaking out.

"Yeah, talk later," I said.

"Yup," he said and ended the call.

I'm losing him. . .

I wanted to call him back immediately, but I didn't trust myself not to fuck things up worse. I let the phone fall to the carpet and went back to doing nothing on the couch while the TV blared nonsense.

Apathy, I learned, was like a ravenous animal. The more you fed it, the hungrier it got. The less I did, the less I felt like doing.

Two days later, I was still on the couch. I had lost all track of time. There was no news from the office. Dad's Halloween party was fast-approaching, and I hadn't gotten in touch with Faith about coming with me. To keep up appearances. To put on the costume of soon-to-be man and wife.

My phone rang. I muted ESPN and rolled over on the couch from where I'd been lying like a slug. I grabbed it without even looking at the incoming number.

"Max. . ."

"It's Sylvia," my assistant said, her voice breathless.

"Oh, hey." I coughed. "Did you get it?"

"I got it. All of it. But Milton knows."

I bolted up straight. "Shit. I thought IT was going to keep it quiet."

"He's got worms everywhere. But holy shit, Silas, these emails. I've only scanned a few, but it's astounding what's been done. What he's *said*. . . I think you have something here. Enough to get him out of your job, but he could also be in real trouble, too. Maybe even do some jail time."

I bit my lip, thinking fast. *None of it matters if he gets to Dad first. Or if he already did.*

"When did IT spill it?"

"Don't know, but a friend in the executive offices told me Milton was going to be out for the day."

Fuck me.

"Go through it all, Sylvia," I said, heading for the bathroom. "Hire a team if you need to and get back to me with the worst of it."

"On it."

I hung up and took a sixty-second shower, threw on jeans and a long-sleeved shirt, then raced to the parking garage. It was hardly eight a.m., but a sinking feeling in my gut told me I was already too late.

This is it, I thought, as I raced the Aston out of the city and to the estate. *Maybe Max was right. I fix this shit with Dad and then I'm free.*

But like an icy nightmare grabbing and shaking me in the night, stepping into the house poked at sleeping demons. A chill broke out over my skin.

"Fuck that," I muttered as I raced through the house to Dad's suite.

I was too late.

Stephen Milton sat in the chair beside Dad's bed. Dad had a laptop propped on his stomach. Stephen smiled placidly, in victory.

The waters of the lake crashed over me, submerged me in their frigid depths as my father shook his head at me, once.

He knows.

"I'm afraid, Silas, we're going to have to send you back."

My head whipped up, my heart stammered in my chest, and terror skimmed along every nerve.

"What did you say?"

My father pursed his lips. "I said, I'm afraid we're going to have to have a chat."

A shaking breath rasped out of me and I attempted to scrape together some composure. A wave of nausea washed over me, though anger burned it away just as quickly. There was nothing in those *Seattle Society* photos to be ashamed about. Not one thing. . .

I strode in, glancing briefly at the nurse in the room and thanking every god in the cosmos it was Dale and not Max. I shot him an icy stare, and he hurried out, muttering something about getting more coffee.

"As I was saying," Milton droned, "*Seattle Society* is a very prolific blog with thousands of followers. Their stories are often shared to other online publications and social media."

"This post is several weeks old," Edward said, his voice toneless. Unreadable.

"Why, yes," Milton said. "I would have brought it to your attention sooner, had I known—"

"That's bullshit," I said, finding my voice, each word out of my mouth layered in frost. "I've uncovered evidence that shows Stephen has not been acting in our best interests, nor that of our customers. He threatened to show you these"—I waved a dismissive hand at the laptop—"if I took further action. Which I have."

"And what are these?" Edward asked slowly. "You and Maxwell. . .?"

I clenched my jaw at those words coming out of my father's mouth. The fear and shame that had haunted me my entire life since Mom died was alive and well and right here in this room.

I swallowed hard.

"Max is a medical professional and has experience in treating overdose victims from his time in the ER. I showed him some preliminary data on the over-prescription of OxyPro to get his advice. That's all."

Yep, that's all, I thought, as I erased everything between us in two words.

A silence fell in which Dad scrutinized me, searching for signs of my weakness. Milton coughed into his fist.

"I must say, the insinuation of the article, not to mention the photos themselves, indicate quite a more personal relationship—"

"That's none of your fucking business," I snapped. "Who gives a crap what a tabloid gossip thinks? There were probably a dozen boring photos of us talking, chewing, or scratching our asses. But those are useless to a gossip-monger who wants to stir up shit, aren't they?"

Milton stammered while Dad's gaze went between us, studying, calculating.

"And where is this *bombshell* documentation about Stephen?" he asked me.

Here, I faltered. "It's being collected."

"Indeed," Milton said, regaining his composure. "Silas has taken it upon himself to abuse his post as Chief Operating Officer in order to raid the server in which I have kept confidential company memos and emails concerning our marketing strategies."

"It's not confidential if it's company property," Dad said.

My shoulders rose and fell with an infinitesimal sigh of relief.

"However," he continued. "I grow tired of this conversation, Silas. I am not interested in your attempts to undermine Stephen or our company's business practices because you're concerned about a few addicts who misused our product. And Mr. Kaufman is to be terminated immediately."

My eyes widened. "What? Why? He did nothing wrong."

"His contract is employment-at-will. I need give no explanation. However. . ." He folded his hands on his stomach. "I cannot violate our state's anti-discrimination laws regarding race, religion or. . . sexual orientation. If you believe Max might have cause to sue for wrongful termination, it would be prudent to tell me." His eyes bored into me. "Is there something you want to tell me?"

A thick silence fell, and I held my breath. Every cell in my body stood at attention, waiting for me to do what Max had said and fight for us. To fight for myself. To say at last, *"Yes, I have something to tell you. Max is with me. I'm with him. He's everything to me. . ."*

I opened my mouth to say the words and saw stairways leading to nowhere. Doors that opened on brick walls. Milton, taking OxyPro to Indonesia. To Asia. All over the fucking world.

I'm sorry, Max. Just a little longer. . .

"No," I said, my eyes forward, my voice as cold as ice. "There's nothing."

CHAPTER TWENTY-FIVE

Max

I dressed for work on automatic, my head stewing in conflict and heartache. I'd slogged through the last few days, trying my damnedest not to let the overthinking control my life. But aside from the one, strained phone call, Silas and I hadn't spoken.

He needed me to wait for him but for how long?

Thanksgiving dinner loomed on the horizon, carrying with it all of my hopes for reuniting with my dad, and Silas couldn't be there. I'd have to show up alone while my brother and sister were surrounded by the families they'd made. Their "stable situations."

"So, Max, where is the special someone you were supposed to bring to dinner?"

"Oh, he can't be seen with me in public, but trust me, we're in a very stable situation."

I snorted a laugh, but as I headed out for my shift with Edward, the unsettling feeling had sunk into my bones. Nothing was stable between Silas and me. The ferocity of my feelings for him scared me shitless. I was supposed to be protecting myself, and yet...

I'm falling in love with him.

"Mr. Kaufman, my good man," Eddie said, meeting me in the grand foyer, startling me out of my thoughts.

"Hey, Eddie."

"I say, it looks like Papa is going to throw a Halloween fete, the likes of which we haven't seen in this household in years."

He indicated the workers who were busy around the clock these last few days. Those in the foyer were lacing the banister with delicate—and realistic-looking—cobwebs and putting in light installations that I was told would suffuse the room with shades of green and purple.

I'd never been to a Halloween party thrown in a billionaire's mansion, but I had a feeling there wasn't going to be a lot of bobbing for apples and people dressed as pregnant nuns.

"Yeah, it looks like it's going to be pretty epic," I said. "Do you have a costume?"

Eddie rocked on his heels, a pleased smile cast to the marble floor. "Indeed, I am going as Charles Dickens."

I smiled. Eddie could've passed for Dickens every day.

"And who shall you be, Mr. Kaufman?"

"Frank-N-Furter from *The Rocky Horror Picture Show*."

I have no idea why that popped out of my mouth, except the sudden image of me bursting into the crowded party in full drag and sending Edward into a fit made me want to laugh. And I needed to laugh.

Eddie tapped his chin thoughtfully. "Can't say I've heard of Frank-N-Furter. Some sort of hot dog, perchance?"

I chuckled again but it faded fast. "No, I'm kidding. I'm not going to the party. In fact, I don't know that staff are even invited."

Not to mention the last thing I want to do is stand across the room from Silas all night, pretending there's nothing between us.

Eddie's glance flickered to me, then back to the floor.

"Hmm, you seem rather down in the dumps, old chap. I have not seen Silas in a few days, myself. I was hoping ever so much we might have another outing, the three of us. Is this the cause of your melancholy as well? His absence?"

"Yeah, I miss him," I admitted, because why not? Eddie was my friend.

"Keep your chin up, my good man. It is always darkest before the dawn, as they say. And I do hope you'll change your mind about attending the party. I would so enjoy seeing your hot dog costume."

He tipped an imaginary cap and strolled on.

Running into Eddie reminded me that I had been so wrapped up in my own misery, I'd forgotten to speak to Edward about Marjorie's request for a group home. I dragged myself up the stairs and to Edward's suite.

Stephen Milton sat beside Edward, and on the other side was Silas. My heart dropped to my knees. Silas stood like a statue. A block of ice. The man I knew—in bed, at the piano, laughing in the kitchen while eating cold chow mein—was gone.

"Ah, Mr. Kaufman," Edward said. "Just in time. We were just discussing your termination."

Heat flamed my skin and Silas whipped his head to his father. "Dad. For fuck's sake. . ."

"What's the issue?" Edward inquired. "You've already explained to me how he means nothing beyond the usefulness of his medical background."

Each word socked me in the gut, adding to the humiliation of three pairs of eyes on me, as Edward stripped me of my job and my experience, ground them to nothing.

"Why am I being terminated?" My eyes were on Edward but I was asking Silas.

"Because I no longer require your services," Edward said. "Nothing more. There's nothing more to be said. Isn't that right, Silas?"

Silas's jaw clenched and pain swam in his eyes. "It doesn't matter what I think or don't think. He shouldn't lose his job—"

Edward folded his paper calmly. "I've heard enough. Stephen, will I see you and Helen at the party?"

A smile of victory oozed over Milton's lips. "Wouldn't miss it."

"Very good. Now if you will both excuse us, I have a few matters to discuss with Maxwell."

Milton nodded and slipped out without another word. Silas hesitated, and I felt the conflicted tension humming in his body. I met his gaze, unblinking, chin up.

Fight for us. . .

"Silas," Edward said. A command that must be obeyed.

And he did.

I watched him walk out the door without a word, dragging my heart behind him.

My eyes fell shut until Edward cleared his throat.

"Do you think I'm stupid?" he asked.

I blinked and forced my stiff neck to look at him. My entire body ached; I felt Silas's departure in my bones.

"What?"

He spoke slowly, enunciating each word as if to a child. "Do you think I'm stupid?"

I straightened, pulling my own armor around me. I inhaled through my nose. "I think you are many things, Mr. Marsh, but stupid is not one of them."

"I don't believe you," Edward said. "I think you listened to what the rest of the staff were saying. That you were my *favorite*." His lips curled around the word. "As if that were possible."

"I didn't believe them," I said, my voice low and controlled. "Because I know it's impossible for you to feel anything for anyone."

He waved my words away as if they were annoying, harmless.

"I've known about you, from the beginning," he said. "Why do you think I've kept you close? Because you're useful to me. You can give a shot better than the rest. Well done."

My face flushed red; my throat went dry. He pushed himself to sit higher in his bed, and I felt as if he were towering over me and not the other way around.

"But I saw how you looked at my son that morning at the pool. I knew then you were one of the degenerates who wanted money, maybe, and seeking to undo all of my plans for my company. My legacy. But do you see?"

He gestured to the door where Silas had walked out. The empty space where he'd been.

"He didn't choose you, Maxwell," Edward said. "He will never choose you."

The humiliation was a roaring fire, the pain its dull glow beneath. Words piled up in my mouth. Graphic descriptions of all that Silas and I had done in his bed, in the shower, in the rain. . .

But it wasn't my place to implode Silas's life. It wasn't right. Not to win a few parting shots on his psychopath of a father and ruin whatever chance he had at helping the people he wanted to help.

He has to fight for us, himself. Not because I forced him to.

"Have you nothing to say?" Edward inquired. "If not, you may collect your belongings and see Cesar about your severance."

I started to go, then stopped at the door. "My name is not Maxwell."

He looked up from his paper. "Hm?"

"My name. It's not fucking Maxwell."

Edward peered at me over his glasses. "Does it really matter?"

I took the stairs down two at a time and then back up to the west wing. I keyed into my room, grabbed my suitcase and started throwing my clothes into it. I kept moving, not giving myself a chance to think. I called an Uber, then hit the bathroom, scraping my soap and shave gel out of the sinks, the shower. Scouring the room of my presence. I gathered my things in an armload, and when I came back out, Silas was there.

Tall, solid, dressed in casual but elegant clothes. He looked beautiful, not at all like a guy who'd just had his guts ripped out, his identity—his humanity—shit on like it was nothing.

"You left the door open," he said.

"And you shut it behind you," I said, then dumped my stuff in the open suitcase. "No one will ever know you're here."

"I didn't want this to happen," he said, his voice rough. "You know that."

"No, I don't know that," I snapped. "But it doesn't fucking matter. I should've quit a long time ago. I should've quit as soon as I recognized you. I should've quit the first time your father said the word 'fag' in my presence."

Silas crossed his arms. "Then nothing would have happened between us. Is that what you'd prefer?"

I whirled on him. "Are you fucking kidding me? You don't get to ask me that, Silas. You can't put that on me. I'm not the one telling your father that what we are is nothing."

Silas swallowed. "What did he say to you?"

"You mean, what did I say to *him*? Did I blow your cover?" I hurled a ball of socks into the suitcase. "No. You're safe. You can go back to your winter hibernation."

"Max," Silas said, his voice low. "Wait. Please."

I stopped my violent yanking of the luggage zipper and put my hands on my hips, head bowed, my breaths coming short.

"What I'm feeling right now?" I said. "It feels like shit. It feels exactly how I promised myself I'd never feel again." A harsh laugh burst out of me. "I was kicked out of my house by my father for being gay. Seven years later, I'm being kicked out of this house by *your* father for being gay. He can't say that's why. *I* can't say that's why, but it is. The fucking circle of life."

I'm right back where I started...

The thought made me sick.

"Max..."

I raised my eyes to his. "He tortured you, Si. Why the hell do you stay?"

He blinked and gave his head a short, baffled shake. "Because he's my father. Are you trying to tell me you don't get that? What about your torture, Max? Your dad kicked you out. You were homeless, doing drugs... You had to sell yourself on the street to survive, right? And yet you're still trying. Again and again, we keep trying because it's family."

"Yeah, I'm trying. One last time. I'm going to a dinner that you can't come to because you can't be seen with me—"

"What dinner? Where?"

"Harvest Inn. Thanksgiving," I muttered, resuming packing. "I'm not home-worthy yet, apparently, so it's at a fucking restaurant, a month away..." I shook my head. "I just have to wait a little longer. Wait for him. Wait for you. I've *been* waiting for seven years."

Silas's jaw worked. "I'm sorry," he said, his voice hardly a whisper. "I hate doing this to you. I really fucking do."

I hated what I was doing too. I'd told Silas I'd be there for him, but what Edward had said to me... The sudden termination, the humiliation and pain of it, the rejection... It all wrapped around me, suffocating, reminding me of why I'd fought so hard to protect myself. The memories of being kicked out of my house and the reasons why were blending and dissolving into the present, becoming indistinguishable.

"It's all the same," I said, an edge of rising anguish to my voice. "I came so far and worked so hard and for what? For it to happen all over again. And I can't do it. I thought I could, but I can't."

"Do what?"

"Us. This. Right now. I can't do it again."

"Don't say that," Silas said. He moved to me, reached for me. "Fuck, Max, please don't say that."

Silas's eyes were shining, his mouth a grim line, as if he were holding back a torrent. He gripped the short sleeve of my uniform, tugged me to him. His second hand joined the first, pulling me in until he had me, arms wrapped around my back, making fists with my shirt, his face buried in my neck.

"I'm sorry," he said. "I'm so sorry. Please. Let me fix it. Please wait for me."

He lifted his head and the tears in his eyes were a mirror of mine. Our lips touched, our mouths brushing, seeking, wanting entry. It would have been so easy to give in. . .

"I can't," I breathed. "I can't. . ."

Wait under the streetlight. Hold on or let go. Hold onto myself or give it away.

Silas pulled away with a curse and wiped his eyes with his shoulder. "What are you saying? You're. . . done?"

"I don't know. But I can't let this go any further until you tell your father the truth. Because if we keep doing this. . . If we keep kissing and sleeping together and then you choose. . ." I swallowed the tears in my throat. "If you choose to go back to your old life, then I'm done for."

"I won't. I won't go back to that."

You're still in it.

Silas read my thoughts, saw them in my eyes. He bit out another curse and paced a small circle.

"I'm trapped. If I walk away from the company, I leave all those people behind. But if I don't break with Dad, I lose you, is that it? An ultimatum?"

"No," I said. "You break with him and you save yourself. And you'll find another way to help—"

"How?"

"I don't know, but it'll find you when you choose the life you want. That's what I'm doing. All my life, I had to choose happiness. It wasn't handed to me. I had to go out and find it. I found a new family who loved me just as I was, and so can you. You can choose a different life. Choose me, Silas. I'll love you for who you are, and we'll have a shot at happy."

The turmoil in him rose to the surface of his eyes. I felt the push and pull in him, and how he wanted to believe me. But he shook his head, eyes hardening.

"I'm so close. I have Milton by the balls. Goddammit, Max, I just need a *little more time.*"

"What am I supposed to do in the meanwhile?" I cried, frustration and pain erupting out of me. "You want to keep me stashed in your apartment, ducking into the next room when the bell rings? Midnight hook-ups? More street corner blowjobs? I'm not your pressure valve. I don't exist so you can express your homosexuality whenever you feel the need and then return to your life without me."

"That's not what's happening here. That night with you. . ." A muscle ticked in his cheek. "It was fucking everything. But there is more at stake here than what I want or who—"

"Who you are?"

Silas's jaw clenched. "There are thousands. . . hundreds of thousands of lives on the line if I don't take control of this company."

"I know," I said. "And I hate that everything I'm saying makes me feel like a selfish asshole, but I can't go on like we have. Being with you. Falling more and more. . ." I bit off my words. "I can't do it, Si. I promised myself I wouldn't, and I won't."

Silas swallowed hard, chin tilted up. "Then I won't ask you to."

A silence fell, and neither of us moved.

"Well?" Silas said, his voice cracking along with my heart. "If you're going to go, go."

I left.

CHAPTER TWENTY-SIX

Max

I sat on the front stoop of Daniel's apartment.
He wasn't home. At work, maybe. I didn't call or text him.
I just sat and waited.

He'd let me back on his couch, or I could go to a hotel. I had plenty of money. Cesar said a "large severance" would be deposited that day.

He also said he hated to see me go.

So did Ramona who got wind of my leaving as she did everything else. She hugged me and wiped away a tear or two.

Marjory wasn't there. She had taken Eddie out on a bicycle ride. He was going out more and more lately. I was glad for that. And glad I didn't have to say goodbye to him.

I don't think I would have handled that very well.

So I sat as the morning haze gave away to an afternoon haze, my own thoughts vague and hazy too. Like they used to be after a long night of partying when the drugs were wearing off. My skin felt hot and stretched tight. My head was stuffed with cotton.

I thought about calling Darlene, but she was in rehearsals for a big show.

It wouldn't be right to show up on her doorstep, no matter how badly I wanted to. So I sat a little longer.

When the first raindrops splattered my leather jacket, I hardly noticed. I was still wearing my Marsh scrubs. I had forgotten that until a passing lady asked if I were just getting off my shift at the hospital.

I fished out my phone to call an Uber and take me. . . somewhere. A hotel after all, I guessed.

I hit the little green receiver icon, and a list of recents popped up. My sister's North Carolina number was at the top of the list.

Before I could think about it, I touched her number and the phone rang.

"Hello?"

"Rach. . ."

Jesus, my voice sounded like I'd been swallowing rocks.

"Max? Is that you? Are you okay?"

"Yeah, it's me," I said. "So hey, I was wondering if that offer still stands."

It took all I had to get the words out.

"What offer?" She sucked in a breath. "Wait, yes. I remember. I'll bundle us up on the couch and we'll cry together. Right?"

I nodded against the phone. "That's the one."

"Yes," Rachel said, from across three thousand miles and so many lost years. "*Yes,* Max. Come here. Come right now. Right this minute."

I turned my back to the busy street; my hand held the phone so tight my knuckles ached.

"I'm on my way."

PART II

The really great men must, I think, have great sadness on earth."
— Fyodor Dostoevsky, *Crime and Punishment*

CHAPTER TWENTY-SEVEN

Silas

"Yoo-hoo! Special delivery!" A woman's sing-song voice filtered in from the front entry of my apartment. "Did someone order a beard?"

I glanced up from the data Sylvia had brought me earlier that day and that lay strewn over my coffee table.

Faith waltzed in dressed in a woman's long skirt, circa 1930—maroon, with a matching, tight-fitting sweater that had beige and gold stripes along the front and sleeves. A cigar dangled out of her red-painted lips, and her hair was coiffed and ironed so that it looked like a helmet of blonde ripples, with a small black beret pinned to the back.

"Whaddya think?" She did a spin, a blue, pin-striped suit in a dry-cleaning bag hanging off her fingers. "We're Bonnie and Clyde. It's perfect, right? It's a couples costume, so that'll please Big Daddy, but there were rumors that Clyde was a repressed gay man. . .win-win! Very meta, don't you think?"

"Great."

Faith tucked the cigar in a pocket of her skirt, kissed my cheek, and handed me the suit.

I tossed it onto the couch beside me. "Thanks."

"I beg your pardon, that's vintage, honey. Be a little careful?" She smoothed the suit on the back of the couch and plopped down beside me. "What's all this?"

"Enough evidence that hopefully proves Milton belongs in jail, not running Marsh Pharma."

Faith rolled her eyes. "Do you ever stop working?"

"This is big," I said, stuffing the printed emails in my briefcase. "Sylvia found me a treasure trove. This is how I get the company back."

"Well, I'm happy if you're happy." She frowned and cocked her head at me. "You don't look happy. In fact, you look like shit, honey. The dark circles under your eyes have circles."

"I haven't been sleeping well."

Or eating, or breathing, or living.

Because I had to keep doing all those things without Max.

"Speaking of not sleeping. . ." Faith said, glancing around. "Since I still have my key, I'd hoped to walk in on you and Max, preferably naked and doing all sorts of. . . Uh oh. Where is he?"

"I don't know."

"Oh dear." Faith laid soft fingers on my arm. "What happened?"

I leaned back on the couch and scrubbed my hands over my face. "I fucked up."

"How?"

"Dad caught us. Sort of. The *Seattle Society* photos finally came to bite me in the ass."

"You could have talked your way around those."

"I did. But Dad fired Max anyway. And I let him."

"Damn." Faith pursed her lips. "But wait a sec. I see a definite upside to Max *not* living in your dad's house. Many upsides. For instance, he suddenly needs a place to live and you happen to have six acres of penthouse. Not to mention that huge bed— "

"I told you, I don't know where he is," I said irritably. "Somewhere in North Carolina. I got one text two weeks ago that said he's okay and that's it. He won't see me until I get this shit sorted out with Dad. Hopefully tonight. I'm going to take all this crap and force him to look at it."

"Sounds like a super fun party," Faith muttered. "Look, I'd love to see

Milton slink back to whatever swamp he came from as much as the next gal, but what if your sneaky corporate caper doesn't work? What if your father keeps dangling that CEO carrot in front of you? What happens to you? What happens to you and Max?"

"Dad has to listen," I said. "If this doesn't end in a reasonable amount of time, there is no me and Max."

God, just the thought made me want to puke.

"Drama queen," Faith said. "It can't be *that* bad."

No, it's worse.

Every night, my hand reached across an empty bed. Instead of hauling him close to me, I hugged a damn pillow that was soft and cold—everything he was not. In the shower, I stroked myself thinking about him, but I couldn't get hard. Remembering him wasn't enough. I needed all of him. His voice, his dumb jokes, his laugh; and that quiet smile of his that made my damn heart beat. I lived for that smile. . .

You hurt him. Live with that.

"Silas?"

"It's bad. Max doesn't want to hide. No, he doesn't want to *be hidden*. And he doesn't deserve to be."

"Have you tried paying him gobs of money?" Faith asked. "Worked for me."

I didn't crack a smile but scrubbed my hands through my hair. "Maybe he's better off."

Faith made an annoying, gameshow buzzer sound. "Wrong answer. You're better *with* him. You're *you* with him." She touched my cheek. "Aren't you?"

I nodded miserably. "But it's not just about me. I have to do what's right. I have to try to make something out of this company. Dad doesn't want a legacy of shit, either. I know he doesn't."

"I hate to break it to you, my darling, but your father is. . . How do you say? Ah, yes. An asshole."

"He wasn't always like this."

"Like what? A raging homophobe that would rather give his company to Milton, a penis with eyes, than his own son?"

She flapped her hand before I could answer.

"It's none of my business anyway," she said, then tapped her tooth with a red lacquered fingernail. "I take it back. . . It sort of is my business. Thank you for the party fee."

"Thanks for handling the costumes."

"They're completely authentic," she said, getting up to go to the kitchen. "Spared no expense."

I smirked. Of course, she didn't; I'd paid for them.

"Silas, baby. Stop pining and go shower, shave, and get changed. You have me until midnight."

"And then what? You turn into a pumpkin?"

"No, silly," she said. "Then I charge time-and-a-half."

"Holy moly," Faith said and gave a whistle between her teeth as the car rolled into the front drive. "I'll say this about Edward, he knows how to throw a party."

The mansion was lit with splashes of orange, purple and green along the stone walls. Guests were arriving in limos and sedans, many wearing evening attire and masquerade masks instead of actual costumes, though I saw plenty of those too. Elaborate, expensive costumes, as if the guests had emerged from wardrobe trailers on a movie set. One group of people were dressed as a Hollywood-ready version of The Addams Family, including a dog dressed as Cousin It, with flowing hair covering its entire body.

We entered the foyer that was draped with cobwebs, expertly swathed on the stair banisters and chandelier. More purple and green lights added an eerie effect. I might've been impressed but the only thing on my mind was that Faith was clinging to my arm instead of Max's strong hand, and if I fucked up tonight. . .

I felt myself bending under the weight of what could be lost if I failed. A flood of OxyPro into Indonesia and losing Max. The actual world and mine, both at stake.

Cesar, wearing an old-fashioned-looking tuxedo, was greeting guests and directing them to a coat check that also took cell phones, as no one was allowed photos of the guests or the house except for pre-approved media.

He greeted Faith and me with a polite smile.

"What is your costume, Cesar?" I asked for lack of something better. "You look like a butler."

"I am a butler, sir."

Faith whacked me in the arm. "He's Mr. Carson, obviously."

"Obviously, I don't know who that is."

"From *Downton Abbey*." Faith beamed. "You look perfect, Cesar."

He bowed. "Thank you, Miss Bonnie. Mr. Clyde."

I excused myself to stow my briefcase of emails and memos in the safe in the library. When I came back, Faith handed me a blue plastic shotgun with a fake wooden stock.

"Do I have to?"

"Yes." She leaned into me. "We're your accessories. Without us, you're nothing but a devastatingly handsome man in a suit secretly pining after same."

"Don't remind me."

I glanced down at the plastic machine gun. But for its coloring, it was designed to be authentic. *Winchester* was inscribed on the stock.

Well played, universe.

In the backyard, a champagne fountain glittered in the spotlights at the entrance to a huge tent, where garlands of yellow and orange lights were strung along the ceiling. Round tables were set up under the tent on the grass, each set for dinner, with elaborate centerpieces of twisting, wrought iron candlesticks that held six fat pillar candles each. Mist flowed over the grass and the pool, where more lights had been installed to give the water a greenish tinge. In the center of the tent was a smaller table piled with skulls, bones, and pumpkins. Three skeletons sat in chairs, posed as if they were chatting.

"What's that?" Faith asked, clutching my arm and pointing at a table in the corner of the tent near the bar. It was laden with gifts, few of which had Halloween-themed wrapping paper.

"Couldn't say," I said. "Get-well gifts for Dad?"

She pouted. "When I was sick with pneumonia six months ago—"

"You had a cold."

"—you only bought me flowers. No gifts."

"I bought you an apartment."

"That came later."

"And eight million dollars. And counting."

She made a face and rolled her eyes. "Don't talk about money, sweetie-darling, it's uncouth."

I chuckled. Of all the chaos in the world, at least I could always rely on Faith to be herself.

As we entered the tent, several guests complimented us on our costumes, and a few others offered congratulations.

"For what?" I demanded of one.

The woman—someone I didn't recognize—gave me a funny look, then tittered with laughter. "Oh, you." She turned to Faith. "He's *so* funny."

Faith cocked her head. "Is he? How can you tell?"

"What was that about?" I asked when we moved on.

She shrugged her slender shoulders. "Maybe we already won the costume contest."

We found Eddie and Marjorie standing near a long table of hors d'oeuvres. Ramona was close by, manning a cheese fondue pot, where the bread chunks on the end of the dipping sticks were artistically burnt to look like little skulls.

Marjorie was dressed as Captain Marvel; Ramona was Mother Goose. The women greeted us with smiles and small talk. My brother was picking olives out of his pâté and throwing them on the grass, careful not to stain the black suit he wore with a ruffled collar and a tall black top hat.

"Silas, my dear brother, so happy to see you." He tipped his hat to Faith, his tone cooling noticeably. "Miss Benson."

"Don't you look dashing?" she said. "And who are you supposed to be?"

"Charles Dickens, of course. I was rather hoping Mr. Kaufman would see my costume, as I know he would quite appreciate it. Is he here yet, brother?"

I closed my eyes at the momentary slug of pain that whacked me in the chest.

"I told you, Eddie," I said, trying to keep the irritation out of my voice. "He's out of town."

"Yes, yes, North Carolina. But I had hoped he would've returned by now."

"Yeah, well—"

"Whatever is he doing there?"

"How the fuck should I know?"

Eddie recoiled as if I'd slapped him, and Marjorie and Ramona averted their eyes. Faith gave my arm a squeeze.

"Sorry," I said to Eddie. "I'm sorry, man. I don't know what he's doing or. . ."

If he's coming back.

Eddie nodded, and his shoulders loosened. "Quite all right, brother. I understand completely. I miss him too."

He said it to the ground. To anyone listening, it would've sounded natural and unremarkable. But Eddie rarely uttered a sentence that wasn't dressed up in fancy language. To utter such a naked sentiment was almost shocking. It stripped my whirling, confusing emotions to the bones.

Tentatively, I reached out and touched Eddie's shoulder. "Me too."

He glanced quickly at me with a small smile, patted my hand, and then slipped out from under my touch.

"This really is quite some party," Marjorie said brightly into the silence that followed. "*Vanity Fair* is here. *Forbes*. And that local one. *Seattle Society*."

Faith perked up. "*Vanity Fair*? Really? Where?"

"They don't have kids they could be taking trick-or-treating?" I said, scowling.

A quick scan of the yard showed me Stephen Milton dressed—appropriately, I thought—as a vampire. His wife, Helen, a thin, frail-looking woman, was dressed as Marie Antoinette in a teal dress and tall wig that looked ready to topple off her head.

I kept scanning and almost didn't recognize Sylvia under a black Cleopatra wig and blue eyeshadow.

"Excuse me for a moment," I said and disentangled myself from Faith.

"Well? What do you think?" Sylvia asked when I joined her. "Do you have enough dirt on Milton? I can get more. I only sent you the worst of the worst—"

"I think you're amazing. And that you've been amazing for a long time and I never told you."

Sylvia took the compliment with a smile and a sip of champagne, but the worry line under the gold circlet on her brow returned.

"I just hope it works. I hope Mr. Marsh can see how reckless Milton's been." She tilted her champagne glass to the entrance of the tent. "There's your father now."

Sylvia indicated to where one of Dad's nurses pushed him in his wheelchair over a temporary walkway. He was dressed as FDR with little round glasses and a plaid shawl over his legs.

"He looks happy," Sylvia said. "In a good mood. That bodes well."

"We'll see. I honestly don't know why he bothered with all this. He hates parties."

"Well, it *is* a special occasion."

I snorted. "Halloween?"

"No, silly. You and Faith. And on that note, congratulations."

"Why does everyone keep saying that?"

She gave me a funny look. "Because. . . you're engaged?"

"That's old news."

"True. But this party makes it official. Doesn't it?"

"What do you mean?" I asked, a cold lump of dread forming in my stomach.

She laughed nervously and did a double-take. "Are you messing with me? Silas, this is your engagement party."

I stared. "Oh fuck me. . ."

"You didn't know? It's on the invitation. . ."

I never saw an invitation. I hadn't needed one.

Because it's my party. Shit. . .

My father tapped a fork to the side of a champagne glass with steady hands. The one hundred and fifty or so guests—executives from Marsh Pharma, a few celebrities and politicians, vultures from *Seattle Society*, photographers from *Vanity Fair* and *Forbes*. . .the entire fucking world gathered close for my father's final act.

"Ladies and gentlemen, friends and colleagues," Dad said, his voice strong and hearty. "I welcome you all and thank you for coming. You may wonder why I had the party moved from that lovely hotel to my own humble abode."

An appreciative laugh rolled through the crowd.

"There are several reasons to hold it here," my father continued. "Firstly, I wanted you to see with your own eyes what our company can do. The miracles we work on a daily basis and the relief we bring to so many."

He handed his champagne glass to a nurse, while another, Dale, grabbed the quilt off Dad's lap and moved the footrests on his wheelchair out of the way. My father's feet touched smooth pavement. Slowly, shakily, with the entire party holding its breath, Dad pushed himself out of the chair to standing.

"They said I would never walk again," he said. "They told me the weakness was permanent. But my medicine—*our* medicine—is the stuff of miracles. I am living proof."

The entire congregation broke into applause and whistles which my father humbly waved off. If I could've moved from my paralyzed state, I would've rolled my eyes at the frou-frou language he only trotted out in front of company. He muttered something at Dale, and Dale handed him back the glass of champagne.

"The second reason I wished to have this party at my house, is because what better way to celebrate our growing family than in our own home? My son, Silas," he said and held his glass in my direction. "He's been very busy, working hard to make me proud. I figured the very least I can do, since I was lying around all day—"

Laughter came on cue.

"—was give him the engagement party we've all been waiting for."

My heart tried to climb out of my throat, and my stomach clenched tight as Faith's hand gripped me in the crook of my elbow. I don't remember her moving beside me; I felt like I was underwater in a murky green and purple pond.

"To Silas and Faith," my father said. "May I be the first to officially congratulate you on what I hope will be a long, happy, and *fruitful* union."

"Hear, hear!" Stephen Milton said, leading the choir of toasts that went up around us.

Dad's eye met mine and he gave me a final, knowing salute with his glass, the smallest smile of triumph curving his lips.

I glared back. How appropriate, I thought, to have this bullshit engagement party in front of a sea of people in costumes. What better way to honor Faith and me; a guy who'd been wearing a costume for years, pretending to be someone I was not, and my "fiancée," a woman I paid to be my accomplice.

My father knew exactly what he was doing. He'd always known. Dancing me on his strings, sending me to Alaska where the true purpose hadn't been to teach me I was broken or defective but to make me believe I couldn't cut myself free when the scissors were in my hand the entire time.

I shook my head at him slowly. His dismissive shrug showed me that he wasn't concerned. I didn't fight back. I never did.

Fight for us, Max whispered in my mind. *Fight for yourself. . .*

I took a step toward my father, but the applause died down quickly. Murmurs began to circulate in a low hum as attention was drawn to Eddie. People were backing away, giving him space as he paced a small circle in the middle of the tent, wringing his hands, head down, shoulders hunched.

"Distressing," he said, in his loud, clear, *angry* voice. "Terribly, terribly distressing."

Faith gripped my arm. "Silas. . ."

"This is codswallop!" Eddie said, his words reaching every corner of the tent. "Flimflam and fiddlesticks!"

"What is happening?" I heard Dad ask Dale, his expression dark. "Go see what he's yammering about. . ."

I hurried to Eddie first, Faith sticking close to me.

"Hey, man. You okay?"

He danced away from my touch, and his voice grew louder as the crowd grew quieter to hear what the commotion was about.

"Father, this is entirely a farce, and I simply won't stand for it," Eddie said, stomping his foot. "Silas *cannot* be wed to Miss Benson."

Oh shit. Oh shit oh shit oh shit. . .

"Hey, Eddie. It's okay. . . " I held a hand to him, but again he flinched and moved out of my reach.

My father smiled for the crowd, but his eyes were daggers. He hadn't wanted Eddie at the party at all, I'd heard, but had relented when Marjory assured him that he'd be only one guest in a sea of guests.

"That's enough now, young man," Dad said, as if his son were a stranger. "Can we find his assistant. . . ?"

"I understand perfectly well, Papa," Eddie said. "It is you who lacks the most basic of enlightenment."

I gaped. Marjorie's champagne glass dropped out of her hand like it had fallen through a trapdoor. I'd never heard him stand up to my father before or raise his voice in defiance. No one had.

Beside me, Faith's eyes were wide as if she didn't want to blink and miss a thing. "Now *this* is a party."

"That is quite enough," our father said harshly, then chuckled tightly. "I mean. . . What in the world are you babbling about?"

Eddie stopped pacing and stood straight, hands clasped behind his back, chin up.

"My brother cannot marry Miss Benson," he stated. An official announcement of unassailable fact.

"Why the hell not?"

Tell them, Eddie, I thought. *Tell them all why not.*

"Because, dear father," Eddie said. "Silas is in love with Mr. Kaufman."

Except for a few gasps, the entire yard—the entire fucking planet—went absolutely silent. For a heartbeat, no one moved but for the glances being exchanged all around me, whizzing over my head like darts.

Then, like an exhalation, magazine reporters began jotting words. Photographers snapped photos. Of Eddie. Of my father. But mostly of Faith and me.

I glanced down at her. She smiled up at me.

"That's my cue," she said. "Goodnight, Silas."

"Goodnight, Faith. Thank you. For everything."

"Lunch, sometime?"

I had to laugh. Even then. In that chaos.

"Absolutely."

"Call me." She kissed her fingertip and touched it to the cleft in my chin. "I'm buying."

And then she stepped back, into the crowd.

"Don't be preposterous," my father was saying. He chuckled nervously. "Eddie has quite an imagination. . ."

"I assure you, what they have is very real," Eddie said. "So very real and true." He turned to me. "I say, my good man. If you please. Tell them the truth."

Another silence descended as if someone had hit the mute button.

The truth. It waited for me, a long-lost piece of myself wanting to find its place.

"Silas. . ." My father warned. He'd sunk back into his wheelchair, his fingers gripping the sides until his knuckles were white like bone.

"*All the colors of my life were changing. . .*" I murmured.

Eddie smiled then. A real smile. One I'd never seen him wear before. Not since before Mom died. I smiled back. I don't think I could've stopped smiling at my brother for anything in the world. I would've hugged him tight if he'd let me.

I lifted my head to meet my father's eyes, and when I spoke, my voice rang out, hard and clear and loud. Loud enough for the entire tent to hear over the gasps and titters and clicking cameras. Because the world was listening.

"He's right," I said. "I'm in love with him."

My Max. All the color in my life. . .

"I'm in love with Max, and this party is over."

CHAPTER TWENTY-EIGHT

Silas

Cesar was put in charge of ushering the party guests off the property. I suppose I could've let them stay and celebrate Halloween, but I wanted a clean slate. They could take their engagement presents and go home.

Dale pushed my father's wheelchair through the house, Dad smiling tightly and waving at departing guests as if the whole thing were a practical joke. Stephen Milton tagged along with us, looking scared under his pasty white vampire makeup.

I led the procession to the library, and once inside, my father's repressed wrath spewed out. I shut the door and he stabbed the air with his finger at me.

"You. . ." Spittle stained his upper lip. "The entire world was in that backyard. Listening to you. . ." he sputtered with rage. "Give me one reason why I shouldn't have you thrown out of here!"

"I'll give you a reason," I said as I went to the safe. "I'm your last fucking hope for redemption. That's a reason."

I'd heard the phrase *step into your power*, but I never understood what it meant until that night. Being with Max, kissing him, touching him, sleeping with him. . . steppingstones to this feeling, this surge of warm, perfect emotion—love for him and for myself. I let it flow. Let it course through my veins, through every cell of my body, pumped by a heart that was filled with him.

With no remnants of cold or fear or shame hanging off of me, I moved calmly to retrieve the briefcase. Everything felt easier. I could breathe.

Wait for me, Max, I sent into the ether. *Wherever you are, please, wait for me. . .*

I set the suitcase on the table and clicked open the latches.

"Under Stephen's direction," I began, "Marsh Pharma has taken a product that was meant to relieve the worst pain for terminal cancer patients and has turned it into a cash cow. The result is we helped ruin and destroy countless families and communities."

Stephen snorted indelicately and tapped his fingertips together. "Edward, please. We've discussed this ad infinitum, ad nauseam. In no way are we responsible for those who abused our product."

"Yeah, we've heard that one before," I said, calmly rifling through the emails and internal memos until I found the one Sylvia had highlighted and tabbed. "You also stated that, 'higher dosages mean better profits.' Oh, and here's a good one: 'It's of little consequence to us if consumers can't read a warning label. We already have their money.'"

My father, his eyes still hard and flinty, glanced between Stephen and me.

Stephen tittered nervously. "That's just internal talk. Braggadocio. Doesn't mean anything."

"Bullshit," I said. "That came from a marketing directive that pushed OxyPro even harder in small, rural communities. You also ignored reports from our own labs about how addictive the opioids are, but I can tell you myself. I've been there."

My father whipped his head to look at me.

"You didn't know that did you?" I said. "Of course not. I was already drinking in high school to deal with your stellar brand of parenting. Then you sent me to Alaska, where I was beaten, shocked, and ground down to nothing. When I came back, OxyPro was everywhere and I dove in headfirst. I only pulled myself out so Eddie wouldn't have to deal with you alone, because after Alaska, being alive wasn't much incentive."

"So you're an addict, too," my father said weakly. "On top of everything else."

"Yes. A recovering addict. I'm recovering from a lot of things, Dad."

I turned to Stephen who was eyeing my briefcase is if he wanted to snatch it and run out the door.

"I have hundreds of damning quotes from you that I'm sure the public, the FDA, and plaintiffs in class-action lawsuits are going to want to hear. And I promise you, they will hear it, because now is the time to clean up the mess we've made."

"You knew," Stephen said. "I'll tell them you knew and tried to cover it up. You researched... You wrote memos..."

"And then you thoughtfully punished me with a leave of absence." I smiled grimly. "Thanks for that."

Stephen stared, then rushed to my father's side. "Edward. You know that everything I have done, I've done for the good of the company."

Dad's gaze was still on me when he said, "Get out. I must speak with Silas."

Stephen's eyes widened with alarm and he backed away slowly. "You'll be hearing from my attorney. Both of you."

When the door shut, my father glared at me and I glared right back.

"What do you want?" my father asked finally. "Forget this drug business, you want me to give you my blessing? You want me to condone the lifestyle you've chosen, despite my best efforts to save you?"

I snorted a laugh. "It's fucking amazing, isn't it? Just yesterday—no, an *hour ago*—I would've fallen to my knees to get your blessing, as warped and twisted as that is. But now?" I shrugged. "My only regret is that I wasted so many years trying to get something that I never needed in the first place."

He narrowed his eyes. "I don't believe you."

"Why would you? I was cowed and bent under your will for years. But that's over. My personal life is *none of your fucking business*." I sat on the edge of the immense desk and crossed my arms. "I'm here to talk *company* business. And the better question is, what do you want?"

His lips made a thin line, and I could see behind his calculating eyes that he was completely baffled as to what tack to take.

"What I want?" he snarled. "I want the company that's been in our family for generations to not be run by a spoiled brat who thinks he can fuck whoever he wants—"

"Stop right there," I said, my hand up. "You've been evicted as my father until further notice. But if you want to talk about Marsh Pharma, then I can tell you that as of right now, the company your grandfather built is on the verge of being relegated to the trash heap of history as a perpetrator of one of the worst epidemics in modern history. And—sorry to burst your bigotry bubble—but the *least* of your problems is its next CEO being gay."

That slapped him in the face, but he recovered quickly. "You still want the job? Or is it the multi-million-dollar paycheck you're after?"

"I want the job so that Marsh Pharma doesn't spend the next decade bleeding people dry, fighting their lawsuits. They need help. We're going to give back."

"Give back? Christ."

"*Yes*. When I am CEO, I will cease and desist all sales of OxyPro. Expansion into Indonesia is dead. We're not going to demonize the addicted. With every settlement made to the victims we will include free medications to help combat the chemical addiction. We will pay every fine, every claim for damages—"

"How do you propose to keep us afloat throwing money around like confetti?"

"Orvale is a breakthrough. You said it yourself. It's not sexy but it'll help. And if we go bankrupt settling the lawsuits, then that's exactly what's supposed to happen. But no matter what, I'm not going to turn my back on those people."

"And if I say no to your *promotion*?"

I scoffed. "And keep Milton as the face of the company? That guy could go to jail for the lies he's spewed to the government. Give it to me and I'll try my best to make something good out of it. Otherwise, I'll join in the chorus to take you out even faster."

"You'd turn on us?" he said with a sneer. "Walk away from billions? Because I'll cut you off. I'll leave you without a cent—"

"I'll walk away with myself. It was never about the money anyway. I'd rather be shit-poor and happy with the man I love than rich and miserable and drowning in lies."

"Love," he snorted.

"Yes, love. What Eddie said tonight was one hundred percent true. I'm completely fucking out of my mind in love with Max. And nothing that was done to me in Alaska could change that. Nothing ever could."

I leaned over him, put both hands on the armrests of his wheelchair.

"But now you have a choice to make. You thought I was the stain on your legacy? I'm your fucking savior. I'm your goddamn knight in shining armor. We are going to pay through the nose to rebuild communities, knowing it might not be enough. That it already might be too late. Or I walk and you sink, and your legacy—your name—sinks with it. I don't have a choice about who I am, no matter how you tried to torture it out of me. But now you get to choose. I'm your last fucking chance at redemption or you will lose everything. That, Dad, is *your* choice."

"Bleed me dry or let the vultures pick at me. That's the choice?"

"Yes. Let me try to fix this. You know that I can. But if you close the door on me now, I walk away for good and I take Eddie with me. *I will disown you.*"

He leaned back in his chair and I backed off.

"You can't give me back what you took from me in Alaska," I said, my chest tightening as even then, the cold memories tried to seep in the cracks. "And I can't communicate what it was like. You have no idea. But I'd like to think that if you knew, you'd be fucking appalled at what they did to me. To the other boys. . ."

I mastered my emotions. "But there is only this moment, right now. The first step in moving forward. Take it or leave it."

My father held my gaze and I held my breath. If he were going to give me what I wanted, it wasn't going to be because of a sudden epiphany of acceptance for his gay son. It would be because his gay son was going to save his tarnished legacy. I was counting on it. . .

"I will call General Counsel to draft a new version of my trust first thing tomorrow morning," Dad said finally. "Stephen Milton will be terminated immediately, and I will name you CEO of Marsh Pharmaceuticals."

I sat back on the edge of the desk, not knowing whether to laugh or cry. Like demanding to be named captain of the *Titanic* in the hopes that this time, I could swerve the ship away from total disaster.

Holy fucking shit, I must be crazy.

Dad held out his hand and I shook it. When I tried to let go, he held on. His eyes—the same color and hue as mine—were softer than I'd ever seen, his thoughts full of sinking ships too.

"Why? Why take this on?"

"Because the house we've built is huge and beautiful, but it has stairs that lead to nowhere and doors that open to brick walls. Dead-ends that have left thousands with nowhere else to turn. I'm going to build places where they can go for help instead."

My dad held on to my hand, and I swear I felt him squeeze harder, hold on tighter, and then he let go, turned his head away.

"Go," he said. "Leave me alone."

Outside the library door, I inhaled through my nose deeply, then exhaled. I'd set one burden down and took up another. So much of what had been broken was unfixable, but I had to try. I had hope. And maybe, I thought as I moved through the quiet house, it would be okay to hold onto a little piece of hope for myself.

Because doing the right things—good things—no matter how hard, was the only way to earn the love of a guy like Max Kaufman.

CHAPTER TWENTY-NINE

Max

"Uncle Max! Uncle Max!"

Jamie tugged on my jacket while Brent wrapped himself around my leg as I came through the front door of my sister's house.

"You're back!" Jamie said. "Can we go to the zoo now?"

"I want to see the monkeys," Brent said. "And eat Dippin' Dots."

"You *are* a monkey," I said, laughing and tried not to whack either one of my six-year-old nephews with the grocery bags in my hands. "The zoo is tomorrow, guys. Remember?"

"Settle down, boys." Rachel came down the front hall and took the bags out of my hands. "They've been climbing the walls. You've been gone entirely too long."

"An hour?" The smile on my face made my cheeks ache.

"They missed you." She gave me a peck on the forehead. "Who could blame them?"

It'd been two weeks since I'd arrived at my sister's house in Raleigh, North Carolina, and those two weeks had done wonders to heal the cracks in our family. Rachel was slammed with work for her magazine that was coming up on its Christmas and Hanukkah issue. Her husband, Ted, worked late hours in a marketing firm. I took advantage and spent as much time as I could with the twins during the day.

"I don't want you to become our live-in nanny," Rachel had said. "You're not here to work."

"It's not work," I'd said. "It's the furthest thing."

My sister moved her work to her home office and loaned me her car. I took the boys to school every morning and picked them up. We spent afternoons and weekends at outdoor parks, trampoline parks, roller rinks. When the boys had gone to bed, I spent long hours at night with my sister on her couch, watching movies or talking and making up for lost time. I told her everything, including the rawest, worst times of my life, when I'd been homeless and on the street.

I talked about everything but Silas.

At the end of every talk, Rachel would say, "And?"

I'd answer, "Not tonight."

I needed a time-out from life. I needed to shoot the shit and joke around with Rachel's husband, Ted. I needed the boys and their wild energy. I needed this house that was warm and homey, and I needed the love of family. I wrapped it all around myself like a blanket and let nothing else in. No texts. No social media. No outside world.

Aside from letting Daniel know I was okay, the only text I'd sent had been to Silas when I first arrived in Raleigh.

I'm out of town visiting my sister in NC for a little while.

Okay, he replied, and that was the end of our conversation.

I couldn't blame him. He'd needed me to stick around but I couldn't be kept like a dirty secret. But now that I was out of that maelstrom of turmoil, that ugly feeling of being right and completely wrong at the same time was the only thing that disturbed the happiness of being here.

A week later, late on Halloween night, long after I'd taken Thing One and Thing Two trick-or-treating and was falling asleep in my guest room bed, my phone chimed a text.

I'm fighting, Max. For me. For us. I'm going to make you proud. Don't have to answer. Be with your sister. I'll talk to you soon. Love, Si

By the time I got to the last sentence, I could hardly see the phone. His words crawled into my heart. I'd done what he'd said, but another week had passed, and the pain of leaving him was wearing me down.

I helped Rachel put the groceries away and she grabbed an hour with the twins while I cooked dinner. Then we sat around the table, passing around baked chicken, peas, salad and bread.

"Ted's working late again," I said.

Rachel cut up Brent's chicken. "A campaign for one of his clients is going live tomorrow and then we get him back. Epically bad timing with my December issue coming up, but that's always how it goes." Her gaze slid to me and then back to the food. "He talked to Morris last night."

"Oh yeah?"

"Yeah. They're buddies. Have been ever since we met."

"Daddy and Uncle Mo are *buddies*." Jamie laughed. "Buddeeeeees."

"Eat your peeeeeeeeas, goofball," I said, ruffling his dark hair.

"Yep, buddies," Rachel said. "Morris tried to call me, but I missed it, so he called Ted instead. You wouldn't believe some of the stories Mo hears from up in his big New York high rise."

I gave her a curious glance. "What kind of stories?"

She forked a bite of chicken. "Oh. . .this and that."

As I'd gotten to know my sister better, I'd learned that she was precise. Journalists write in narrow columns, using only the most important words, cutting the rest. Rachel carried that over into her life.

This and that was her version of *article cont'd on page 12*. Or ten p.m. tonight when the boys were asleep.

She washed the dishes while I got the twins in their pajamas, helped them brush their teeth, and read them a story in their room. *The Grouchy Ladybug* got a smack-down from the whale's tail and ended a long day.

"Get some sleep for the zoo tomorrow, guys," I said, shutting off the light.

"Uncle Max?" Brent asked.

"Yep."

"Are you going to live with us?"

"No, buddy. I'm going back to Seattle in a few days."

To where and what, I have no idea.

"I don't want you to go."

"Me neither," Jamie said, sleepily. "I'll miss you."

I was glad that the only light in the room was from an Iron Man nightlight. "I'll miss you, too. But before you know it, it'll be Thanksgiving and you guys will be coming to see me."

"And Grandpa and Grandma," Brent said.

I stiffened. "Yep. Them too."

I said goodnight and went to the guestroom to change into flannel pants and a T-shirt. Downstairs, Rachel was already in her yoga pants and one of Ted's shirts, sipping from one of two mugs of tea.

"How do you feel about chamomile?" she asked when I came in. "It's not wine and ice cream, but. . ."

I sat down beside her. "Okay. Spill it."

She set her mug down carefully. "I'm not sure how to tell you this."

"Tell me what?"

"You're kind of famous."

"Say what now?"

Rachel settled herself sideways on the couch to face me. "Morris does a lot of business in a lot of different sectors. I'm not going to bore you with the details—he'll do that at Thanksgiving dinner. But suffice to say, not a lot goes unnoticed in his world, especially where big money is concerned."

"Okay," I said. "I'm listening."

"Apparently, on Halloween night, Marsh Pharma's chairman threw a huge engagement party for his son, Silas. Everyone was there."

My jaw clenched at the name, and my heart ached. As if his name were a call and my damn soul were answering. Then the rest of her sentence sunk in.

An engagement party. For him and Faith. Of course.

Rachel sighed through her nose. "Oh sweetheart, you should move to Hollywood. Everything you're feeling is all over your face." She took my hand. "You don't have to keep it secret from me anymore. It's all moot. The press was there. Everyone knows."

"Everyone knows what?"

"Silas Marsh told the entire world he was in love with you."

I stared as my heart took off at a gallop so fast, I lost my breath. "He did *what*?"

"Mo nearly lost his shit when he heard it was you. Apparently, the acting CEO of Marsh Pharma has been given the boot and Silas has taken over."

I faced forward, my head—and heart—swimming. "So. . . wait. Silas is the CEO?"

"Yes. And he's in love with you." She smiled at my reaction. "You looked like you needed to hear that part again."

I stared at nothing, my heart full and breaking at the same time. "He. . . came out?"

"You could say that. Something about his brother being involved but I'm hearing it third hand."

"Oh my God."

"So." Rachel bundled herself in the blanket. "Now can you tell me about him? I'm pretty sure your NDA has been rendered null and void."

I told my sister about Silas and me, starting with my job at the estate and ending with my being fired, leaving out his time in Alaska and his fight against opioid addiction.

"Now, given all that's happened. . . Fuck, Rach. I should've stayed. I should have waited for him. I promised myself I wouldn't hide anymore, and that's the truth. But honestly, I freaked out because of how I feel about him."

"Because. . ." Rachel prompted gently. "You're in love with him too."

I nodded. "I told him to fight for us, but *I* didn't fight for us. I ran away, telling myself it's because I'd been burned before."

"Burned before?" Rachel said. "Sweetheart, Dad kicked you out of our home. You were on the streets, fighting for survival. That's not a little burn, that's a scorching. Anyone would protect themselves after that. And honestly, after all you've been through, Max, I can't believe you're even willing to be in the same room with me."

"Don't say that," I said, taking her hand. "I wouldn't trade these last two weeks for anything."

"Me neither, except that we might've had more of them. You wouldn't have been out there. . . in the cold." She sniffed and wiped her eyes. "The point is, you give so much. I see it with my boys. With us. That's who you are. But the problem with giving so much of yourself is that you could end up with nothing left."

"I needed this time. For a lot of reasons. But. . ."

"But now you can go back to your beautiful billionaire who's in love with you."

"I don't know," I said. "I might've fucked it up. I kept telling him, he needs to be who he is. As if I had all my shit together myself. I didn't. I don't. I don't know what I'm going back to. I have no place to live, no job. . ."

"Is it a matter of money because Ted and I—"

"No, I'm good. I have savings and severance. I just don't know what to do with it. I don't know what to do with my life."

"Back to the ER?" Rachel asked.

I shuddered at the thought. "God, no. Maybe work in a clinic somewhere. Taking care of only one patient isn't enough, but the chaos of a hospital is too much."

"Maybe go back to school?"

"Maybe," I said. "But it's time to go back to Seattle."

Rachel's eyes widened in alarm.

I laughed. "*After* I take the twins to the zoo."

Two days later, Rachel drove me to the airport while Ted stayed home with the twins. I'd hated saying goodbye and reminded myself constantly on the drive that I'd see them all in a week.

At the curb, my sister hugged me tight. "That was the best two weeks," she said. "For all of us."

"For me too," I said.

She cupped my face. "You going to be okay? Don't give me that look; you're my baby brother and my days of being absorbed in my own life are *over*."

"You're going to be all up in my business now?"

"Every minute." She hugged me again, and I felt her inhale a shaky breath. "Can you ever forgive me?"

I squeezed my eyes shut. "There's nothing to forgive—"

"I knew you were going to say that. But there is. I need to hear it."

"Then I forgive you," I said.

"Okay, then. You take care of yourself. Call me when you land, and when we get to Seattle next week, I'm going to march straight to Dad and—"

"No, it's okay, Rach," I said. "Let him be who he is. If you yell at him, he'll just retreat further away."

"Probably." She tucked a lock of hair behind her ear. "Listen. I said an awful thing at lunch with you and me and Mo, talking about Thanksgiving and balancing out your side."

I nodded.

"That was a horrible thing to say. I'm on your side. Mo is on your side. And Ted and the boys. . . " Tears filled her eyes. "We're all on your side. Okay?"

"God, Rach. . ."

My chest felt an incredible lightness despite how her words filled my heart. In a perfect family there shouldn't be any sides at all, but what was perfect? I felt my sister's intentions, her love for me, and I knew that whatever happened next, I was going to be okay.

The police monitoring the curb drop-off motioned at us to wrap things up.

"Love you, Rach."

"Love you, Max. We'll see you next week." She gave my cheek a final pat, then moved to her car. "But you're calling me the second you land. And to let me know where you're staying. And you have to tell me about You Know Who."

"You sound like a Jewish mother," I said, laughing.

"I am a Jewish mother," she shot back, then made the "call me" sign with her fingers and got in the car.

I flew back to Seattle and Daniel set me up on his couch. Again. He hadn't heard about Silas; corporate news wasn't exactly TMZ-worthy, and since no video had been taken of that night, there was nothing in detail except the article in *Seattle Society*.

"I have been positively slammed at work," Daniel told me. "Which is why I'm taking this Monday night to go out. Come with. The boys miss you. I've missed you."

"No, thanks," I said. "I'm a little jetlagged. Going to hit the couch early."

"Suit yourself."

He went out and when he'd been gone an hour, I called Silas.

"Max," he said, answering quickly. Nervously. "Hey."

"Hey." God, just hearing the low timbre of his voice slugged me right in the chest and made it ache.

"How've you been?"

"Nope, I refuse to do small talk with you," I said. "I'll get straight to the point, Si. I miss you."

He eased a breath with a short laugh. "God, me too. I miss you so much. I suppose you heard about what happened?"

"Some. I want to hear it from you."

"I did it," he said. "I got the company. Which is sort of like being happy about inheriting a landfill, but. . ."

"You did it. You did what you set out to do, and now a lot of people are going to get help."

"Yeah, well. . . Some other things happened that night." He exhaled over the line. "Basically, Eddie took it upon himself to out me in front of God and everybody."

I laughed a little. "Sounds like Eddie."

"It wasn't exactly my plan, but I'm glad. I'm so fucking glad. And I said some stuff. But. . ."

But. . . I filled in the rest.

I didn't mean it.

I changed my mind.

You weren't there. . .

"I wasn't there," I murmured.

"What?" Silas said. "This connection is shit, and I can't do this over the phone. I fucking can't."

"Okay," I said.

"You're in Raleigh, right? That's not too far—"

"No, I'm back in Seattle."

"*What?*" Silas bit off a curse. "Goddammit, Maximilian, I'm in Virginia."

I had to laugh, even as I felt whacked in the stomach to hear there were so many miles between us.

"What are you doing out there?"

"I'm using a mop to clean up a flood. You remember that doctor I gave fifteen million dollars to?"

"I thought it was ten," I said, smiling. "Five million extra must've fallen out of your pocket."

"Don't wealth-shame me, Kaufman. I'm going to end up in the poorhouse after all this shit is said and done, and then you'll be sorry."

I smiled wider. Silas didn't give a shit about losing money. He sounded happy. Not that what he was doing was fun, but it created a deeper kind of happiness that comes from doing the right thing.

"Anyway," he said. "This doc. . . Turns out he had no idea what to do with fifteen million dollars so we're building a clinic. The first of many."

"That's great, Si. Really incredible."

"It's not enough, but it's something." His voice downshifted. "So listen, I don't know when I'll be back in Seattle. This project has me busy until December, and then I have Congressional hearings the week after that."

"Holy shit. You're not in trouble, are you?"

"No. Milton and his cronies are in deep, but I still have to answer some questions. Lay out my plans for restitution. Anyway. . ."

Thanksgiving.

I rubbed my chest. "It's okay, Si. I get it. You have to do what you set out to do. It's important."

"Yeah, but it's not the only thing that's important," he said. "Max. . . Fuck, I really hate phones."

"Same," I said.

I want to see your face, touch your skin, inhale you. . .

"I should go."

"Go," I said. "Call me. . .when you can."

When it's right.

"I will." Another inhale. "Goodnight."

"Goodnight."

We hung up and I stared at the phone in my hand, feeling a distance between us that was so much more than miles and time zones.

Silas Marsh told the entire world he was in love with you.

But maybe it was too much, too soon. I'd been yanked out of the closet in front of my family. Silas had been thrust under a spotlight in front of the entire world. Especially after all he'd been through, I couldn't imagine that level of scrutiny.

He'd flung his heart into the world, while I'd taken mine and run away.

CHAPTER THIRTY

Max

"Max, get over here," Daniel said. "You have to see this."

It was Thanksgiving Day. I'd been back on Daniel's couch for the last week and had emerged from his shower dressed in black jeans, a dark button-down, and my black leather jacket for the family dinner.

"You look. . . " Daniel kissed the tips of his fingers. "You and your jacket. . ."

"It's waterproof, which is good, since I feel like I'm going to puke." I nodded at the TV where an empty podium in front of a small building was surrounded by press in the late afternoon sunshine. The chyron at the bottom read, Richmond, Virginia. "What's this?"

"Your billionaire lover is on the news," Daniel said. "Maybe he's going to tell everyone how much he loves you again and then take a few questions."

"Very funny," I said without energy. Daniel had learned about the Halloween party after all, and I'd taken no end of shit from him and the guys for it. "Turn it up."

Daniel grabbed the remote and the screen switched back to the news anchor.

"In a surprise move, Marsh Pharma's chairman, Edward Marsh has made his son, Silas Marsh, CEO of the company, ousting interim CEO, Stephen Milton. Milton has been the subject of scrutiny lately, as internal memos reveal his shocking and callous directives to push the company's top-selling drug, the opioid pain killer, OxyPro, into communities with reckless disregard for the drug's potency and potential for misuse."

The screen cut to footage of Silas walking with a group of people through a small town, a sheriff and a woman in a lab coat among them.

"More shocking, Silas Marsh has vowed not to fight the torrent of lawsuits against Marsh Pharma but has stated he is committed to quote, 'help clean up the mess we made.' He's been touring some of the communities, talking to bereaved parents of overdose victims, and working with local doctors and law enforcement to build rehab centers and bring awareness about this sweeping epidemic that his own father's company helped to create."

The screen switched again to Silas Marsh at the podium, looking devastating in a light gray suit with a pale blue tie.

"Good lord, your man is hot," Daniel said. "You could get lost in the cleft in his chin."

"Addicts need help, not jail," Silas was saying on the TV. "They need better, longer rehabilitation stays and access to the medicine that helps curb the addictive morphine molecule. Fighting drugs with more drugs might seem counterintuitive, but the addicted person's brain is battling a disease, and addiction of this magnitude needs to be treated as such. And it is my intention to help fight this epidemic using every resource available."

The screen cut back to the reporter. "That was the scene two days ago—"

Daniel shut off the TV.

"Wow. He's really making a stand. And he could've walked away." Daniel gave my shoulders a squeeze. "Gorgeous, rich, ethical. You're one lucky bastard."

I smiled faintly and Daniel mistook my expression for apprehension about the dinner I was about to walk into.

"You'll be fine. Your brother and sister will be there, yes? They'll have your back." He put his arm around me. "You sure you don't want me as your date? I can take out my eyebrow piercing. . . ?"

"You have your own family dinner. And I wouldn't let you change a thing anyway. That's the whole point. I have to keep reminding myself that my dad's the one that has to take the next step."

With or without me bringing someone.

The idea had been ludicrous to me all along, that after all these years of exile because I'd had a guy over, now he wanted me to have a guy over, but without actually having to talk to me about it. Instead of it feeling welcoming and inclusive, it felt exploitative. As if Dad needed to witness a gay couple firsthand, the way you visit exotic animals in the zoo—to see them with your own eyes. But it was a moot point anyway.

Silas is in Virginia.

My phone had been silent, and every day that passed, I was more certain that Silas had thrown himself into his work to distance himself from the spectacle of the Halloween party and how he'd laid his heart and soul bare for the entire world to see. He'd fought for himself and won, and I hadn't even been there. It was ridiculous—and selfish—to be upset he wasn't here now.

He reconciled himself to his father. It's my turn to do the same.

The Harvest Inn was on the other side of the city from Daniel's Capitol Hill neighborhood, and my Uber driver's route took us to a road that was closed for a broken hydrant.

"Shit, sorry," he said. "Rerouting."

I felt the minutes ticking away, and it was all I could do to keep from jumping out of the car. The fucking last thing I wanted was to be late. To have my family already sitting together at the table, talking and going about their business. If I was late, I wouldn't have even one minute alone with my dad.

But the universe was not on board with my wishes.

I arrived fifteen minutes late and I bit off a curse when the hostess told me that, yes indeed, the family was all here and waiting. I followed her to the table; my heart was clanging so loud, I could barely hear the noise of the crowded, bustling restaurant. It was a nice family-style place with wood-paneled walls and flowering wallpaper. Little cornucopias sat on every table in bursts of yellow and orange.

My family was seated at a table smack in the middle of the restaurant, down a short flight of stairs that separated the two levels. Rachel, Ted and the twins sat along one side of the long, rectangular table. Morris, his wife, Angela, and their two-year-old daughter, Amy, in a highchair, sat along the other side My parents flanked the ends. Two empty place settings—for me and my 'date'—were on the opposite end from my dad, as far away as possible, so that any conversation would have to be shouted.

My dad. . .

I stopped and gripped the railing on the stairs.

He showed every one of the seven years that had passed since the night he kicked me out. His hair was graying on the sides and thinning on top. His stomach was rounder than before, his jowls heavier. He watched the happy chaos of the kids and the bickering between Mo and Rachel with a placid, emotionless face. If he were nervous about seeing me, he didn't show it.

I sucked in a breath and headed down the stairs.

"Hey," I said, my voice gruff and nearly drowned out by the noise around us. "Sorry, I'm late."

My dad turned his gaze to me, and I saw his eyes widen slightly. But he didn't speak or move. No one did. A bubble of silence fell around the table—even the baby grew quiet.

Rachel popped out of her seat, bursting the bubble.

"You're here!" she practically shouted and raced over to me, hugging me tight. "I'm so proud of you."

A deep sadness panged in my stomach. Showing up for dinner with family shouldn't have to be this difficult. It should just be.

"Uncle Max! Uncle Max!"

The twins scrambled out of their chairs to cling to my legs.

"Hey, guys. I missed my little monkeys."

Ted and Morris got up next to shake my hand, and Angela kissed my cheek and introduced me to Amy who ran her chubby little fingers over my stubble.

Mom, her eyes streaming, stood and took my face in her hands. "Beautiful boy," she said and hugged me. "Oh, Max. I'm so happy you're here. . ."

"Me too, Mom."

"Things are going to be different from now on. I promise," she said against my cheek, then gave me a kiss.

God, I hope so.

I heaved a breath and turned to my father. He'd stood up and was waiting for the hubbub to die down.

"Hey, Dad."

"Max," he replied in a tone I couldn't decipher.

The last time I'd heard that voice, it was raised in anger, telling me I was no longer welcome. . . The memory sniped and bit at me, and for a second my brain couldn't reconcile that the same man was now holding his hand out to me.

I reached out and took it, and it took everything in my power to not break down at the touch of his skin against mine, his skin dry and hard. Before I could squeeze it, hold on a little longer, he let go.

"Well, now, is everyone hungry?" he said. "I know I am."

And just like that, our "reunion" was over. He resumed his seat and I had no choice but to do the same at one of the empty place settings. I opened the menu that was sitting on my plate, wondering with humiliation burning my skin why I had agreed to this.

"Well," Mom said. "I think this is going to be a wonderful holiday, yes? So much to be grateful for."

The waitress came in her green apron, yellow shirt. "Everyone here? Should I take a setting away?"

"Should we?" Mom asked me. "Are you. . .?"

"Take it," I said. "It's just me today."

Another silence fell and I felt like crawling into a hole.

"Well, okay," Mom said. "That's perfectly fine. Isn't it, Lou?"

I couldn't look at my father. Heat burned my neck, and the sense of failure washed over me, followed by anger.

Why wouldn't it be fine? It's not enough I'm here?

From across the table, Rachel gave me a commiserating smile, then something over my shoulder caught her eyes. They widened until I thought they were going to pop out of her head.

"Sorry I'm late," said a deep voice. "I couldn't remember the name of the restaurant. But anyway, hi, I'm Silas Marsh."

I turned around and my heart crashed so hard against my chest, I thought it was trying to break free.

Silas was here, looking like an Adonis, wearing dark gray slacks, a black turtleneck, and a dark gray long coat. His gold hair was still wet from a shower, and against the black of his sweater, his eyes were more crystalline blue than I'd ever seen them.

The men at the table stood up, myself on weak legs, to greet him. Angela stared. Rachel stared. Everyone in the restaurant stared at Silas, tall, reeking of power and wealth, devastatingly beautiful, and fully inhabiting his body. He was powerful in his confidence, and no one could tear their eyes away, least of all me, as he strode over and kissed me on the mouth.

"Hey, babe," he said. "Sorry I'm late." He pulled me in for a hug and whispered, "Am I too late?"

"No," I managed. "No, God, Si. You're not too late."

He gave me a final squeeze that felt as if he were reluctant to let me go, then turned to the others.

"Morris? Good to meet you. Rachel, heard so much about you."

I met my sister's eye as Silas greeted our mom, then Angela, making his way down the table toward my father.

Are you kidding me? Rachel mouthed and pulled her maroon blouse away from her skin a couple of times as if the temperature in the room had increased twenty degrees.

Brent and Jamie both had their hands out across the table, waiting for their turn to shake like the grown-ups.

"Double trouble," Silas said to the twins. "Which one are you?"

"Brent," Brent said and hooked a thumb at Jamie. "This is Jamie."

"Why did you kiss Uncle Max?" Jamie wanted to know. Loudly.

Silas didn't blink an eye. "Because I'm his boyfriend."

Boyfriend. . .

I sank down into my chair, and Rachel kicked me under the table. Morris, on my right, socked me in the shoulder.

"Boys can be boyfriends with other boys?" Brent wanted to know.

"Sure, they can," Rachel said. "And girls can have girlfriends. There aren't rules about love." She didn't look at our father, but the words were for him. "Or shouldn't be, anyway."

Brent thought about this for a moment, then shrugged. "Okay."

I smiled at my nephews, amazed that the six-year-olds accepted this basic human concept of love that my sixty-two-year-old father had been wrestling with for decades.

Because hate has to be taught. You're not born with it.

Silas had finished greeting Ted and Angela and had made it to my father, hand outstretched. "Mr. Kaufman? I'm Silas Marsh."

"Silas," my father said, looking him up and down with a strange curiosity. "Good to meet you."

"Likewise," Silas said politely but not overly friendly.

The two men let go, and Silas took off his coat and gave it to a passing waiter to hang up. He sat in the chair on my left at my mom's right hand. The black turtleneck clung to his body, both elegantly conservative and completely drive-me-out-of-my-mind sexy at the same time.

The waitress reappeared and took our drink orders, gave the Thanksgiving specials, and then we all got busy perusing our menus. A half-dozen different conversations sprang up around us. From behind the barricade of my own menu, I drank Silas in.

"I feel you staring at me, Kaufman," Silas whispered out of the corner of his mouth. "Cut it out. I'm a goddamn titan of industry now. I can't be melting into a puddle of goop in the middle of a restaurant." He leaned in until his lips were a hairsbreadth away from my ear. "A puddle of goop with a raging hard-on, no less."

"What are you doing here?"

"What am I . . . ?" He fumed. "I called you like a hundred times."

I had to bite back a sudden laugh; he was so goddamn sexy when he was grouchy.

"Like hell you did."

"Check your phone, dummy. I wanted to surprise you, but not *this* much of a surprise."

I dug my phone out. "Look. It's right here. No calls. . . Oh shit."

The screen was black and not coming to life.

"Out of juice?" Silas scowled and lowered his voice even more. "That's because you're crashing on someone's couch, right? You don't even have a place to plug in your phone. . ." He shook his head and whispered, "Eff that noise. You're moving in with me."

"Is that a fact?" I whispered back, trying to stand my ground with him despite that euphoric happiness that was filling every part of me.

"Fact. And don't argue with me, Maximilian. We've been apart long enough, thanks. I can't stand being without you for one more fucking minute."

His eyes were on his menu, so he missed how deep his words sunk in and how the love I felt for this guy was taking over my entire being.

Fling away, Max! Darlene whispered in my mind. *Grab happy and run like hell.*

I set my menu down with a slap. "Silas, may I speak to you for a moment?" I addressed the rest of the table. "Will you excuse us? Be right back."

I got up, and Silas followed, tossing his napkin on his chair. I led us through the crowded restaurant, to the bathroom alcove, that was dark with maroon wallpaper and mercifully empty.

"Look, Max, I'm sorry. I should've spoken up when Dad fired you—"

His words cut off as I slammed him against the wall and kissed him hard. He stiffened in shock for a second and then melted against me, his arms wrapping around me and his mouth softening to let in my kiss.

"Oh, thank fuck," he groaned against my lips, his fingers sinking into my hair. "Jesus, I missed you."

I kissed him long and deep, inhaling him, drinking him in, tasting him with long sweeps of my tongue. I'd been starved of him, dying of thirst, suffocating without him.

The kiss quickly turned dire and I broke away before it got us in trouble.

"I'm so sorry," I said, breathlessly. "I'm sorry I wasn't there. You're so fucking brave, Silas. So brave, and I wasn't there. . ."

He shook his head. "No, you were right. About everything. Until I stood up to my dad, I wasn't there either." His blue eyes swam, and he inhaled a shaky breath. "Max, I—"

A woman entered the little alcove, her eyes on her phone. We jumped apart, and she stopped short, taking in our rumpled clothes and close proximity. Then she smiled to herself and continued to the ladies' room.

"We better get back," Silas said. "I don't want your dad getting suspicious of my intentions toward his son."

"I don't know that it matters. I don't know what the hell we're doing here. We can't talk, it's so loud, and I hate feeling like we're on display."

Silas frowned. "So, let's leave."

"Leave?"

"Well. . ." He thought about it. "Yeah."

"Just walk out of Thanksgiving dinner. I've been waiting for this moment with my dad for over seven years."

"But is it your moment or his?" He shrugged. "I can tell you one thing I learned from my little Halloween extravaganza, you have to reach out and seize your moment, Max. Your power." He grinned. "I could call Eddie over here to get the ball rolling for you."

I laughed but it faded fast.

"Whatever you want to do, Max. It's your party." He held the back of my neck in his large hand, his thumb brushing over my cheek. "I'm here for you. Period."

I thought about going back to the table and how my family would ask Silas about himself and his work over turkey and stuffing. A blanket of superficiality would lay over all of it, because my years on the streets, my addictions, what I'd had to do to survive. . . None of that was polite restaurant conversation. Carl, the man who treated me more like a son than my own father, didn't have a seat at the table, not even in spirit. Because this night had been orchestrated specifically to keep my past—what had made me who I was—neatly tucked away, where it couldn't spoil the pumpkin pie.

"Let's get out of here," I told Silas.

"You sure? They're going to think we left just so we could screw our brains out." He tapped his chin thoughtfully. "Not that they'd be *wrong*. . ."

"This isn't a moment. It's a show. I want the real deal."

Silas smiled. "You should have it."

We returned to the table, hand in hand.

"Mom, Dad, everyone, sorry, but we have to go. I love you all, and I'm happy to see you again, but too much time has passed and this. . . It doesn't feel right. It feels like we're picking up where we left off without acknowledging what I had to do to get here. I'm not trying to make it all about me. It's supposed to be about *us*. But it can't be. Not in this loud, crowded restaurant."

"You're... leaving?" Mom's eyes widened in alarm.

"Let him go, Mom," Rachel said, her eyes shining. "He's right. This isn't home. Max needs—d*eserves*—to be home, bundled up on the couch to cry and yell at us."

"Cry, maybe," I said, smiling at my sister. "No yelling required."

"But... Lou?" Mom implored my dad.

I bent and kissed her cheek. "Sorry, Mom. I love you."

"I love you too, but Max. . ." She wrestled with herself for a moment, then stood up and hugged me tight. "No, I know. I think I understand. I do."

"We'll talk soon, okay?"

"We will. I'll make sure of it."

"See you, Mo." I thumped him on the back, and he mumbled something around a bite of breadstick while giving me a thumbs up.

"Rach. . ."

"We're here until Sunday," she said pointedly. "I'll see you before then or I'll hunt you down."

"You will."

I went to Dad and squatted in front of him, this stranger who'd said three words to me in seven years.

"I appreciate what you tried to do, but this. . . It isn't right. We're not fixing anything. We're sitting at the same table, not talking, pretending like you're suddenly cool with me being who I am."

"Max," Dad said. He looked as if he had something to say but glanced around the crowded restaurant and shut his mouth again.

"It's okay. We can still try." My throat started to close. "I'm. . . here. I'm always here. But not like this. Not playing pretend and definitely not without saying what needs to be said. Okay?"

He nodded faintly, then cleared his throat. "If that's what you want."

"It is," I said, knowing I was taking a risk. Knowing this might be my dad's only offer, but I wasn't buying, I wanted more. I deserved more.

I gave his hand an awkward pat, said goodbye to Angela and the baby, ruffled the twins' hair. Rachel smacked a kiss on Silas's cheek and blew me one with both hands. Then Silas got his coat back from the hostess and we left.

Out on the street, Silas hauled me to him and hugged me tight.

"How'd that feel?" he asked.

"I don't know. Like I put everything on hold. Maybe I should've sucked it up and sat through the meal but. . ."

"But you have integrity," Silas said, taking my hand and holding on as we resumed walking. "And you don't compromise yourself. Both of which are your defining characteristics. Except now we have no Thanksgiving feast. Didn't think that one through, Maximilian. I already popped in with Dad and Eddie, and I don't feel like sharing you right now anyway."

"Is that Chinese place by your apartment open?"

"You mean *our* apartment? Yes."

"Then let's go. We'll talk about living-situation pronouns later."

"Sure, we can talk about it. Right after you get your shit moved in."

"Silas. . ."

He stopped, and we pressed against a wall, out of the flow of light, pedestrian traffic. He moved in close, the scent of his aftershave—masculine and clean—wafted over me, and his eyes. . . Christ, I'd never seen Silas's eyes as they were at that moment. The light blue now more like a multi-faceted gemstone instead of ice. They refracted and reflected the depths of him, and the love that suffused them as he looked at me.

"I'm serious Max," he said, his voice gruff. "I know what I want and it's you. No one else. You're it for me." He swallowed. "Maybe. . . forever. And if it's too soon for you to move in, then okay. That sucks but. . . I want whatever you want. Because when you boil it all down, that's really the only thing that matters to me. That you're happy. I just want you to be happy." He carved his hand through his hair. "I'm not romantic, I just. . . know what I feel. And I. . . I love you, Maximilian. I'm *in* love with you. So. . . there you go."

Flustered Silas, I thought through the warm haze of his words. *There are few things sexier.*

I held his gaze, held his hand in mine, and just took it in. This moment with him. The first of a thousand, I hoped. Millions. I basked in it for a little longer, like a lovesick dope, until Silas lost his patience. And that was cute as fuck too.

"Well?" he said. "Aren't you going to say something?"

"Yeah, I am." I took his face in both my hands. "I love you, Silas. I'm stupidly, crazy in love with you. You're it for me, too. Maybe forever, and I don't want to be anywhere but where you are."

I smiled, kissed him softly, my lips reverently touching and moving over his, my tongue gently tasting him, letting every emotion in me breathe into his mouth and taking his into mine with gentle, sucking pulls.

When we broke apart, I half-expected someone on the street to sneer or make a comment. But we had that perfect moment, and no one ruined it. It was ours.

Silas heaved a breath and glanced around the city street, then back to me.

"Jesus, look at us. We're kissing in public and holding hands, and instead of feeling like I'm jumping in a cold lake, I feel. . . fearless. And scared shitless at the same time. Not about what others think but because of us. You. I love you. I fucking love you so much. . . Hell, I love you so much, I told *Forbes* about it."

I laughed and it mellowed into a deep, warm happiness. His courage struck me all over again, and I knew with every particle of my being that if there was a man worth risking everything for, it was this one.

"And I want you to know, Max. . . I'm still fighting. For myself."

"What do you mean?"

"All that shit that happened to me in Alaska? It doesn't have a hold on me anymore, but it's still there. And it might jump out at me. At us."

"I know. And if it does, I'll be there for you, Si. I swear it."

"I'm going to be there for myself too, if that's even a thing." His glance darted away. "I've found a therapist. God, I feel lame just saying it. . ."

"Fuck no," I said, gripping his hand tighter. "Silas, that's what you deserve. And yes, being there for yourself is a thing. It's the most important thing." I held him tight. "I'm so fucking proud of you."

"Okay, okay, let's get out of here. Kissing and holding hands in public is one thing. I draw the line at crying like a baby."

We peeled ourselves off the wall and walked down the street together, hand in hand, our fingers entwined.

After a few minutes, I couldn't help myself. A small laugh escaped me. He glowered. "Don't say it."

"Silas..."

"Christ, here we go."

"I love you..."

"Get it out of your system."

"So... there you go."

He snorted and rolled his eyes while I cackled a laugh.

"Shut up." He slung his arm around my neck, scowling but with a smile peeking through.

We went to the Chinese place, and ate at a tiny table, sitting close, sharing the food. I teased Silas about how bad he was with his chopsticks.

The night fell outside, and it was growing too hard to be so close to each other and not do anything about it. My body hummed, every brush of our fingers caused sparks. I looked up at Silas in the dim light over our plates. His eyes were dilated and dark. Grease from the food stained his lips, and I leaned over the table and kissed him, licking it off with one swipe and sucking his lower lip into my mouth before letting go.

"Goddammit, Maximilian," Silas growled and looked for the waiter. "Check, please."

He ordered the food boxed up and we walked around the corner in a night that was brisk and cold. It mellowed us a little so that we didn't attack each other once we got inside.

"This is your entry," Silas said, taking off his coat. "Closet is here."

"You're giving me the tour?"

He ignored me, stripped me out of my jacket and hung it in the closet. "Over there is the kitchen. Living room. Piano. Please don't play too loudly; the neighbors will think I've had a stroke."

"Ha ha."

He took me by the hand and led me through the apartment. "Guest bedroom, guest bathroom..."

"I've been here before, you dope."

"And this is our bedroom," he said inside the master. "Bathroom is there, dresser is there. . . I'll clean out room in the closet. Or build a bigger one if you need it."

"For my one leather jacket?"

"Well, I wasn't sure if you had a Steve Jobs-kind of situation going, where you have a hundred of the same jacket, white T-shirt, and jeans."

"Nope. And get any kind of *Pretty Woman* shopping montage out of your head. I'm good, thanks."

"I have no idea what you're talking about."

I flopped onto the bed, and he lay down with me. On our sides, our heads on the pillows, face to face. An unspoken understanding passed between us that we needed a little time. There was no rush. Being in each other's space was enough—for now.

I traced my fingers over the contours of his face.

"Something on your mind?" Silas said.

"I'm still thinking about what happened at the Halloween party. How fucking brave you are. And I wish I'd been there to see it. To be there for you."

"First, it wasn't all that brave," Silas said. "I climbed up the high dive, but Eddie shoved me over."

I smiled. "Love that guy."

"Second, I think everything happened the way it was supposed to. Even the parts that fucking hurt. I hate that I hurt you, but it would've been worse had you stayed. I would've done what your dad did today—pretended like everything was okay instead of taking a stand. It would have chipped away at you to hide. Because you're too fucking good for that shit, Max."

"I've been waiting my whole life to feel what I'm feeling right now. I could've waited longer."

He shook his head against the pillow. "No more waiting."

We kissed then. For a long time, we just kissed. Our mouths moved in perfect tandem, tongues sliding softly, teeth grazing, while our hands ventured no lower than each other's shoulders.

I inhaled him, smelled the warmth of his skin and the scent of him, swallowed down the little sounds of want he made, and answered with my own.

In moments, our breathing grew labored as our kissing deepened and became not enough. Now hands tugged at shirts, seeking naked skin. Silas slipped out of his turtleneck and it left his hair messy.

"Damn, Si," I said between kisses, smiling against his mouth. "You're doing that on purpose."

"And you're not getting naked fast enough."

He stripped me out of my shirt, and our hands roamed over defined muscle and smooth skin, then migrated south, undoing buttons and zippers.

My need for him was growing urgent, but I wanted to go slow. To savor every second. Still kissing, his hand went to my groin, stroked my rock-hard erection over my pants. I did the same to him, and our bodies began to move, hips grinding.

I pushed Silas onto his back and straddled him, giving him one last lingering kiss before moving down to his chin, his throat. I kissed his Adam's apple, swept my tongue along the hollow beneath where his heart pulsed against my mouth. Down, along the smooth plains of his chest to one small nipple. I took the tiny nub between my teeth and sucked.

Silas's breath hitched, his body undulating beneath mine in repressed need.

"Jesus, Max," he said, pleading.

"I will not be rushed."

"Bastard..."

I moved to the other nipple, biting softly and sucking and licking. The sounds in Silas's chest and that were escaping from his throat spurred me on. Lower, I dragged my lips over the hard ridges of his abdomen that clenched and grew more defined under my mouth. I traced his abs with my tongue, moving lower still, until I reached the course material of his slacks.

"Wait..." Silas sat up, breathing hard, his eyes dark with lust. "Wait, fuck..." He got to his knees so we could face each other, kneeling on the bed. "I've missed you too much," he said. "Before you put your mouth on me and I lose my goddamn mind, I want to ask you something."

"Okay."

"Have you ever...? I mean, do you prefer being...?"

"What?" I asked, smiling. "Are you asking if I've ever topped?"

"I don't know all the goddamn terminology, okay? I don't know the rules."

"There are no rules. There's only what feels comfortable and right."

"Then I don't want to talk about it anymore," he said. "I just want you. I want you, Max." He pulled me closer, our chests touching, his eyes boring into mine, darkened by lust but electric with nervousness too. "Do you get what I'm saying?"

"You want me to fuck you," I whispered hoarsely.

He nodded. "Yeah. That's exactly what I want."

God, I'd never in my entire life seen anything as beautiful or sexy as Silas Marsh on his knees, offering his body to me.

I nodded and kissed him with a deep sweep of my tongue, gentle, to show him that's what I would be. Though if I knew Silas, he wouldn't want it gentle for long. My cock felt harder than it had ever been, and I doubted I could be gentle, either.

"Max. . . damn," he said. "I'm not going to last eight seconds when. . ."

When I'm inside him.

Jesus, the thought made me dizzy.

"I'll take care of you, Si," I said, and pushed him onto his back.

I stripped him of his pants and underwear, and his cock sprang free. I wrapped my hand around him, then kissed the tip before running my tongue just under the little slit.

"Oh fuck," Silas ground out, his back arching.

I took him in my mouth deep and he was right. A few long sucks and my hands pumping the perfect length of him, and he came hot and fast. He lay on the bed, his broad chest expanding and contracting with each shuddering breath.

"This time," he said between gasps, "I'm prepared." He hauled himself sideways to the nightstand drawer and withdrew a bottle of lube and a condom.

"Housewarming gifts?" I asked with a dry smile.

"Yes, smartass," he said, chucking them at me.

My smile dropped away, all teasing aside. "Are you sure?"

"In the last two weeks," he said, "I fantasized about fucking you in every position imaginable. But now. . . Having you here. . . I don't know what's wrong with me, Maximilian, I just want to give you everything. My house, my money, whatever you want. Right now."

"I don't need any of that, Silas," I said. "I just want you."

"And you don't have to wonder if I'm sure, Max," he said, his voice turning gruff. "Get over here."

He lay back on the pillows and I knelt over him, kissing him. I kissed him while he rolled a condom on me and slathered lube over my cock. He stroked me until I knocked his hand away and did it myself, my eyes never leaving his. I worked myself until my fingers were coated, and then moved my hand down, kissing him and working him open, slowly. It had been a long time since I'd been inside someone. The trust Silas was giving me, after all he'd been through, was overwhelming, and I vowed in that moment to give him everything. My entire self, because holy shit, I loved him. I loved him so much, that when we were joined, I nearly cried.

"Oh, God. . . Max," Silas said, his words choppy and tight, his hands gripping my forearms painfully.

"You okay? Breathe, baby."

"Don't stop. Jesus. . . don't stop."

Slowly, I moved in him. God, he was so tight and perfect. I kissed him deep while my hips ground against him and withdrew, gently, until it wasn't enough. I let him tell me what he needed, show me what he wanted, and he did. Our kisses became messier as he gripped my hips, seeking to drive me into him harder and harder.

"I don't. . . want to hurt you," I gritted out, using every ounce of restraint to hold myself back. It was his first time taking a man inside him; giving himself up, not just to me, but to his truest self, and it had to be fucking perfect.

But Silas defied any shame or guilt that had been ingrained in him with the same untamed power, the same ferocity in which he embraced everything in this life. . . including how he loved me.

"I want it," he growled. "All of it. . . You." His hand snaked out to grip my jaw, to bring my mouth to his in a crushing kiss. "Fuck me, Max," he ground out against my lips. "Fuck me hard."

His rough, commanding words and the euphoria that was painted across his beautiful features told me everything. No pain, only this perfection of us, and I gave myself up to it and to him.

"Max," he grunted, pressing me in deeper. "I'm going to. . . oh, Christ. . ."

I reached down and stroked him, watching his beautiful face contort with the ecstasy welling between us. He came again, his release spurting hotly, and I released my hold on him; I needed both hands to press myself into the bed, to thrust into him with abandon.

Every fear I had about protecting myself was burned to ash in the fire of this moment, in these heated touches, in the molten hot pleasure that surged through me. I bent down on shaking limbs to kiss him as the orgasm reached its peak.

"Love you," I whispered against his mouth and then kissed him hard, buried my face in his neck. He wrapped his arms around me, holding me, sealing me to him as I came shuddering in a white-hot release.

We lay that way for a long time after, breathing heavily, tangled up in each other—strong muscle, hard bone and sinew and soft skin. Warm and safe. And I vowed with my heart and soul that I'd never let the cold touch Silas Marsh again.

CHAPTER THIRTY-ONE

Max

We spent the night in tangled sheets, grasping at each other, insatiable. Silas had to go to DC in a week and I had to figure out what the hell to do with my life, but for a few days, we had only each other.

After a shower, we called a truce in order to eat and drink and refuel. Silas loaned me a pair of his sleep pants and we both stood in the kitchen, shirtless, eating cold chow mein out of the boxes with chopsticks.

I fed Silas a piece of baby corn, since I knew he liked those best, and he reciprocated with a small pile of noodles. His chopsticks slipped, and half of the noodles made it into my mouth, the rest hitting my chin.

"You're probably one of the most incredible, agile piano players on the planet," I said, reaching for a napkin. "How can you suck so bad at chopsticks?"

He stopped my hand. "Shows what you know. Maybe I did that on purpose." Silas leaned in, his eyes suddenly dark and hooded as he sucked the noodles into his mouth and then kissed me.

My blood ignited immediately, and I set my food down to hold him to me.

So much for our truce.

"Are you *Lady and the Tramp*-ing me?" I asked.

"I don't know what you're talking about."

"It's another classic movie you haven't seen."

"Oh yeah?" He kissed my chin, sucked my lower lip. "Who's the lady and who's the tramp in this scenario?"

"We're both the tramp. *Tramp and the Tramp: The Reboot*."

"Mm," Silas said, kissing me harder. "Your cinematic expertise is such a turn-on."

"Yeah?" I grabbed his hips, ground him against me.

"Yeah." His tongue invaded my mouth while his hand ventured down to stroke my erection. "I have an overwhelming urge to suck you off right now."

"Such a romantic."

"Do you want romance or do you want a blowjob?"

"Is this a trick question? On your knees, Marsh."

"That's what I thought."

That morning, we toured the Valley Village group home with Eddie. He followed behind us nervously, hands twisting, as the director showed us the facility and the grounds. The place was beautiful, immaculate, clean. It had space for twenty residents, each with their own room and bathroom. We toured the dining room, kitchen, art rooms, rec rooms, and the library.

"How about it, Eddie?" Silas asked. "This is some library, right?"

Eddie nodded, not lifting his eyes. "Yes, quite. A lovely place, indeed."

Silas and I exchanged glances. Eddie seemed torn between wanting to investigate further and wanting to run out the door.

"What do you think?" Silas asked me out in the sprawling yard in front of the director, a middle-aged woman named Odette, with a kind face. "Max is a medical professional," he explained to her. "What he says, goes."

"I think it's clean, professional, first class. The residents seem happy." I turned to Odette. "There's not another facility like this for miles, is there?"

"I'm afraid not. We are quite special, and the fact that we have a vacancy is incredibly serendipitous. We have to conduct a few more interviews with

Eddie, but it's apparent to me already that he'd be a wonderful addition to our community."

"If he's willing," Silas said. "What do you think, Eddie? Want to give it a try?"

"Would I be permitted to keep my attire?" he asked. "I daresay, there isn't some sort of uniform I'd be forced to don?"

"Not at all," Odette said. "You're welcome just as you are."

Eddie rocked back on his heels. "I have to say, I'm quite torn. I feel ever so much intrigued by the notion of residing here, and yet I have lingering concerns." He turned in my general direction. "Mr. Kaufman, perhaps you might stay awhile. Allow me the time to become acclimated to my new environs?"

"I don't think that's possible, Eddie."

"If I might ask, what is your line of work, Mr. Kaufman?" Odette asked.

"My training is in nursing," I said. "I worked in an ER for a time, here and in San Francisco."

"I see. And have you ever thought about personal care at a facility such as this?"

Eddie's eyes, still trained on the ground, widened.

"Not exactly," I said. "But I haven't *not* thought about it either."

Silas was staring at me. "What are you saying?"

"I don't know what I'm saying," I said, a smile on my lips that wouldn't quit. "I'm not saying anything. Just. . . talking out loud."

"Since we're talking out loud," Odette said, "we are always looking to expand our family of specialists."

I held up my hands. "I have no training or experience with ASD patients."

The director nodded. "We require a master's degree in behavioral sciences, and all employees must become board certified by passing the Behavior Analyst Certification program."

"So, a lot more school," I said.

"We have volunteer programs as well," Odette said. "That might be a good way of getting one's feet wet." She smiled. "If one were interested."

I nodded, thinking. Eddie was smiling at the grass, his hands clenched tight, like in prayer. Silas and Odette were staring at me.

"One could be interested," I said, laughing. "But let's get Eddie squared away first. What do you say, old chap? Want to give it the old college try?"

"I say, Mr. Kaufman, my fears would be much allayed to know you were on the premises. Even on a voluntary basis."

"I think that can be arranged, Eddie. Especially if this is what you want."

Silas abruptly turned away, hands on his hips, head tilted up.

"Wonderful," Odette said. "Let's see about some paperwork."

We dropped Eddie back at the estate where Marjory and Ramona took him in their care and asked him all sorts of questions while Silas went up to talk to his father.

When we left and drove back into the city, Silas was quiet, his eyes on the road. In the underground parking of the apartment complex, he shut the door to the Aston and looked at me across the hood.

"I can't believe you volunteered at that home."

"Just a trial basis," I said. "For both Eddie and me."

"But you're really considering working there, permanently?" Silas asked, coming around to my side. "No shit?"

I shrugged. "I hadn't planned on it. If you'd told me a year ago I'd end up there, I wouldn't have believed you. I don't have experience or training with ASD patients, but I love Eddie. I love the idea of helping him and the others. . ."

Silas cut me off with a bear hug that left me breathless.

"Hold on," I said laughing. "I'm not saying I am. The last fucking thing I want to do is commit to more school and then learn that's not my purpose either. I can't do that to Eddie."

"I get that," Silas said. "But whatever you want to do, Max. I support you. Even if it's not working with Eddie." I started to speak but he held up his hand. "And don't even start with me about money. It's not an issue."

"It is to me, Si. We need some ground rules if I'm going to be living here."

He rolled his eyes, and we started walking to the elevators. "Sure, sure.

Go back to school and rack up a bunch of student loan debt if it makes you feel better. I'll just pay it all off when we're married."

The elevator opened, and he stepped inside, then shook his head at me, still standing outside the door.

"Are you coming?" He huffed a sigh, reached out and hauled me in as the doors closed.

"You're really damn bossy, you know that?" I said.

He shrugged and moved in to kiss me. "I just know what I want."

"Married, eh?" I asked, arching a brow.

He snorted. "I'm not proposing to you, Maximilian. I'm just predicting the future."

I grinned.

Our future.

We stepped inside, and all that marriage talk—which was silly and yet not—was making me want to grab Silas and spend the rest of the afternoon bringing each other to one mind-blowing orgasm after another, but my phone rang with my mom's number.

"Hey, Mom," I said. "Everything okay?"

"Fine, dear," she said. "Are you busy right now?"

I glanced at Silas who was popping the caps off two Topo Chico sparkling waters in the kitchen.

"No, what's up?"

"Well. . . your father and I would like to invite you over to Thanksgiving dinner."

"Ummm, Mom. . .?"

"Yes, silly, I'm aware it was yesterday but. . ." She sighed. "It wasn't right, was it? Your father and I agree—"

"Wait, Dad agrees?"

Silas handed me a bottle, shooting me a curious glance.

"Yes. We would like you to come over for what you kids would call a do-over. Just you, me and your father. Today."

My pulse quickened and I swallowed through a throat that had gone dry. "Just us?"

"Rachel and Morris took their clans to the museum. And as much as we were impressed by your friend, Silas, we want. . . We'd like to have you all to ourselves for a few hours. How does that sound?"

My eyes swam, and Silas, sitting on the couch, sat up on high alert.

"Uh, yeah, that sounds. . . great." It sounded too fucking good to be true.

"Dad's on board with this?"

"It was his idea."

Holy shit. I stared at Silas, shaking my head.

"Will you come?" Mom asked.

This is it. This is my moment.

I nodded. "Yeah, uh, yes. I'll be right over."

"I'm so glad," Mom said, her voice thick. "See you soon, sweetheart."

"Yep." I hung up and my hand dropped. "They want me to come over for dinner. Just me. No siblings, no kids. . . Holy shit."

"Right now?"

"Right now. Mom said it was Dad's idea."

Silas set his bottle down and came over to me. "What do you need? A ride? A car? What can I do?"

"Nothing, just. . ."

"I'll be here when you get back. Or you can call me. Or text me if shit gets bad, okay?" He held me tight. "I'll be here for you."

I eased a shaky breath. "That's all I need."

I took an Uber to Mom and Dad's house on Plum Street in the Beacon Hill neighborhood, south of the city. My house. My home—or it had been. It hadn't changed at all on the outside—set a little back from the street by a short lawn and two oak trees that buffered it on either side. The yellow paint had been retouched at some point but Mom's yellow curtains with the small red flowers were the same.

I climbed the two steps up to the front door and knocked. My damn heart was beating so fast, the blood rushed in my ears. Mom opened the door wearing an orange sweater and beige pants. She hugged me close and I smelled turkey, stuffing, and hot bread wafting out from behind her.

"Come in, dear," she said, wiping her eyes. She took my hand, every one of the seven years standing between me and those first few steps. "Come in."

I followed her in.

The sense memories swamped me, as those same seven years collapsed like an accordion's bellows. The living room was the same—same beige couch I watched Saturday morning cartoons on. Same carpet I spilled Kool-Aid on, though the stain was washed out now. Same wooden coffee table I'd bonked my head on that time I'd been horsing around with Morris when he was thirteen and I was three, and he decided to launch me—laughing—through the air at the couch. And missed.

The pictures on the wall were still there, even those of me as a kid with braces, in Little League, where I'd had a crush on Billy Sturgeon and no one had known it, least of all me. Only feelings. Stirrings of who I was and what would lead to so much confusion and eventual exile from this, my home.

Mom led me to the kitchen that was another round of sensory assault. The counter tile—the same white squares that had been popular forever were there, every few painted with a blue fleur-de-lis.

"I'm heating up leftovers from the restaurant yesterday," Mom said, sitting me down at the small, round wooden table. It was near the sliding glass door that overlooked the yard where I'd spent countless hours with friends or by myself, reading on my back in the grass. The table was set for three.

"We have everything," Mom said. "Cranberry sauce, green beans, but the bread I made myself. Have to have fresh bread."

"Where. . ." I swallowed. "Where's Dad?"

The door that led to the garage opened and Dad came in, carrying a bottle of Martinelli's sparkling cider in each hand. He stopped when he saw me. "Oh, you're here."

"Yeah, hi."

A short silence descended.

"Can I help?" I asked.

"No, no, I think we got it. We got it, right, Barbara?"

"*I* have it," she said, pulling a large tray of tinfoil wrapped turkey out of the oven. "Max can help. Get the glasses, would you, dear? Lou, you pour, then everyone wash your hands. We're about ready to eat."

I went to the cabinet above the sink where the glasses had been seven years ago. They were still there.

"I got this instead of champagne," Dad said when I came back to the table with three wine glasses. "I understand you don't drink."

"That's true," I said. "Thank you."

"Of course, yes."

He poured the bubbling cider and Mom rejoined us with leftovers and then set a bowl of fresh bread on the table. We took our turns washing our hands at the sink.

My family wasn't Orthodox, but we practiced many of the little rituals, and it wasn't until that moment, I realize how much I had missed that part of my life too.

We sat at the table and Mom smiled at me.

"Max. Will you say the blessing?"

"Uh, sure. If I remember."

She held out her hands and Dad and I each took one. After a moment of hesitation, Dad did the same to me and the circle was joined.

I closed my eyes and the words came flooding back to me, though I hadn't recited in Hebrew in seven years.

Blessed are You, Lord our God, King of the universe, through Whose word everything comes into being...

"Barukh ata Adonai Eloheinu, Melekh ha'olam, shehakol nih'ye bidvaro."

"Omein," we all said together.

Mom opened her eyes and we let go of each other's hands. "Lovely. Let's eat."

For a while, the only sounds were the clattering of silverware and commentary that the leftovers from the restaurant were surprisingly good.

"I've seen a little bit of Silas in the news. How did you two meet?" Mom asked.

We met at a Narcotics Anonymous meeting. I was telling the group how I sold myself for drug money and he shared how he'd used pain pills to cope with PTSD from conversion therapy. Classic American love story.

I coughed a laugh into my napkin and made a mental note to tell Silas we needed a cute story to answer this question.

"I met him while working for his father."

Mom scooped green beans onto my plate. "And you two are... serious?"

"Yeah, we are," I said. "I love him and he loves me. And... I guess that makes me the luckiest guy on the planet."

Sheer poetry, Maximilian.

I could see Silas rolling his eyes, but there wasn't any way to encompass all that Silas meant to me or who he was, so I'd stuck to the basics.

Mom reached over and took my hand. "I'm so happy if he makes you happy. He seems like such a *lovely* young man. Doesn't he, Lou?"

My father nodded, leaned over his dinner plate and pursed his lips thoughtfully. "On that note, I suppose you're wondering why I asked you here."

I froze and the food I'd just eaten turned to stone in my stomach.

"Yeah, I was curious," I said. "It's been a long time."

Mom dabbed her mouth with a napkin and cleared our plates. "I have some chocolate babka in the fridge in the garage. I'll just go get it..."

She left us, and the silence, distance, and years between my father and me were there with us, staring us in the face.

"Yesterday was a bit of an eye-opener for me," Dad said. "There at the restaurant."

"Okay."

"Truth be told, when you came in alone, I didn't know what to say. It felt like what happened that night... seven years ago. It was too much. I'd picked the wrong place and time to try to fix it and... well. It was cowardly of me. Because *I* did wrong, Max. For a long time, I've known that what I did those seven years ago was wrong. And I didn't know how to fix it."

I nodded, not daring to speak. Not wanting to take him off his trajectory.

He pursed his lips, elbows propped, his fingers laced over the tablecloth.

"Then Silas came in," he said. "Rich, successful, handsome young man. I didn't get to know him; you walked out of there pretty quick. But what I did see was how he looked at you and how you looked at him. And it gave me a feeling. The same feeling I had when Ted asked for my permission to marry Rachel. The same feeling I had when Morris put his baby girl in my arms.

"And I told myself, sitting there at the table, that it wasn't the same. It couldn't be. But it was. It was the exact same feeling a parent has when they see that their child is happy. It's all the damn same. And when it boils down to it, isn't that all that matters?"

I nodded. "Yeah," I said. "I think so."

Dad reached across the table and his hand hovered over mine for a second, then landed. He held on, gently at first and then harder. Harder, like he didn't want to let go.

"I'm sorry," he whispered. "I'm so very sorry, and if it's not enough, I'll understand. If too much time is gone by or if it's too late. . ."

"It's not too late," I said, my voice gruff. "There's no such thing."

"There is," he said. "Some things are unforgivable."

He looked at me then, and for the first time, I felt him see me. The boy I'd been and the man I was.

"I can't take any credit for who you turned out to be, Max," Dad said. "None. But I wish I could. More than anything." He inhaled sharply. "I'm proud of you, son. I'm proud that you *are* my son. And I'm really glad you came."

I let out a shaky breath that felt seven years old. "Me too."

A silence fell and then a sniffle came from the kitchen door. Mom, pretending like she hadn't been standing there for who knew how long, hefted a loaf of chocolate bread.

"Who's got room for babka?"

I keyed into Silas's apartment—our apartment—and hung up my leather jacket in the entry.

Silas looked up from the book he was reading. "Well? How did it go? Why didn't you text me? I've been a fucking nervous wreck." He stopped, studied my dazed expression. "Oh shit, it was bad. Was it bad? No. . . it was good? It was good. I can read your face and it was good."

I nodded. "It was good."

"Holy fucking shit."

He shot off the couch and held me so tight I couldn't lift my arms to hug him back. I sagged against him, soaked him up, melted into him with my face in the crook of his neck.

"Thank God," he said, still squeezing me tight. "I was imagining the worst."

"Silas. . ."

"Yeah, baby, what is it? Anything. Tell me."

"I can't breathe."

He let me go with a watery laugh.

"I'm so happy for you. And so happy for *me* now that I don't have to go over there and murder someone, because that would have really complicated my plans for our future."

I laughed but it tapered out. "Damn, I'm exhausted."

"Come on," Silas said, leading me to the couch. He sat down and I stretched out beside him, my head on his shoulder. His arm around me. With his free hand he picked up the TV remote.

"Let's Netflix and chill, emphasis on the Netflix. Any requests?"

"Yes, we can't proceed one second more with this relationship until you watch *Ferris Bueller's Day Off*."

"Whatever you want."

Silas kissed the top of my head and put on the movie. I settled against him, thinking about what he'd said—about us getting married. . . our future. Our future was wide open. No one was going to stand in the way of how much we loved each other.

And as the world slowly changed, it was the deepest hope of my heart that someday, no one would want to.

EPILOGUE

Silas

"Quiet, everyone, please!" Phoebe adjusted her headset and glanced around the room and the people in it. "Max? Silas? Are we missing anyone?"

I scanned the anteroom of the Rooftop Pavilion, taking inventory and basking in the wealth of people surrounding us. The people Max and I loved most in the world. Half of them, anyway. The others would arrive tonight for the rehearsal dinner.

Max's mom and dad were chatting with his friend Daniel. The twins, now nine, stood with their five-year-old cousin, Amy. Eddie was with Faith, my brother holding a conversation with her while keeping his eyes on the ground. My chest swelled with pride and love for him. After three years at Valley Village group home, he was finally comfortable enough to work with me in the MP offices, and rumor had it, he was bringing *a date* to the rehearsal dinner.

"Not everyone is here," Max said, checking his phone with a worried frown. "Darlene is—"

"I'm here! I'm here! Sorry we're late," called a feminine voice from the back.

Darlene Montgomery-Haas, her brown hair in a ponytail and large gold hoop earrings in her ears, came flying into the room. She scanned the small assembly, found Max, and an expression of the purest joy came over her face. I watched her race to him, wrap her arms around his neck. He hugged her back, eyes closed against her shoulder—the look of a man whose life just became complete.

My damn heart ached to witness it. I'd met Darlene at her own wedding to Sawyer Haas and liked her immediately. She was funny, smart, and bursting with energy. But to me, her most endearing quality was how much she loved my Max.

"Hi, honey," Darlene said to him, tears in her eyes.

"Hey, Dar," he said softly. "Glad you made it."

"You couldn't pay me to stay away." She hugged him again and then turned. "Hi, everyone. I've met some of you, but for those who don't know me, I'm Darlene. Max is my best friend and I love him so much and I'm just out of my mind happy for him that he's getting married."

There were appreciative murmurs and smiles all around.

"And you," she said, turning to me. "Come here, you big lug."

I grinned and took my turn being enveloped in her embrace.

"I'm so happy for you," she whispered against my neck.

"So am I," I said as we both watched Max kneel in front of Jamie and Brent, our ringbearers, and make them laugh.

Darlene spoke with her eyes on Max. "I was going to make a joke about how I'd hunt you down like a dog if you didn't take care of him, but. . ." She glanced up at me. "I don't have to worry about anything, do I? The way you look at him. . . I've wanted that for Max since the day we met. For someone to look at him and really see him, you know?" She shrugged her shoulders up and let them go with a sigh. "I love that I don't have to worry anymore."

I swallowed a lump in my throat. "You don't have to worry about a thing."

She smiled and kissed my cheek. "Thank you."

Max joined us and gave our watery eyes an arch look. "Uh oh. She got you too, didn't she? I still maintain that when it comes to making people cry, Darlene is worse than Oprah."

"Silas and I were just talking about what a tremendous sap you make everybody because we all love you so much."

Max tried to shrug it off, but I could read his face better than anyone. Darlene's words had sunk in and he held them close.

Even after all this time, it still surprised my fiancé how well-loved he was by nearly everyone who met him. After volunteering at Eddie's group home, he'd found his calling among the ASD residents and had gone back to school to become certified as a behavioral specialist. Three years of work and he'd graduated with honors. The home had immediately hired him as their assistant director, where the residents and their families—as well as the rest of the staff—all sang his praises as one of the most compassionate, competent caregivers they'd ever had.

I wasn't surprised in the least, and my own love for him skyrocketed higher, if that were possible, for what he'd done to make my brother's life better.

"Sorry for holding up the festivities," came the deeper voice of Darlene's husband, Sawyer, from the door. He came in wearing a suit and holding the hand of their four-and-a-half-year-old daughter, Olivia. They were absorbed into the crowd, greetings and hugs were exchanged, and then Olivia and Amy huddled up, giggling together.

Sawyer joined us, and he and Max hugged like old friends.

"Sawyer the Lawyer in the flesh," Max said.

Sawyer rolled his eyes. "Gee, *that* never gets old."

I shook his hand. "Thanks for being one half of our officiating team."

"Honored to do it," he said. "You're my first wedding."

"Hopefully, not your last," Darlene said. "He works so hard in the courtroom, lawyering day in, day out." She gazed up at her husband lovingly. "Don't get me wrong, he's the best at what he does, but this is much more fun, isn't it, honey?"

Max rubbed his chin in mock thoughtfulness. "Sawyer the Officiant just doesn't have the same ring to it. . ."

Sawyer made a face at his wife who giggled behind her hand. "See what you started?"

"Speaking of Sawyer's expertise. . ." Darlene turned to us. "Do you have any other official legal work you need done while we're here this weekend?"

She batted her eyes. "Perhaps some preliminary adoption papers you need drawn up?"

Sawyer's dark eyes widened. "*Babe...*"

"Oh, don't worry," she said with a wave of her hand. "Max and I talk about this all the time."

I swung my gaze to Max. "Do you, now?"

He held up his hands, looking chagrined. "*All the time* is a typical, Darlene-sized exaggeration," he said, shooting daggers at his best friend. "She brought it up *once,* and I said that you and I... I mean, obviously, we'd have to discuss things..."

"*Obviously*," I said, grinning but not letting him off the hook. A flustered Mighty Max is a rare sight and I wasn't going to miss a second.

"Anyway," Max said, coughing. "Yes, I need your lawyering expertise. I need you to draw up a prenup. Silas only wants me for my money."

"Fair," I said. "Max only wants me for my body."

"That's one hundred percent true."

"Ugh, stop it, you two," Darlene said. "You're too precious... Uh oh, your wedding planner is glaring at us."

"At me," Sawyer said. "I need to get to my post. Through that door?"

Max nodded. "Follow the path to the podiums. If you pass the rabbi, you've gone too far."

Sawyer kissed Darlene, checked in on his daughter, then headed past Phoebe who was tapping her foot impatiently.

"*Now* is everyone here?"

My smile slipped. Not *everyone* was here.

My father didn't want anything to do with this wedding. With Eddie out of the house, our relationship over the last few years had been mostly business, as I used the company's resources to give back to those we hurt. Marsh Pharma had been broken into pieces and sold off to pay for the damage we'd done, and now all that remained was the division that manufactured diabetes drugs, the Orvale, which had proven to work so well against MS, and our latest, Hazarin. I'd negotiated contracts with an Australian doctor on an experimental new drug that helped patients with severe amnesia. His first round of trials had mixed results, but round two, using our labs, had been a success. I was confident about the future.

But Dad wasn't here. He'd sent me to a torture camp and had generally made it clear that I was unacceptable in his eyes, and yet. . .

My dad's not here.

Max gave me a studying glance and slipped his hand in mine. "How're you doing?"

I forced a smile that a moment ago I couldn't have kept off my face if you paid me. "Great."

Max's hand tightened. "Hey, I know."

I looked down at him, and the love that swelled through me was staggering. I gave him a soft, quick kiss, shaking out of my low spirits. "Let's do this. I don't know about you, but I'm glad we're rehearsing walking down an aisle. I'm so out of practice."

"I know all this hoopla isn't your thing, but if we get through the rehearsal, we get rehearsal dinner."

"Silas? Max?" Phoebe asked. "Ready to start?"

"We're good," I said. "Let's do this."

Max gave my hand a final squeeze and went to take his place with his father, the two men linking arms. Max's mom, Barbara, sidled up to me.

"Ready, handsome?"

"Ready," I said, covering her hand on my arm with my own.

Barbara and Lou would have walked Max down the aisle, but I had no parental figure to do the same, so I borrowed Max's mom. They'd made huge strides in the last three years repairing their relationship with Max, and I couldn't be happier for him.

He deserves all the good things. Including this big fat wedding.

In truth, it wasn't all that big. Fifty guests atop the rooftop Pavilion, overlooking all of Seattle. Nothing fancy, nothing elaborate—even though I would've paid for fireworks, crates of doves, tons of confetti, balloons, writing his name in the sky. . .whatever shit necessary to show him how much I loved him. But Max didn't want all that. He'd said he only wanted to celebrate us and have a party after.

The last fucking thing on this earth I ever wanted to do was deny him anything.

Phoebe adjusted her headset. "And. . . cue flower girls."

Olivia and Amy, holding empty baskets that would have flower petals tomorrow, walked out of the anteroom toward the outdoor deck, still giggling.

Phoebe gave an eight-second count. "And now the ringbearers. . ."

Brent and Jamie held small, empty boxes stiffly in front of them, taking their job very seriously. Tomorrow, the boxes would hold identical silvery tungsten rings with a small inlay of braided eighteen karat gold down the middle.

Never in my life had I wanted to wear a piece of jewelry so damn badly.

"And now the groomsmen. . . Groomspeople," Phoebe said.

Daniel hooked arms with Faith. "My lady."

"You're the sweetest," Faith said, and shot me a wink over her shoulder.

"And now the best man and maid of honor," Phoebe said.

"Best *woman*," Darlene corrected, gently taking Eddie's arm.

Eddie paused in front of us, his gaze cast downward.

"Max. Silas. Mr. Kaufman, the elder, and Mrs. Kaufman," he said. "Traditionally, the best man gives a speech in front of the entire assembly. However, Miss Darlene and I have discussed it and have agreed she'll be taking on the sole speech-making duty tomorrow at the reception. I hope you don't mind but speaking in front of large groups isn't my thing."

"Oh really?" I said. "You didn't seem to have a problem talking in front of *large groups* at a certain Halloween party a few years back."

Eddie blushed and grinned. His eyes met mine and Max's for a quick second before retreating to the floor. "True, but that was an emergency. . ."

Since he'd been at the group home—and with Max's help—Eddie had stripped his language of the affected, Victorian-speak. He no longer felt the need to hide behind the fancy talk or play make-believe. He was himself now.

You and me both, brother.

"We don't mind, Eddie," Max interjected. "Darlene can talk enough for two people. Or more, if necessary. . ."

She scoffed and rolled her eyes. "Hilarious, Maximilian. But not wrong."

Phoebe cleared her throat.

"Oops," Darlene said. "We're holding up traffic."

She and Eddie proceeded out.

"Max and Dad," Phoebe said. "Go."

Max gave me a parting smile over his shoulder and walked out with his father.

"Silas," Barbara said. "I know this is only the practice run, but I can tell already I'm going to be a little bit of a mess tomorrow and might not be able to say what I want to say."

"Okay," I said, bracing myself. All of the deep emotions swirling around this event were getting to me too, and I was beginning to have serious doubts about my ability to hold my shit together during the ceremony tomorrow.

Barbara ignored Phoebe who was mutely urging us out the door.

"I wanted to tell you that it has not gone unnoticed by anyone in the Kaufman family how happy our son is with you. He glows with it. And as a mother, there is no greater gift than to see your child like that—happy, safe, loved."

Oh shit...

I bit the inside of my cheek.

"We failed in that for a long time," she said, her eyes shining. "And I honestly can't remember why. Whatever could have been so wrong to deny him those things...It seems impossible that there could have been anything at all." She put her hands over her heart, as if the pain that lingered there had woken at her words. "I could go on and on, but what I'm truly saying is thank you. Thank you for doing that for him and thank you for letting us celebrate with you like this."

Phoebe gave us a look.

"Okay, I'm done," Barbara said, taking a long, deep breath as she dabbed her eyes. "Let's walk, shall we?"

Sure, after a speech like that, let's walk. Fucking hell.

Barbara's words had brought me to the brink, and it took everything I had to suck it up and not fall apart when the doors opened. The warm sunshine fell over me, and there was Max at the end of the aisle, waiting for me with that smile on his face that made my heart swell.

And this is just the damn rehearsal. I'm so fucked.

I walked with Barbara down the narrow stretch of polished wood that was flanked with chairs. On every side of us the city of Seattle stretched out under a brilliant June sky. Eddie and Faith were waiting on my side, Darlene and Daniel on Max's.

There were two small podiums under an awning to give cover. Sawyer the Lawyer stood behind one and Rabbi Soloff behind the other. Max had explained to me that we were lucky to find Soloff, who performed interfaith weddings. It was important to his parents that we have some of the Jewish traditions in our ceremony, and therefore important to Max. Which made it important to me.

Somehow, I made it to the end of the aisle where Barbara gave my hand a squeeze and a kiss on the cheek, then took her seat next to Lou in the front row. I had to pull an Eddie and keep my eyes on the polished wooden floor as I took my position facing Max.

"And now you take each other's hands. . ." Phoebe instructed.

"Si. . ." Max said softly.

"Don't say a word," I said gruffly, taking his hands in mine. "Tomorrow, *I'm* walking down the aisle first."

"Why?" Max said. "You think it's easier going first? I had to watch you come toward me and nearly lost my shit."

I lifted my gaze to meet Max's. His deep brown eyes were watching me with all the warmth and love a guy could hope to see in the person he was going to spend the rest of his life with.

"And cue Rabbi's opening remarks," Phoebe said, pacing beside us. "Then Officiant number two speaks. . ."

"Great," Sawyer mumbled under his breath. "I went from 'the Lawyer' to 'Number Two.' I have a name, people."

Max and I both chuckled, and I stepped back from the precipice of crying my damn eyes out.

"The rings and then the vows," Phoebe said. "I assume you want to save those until tomorrow?"

"*Yes*," we said together.

"Then you both smash a glass, kiss the grooms, and boom. You're married."

Max smiled that quiet smile of his. "Then we're married."

Rehearsal dinner was also at the Pavilion; a long table with a white cloth was set for twenty-nine people: the Kaufman family, my assistant Sylvia—who I'd promoted to Vice President of Marketing immediately upon taking over as CEO—Cesar, Ramona, Marjory, Odette from the Valley Village group home, and their plus-ones. Faith had a date for the wedding but had said he wasn't quite rehearsal dinner material. Yet.

"He has potential," she'd told me on the phone a few weeks before. "At least with him I get to have sexual relations."

"I don't recall you being at a lack for sexual relations when we were together."

"True, honey. They just weren't with you."

Since breaking off our "engagement," our friendship had grown into something real and honest, and she took to calling me her gay best friend. I hoped this guy she was bringing tomorrow was good for her, or I'd have to kick his ass.

As gay best friends do.

The elegant room was buzzing with our guests, and Max extricated himself from his sister Rachel, Darlene, and Faith—the three women having become inseparable over the course of twenty minutes. He sidled up to me and handed me a glass of sparkling water.

"Okay, spill it," I said. "Is that her?"

We both looked to where Eddie stood beside a young woman with her light brown hair in a braid and piercing blue eyes. Both of them smiled shyly. Eddie stole glances at her now and then, but the woman made stronger eye contact with him and the rest of the group.

"Yep, that's Carly. She moved into the home about six weeks ago," Max said. "They were friends right away, talking about Dickens, Chaucer. . . They've been thick as thieves ever since."

"Thick as thieves?" I said, fixing him a stern look. "Why haven't I met her yet?"

"Maybe because Eddie is afraid you're going to scare her off with that glower of yours."

I fixed my face. "Shit, I don't want that. But if he gets attached and she hurts him. . ."

Max smiled. "That's the chance we all take, Si. Eddie's a grown man. He can take care of himself. . . He just needs a little bit of guidance." He took a pull from his water. "Hell, don't we all?"

I marveled at Max. Eddie had come as far as he had because he felt safe with Max there to help him. He might've gotten to this point—standing more or less comfortably in a room full of people, holding hands with a girl—but it would've taken a hell of a lot longer.

"Introduce me. I'll put the glower away."

We went to where Eddie and Carly were talking in low voices.

"Ah, Silas," Eddie said, straightening and clearing his throat nervously. "I'd like you to meet Carly. Carly is my girlfriend of approximately three weeks. And those have been the happiest three weeks of my life, given how she fills every minute with her beauty and wit and companionship."

I stared while Max hid a smile in my shoulder.

"And Carly, this is one of the men of the hour, my brother, Silas. You know Max, of course. This great event that we are now attending had its roots in the night Silas declared for all the world, including major media publications like *Vanity Fair*, that he was in love with Max. Really made for quite a memorable evening."

I fumed. "I'm never going to live that down, am I?"

"'Fraid not," Max said.

Carly made direct contact and stuck out her hand stiffly. "Hello, I'm Carly Moreno, and it's a pleasure to meet you. Congratulations to you both on your impending nuptials."

"Thank you," I said.

"Eddie tells me that you're a masterclass pianist," Carly said. "And that you sometimes play large events and concerts. . . as sort of a hobby?"

"Pretty much," I said. "I'm not a pro."

Max snorted and muttered under his breath, "I'll let that one slide."

Eddie had no such intentions. "Silas is being ridiculously modest."

"Agreed," Max said.

"My brother could play Carnegie Hall if he wanted to but chooses to limit his engagements to charity events."

"I hope to hear you play one day, Silas. Maybe at the home?"

"Excellent idea, my dear," Eddie said, and I watched in astonishment—Max clutching my arm—as he pecked a kiss on the back of her hand.

Carly's gaze dropped to the ground and a blush colored her cheeks.

"Did you see that?" I asked, dumbfounded, as the group trickled into their chairs.

"I totally saw that," Max said, grinning ear to ear.

"You helped make that happen," I said.

Max shrugged. "That's my job. But truthfully, Eddie made that happen. And he's going to be just fine."

I shook my head, my eyes stinging as my brother took a seat beside his girl.

We took our own seats together at one end, next to Lou who bookended the table with Barbara, and Max put his arm around me, leaned in.

"You're sexy as hell when you're grouchy, but I have to say, Emotionally Vulnerable Silas is a good look for you too."

"This is all your fault," I muttered. "This night is trying to kill me."

"Well, buckle up, baby, since it's time for us to give our speeches."

"Oh, fuck me."

Reluctantly, we got to our feet, sparkling water glasses in our hands.

"Silas and I would like to thank you all for coming," Max said. "It's a beautiful thing, to look out over this table and see the faces of so many we love. Silas will be the first to tell you that this is a lot of fuss for him, but he's putting up with it because I asked him to."

Max's voice grew rough.

"When you love someone as much as I love Silas, and if you're the luckiest man alive because he loves you back. . . I feel like that is something to celebrate." He turned to me, his eyes full. "I love you, Si. More and more every day, when I didn't think that was possible. Thank you for making a life with me. Thank you for choosing me." He raised his glass to the group. "And thank you all for being here."

The guests raised their glasses, too, in a happy, tearful toast. Rachel handed Darlene a tissue.

Max leaned in to kiss me. "Your turn."

I had no words. They'd all gotten tangled up in my heart. I'd already declared for the entire world to hear that I was in love with him. But doing it in this room was a million times more important.

"He's right," I said. "I didn't want a big deal of a wedding, not because I didn't want to see you all and not that Max doesn't deserve everything he could ever possibly want. That's all I want to give him. Everything."

Darlene let out a sob and buried her face in Sawyer's shoulder.

"But the reason I would've been perfectly happy with Vegas or a piece of paper at City Hall or nothing at all is because. . ." I turned to Max, my heart and eyes overflowing. "I just want to spend the rest of my life with you, Maximilian, and I don't care how, so long as we do."

Max swallowed hard and his hand in mine squeezed.

I coughed and turned to the group. "But this works too."

Everybody laughed, and a few of the women dabbed their eyes. Eddie smiled down at his plate, still holding hands with Carly.

"I love you," I said to Max and kissed him. "Cheers everyone, thanks for coming."

We sat down and the dinner began, waiters delivering filet mignon, halibut, or pasta for the vegetarians—Carly and Sylvia—among us. Along the table, eating and talking and laughing, were twenty-nine faces lit by amber light candles.

An even thirty if Dad were here.

And then he was.

My hand gripped Max's and my heart nearly stopped to see my father across the room, just outside the door.

"What. . .?" Max looked to where I was staring. "Oh, shit."

The moment froze. No one but Max saw my father. A large, flat present wrapped in purple and gold sat in his lap. He nodded at me, once, and then motioned for the nurse pushing his wheelchair to move. They vanished from sight, and I wondered if all the damn emotion of the night made me hallucinate him.

I felt Max's arm around my back as he leaned into me. "What do you need? Do you want me to talk to him? See what he wants? You want me to get rid of him? Or do you want. . ." He pressed his lips together. "Do *you* want to talk to him, Si?"

"He shouldn't be here," I said, anger burning away my shock. "We invited him to the wedding to be fucking polite—not that he bothered to answer or that I even expected him to. But he's not supposed to be here. This dinner is for family, and after the way he's treated me and Eddie. . . treated *you...* He clearly isn't family. He has no right... not on your night. Our night..."

But Max, who didn't have a vindictive bone in his body, held me closer. To the rest of the table, we were the happy couple, talking intimately.

"Don't worry about me," he said. "It only sucks if it hurts you. I hate if he's hurting you. But maybe, Si..."

Maybe this is my moment.

Like what Max had with Lou.

But the sliver of hope was the match to the fire. He had to be toying with me, getting my hopes up and for what? To make amends? For Alaska?

That had better be some fucking wedding present...

I barked a harsh laugh, stood up, and tossed my napkin on the chair. "Be right back."

I strode out of the room, followed the path down a short hallway. "Where is he?" I demanded of a staff member. "Old man in a wheelchair?"

"In the sitting room, sir."

I busted into the room and towered over my father. A nurse I didn't recognize scurried out.

"What the hell are you doing here?"

"I brought you something," he said. "For you and Max." He indicated the present in his lap.

"A wedding gift," I said stonily. "What is it? A round-trip ticket for two to Alaska?"

He flinched. "Something I thought should belong to you." He set the present on the nearest table. "Can we talk?"

I glared, my heart jackrabbiting in my chest. "Are you fucking kidding me? I'm a little tied up right now. At the rehearsal dinner for my *wedding*."

"I know," he said. "I waited too long. Tomorrow at the wedding would've been out of the question and after that, you'll be on your honeymoon, I assume. I needed to talk to you before..."

"Before I married a man?"

Emotions were bubbling up in me, a potent mix of anger, pain, regret, pity...and something softer I didn't want to acknowledge. I held on to the anger tightly.

"What could you possibly have to say to me at my fucking rehearsal dinner?"

"It's important," he said in that maddeningly unruffled way of his. "It's something I think you should hear."

I crossed my arms over my chest, bracing myself, and leaned against a table. "You have five minutes."

"Do you want to sit down?"

"No. Say whatever it is you're going to say, but I swear to God, Dad, if you've come here to play some kind of mind game with me. . . or shit on my night, or what I have with Max—"

"They caught Coach Braun."

My hands dropped to my sides, even as a cold shiver ran up my spine. "What?"

"The FBI came to me six months ago. They knew I'd participated in his program and thought I might have information as to his whereabouts. Jerry Needler is his name, they said, and he was wanted in six states."

My breath was coming short. "Why the fuck are you telling me this right now?"

"The FBI wanted my help snaring him. So I got in touch with Needler, told him I'd give him some money. My ploy worked and he was arrested. You haven't heard?"

I shook my head, my neck feeling as if it were made of stone.

"It wasn't big news here. But the point is," my father said, "as part of the process of catching Needler, I had to tell the FBI what. . . what he'd done to you. What *I* had done to you."

I sank into the nearest chair; my legs having ceased to work. I couldn't speak, couldn't say a word.

"I had to tell the FBI that I had hired this man to take my son to Alaska for six months. Over the winter. Over Christmas. I had to admit that I didn't know all of the details of what was done to you—but that when you came back you had to go to the hospital. I told them how you had pneumonia, how you were screaming, not letting anyone touch you." He swallowed. "I had to tell them that my son tried to hurt himself because he didn't want to be alive anymore."

Only the three years of therapy I'd had were keeping me from storming out of the room. I listened, following the trail of my father's story to whatever end he had, half scared shitless and half hopeful. Even then. Even there.

"I told the FBI everything, and the agents looked at me as if I was the scum of the earth.

No one's ever looked at me that way before." He tilted a dry grin. "Kind of like how you're looking at me now."

"Why are you telling me this? Why are you telling me this the night before my wedding? Why are you coming in here and bringing up all of this horrible shit. . .?"

"I wanted you to know—"

"That you helped catch him? You want thanks for that? Gratitude? A medal? Do you want a seat at the table?"

"I'm telling you," my father said, his voice low, "because I wanted you to know that I helped put him behind bars. I tried, in some small way, to right a wrong. To do what you did with our company. The damage has been done, but he's not going to hurt anyone else. That's what I wanted to tell you."

"Well," I said, crossing my arms tighter. "You told me. So. . . thanks for that."

A short silence fell and then my father shifted in his wheelchair.

"I heard your speech," he said. "I heard Max's speech and I felt your mother in that room. She was like Max. She didn't want a big party for our wedding, but she wanted to celebrate us. I was like you. I didn't care one way or the other, but I wanted to give her everything. I loved her so much. So much."

He sighed heavily.

"And she loved you both, you and Eddie. She would not be happy with me, I don't think. How I've handled things. I did what I could to put Braun behind bars, not just for me or you or those boys. It was for her too. To get right with her because she never would've let that happen to you, Silas."

My teeth clenched as I fought down a wave of grief. For her. Me. Even my dad.

"My life fell apart when she died," Dad continued. "I couldn't control it. So I tried to put things back the way they were before. To put my life back together. To keep anything bad from happening again. I took it all out on you and your brother."

"That's one way of putting it," I said, my voice gruff.

"I don't understand how it works. I don't understand how it happens between two men or two women. It seems to me like it's counter to the natural urges of the species. I'm not going to tell you I fully understand but. . ."

"But?" I spat.

"But I've spent the last three years alone in a big house, and then I came here to tell you what I told you and. . ." He gestured vaguely to the dining room. "There's so much warmth in those people. At that table. They're all happy for you and Max, and it just seems so easy. More *natural* to be happy for you than to hold on to hate. And that's the long and short of it, isn't it? Maybe what's really unnatural is hating someone for a reason that has nothing to do with you. For a difference or preference you don't share. So what?"

"It's been a little bit more than *so what* for me, Dad. Since I was seventeen years old."

"I know. I just wanted you to know that there is a little less hate in the world now. That's what I came here to tell you. On the night before your wedding."

He folded his hands in his lap, while I sat immobile, no clue what to say or feel or think. Something Max told me once when we were talking about his own father came to me, drifting calmly atop the sea of turmoil in my heart.

Forgiveness isn't for the person you're forgiving. It's for yourself. To set the burden down and move on.

"Would you mind calling my nurse, please?"

My father's words jolted me out of my thoughts, and I went to the door. I motioned for the guy to come in, feeling like I was in a dream, having an out of body experience; a thousand emotions crowding in, each vying for attention.

The nurse came in and started pushing my father out the door.

"Wait."

I heard the word fall out of my mouth. He stopped.

"I don't... I don't know what happens next."

"I'm going to go home," Edward said. "I'm not going to spoil your dinner any more than I already have. Tomorrow, you get married and then go on your honeymoon, and when you get back... Maybe we can talk."

He studied me for a moment, his icy blue eyes softer than I'd seen in a long time.

"You're a good man, Silas. And I know there is a part of you that's wrestling with everything I've dumped in your lap, and you're debating whether or not the wedding invitation you sent me was a formality or if you really want me there."

"I..." I swallowed. "Shit, Dad..."

"Don't," he said. "I haven't earned the right to come. I shouldn't be here now. That's selfish enough. When you get back. Maybe you and Max can come to dinner."

At that moment, Max appeared at the door, his glance going between me and my dad. "Everything okay?" he said in a low, warning tone.

"I was just leaving," Edward said. "Dropping off a present." He pointed at the gift on the table and then looked up at Max.

"Congratulations, Maximilian. I'm sure it'll be a beautiful ceremony."

Max blinked and watched him go out, then rushed to me.

"Are you okay?"

"I think so." I shook my head with a dazed laugh. "Not perfect. But... better. I feel better. Lighter, somehow."

Max nodded, still wary. "Okay. You want to talk about it? Or head back to dinner? Whatever you want."

"I want to open this gift."

Max nodded again and brought the package over. I tore the paper to reveal Mom's portrait, the oil painting that had been hanging over the piano in the sitting room at the estate.

"God..." My eyes filled and my throat closed. "She was so beautiful, wasn't she?"

"She *is* beautiful," Max said.

"She would have loved you."

I heard a sniff and glanced up. Max was hurriedly wiping his eyes.

He saw me staring at him with a pointed look and gave watery laugh. "Okay, fine, we're both saps."

"Saps? Maximilian Kalonymus Kaufman. . ." I hauled him to me and kissed him. "We're not going to make it out of tomorrow's ceremony alive."

That night, the night before I was going to marry Max Kaufman, I sat at the Steinway in our apartment and played my mother's favorite, the Ravel. I'd hung her painting over the piano. She couldn't be there except in spirit, but playing her favorite piece, I felt like maybe it would call her to me. Maybe she was there already, watching over me. And maybe she was proud of me. I was doing my best, trying to make things better for the people who'd been hurt. Marrying Max. . .I was going to do my best by him too, to make him happy, to make sure he knew he was always loved. To thank him for being responsible for all the changing colors of my life. A rainbow of color, brighter and warmer than the cold gray of my life before him.

"Hey."

Max sat beside me on the bench but facing away, his back to the piano. He leaned his cheek against my shoulder. I brought the piece to its end and we sat for a minute in the stillness.

Then I glanced down at him.

"Adoption, eh?" I asked. I was trying for sarcastic, but my throat caught.

"It came up," he said, his voice soft. "Just a conversation."

I nodded and moved so that my arm crossed over his chest as I held him to me. "You want to keep having that conversation?"

"Do you?"

I shrugged. "We can have a conversation. . . But damn, a baby? A kid? You and me being. . . dads?"

"To a little boy," Max said. "Or a girl. It actually doesn't matter. The only important thing is that he or she knows. . ."

I nodded against his hair. "Yes, baby. . ."

"No matter what."

"No matter what." I heaved a shaking breath.

No matter what, he or she will know we love them. Unconditionally.

Our child, Max's and mine, would never, ever be left out in the cold.

"Maybe, though. . ." I said, ". . . and hear me out. Maybe we should get married first."

I felt the soft rumble of Max's chuckle against my arm, and then he pulled away to face me.

"Good thing I planned a big ole wedding, then."

I smiled and kissed him, and my heart was so full of him. Saturated. Only I knew it wasn't going to shatter into a million pieces.

Because it was in his safekeeping.

AUTHOR'S NOTE

When the ideas for this book began to solidify in me, I thought (hoped) that I might have to take a different tack with Silas's character because surely, I thought, conversion therapy is a thing of the past. Unfortunately, according to The Trevor Project, more than 80,000 LGBTQ youth will be forced to endure conversion therapy in the coming years, and nearly a million have already been subjected to the practice that has been scientifically proven to be ineffectual, has been disavowed by every medical and psychiatric institute, and moreover, is incredibly harmful to those forced to participate. The CT that Silas endured is fictional in its physical setting, and to my knowledge there has been no program that severe in terms of location and environmental hardships. However, the ideas and beliefs—the idea of being unnatural, the shaming, the reprogramming (as well as electric shock) are still very much part of many CT programs, and the detriment to the young LGBTQ person is very real and long-lasting.

Max's story has real-world reflections as well, as homelessness among LGBTQ youth are higher than the national average by a margin of 120%, and LGBTQ youth are reported to have attempted suicide at a rate five times higher than their straight peers.

You can read the facts here:

AUTHOR'S NOTE

http://bit.ly/33U5LVO

Anyone wishing to make a difference can do so here:
http://bit.ly/33UoVee

And if you or someone you know is struggling, The Trevor Project's national helpline:
1-866-488-7386

In this book, I have also tried to address, in a microcosmic way, the opioid crises that has ravaged this country for the last twenty years. There is no way to encompass the entire tragedy, so I attempted to boil it down to some of its most basic (yet still horrific) parts in order to bring awareness to a crisis I myself had been ignorant of. The treatment for those addicted to opioids is woefully inadequate and the stigma of an addicted person being seen as a criminal comes from a lack of awareness as to how the drug alters brain chemistry. The drug companies responsible for helping to create this epidemic are now paying, but their victims deserve help, not jail. I gratefully acknowledge Beth Macy's book, Dopesick, which helped elucidate this crisis.

For those struggling with addiction, there is help: 1-800-662-HELP (4357)

ALSO BY EMMA SCOTT

Read the beginnings of Max's story, and meet Sawyer the Lawyer and Darlene in:

Forever Right Now
You're a tornado, Darlene. I'm swept up.

"Forever Right Now is full of heart and soul--rarely does a book impact me like this one did. Emma Scott has a new forever fan in me." --*New York Times* bestselling author of *Archer's Voice,* **Mia Sheridan**

A Five-Minute Life
Keep me wild, keep me safe
It's one of the best books I've ever read.--T.M. Frazier, USA Today Bestselling author of King

Bring Down the Stars (Beautiful Hearts Book 1)
*I was not expecting to feel so lost. So emotional. So desperately in love with EVERYONE AND EVERYTHING about this novel." -**Angie & Jessica's Dreamy Reads***

Long Live the Beautiful Hearts (Beautiful Hearts Book 2)

*"***INFINITE STARS*** BEAUTIFUL. EXQUISITE. LITERARY PERFECTION!!" --**Patty Belongs to....Top Goodreads Reviewer***

In Harmony

"*I am irrevocably in love with IN HARMONY.*" —**Katy Regnery,** *New York Times* **Bestselling Author**
"Told through Shakespeare's masterful Hamlet in the era of #metoo, In Harmony is a deeply moving and brutally honest story of survival after shattering, of life after feeling dead inside. If you've ever been a victim of abuse or assault, this book speaks directly to you. This is a 6 star and LIFETIME READ!!!--**Karen, Bookalicious Babes Blog**

How to Save a Life (Dreamcatcher #1)
Let's do something really crazy and trust each other.

"You're in for a roller coaster of emotions and a story that will grip you from the beginning to the very end. This is a MUST READ…"—**Book Boyfriend Blog**

Full Tilt
I would love you forever, if I only had the chance…

"Full of life, love and glorious feels."—**New York Daily News, Top Ten Hottest Reads of 2016**

All In (Full Tilt #2)
Love has no limits…

"A masterpiece!" –**AC Book Blog**

Never miss a new release or sale!
Subscribe to Emma's super cute, non-spammy newsletter: http://bit.ly/2nTGLf6

Printed in Great Britain
by Amazon